D0960702

The St. Ambrose School for Girls

The St. Ambrose School for Girls

Jessica Ward

GALLERY BOOKS

New York London Toronto Sydney New Delhi

G

Gallery Books
An Imprint of Simon & Schuster, Inc.
1230 Avenue of the Americas
New York, NY 10020

First Gallery Books hardcover edition July 2023

Interior design by Davina Mock-Maniscalco

Manufactured in the United States of America

10 9 8 7 6 5 4 3 2 1

Library of Congress Cataloging-in-Publication Data is available.

ISBN 978-1-9821-9486-4
ISBN 978-1-9821-9488-8 (ebook)

Dedicated to
Sarah M. Taylor.
Thank you for coming and finding me.

The St. Ambrose School for Girls

He who has a why to live can bear almost any how.

—Friedrich Nietzsche

In some causes, silence is dangerous.

—St. Ambrose

Arrange whatever pieces come your way.

—Virginia Woolf

chapter ONE

The St. Ambrose School for Girls
Greensboro Falls, Massachusetts
1991

My first view of the St. Ambrose School for Girls is from the back seat of my mother's 1981 Mercury Marquis. The ten-year-old car is utterly unremarkable except for being reliable, and the reason I'm in the back is because I put the laundry basket full of my bedding in the front passenger seat. My mother is a smoker and I can't stand the smell. I have a theory that I can put my head out the rear window and get better air because I'm farther away from her.

I'm wrong.

We pull through a pair of stone pillars that are united by a graceful arch of black iron filigree, a necklace overturned, the perfect welcome to a pearls-and-sweater-set institution of learning. I'm being dropped off here for my sophomore year of high school. I'm a fifteen-year-old charity case on scholarship because I won a spot I was not aware of having competed for. My mother filled out the application and put a piece of writing of mine into the pool of candidates. Those five thousand words, which I had no intention of anyone ever reading, coupled with my idiot savant grades, were the key to unlock this door I do not want to enter.

"Look at this lawn," my mother remarks. She gestures around with her left hand, the lit cigarette between the fore- and middle fingers a laser pointer with an angry orange end. "This is a *lawn*. I'll bet they mow it every morning."

I am not as impressed with the *lawn*. I am not impressed with any of the brick buildings or the sidewalks that wind around the campus, either. All of this, from the acceptance to the packed sheets in that basket to the two-hour trip from where she and I live, has little to do with me, and everything to do with my mother's need to upgrade something in her life. Our tiny two-bedroom house is cluttered with issues of *People*, *Star*, *Us Weekly*, the *National Enquirer*, the *Globe*. Each one of them is a pulpy, soft-spined vacation into another, better world for her, and after she's done reading them, she keeps them like they're diaries of a trip she never wants to forget.

I wonder sometimes if she isn't moving me out of her house so that she can use my bedroom for storage space. I know this isn't true. The real story is that I'm the ninety-nine-cent houseplant she is shifting to a better, more sunny spot on the sill by the sink. I'm the pragmatism that I doubt she will admit to consciously, a recognition that her own life is a stagnation of going-nowhere, but damn it, she can figure out how to get her fucked-up daughter into Ambrose.

"Look at this campus. I tell you, Sally." She flicks her Virginia Slim out of her window, ashing onto the *lawn* and evidently missing the irony that she's crapping up the very thing she's admiring. "They know how to *do* things at this school."

My mother puts a push into a lot of her words, as if her tongue is frantically shoving the syllables out of her lipstick-slicked mouth, like someone trying to bail out a boat. For her, an ocean of unspoken urgency surrounds the hull of her leaky skiff of nervous chatter, so there are always words for her, and rarely a pause for consideration of content. She speaks like the magazines she reads, everything headlined, drama manufactured out of her dull and endlessly reconstituted reality of being a school lunch lady at Lincoln Elementary.

"Where are we going?" she asks. When I don't answer her, she looks over her shoulder. "Sally, help me here. *Where* are we going?"

My name is Sarah, not Sally. I'm not sure how I got the nickname, but I hate it, and the first thing I'm going to do here is introduce myself as Bo. Bo is a cool name for a girl, unisex and unusual, just as I am fairly unisex and definitely unusual. Unlike the other girls I see walking around the campus—who look like they've stepped out of the rainbow page of a United Colors of Benetton ad—I'm dressed in black and loose clothing. I'm also not wearing shoes, but lace-up boots with steel toes. My hair is dyed jet black, although my mouse-brown roots are starting to show already, a trail of mud at night.

My mother, whose name is Theresa, goes by Tera. Tera Taylor. Like a movie star. She said she named me Sarah so it rhymed, so we could be twins forever. She's told me over and over again she wants me to have a little girl and name it Lara to keep the tradition going, even though, technically, Lara does not rhyme with Tera or Sarah. It would have to be Lera. The fact that my mother can only get sort-of-there with her own construct is the kind of thing that should go on her driver's license.

I'm just hoping to make it to sixteen at this point.

"Sally, come *on*."

It's pointless to mention that I have not been on this campus before either, and there's no map to consult.

"I think it's over there," I say, pointing in any direction.

This mollifies her and we find the correct dorm by luck. Tellmer Hall is right out of the brochure of any New England prep school: brick, three stories, two wings, and one main entry with a limestone pediment bearing its name. Just below the slate roofline, there is a marble frieze bearing the names and profiles of musical luminaries: Bach, Mozart, Mendelssohn. As I get out of the back of my mother's Mercury, I stare up at the faces and start counting down to Thursday, June 4, when, according to this year's school calendar, summer vacation starts.

"Look at this building. Just *look* at it."

My mother slams the driver's side door to add an exclamation point, and the sound of the hollow bang brings us attention from the other girls who are unpacking from their parents' cars. As my mother smiles in the direction of a Volvo station wagon and then a Mercedes sedan, there's expectation and relish in her still-attractive features, like she's prepared to be invited to dine with the Izod-wearing fathers and the Talbots-clad mothers. What she fails to notice, and maybe this is a blessing, is that their perusal of us is of short and disinterested duration, a cursory assessment of my black Goth-ness and my mother's synthetic-fiber, fake von Furstenberg dress. They don't even bother to reject us. We're not significant enough for that. We're something they look through, ghosts of the lower middle class.

"Go introduce yourself to the girls."

When I don't respond, my mother glares over at me, and then refocuses on the Mercedes as if she's trying out the logistics of dragging me to it.

She's going to need a fireman's hold.

"We have to unpack the car," I say.

The Mercury's trunk has two suitcases in it. One a battered black, the other a winsome blue that has inexplicably fared better with age—black seems like it would be stronger, more durable. I take them out one by one. As I straighten, I see around the corner of the dorm. There is a plumbing truck parked in the back. *Albrecht & Sons.* It is white with blue lettering, the telephone number starting with an area code I am not familiar with.

"You really need to introduce yourself," my mother says.

"Why do the plumbers need to meet me?"

"What the heck are you talking about?"

She exhales over her shoulder, flicks the butt onto the *lawn*, and lights another cigarette. She smokes when she's frustrated with me, but she also smokes for a lot of other reasons.

I look over to the Mercedes that has commanded her attention. The car has a rich, creamy yellow body, and its hubcaps are painted to match the sunny shade. The fact that, at this moment, there isn't a fellow student of my own age to introduce myself to anywhere near it is irrelevant. My mother wants to go over and make acquaintances between adults, and as she stares at the mother and father, she gleams like lamé. In her mind, she's no doubt advancing way past dinner in the small town we went through about two miles down the road. She's spending a late-season week at their summer house. Then they're all skiing together wherever people like that ski together in Colorado during Christmas break. Finally, three years from now, she sees them all sitting together at graduation, sharing in-jokes and reminiscing with a tear about how fast the young ones have grown up, and how lucky they are to have found each other.

Lifelong friends in a blink, the assumptions and the fantasy as real to her as my own assessment that the last thing those two wealthy people want is for a pair of scrubs like us to do anything other than wash that pretty, buttercup-colored sedan of theirs.

"You're being ridiculous," she announces. "We're going over there."

My mother links her lower arm through mine, and I think of the old-fashioned *Wizard of Oz* movie, Dorothy lined up with her friends, skipping down the yellow brick road. It's an apt image on one level, at least. We're going to my mother's version of the wizard, and out of the two of us, I'm the only one who cares what's behind the curtain. My mother is not just content to be on the surface; staying superficial is necessary for her survival.

The parents of the Mercedes—and, presumably, a student who's also in this dorm—look at us a second time as we approach. I'm embarrassed by everything about my mother: the dress, the lipstick stain on her cigarette, her peroxide yellow hair, this Hail Mary "introduction" that has taken us over a boundary line that to me is as obvious as a border wall. I'm also ashamed of my cheap black clothes, even though they are a persistent expression of my inner self, a signal to the world that I am different and apart from the crowd. Armor.

The good news about looking like a freak is no one tries to talk to you.

"Isn't this a *marvelous* campus!" my mother says. "I'm Theresa—Tera Taylor. This is Sarah Taylor. She goes by Sally. How do you do."

Ah. She's switched into Rich Person Dialect. I've heard her do this before. She picked it up while watching Robin Leach.

And so much for my going as Bo here.

The father's eyes go to the V in the top of my mother's dress. Then he looks at her mouth. My mother recognizes this perusal and shifts her body so that one hip moves out of place, the inquiry on his part answered with an affirmative on hers. Meanwhile, the wife notices no part of this currency exchange between her husband and what could arguably be called a tart. The other mother's eyes land on me, and the pity in them makes me look at the pavement.

I don't want any part of this. But this whole thing, from the clandestine application and shocking admission to the excited way my mother talked all summer long about my coming "to St. Ambrose" to this "introduction," is the same rabbit hole for Tera Taylor, a glossy magazine she is creating for herself. The defect in her reasoning, which is a blindness similar to the other mother failing to see her husband's flirtation, is that no one else is going to buy this bullshit. I'm no more a St. Ambrose girl than Tera Taylor could be.

"Greta will be down in a minute, I'm sure," the mother of the Mercedes is saying. "She was here last year as a freshman so she's excited to see everyone."

"Greta and Sarah!" My mother claps and ash falls on the back of her hand. She shakes it off with a grimace she almost hides. "The two of them will be the *best* of friends. It's fate."

"Here is Greta now."

My eyes swing like the boom of a sailboat, an attempt to come about and salvage this poor tack I'm on. What I see emerging from the darkened interior of the dorm gives me no relief. It is blond. It is tall. It has limbs that would be described as willowy in a supermarket romance novel.

It has the eyes of a predator.

Even, if not especially, as it assumes the facsimile of a pleasant expression.

"Greta's" smile is shiny and white, a second sun. She has freckles dusting across a nose that is so straight and perfectly proportioned, you might assume she'd had it done—until you look at her father and realize that all that aquiline is the result of breeding, no donkey in this bloodline of thoroughbreds. She also has cheekbones with hollows under them—which makes me decide her baby fat was ordered to vacate the premises years ago—and her clothes are expensive and right out of *Seventeen* magazine: a boxy turquoise jacket, a coral crop top, a kicky skirt with contrast leggings, ballet flats.

She is a jewel.

"Greta," her mother says, "this is your new best friend, Sally."

There is no awkward pause because the girl puts her hand right out. "Welcome to Ambrose."

My mother golf-claps around her cigarette again, but doesn't burn herself this time.

I glance at Greta once more in case I was wrong, in case my insecurities have misconstrued what is actually going on. As our eyes meet, she somehow manages to smile wider and narrow her stare at the same time. It's a cute trick.

If you're Cujo.

My heart pounds sure as if I am already running in the opposite direction, throwing myself in the trunk of the Mercury, and refusing to come out until I am released from this ruse.

My mother is wrong. Greta and I will never be friends.

And one of us is going to be dead by the end of the semester.

chapter TWO

It is forty-five minutes later. I'm back down by the car, and the Mercury is empty of my things, the laundry basket returned to the front seat without its load of folded sheets and blankets. My mother is embracing me, and I breathe in the familiar scent of cigarette smoke and Primo, the knockoff Giorgio perfume she buys at CVS. She's leaving not because I have unpacked, but because she is getting no further than the introduction stage with Greta's parents. They've made the disappointing choice to help their daughter settle in across the hall, ignoring the incredible opportunity of forging a relationship with Theresa who goes by Tera.

I know this dose of reality is challenging my mother's imaginary world so she's got to go before the spell is broken, Cinderella pulling out of the ball early before she realizes she's actually at a pool hall. I'm the glass slipper in this analogy, and I'm very certain that my mother's already anticipating a Parents' Weekend reunion with her new best friends, my residence at Tellmer the thread that will connect her once again with the objects of her aspiration.

Things are going to work out for her. She just knows this.

She's getting behind the wheel now. She's lighting another cigarette. Absently, I note that she has only four left in the pack. She'll stop for gas and more Virginia Slims at the Sunoco down in the little town, but

I have to believe the fumes of her fantasy are what will really carry her back to our meager existence, not whatever unleaded she pumps into the tank of her old car.

My mother looks up at me, and for an instant, the façade breaks and I see what is underneath. She's worried about me. So am I. But my reality is not one that I can invite her into because this flare-up of motherly concern will not last more than a moment for her. The split in the clouds of her busy internal life is something I cannot trust and not because she's abusive. She's far from cruel; she's just self-absorbed. Accordingly, I've learned the hard way that I'm the only savior I've got in this world.

"You're going to be fine," she says through an exhale of smoke.

She has to believe this because to entertain the opposing option that I will not be fine and leave me here anyway means she's a negligent mother. Which she's not. I have been fed, watered, clothed, and housed since the moment of my birth. The damage she does is never intentional, and besides, her desperate, twitchy, clawing need to distinguish herself from her lot in life tortures her much more than it does me.

I've always felt sorry for her.

"I'll call you every Sunday at two p.m.," she tells me.

"Okay."

"You have the money I gave you."

"Yes."

There's a long pause, and as things become uncomfortable, her eyes skip out to the *lawn*. The sight of the grass she is so taken with must calm her because she nods once, the sharp head bob like a gavel coming down on a court case, the verdict in. Then she waves at me with her cigarette and I step back to watch the Mercury pull away. In the wake of her departure, I link my arms around my middle. I blink in the lightning-bright sunshine of fall. I smell clean air.

The leaves on the trees are still green. This will not last.

I turn and face the dorm, seeing it properly for the first time. The glossy black door has been propped wide with a brass weight, and there are windows open all across the front of the building, the lower sashes pushed high, no screens to buffer the sounds inside. Voices, high and low, form a symphony that could have been written by the members of the roofline's frieze, and I close my eyes, trying to find the repeating sequence that pulls all of it together. There is none.

My stomach cramps as I walk into the dorm's cool interior. Straight ahead is the main staircase, and beyond it, through a broad archway, I see a big open area with no furniture and floor-to-ceiling windows. To the left is a room with several mismatched tables, a couple of chairs, and eight phones with long cords that crisscross institutional-grade carpeting.

Okay, so that is where I have to be every Sunday at two p.m.

To the right, on the wall, is a varnished wooden rack of open-air mailboxes, each cubbyhole marked at its top with a name tag slid into a brass holder. There are missives in each of the slots already, a multicolored assortment of notices that have lollygagged in their compartments, forming rows upon rows of the letter *c*.

I leave my set of papers where they are because no one else has picked up theirs, and in my disinterest in the communiques, I figure I am fitting in with the crowd here for my first, and maybe only, time. The stairs are made of the same dark-colored and varnished wood as the mailboxes, each step protected against wear by a black-treaded pad that will also provide purchase when students come in with rain on their sneakers or snow on their winter boots. The banister is the same kind of wood again, and I wonder what sort it is as I troll my hand up the smooth and spindled support.

When I get to the second floor, I stop on the landing. Ahead, there is a closed door with a brass plate on it that reads *Residential Advisor*. I look to the long halls on the left and the right. The student rooms are set at equidistant measures down both sides of the pale-brown-carpeted corridors. For a moment, I panic because I can't remember which way I should go and I can't think of how to come up with the correct analysis. There are too many excited voices, too many people walking around with suitcases and duffels, and too many perfumes and colognes mingling in the humid, still-summer air, a department store's fragrance counter come to Christmastime's agitating life.

Everyone is energized by the fresh start that the new school year brings. New notebooks and packs of pens, new textbooks with bindings that are uncracked. New teachers, new subjects. New friends, new boyfriends. I recognize this phenomenon because a similar buzzy buoyancy infected everyone on the first day of my public high school a year ago. I witnessed it from afar then, too.

Right. I go to the right.

As I make my way down to my room, I realize I'm more like my mother than I'm comfortable with. We're both outsiders to so much, although at least I am content to stay where I am on the far-flung fringes.

My room is not that far down, located just past the bathroom that services our wing with six shower stalls, six toilet stalls, and six sinks. As I pass by, two men in work uniforms come out with buckets of tools and a coiled snakelike contraption. They don't look at me. They're sweaty and they are clearly ready to have whatever job they are doing over with. Perhaps their wish has been granted, I think, because they seem to have packed up.

"Are you boys done?"

At the sound of the male voice, I turn back around. There's a man standing in the juncture of the hallways, by the stairs. He has his hands on his jean-clad hips as if he's in charge, but he's got a Nirvana *Bleach* tour T-shirt on. His dark hair is a grow-out of a much shorter cut, the ends perking up as if they are making a break for it, the brown color deepened by dampness and lightened by streaks of copper. His cheeks are shaved. His face is breathtakingly handsome. He is wearing a wedding ring.

I am glad my mother left before meeting him. And I am curious how he can call two men in their fifties "boys." He is at least twenty-five years younger than they are, fully mature, yet nowhere near dad status.

The plumbers walk over and talk to him about pipes. He asks questions. I hear nothing.

The more I look at him, the more I feel strangely excited and a little nauseous. My palms sweat and a giggle trembles up between my lungs even though there is no joke anywhere near me.

He doesn't notice my presence, and this makes sense. For one thing, there clearly are some issues with the pipes—not the sort of thing you want with twenty rooms full of young women. But I'm also not the kind of girl that people notice for the reason I'd want someone like him to notice me.

As I continue on to my room, a residual of the man follows me, my molecules supercharged and vibrating even as I leave the sight of him behind.

The room I've been assigned to is 213, and as I pass through its open doorway, I want to close things up. I have a paranoia about open doors. About people staring at me. About my secret getting out. My roommate hasn't arrived yet, though, and it seems rude to shut her out before she even gets here.

Our space is generously sized and split down the middle by an invisible line. The walls are whitewashed down to the chair rail that runs around about four feet off the floor, and under that rail there's beadboard that's varnished the same color as the floor, as the banister, as the stairs, as the mailbox cubbies. The arrangement of what is mine and what is my roommate's is a mirror image, the beds wedged into the corners on either side, the bureaus at the foot of the beds, the narrow desks pushed together in front of the tremendous, many-paned window that makes up the whole wall opposite the door.

The furniture is not fancy. The beds have no box springs, just mattresses, and even those are covered with a practical plastic barrier that is stitched into the batting. The bed frames are metal and the headers and footers rise up on both ends to the chair rail level, as if that piece of molding is a height restrictor. The bureaus are old wood. So are the chairs that go with the desks.

I'd chosen the right side for no practical reason and every superstitious one. As I first entered with the laundry basket of bedding suspended between my cramped, stinging hands, it was immediately apparent that I had to be on the right side or everything would go badly. If I ended up on the left, these next nine months were going to be consumed by academic trials I cannot best, pretty girls who hate me, and an enduring, baseless homesickness that cannot ever be cured because I don't actually enjoy living with my mother in our home. As long as I'm on the right, though, there's a chance I'll come out on the June side of this sophomore year with, if not a glowing experience, then at least something I tolerated.

Something I lived through.

I glance over my shoulder at the door. The 213 on it bothers me tremendously and I stare across the hall at the closed-up room opposite me. It bears the more coveted 14 after its 2, and I wish I could change rooms with that Greta girl who is not my best friend. I can't, of course. I'm a cog in this wheel of pairings and location assignments, and if childhood has taught me anything, it's the reality of endurance.

Behind 214's closed door, there are voices. High, shrill, bubbly. There is music, too. Paula Abdul, bright, cheerful, danceable. Parents venture past the members-only party and ignore the muffled sounds. Every single girl who passes by looks and lingers, like she's trying to figure out how to get in there, the code to that vault of valuables.

I find myself yearning to be welcomed into room 214, too, and I hate it. This hollow coveting is my mother's persistent hobby, and after watching her want things she cannot, and will never, have, I'm not interested in impotent cravings. If I start with that stuff now I'll be just like her as a grown-up, greasy-lipped, smoking a Virginia Slim, wearing a cheap knockoff dress as I flirt with the father of one of my daughter's schoolmates. The good news is that I know damn well that my black wardrobe and my matte, dyed-black hair are, among other things, guaranteed to cut off access to 214 right at the pass. This justifies my aesthetics. I'd rather make things like that Paula Abdul dance party an impossibility than be tortured with a string of maybe-I-mights that are forever defeated.

I walk over to the window, lean across my shallow desk, and check out what's behind the dorm. I see a parking lot with three spaces and a tremendous oak that seems as big as our whole building. Then there's a stretch of mowed grass that declines to a thick border of unruly vegetation that is ready to give someone ticks or at least poison ivy. Through the rare breaks in its entwined growth, I can make out a stream that is flowing fairly fast.

The longer I stare at my short-stack view, the more my mind begins to stir in ways that I need to watch out for, and I wonder, not for the first time, whether I can do this. And not from a social or academic standpoint. My fault lines run very deep, and keeping them quiet is something I have failed at before.

"So we're roommates."

In the moment where I am suspended between hearing the voice behind me and seeing whoever spoke the words, I am convinced, in the same way I knew I had to be on the right side of this room, that the girl who has entered is my tea leaf reading on how things are going to go. Her appearance, her short skirt or sensible shorts, her belly shirt or her polo, will determine whether I make it out of here in one piece.

As I turn around, there is a loud thump, her duffel bag hitting the floor, and I am instantly relieved. She is not like me, but she is not like the blond girl across the hall, either. She is tall, and her shorts reveal the thick ankles and calves of a field hockey player. She is brown-haired, only the wisps that escape her ponytail blond. She is wearing a blue T-shirt that has no words on it, no appliques of a joke or a concert cluttering what covers up her strong upper body. She has no glasses, a square face, and blue eyes that are the color of a Sunoco sign's lettering.

"I'm Ellen. Last name Strotsberry. People here call me Strots."

She puts her hand out. She is not smiling, but she's not looking at me with disdain. As I step forward, I want to tell her my name is Bo. I want a nickname like hers, punchy, powerful, a declaration that I'm not going to be snowed by bullshit and I can handle anything.

"Sarah Taylor," I say as we shake. "But my mother calls me Sally."

As I tack on the second half because it's what I've been doing all my life, I realize that it is odd that my mother named me to rhyme with Tera, yet calls me something that ends in *-ly*.

My roommate's handshake is dry and firm, not a bone-crusher, but not anything I want to hold on to for very long because I don't want her to feel the moisture of my own palm. She nods as we drop our arms, as if that greeting malarkey is off her list, and sure enough, she moves on fast. She kicks the door shut, goes over to the bed on the left side, and throws open a portion of the window. Dropping an enormous, camping-sized backpack onto the bare, plastic-coated mattress, she curses as she unzips a compartment.

"I can't believe it's so damn hot."

She takes out a pack of Marlboros and a red Bic lighter. Tilting the cigarettes toward me, she says, "Want one?"

I shake my head. She doesn't ask me if it's okay if she smokes in our room, but even if she had, like I would ever presume to tell her she couldn't? I may have unpacked and have my thin sheets and a blanket covering the right, correct-sided, bed, but Strots is in charge here. I am relieved by this. I picture myself drafting behind her in a bike race, her larger, more powerful body creating a lee in the wind that I am permitted to take advantage of, thanks to the room assignment gods.

She exhales out the open window. "So what's with the black clothes, Taylor."

Her eyes are direct as they focus on me, and to duck the spotlight in them, because I love that she's calling me by my last name, I focus on her hands. Her nails are cut to the quick, her fingers blunt and veined, her forearms strong, but not in a manly way. She has moles in the bed of her tan, darker spots that announce her Eastern European ancestry. No doubt all her time in the sun is from sports.

My roommate does not smoke like my mother, all flourish and false-fancy. She inhales, she exhales, she rests the hand doing the nicotine delivery on her bare knee in between draws. When the smoke comes out of her mouth, she kind of shoots it in the direction of the open window, but she doesn't seem concerned about being caught and her casualness makes me wonder whether we're allowed to do this in our rooms? That can't be right. I think of the hot residential advisor with the Nirvana T-shirt and wonder how much he is going to let us get away with.

I decide he'd probably just let her carry on, too.

"Do we have a problem with the smoking?" Strots asks me.

I realize my eyes are on her lighter and the soft pack of Marlboros, and in the silence that follows, I know I've got to explain myself to her satisfaction. I look at her face, but do not make it past her nose, which is slightly sunburned. Her stare is an intimidation ray.

"No," I say. "I'm just wondering whether you matched your Bic to the Marlboros on purpose. It's something I would do."

Strots glances down at where she's placed the red twosome on the mattress. "Huh, hadn't noticed."

My roommate smiles, revealing teeth as straight and white as a picket fence, although not from any kind of expensive dentistry, it seems. Like her mannerisms and her voice, every piece of her is sturdy, functional, and, in the manner of reliability, attractive.

"So you wear black because you can't handle not matching?"

I look down at myself in the same way she assessed her smoking paraphernalia. I sift through possible responses, and then decide, again, to be honest.

"I'm angry at the world."

It's almost the truth. I can't finish the second part. I'm mad, but I'm powerless. I am fifteen years old, the product of a man who doesn't care and isn't around, and a woman who cares too much, just not about me. In addition to being my social defensive mechanism, black seems like the only way to express my inner rage at living in a house full of magazines and cigarette smoke with nowhere else to go. Well, nowhere except Ambrose, and I did not choose this escape hatch.

"Everyone's pissed off when they're fifteen," Strots announces. "It comes with the territory."

"You don't look mad."

"You don't know me yet and people are weird." But then she smiles. "Don't worry, I let it all out on the field."

"On what?"

She laughs. "The opposition, dummy. You don't do sports, do you."

"No."

As she cocks one eyebrow, like she can't fathom my reality, I take a deep, disappointed breath and smell smoke, but I'm not resentful because it is Strots's. We do not have a problem with her smoking. On the contrary, as I stand in front of her, I want to change into loose khaki shorts and a loose blue, unmarked T-shirt. I want to have a by-mistake matching set of lighter and pack of cigarettes, although something different than Marlboros so we are not matchy-matchy.

I want to throw out my black clothes and armor myself in everything Strots.

All of this is bullshit, of course. And I've got to keep this kind of characteristic crazy thinking, among many things, from Strots. She cannot know how my mind actually works, the connections it makes, the places it goes without my permission. If she finds out, she'll demand to be assigned to another room, and I don't want to live alone when everybody else has someone.

The sound of a toilet flushing on the other side of the wall next to her mattress makes Strots roll her eyes. "This room sucks."

"Do you want to switch?" I ask, pointing to the bed I have made and praying she doesn't want to.

"Nah. I can sleep through anything. But the toilet flushing is annoying."

"Were you in this room last year?"

"I was on the first floor and farther down the hall. But I had a friend in here and I spent a lot of time at her place."

"Did you like your roommate?"

I'm hoping she did, as if it might be a warm-up for tolerating me.

"Nope." Strots gets to her feet and returns her cigarettes and her lighter into the pocket of the backpack. "I did not."

In that moment, I am desperate for her to tell me she feels differently about me. I want her to give me a gold seal of approval, a stamp on my forehead that announces I have passed quality control.

I am my mother, giving my power over to a stranger, all because of a self-created myth of their authority and higher status over me. I am a shadow in my black clothes, looking to conform to another's contours on the ground, following them wherever they go.

The only benefit to Ambrose that I'd seen was getting a break from Tera Taylor, undiscovered movie star. Now it seems I have brought all my own baggage along with my two suitcases.

On the far side of the door that Strots closed with her foot, there is a burst of laughter and chatter. Greta has broken the seal of her privacy and I have a sense of many girls skipping out, the pressure released, a cascade of Benetton and Esprit like sequins spilled from a dressmaker's pocket.

When I look back at Strots, she's staring at me in the same way I assessed her lighter and soft pack. I'm used to this expression on people. Behind their eyes, they're wondering about me, connecting dots that, if I could read minds, I suspect would make me defensive and sad, even though they're probably somewhat close to the truth.

"I'm going to give you a piece of advice," Strots says in a low voice. "Don't give them what they want."

"Who is they?"

"You'll know who I'm talking about," Strots mutters as she puts her cigarette between her teeth and unclips the flap on the top of the backpack. "Just don't give 'em what they're looking for and they'll get bored. They only like chew toys with the squeakers still in 'em."

chapter
THREE

Two nights later, I'm asleep on my back in bed when my eyes flip open. My first thought is that I'm glad I was in any sort of REM state. Settling here in the midst of all the dorm activity is proving to be a challenge, and I've never had a roommate before. And then there is the incessant traffic in the bathroom.

I turn my head on my thin pillow. Moonlight is streaming in the central window that I've come to think of as a referee that holds Strots's furniture on her side and mine on my side. Across the floor between our line of scrimmage, geometric shadows thrown by the frames of the panes cut the lunar glow into blond brownie pieces on the pine boards.

Strots is curled tightly on her side facing me, her head ducked into her hugging arms, her legs drawn up, yet scissored below the knees. It is not a fetal position. It's as if she has a ball in her grip and is rushing through players on an opposing team. Her drawn brows confirm this impression and so does what I've gleaned about her character over these forty-eight hours of our cohabitation. She is an athlete in everything she does. The world is her overtime.

Sitting up, I slip my bare feet out from my scratchy sheets and place them on the blond brownies. I am quiet as I go to the door, but I'm not as worried about waking Strots up as I was the first night. She's not disturbed by much, and I envy how that generalizes from her waking hours into her dreamscapes.

Our door doesn't make a sound as I open it, and thanks to the moonlight, there's no adjustment of my eyes as I step out into the hall. Looking both ways, as if I'm at a busy intersection and trying to cross with no pedestrian light, I'm struck by how many girls my age are sleeping right now. Slumber is an intimate state, marked by vulnerability. To be so close to so many strangers as they twitch like dogs on a rug, separated only by doors that have no locks on them, makes me feel as if I'm an intruder in all of their houses at once.

I don't have far to go to get to the bathroom, and that's the problem Strots pointed out that first day. No one is inside when I enter and the details of the buttercup-yellow facility don't really register in my fog, other than it, as always, reminds me of that Mercedes. One thing does stand out, however. The florist-shop air in here, heavy with humidity and the bouquets of so many soaps, shampoos, and conditioners, is the kind of thing that I haven't decided whether I find noxious or magical.

After I use the toilet and wash my hands, I stand over one of the trash bins at the row of sinks to dry things off and hope that I can go back to sleep. I still don't know what woke me.

Voices register and I look up. Over the sinks, there is a row of mirrors that are lock-in-step with the basins, dancing partners that are the flash to the static porcelain. The sounds of an argument are coming through the wall.

In my groggy state, my first thought is that it's my mother and one of her boyfriends. This conclusion is immediately discarded. Wrong bathroom, for one. For another, there's only the male part, low and defensive, the shriller, female counterbalance noticeably absent. There are plenty of pauses, however, which suggests the woman both has a lot to say and fights in the carpet-bombing manner Tera Taylor does.

I lean toward the wall to try to catch the words. Eavesdropping like this feels both wrong and delicious, a second piece of cake stolen out of the fridge after the party is over. I am suddenly much more awake.

"—please, don't do this again with that Molly Jansen thing." The tone turns exhausted. "It's been a goddamn year and the charges were dropped—I'm sorry, what was that?" Pause. And then things get sharper. "You're the one on the road, Sandra. You chose that job—look, I have to go." There is a short silence. "I'm—because I need to clear my head, that's why. I love you, but—have you been drinking again? You're slurring . . ."

With a flush, I recognize who it is. It's my residential advisor, and he's fighting with his wife.

"I'm hanging up the phone, Sandra. I—" Another pause. "I'm not doing this tonight. I'm just not. I love you and we'll talk in the morning."

As he ends the call, my conscience gets the best of me. It was wrong of me to listen in, but the lives of adults fascinate me.

When I turn to go, I have a pause of my own. Between the mirrors and the sinks, there's a frosted glass shelf that runs all the way down the lineup. At the far end, a curling iron is sitting on it, like an abandoned child, and on a hunch, I walk over to the wand. I'm not surprised to find that it's still plugged in and turned on, despite some fifty girls having come here to wash their faces and brush their teeth before bed. No doubt it's been smoldering and making plans to fall into a bin full of combustible paper towels since before dinner.

I yank the cord out of the socket, and reflect on how pretty girls who feel the need to dress up for meals at an all-girls school don't worry about things like fire hazards. I believe it's because with them having won a genetic lottery when it comes to their looks, they assume all of chaos theory's consequences will inure to their benefit. For them, there is no tripping, no falling, no fender benders, and no lost car keys, sunglasses, or library books. All of their scratch-off tickets yield hundred-dollar payouts, any line they step into moves the fastest, and neglected responsibilities never come back to haunt them.

There's an unintended consequence to all this entitlement, however. The attractive are often agents of the very thing that blesses them, stewardesses coming down the aisle with rolling carts of collateral damage.

Curling irons left unattended are dangerous, for example, and even if my hypothesis is correct and their own rooms are not at risk, there are plenty of average- or below-average-looking girls trying to sleep within this nearly hundred-year-old dorm's nest of kindling wood.

At least this night, I have saved my homely cohort with my vigilance, and as I exit out into the hall, I feel like a fire safety inspector who has protected the lives of the acne-prone, the pudgy, the socially awkward, and the slope-chinned. I want a medal—

Someone else is emerging at the same time I am. They are to the right of me, but I can't see around the molding that sets apart the hallway from the main stairwell's second-floor landing. I hear the creak of floorboards, however, as well as the subtle squeak of a set of door hinges.

Tilting forward out of curiosity, I freeze as my residential advisor turns toward me. Standing on the threshold of his apartment, he is in loose blue jeans that have been washed many, many times; what once was hardy denim is now more like thin cotton. His T-shirt is gray and of a similar, faded vintage as the jeans, the Snoopy silkscreen merely a fog of what it once was. On his feet are leather sandals that braid over his tanned toes, and I have to admit that on anybody else, I would have found the look hippie-ish and unattractive. On him, it is hipper-than-I and way out of my league.

His eyes are so very, very green, beneath the brown fall of his longish hair.

I'm not surprised my body vibrates with warmth again. Our paths have not crossed in a one-on-one fashion since that first day, although I did get a lot out of our dorm orientation meeting for the sole reason that I could stare at him as he did most of the talking about the rules and regulations of Tellmer Hall.

"Well, hello," he says in an easygoing way. Like running into a student in the middle of the night is no big deal.

Then again, in spite of our curfew, there is no rule against using the bathroom after ten thirty p.m. We girls are wards of St. Ambrose, not prisoners.

"Hi," I say back.

My voice is so soft, I'm not even sure it registers for my own ears. But I'm worried that he can guess what I heard through the wall and this makes me timid.

"Having trouble sleeping?" he says as he reaches back and closes his apartment up.

His car keys jangle as he locks the deadbolt and I wonder where he's going. I also want to ask him if he's okay, a reflex born from years of being a spectator to all the one true loves of Tera Taylor, undiscovered movie star.

Instead, I go with, "Huh?"

"I can't sleep, either." He draws a hand through his hair, and that which was spilling forward obligingly reorganizes around a cowlick that is off to the side. "I don't know what my problem is. So I've decided to go for a drive. Have you seen the moonlight? It's incredible tonight."

His eyes shift to focus on the hall behind me, then go to the ornate window on the far side of the stairwell, and after that to the carpet runner beneath his funky sandals. This is what happens when someone is trying to manifest composure when on the inside, they're stressed. I'm fascinated that somebody as beautiful as him has anything wrong in his life.

"I'm Sarah," I blurt. Even though he didn't ask me my name.

"I'm pleased to meet you." He refocuses on me and puts his hand on the center of his chest. "I'm your RA, Nick, but you already know that."

"Yes, Mr. Hollis," I say. Because I'm clearly practicing for my future in public speaking.

"Call me Nick. Mr. Hollis is my father."

As I flush, I look down at his sandals. He has perfect toes with nicely trimmed nails. "Okay."

"I just have to go for a drive," he says like it's an afterthought. "Anyway, I hope you get some sleep."

"Thank you. You, too."

"Thanks." As he starts down the stairs, he says over his shoulder, "Let me know if you need anything, 'kay?"

Nick Hollis, call-him-Nick, gives me a little wave and jogs off, lithe as someone who is a gold medal winner in descent decathlons around the world. In his wake, I stay where I am, rather as one would if one encountered a unicorn in the woods without a camera: I memorize exactly where I stand, and the sounds of him bottoming out down below and then continuing to the full stairs that will take him to the basement and the back exit of Tellmer are like a symphony in my ears.

Or perhaps a sad opera, where there are asps involved at the end and everybody dies.

When there is nothing left to hear and my recollections have started to harden in my mind, I pivot on one foot.

And find that I am not alone for the second time.

Directly across the hall from my room, Greta Stanhope is in her own doorway, and in spite of the late hour, she is dressed in high-waisted jeans and a jacket that's the color of the inside of a cantaloupe. She is glaring down at me, as if I've trespassed into her house, and I brace myself for a confrontation that I am not ready to have.

All she does is recede like a sea monster, back to the briny depths of Ralph Lauren separates and Laura Ashley bedding.

I look back at the stairs. And promptly dismiss implications that make me feel uncomfortable.

I put my own door to very good use and take cover in my room. Going over to my bed, I don't lie down. I lean on the windowsill, bracing my palms on the cool wood and pressing my nose up against the even cooler glass.

I don't have to wait long until my residential advisor emerges down below.

Overcome by the knowledge that I've spied on him once unintentionally, and now I'm repeating the privacy violation very intentionally, I quickly duck back and make a messy fumble over the surface of my desk, bumping into notebooks and textbooks, the disruption causing a pen to roll off and chatter across the floorboards like it has four legs and is wearing a quartet of tap shoes.

"Jesus, Magda. Will you quit it with the noise," Strots mutters. "Granny's going to sic the butler on us."

My head whips around to my roommate. She is still on her side, in her running repose pose, and though she chastises me in her sleep using a different name, that's as far as it goes for her rousing. I lie down and try to mimic her. I suppose it's a testament to the physical attributes of my residential advisor that I don't dwell on the girl across the hall, even though she looked at me as if she'd made a target of me.

Nick Hollis is all I can think about.

chapter FOUR

I'm sitting at my desk, alone in the room I share with Strots. It's three nights later, and I'm trying not to think about the way Greta looked at me out in the hall. Although Nick Hollis held my attention at the time, the aftertaste is all about the girl who lives across from me. I cannot understand why she was so offended by my presence. Unless what I suspected was going on was actually happening.

But maybe the two of them know each other from life outside of Ambrose. Distant cousins? Yes, that has to be it. Two cousins, going out after curfew, for a drive.

Right after the married, mature-adult side of things had a fight with his wife who's out of town.

As I attempt, and fail, to concentrate on my geometry homework, I glance over my shoulder. The door is open. I would prefer that it be shut, but it's hot and I need the breeze flowing through the open slat windows above the beds. The voices that intrude are uninvited visitations, and I'm both trying to tune them out and paranoid that Greta's will be in the mix.

There are also perpetual footsteps, and opening and closing doors.

A toilet flushes. And then another.

This is one of the rush hour periods for activity. It is seven-oh-five and most of us have just come back to the dorm from dinner. The largest residential halls have big restaurant-sized kitchens in them and dining areas with the square footage of a soccer field. We're assigned to eat at Wycliffe, which is next door to us. I don't eat with Strots. She sits at a table that is full, all ten spindle-backed chairs occupied by girls who wear Ambrose Huskies sweatshirts even when it's eighty degrees out.

As far as I've seen, there are only two types of girls here. The ones who play sports and the ones who dress like getting a date is their sport even though there are no boys around to compete over. The former use no curling irons, ever, and the strict two-party system is strange to me. In my public high school, you had many divisions and strata. Not at Ambrose.

For the past three evenings, Strots hasn't returned immediately from dinner because she's hanging out in front of the dorm on the *lawn*. I come back here as soon as I'm finished with whatever is on my plate, desperate to get away from the pungent chaos of the dining hall and the fact that I don't know anybody and eat at a table alone with a book that's a prop.

Looking down at the notes I took in class, I contemplate the idea of sneaking food back to my room. I vow I will try this at breakfast.

A toilet flushes again. Down the hall, someone laughs.

It's then I hear the voice I have been dreading.

I look over my shoulder. Through the open door, I see Greta standing outside of her room with two brunettes. She's in the middle and prominent not only because of her blond coloring but also due to her superior physical attributes. Arranged like that, they remind me of a three-stone engagement ring, where the side diamonds are mounted only to enhance the larger, more valuable center.

The way they stare across the hall at me makes my throat tighten with fear. I wonder if she told her pals about our nocturnal meeting, and decide if she did, she clearly framed it that I interrupted something private, that I cheated her out of something: Those girls have the circle-the-wagons vengeance of best friends protecting the interests of their other half. The fact that residential advisors and students are two chemical compounds that are explosive if mixed seems not to matter.

Then again, I could be constructing a reality because, like my mother, I am possessive of things I will never, ever have, no matter my age.

"Hi, Sal," Greta says with a smile. "How are you? Adjusting okay?"

She's the only one who calls me that, a hangover from my mother introducing me that first day. And as the girl sends out her inquiries as to my welfare, her pretty face is arranged into a composition of concern. Her eyes sparkle like something that can burn me down, however, turning the toothbrush and tube of toothpaste in her hand into weapons that fight more than dental caries.

"Cat got your tongue?" she asks. "Just kidding. Let me know if I can help you get settled, okay?"

"Okay," I say. "Thanks."

"You're so welcome."

The pair of brunettes—Stacia and Francesca, if I have the names right—tilt inward and cover their mouths with a cup of their hand. Both of them have colorful woven bracelets on and I have a thought that Greta must also wear one. She does. As well as a gold bangle that is thin and delicate.

Greta ignores whatever the girls are whispering to her. She is staring at me, recording me, filing some kind of assessment report in her head. And then she turns away, and the brunettes follow, flags tied to the stern of the mother ship. The door to the vault is closed.

Strots walks into our room. "Hey. What's up, Taylor."

Her presence is a jarring relief, pulling me out of my head, and yet I'm saddened by seeing her, too. Five days after I first met my roommate, I've realized that as nice as she is to me, there's no opportunity to be her friend. She's busy with her fellow athletes, busy with her sports, busy with her busyness. I still want to be her, but I am no longer actively mourning my lack of khaki shorts and blue T-shirts.

"Mind if I close this?" she asks at the door.

"Sure."

She shuts the thing with her foot, and goes over to smoke by her open window. As usual, she solves the ashtray issue with Coca-Cola, which she drinks all the time. Leaving two inches in the bottom of the plastic bottles does the ticket, her butts drowning in sugar and carbonated caffeine.

"You got Crenshaw for geometry?" she asks.

I look at my textbook. "Yes, I do."

"She's a pushover. My friend had her last year. I got Thomas."

I feel compelled to offer an opinion on Mr. Thomas. "I've heard he's good, though."

"Her. It's Ms. Thomas."

I flush and go quiet. As we sit in silence, I try to think of something, anything that would be normal to say.

"You gotta meet some people, Taylor," Strots tells me. "You gotta get out more."

An image of the dining hall comes to mind, and my memory of the two hundred girls in there, all of them talking at once, eating, drinking, scraping their chairs back and their trays off, is an electrical shock down my spinal cord.

"I'd ask you to sit you with me, but we don't have room," Strots says like she's reading my mind. "They don't let us pull chairs."

This is not true. I've seen other tables that have a Saturn's ring of seats around the core. Greta's is one. But I appreciate Strots trying not to hurt my feelings, and have a sense that she feels as though I am a responsibility of hers that she wouldn't have chosen, but will not shirk.

"It's okay," I say.

"You don't talk much."

"I don't have much to say." I look back at her. "I'm sorry."

"Doesn't bother me." She taps her ash into the soda bottle. "You need friends, though."

"Greta and the two brunettes?" I say in a wry tone.

Strots laughs. "Oh, my God, like it's a band and they're the backup singers. That's fucking perfect."

The idea Strots has found something I've said funny makes me tingle with happiness, and I realize I want to be my roommate not because she's sporty. I want to be Greta not because she's popular or pretty. I just want to be something, anything, as opposed to in the "other" category I inhabit. I want a full table of people who are from the same dye lot as myself, whose voices I recognize, whose ears want to hear what I have to say, whose eyes seek out mine to acknowledge inside jokes.

There's no one in my orbit for sure, and there's another reason I keep my mouth closed. I have a secret I'm ashamed of, and pride is the only thing that the poor have plenty of in their wallets and their cupboards, and I am destitute not just from a money standpoint, I am poor all over, in all ways, I am Tiny Tim, I am disabled by a fireplace, hungry at Christmas, begging for—

I stop my thoughts as a cold rush hits the top of my head.

It's too late. My mind coughs up countless Tiny Tim images, Tiny Tim syllables, a deluge of the spines of Dickens novels along with that old movie my mother made me watch on the TV with turkey meat TV dinners—

I squeeze my eyes shut.

I take a deep breath and do what Dr. Warten taught me to do. I label this behavior. This is a prodromal symptom I must rein in. I am not Tiny Tim. I am not Charles Dickens. I am not a starving, peg-legged child on a stool before a crackling fire, with an empty belly, dirty clothes, a smudge of soot on my too-lean, baby boy face—

My heart begins to pound. My mouth goes dry. I find it interesting that I can be on such a precipice and yet my roommate is calmly easing back against the wall on her bed, cracking open a book, taking out a notebook and a blue Bic pen—

It's a Bic. Just like her lighter. A Bic. Two Bics.

Lighter and pen. A lighter pen. AlighterpenBic. Bic, Bic, Bic . . . two Bics, a Bic, a Bic, a BicaBicaBic—

I jump to my feet and knock my chair over. On her bed, Strots looks up in surprise. I turn to reassure her, but cannot hear what I say to her or what she says back to me. Her lips are moving, and so are mine, but I cannot—

—BicBicBic. Red. Blue. RedBlue. Pen.Pen.Lighterlighterbluered—

The next thing I know, I am in the shower, standing under cold water. I have no idea how I got here. I'm naked, so I clearly had enough presence of mind to remove my clothes somewhere along the way—please, God, not outside my room, in the hallway—and my teeth are chattering. My arms are locked under my unremarkable, ant-mound breasts, and my fake-black hair has rivered down onto my collarbones, forming oil streaks on top of my pale skin . . .

I lose my grasp on those thoughts. Whatever they were.

Taking a deep breath, I close my eyes and concentrate more on what my lungs are doing. In and out. In and out. I ride as best I can the tremors of the currently receding cognitive earthquake, those hoppity-skippity-thought-ities that will take me back down the road I do not want to go down again, down, again, downagain—

More breathing, as I fight the filaments of madness that are attaching to me and trying to pull me through the reality fence into a playground with sharp knives and sandpaper, broken glass and rusty nails.

Desperate to save myself, I picture Strots sitting on her bed in our room, blowing smoke in the direction of the open window, her bare legs crossed, her other hand holding the pack of cigarettes and the lighter on one of her knees. I see the new bruise on her shin from field hockey practice. I see the scrape on the outside of her thigh. I see the raw patch on her elbow.

This is what does it. The image of my roommate, with all its accurate, short-term memory details, is what unplugs the electrical current.

As I land more solidly back in my body, this is the most important reason I don't talk much: It takes so much effort to keep myself connected to reality that I don't have much left over for casual conversation. I am in a perpetual inner loop, my mental illness a centrifuge that tries to draw me into myself, the outside world and other people a Polo to my Marco that in best-case scenarios can bring me back.

As long as I am measuring my environment and the people in it, I am a tethered air balloon.

And it has worked again. This time.

As my physical awareness resurges, the temperature of the spray becomes painful and I shiver. I reach behind and fumble with the faucet's single handle, cranking it all the way up to the *H*, after which I regulate things so I'm comfortable. I'm relieved that there seems to be no one else in the bathroom. I hear no voices in the larger space and the girls here are incapable of going anywhere singly or in silence, their endless expulsion of syllables part of their respiratory function. There are also no fruity, flowery smells emanating from the showers on either side of me, no toilets flushing with a choked gasp, no minty fresh goings-on at the sinks.

I dread what Strots thinks of me right now and I hope no one else witnessed my shambled trip in here. I'm also surprised to find that I remembered to get my shampoo and soap from my cubby and bring them with me. They're at my feet on the tile, loners in a wet desert. Unlike the other girls, I don't have a red bucket with a handle to keep corralled bottles of Herbal Essences along with razors, moisturizers, and the ubiquitous Clinique facial soap that comes in those pale green plastic-train-tunnel containers.

I didn't know I needed a bucket.

Bending down, I pick up my shampoo bottle. Like my mother's Primo perfume—an almost Giorgio—this is a value brand of some kind, a knockoff of what the other girls have.

As I tilt the fluted plastic container over my palm, a loose rush comes out and the dispenser top falls free to the drain, dancing in the rain to a diminishing beat. I look up at the curtain that I had at some point pulled into place, but as it answers no questions, I go back to staring at my palm. Most of the totally diluted shampoo has run through my fingers, but there is a gloss of it left. I lift my hand to my nose and my heart pounds. There are so many things to tamper a bottle with, and I am terrified it is urine.

I sniff, trying to suss out the nutty, acidic bouquet of pee.

There is none. It's just water.

I'm going to give you a piece of advice. Don't give them what they want.

As I hear my roommate's voice in my head, I think of Greta's expression out in the hall just now and I'm willing to bet she did this—or maybe ordered one of the Brunettes to do the tampering—in retaliation for my unintended nocturnal interruption of whatever she was doing. Or maybe she just hated me on sight.

I am not using anything that comes out of that bottle.

Instead, I rub my rotgut bar soap on my head, aware that I'm likely to strip even more of the black Clairol color out of my hair. Then I use the stuff on my body, and that's that. I have no razor to shave with. I never do my armpits or my legs or my privacy, as my mother calls it. I can't be trusted with razors. Knives. Scissors.

I turn the water off. I pull the plastic curtain back. I remain mentally present for the drying off and the donning of my long-sleeved nightshirt and pj bottoms. I marvel at how, even in the flight from my room, I had the presence of mind to bring the change of clothes.

I promptly become obsessed with when the tampering occurred. During their teeth brushing after dinner, maybe? I've noticed that all three of them go to the bathroom with their Colgate and Crest right after the nightly meal. It's not because they're worried about their dental health. They have to vomit out whatever they've eaten and the dental artifacts are to clean up after the evacuation. They're not the only ones who do this on my floor.

As I take note of my thoughts, I am relieved. Where my brain is now, in this very non-Tiny-Tim, anti-Dickens, no-turkey-TV-dinner kind of place? If I am to survive here at Ambrose, this is where I must stay, and in a weird twist of fate—or perhaps inevitably, given the principles of chaos theory—I have Greta to thank for the return to the real world.

The threat of her has put me back in my skin, back with everyone else.

As I step out of the stall with my things, I look around. The bank of sinks is across the way and there are trash receptacles between each of the basins. I toss out the shampoo bottle in the nearest one and look toward the exit. Just like downstairs with the mail cubbies, there is an entire wall of cubicles by the door. They're not marked with our names up here, but rather with our room numbers, an A and a B denoting which roommate's is which.

I can guess Greta's spot. Undoubtedly, she took the A—214A.

In a fit of paranoia, I go over to 213B and take my toothbrush in hand. The bristles are dry, and, upon a close inspection of each and every stalked group of them, I find no evidence of toilet scum. After I tuck my Oral-B-ish brush and generic paste into the load I am balancing, I leave the bathroom.

Out in the hall, I measure the brown and gray flecks in the heavy-duty carpet I walk on. And the smudges on the painted walls. And note how uneven the ceiling is because it was plastered in the twenties and has had to be repaired over the last seventy years.

All of what continues to go through my mind is in the world that others inhabit, the one that I have just involuntarily left and, for the moment and courtesy of Greta, returned to. Dr. Warten, my psychiatrist, warned me before he signed off on my attending Ambrose that disruptions in sleep and schedule can create a fermenting ground for the bad side of my brain. He told me to be on the lookout for signs that I'm becoming symptomatic again. Frankly, I was surprised he was okay with my coming here at all. But I think he knows that with a brain like mine, all of life is an experiment with a low likelihood of success. It doesn't matter where I am, so I might as well get a good education in the process.

This Bic-a-Bic, Tiny Tim thing was just a hiccup. Nothing to get hysterical about.

As I come up to 213, I am aware that Greta's door is now open again, and in my peripheral vision, I register how she is sitting on her pink and white bed. She is brushing her long, luxurious, properly washed and conditioned blond hair. She is wearing a silky pink and red robe, the halves of which have parted to reveal her shapely legs. Music is playing from a portable stereo that is big as a desk, Boyz II Men.

I don't have to see her face to know she is looking at me and feeling triumphant over my ruination.

But she is incorrect. I am not cowed by her actions. When it comes to her, my eternal vigilance is going to help keep me where I need to stay. In this regard, I should be grateful.

"Have a good shower, Sal?" she says with a smile.

I meet her right in the eye. "Yes. Thank you."

chapter FIVE

Two weeks later, I'm in geometry class. Ms. Crenshaw, who also happens to be the RA on the first floor of Tellmer, is at the board. She is like my mother because she is forty, but other than that, they have little in common. For Ms. Crenshaw, there is no wrap-dress-thing going on. No highlighted hair. No makeup. She looks like a tour guide at a zoo, all khaki-colored and sturdy-shoed, her ashy hair in a bowl cut that somehow still manages to look uneven at the ends.

The room we are in is on the ground floor, in the front corner of Palmer Hall, a grand old brick building that looks like something you'd find on the cover of a book about higher education. All of the windows are open and it's not helping the heat. Summer's last thermal assault has arrived in this part of New England and it feels like August, the air a suffocating solid that you break sweaty pieces off of as you inhale.

"Come on, you guys," Ms. Crenshaw says. "I know it's sweltering in here, but let's try to pay attention. This is a review for your test on Friday. Who can tell me what the difference between a line and a ray is?"

As I shift my position to try to rouse myself, the capsule desk does not accommodate me in the slightest.

"How about you, Sarah?"

I look up from my book. Ms. Crenshaw is staring over the heads of the twelve other students who have likewise melted into their table-chairs. In my teacher's unremarkable brown eyes, I see stress kindling, and I have the sense that if she doesn't get a reply, her head will vibrate and explode like the guy from that movie *Scanners*.

Her apartment back at Tellmer is directly under Nick Hollis's, and the instant this mental connection is made, my mind slides into a familiar home base. Like all the others who live where I do, my eyes follow Hot RA around our floor, around the dorm, around campus. Every time I catch sight of him, it's as if I am in a convertible with the top down and the music turned up loud. It's a secret, private thrill, and of that, I'm glad.

Ms. Crenshaw, on the other hand, has likely made no one tingle in the course of her life, and it's not a surprise that she wears no wedding band.

"What's the difference between a line and a ray?" she prompts.

"A line has two fixed points," I say. "A ray has one fixed point and then infinitely extends in the other direction."

"Exactly." She exhales as if she's been rescued out of the jaws of a bear. "Thank you, Sarah."

I nod to her and then refocus on my book. Or pretend to.

One of Greta's Brunettes is sitting in front of me, her long, long hair blanketing her back like dark silk. Francesca is enviably slim, with a tiny waist and long, long legs, and I have a feeling she must be stuffing her bra because at her swizzle stick body weight, I can't imagine her breasts are as big as they seem.

I have been stalking her at night and I wonder if she knows it.

Actually, no, it's Greta I've been following. She and Stacia are collateral foci.

Every evening, about an hour before curfew, Greta and her Brunettes leave out the back of the dorm. A week ago, I decided to follow them. At the appointed hour, I hid down on the lawn, and when they emerged, I slid into the shadows behind them, making sure that I stayed out of earshot as I tracked their progress. They ended up going to the river behind Tellmer and Wycliffe, penetrating the brushy overgrowth and hooking up with a well-trod path of which I was previously unaware.

Their destination was an outcropping of flat broad stones within the waterway, and they sat in a circle and smoked.

It was a window into another world, and their nightly tradition has become my own. I have discovered the perfect hiding place from which to eavesdrop. Right by their perch, there is a great sugar maple with a bifurcated trunk, and as they talk and gesture theatrically, I watch from behind its craggy cover the firefly ends of their dancing, flaring cigarettes, and I listen in on their conversations. Mostly they talk about the boyfriends they're with when they return home on breaks or are off during the summers. These boys go to boys' schools just like Ambrose, and letters and phone calls are dissected within the group, picked apart for hidden meaning and any evidence that some other girl may have entered the picture when their back was turned. They also talk about giving head, and third base, and going all the way, something the three of them have done more than once.

In the darkness, with their lit cigarettes, Greta and the Brunettes blow smoke with extravagance, ever ready for their close-ups though there are no cameras around. I wondered, in the beginning, whether they even noticed the lack of audience. Now, I realize that narcissism provides a perpetual one.

Overhead, the classroom bell rings and there's an instant rush of girls jamming their feet into the floor as they slam shut their textbooks, scoop up their backpacks, and shoot themselves free of the uni-desks.

"Quiz on Friday," Ms. Crenshaw calls out. "Don't forget!"

In other classes, I am slower to extract myself, preferring to let my classmates tangle into a traffic jam at the door. With Ms. Crenshaw, I leave inside the great exodus, making sure there's a blur of students between us. I worry that she'll trap me into a heart-to-heart, two misfits catching up on what it's like to be an outcast.

I do not want to bond with an adult over the very thing I'd change most about myself.

The front entrance of Palmer is opened wide, students blindly holding the heavy wooden doors for the girls behind them, the torrent released by the bell like a storm-swollen brook flowing down stone steps that have worn grooves in them from countless years of this phenomenon. I am pushed to the side because I don't fight for a position in the middle, but I must keep with the pace or I'll be trampled.

As soon as I'm on the sidewalk, the tsunami disperses into a trickle, students heading off in all directions to their assigned dining halls. I meander now. Overhead, the sun is brutally hot behind a translucent veil of thin clouds. I assess the heavily leaved maple trees for signs of color change. There still are none. I'm disappointed.

It's lunchtime, but I don't feel any urgency in this regard. My enthusiasm for food has waned for a variety of reasons, and my gastronomic ennui has been heightened by the fact that late last week I was informed that, in fact, I may not remove food, silverware, or plates from the dining hall. This is a problem, but what can I do?

I am stuck eating as quickly as I can, sitting at my table alone and trying to tune out the sensory overload. Maybe if I had someone to talk to it might be easier, but no one's volunteered to take a chance on me and I won't take a chance on anyone else. I always perch at the table closest to the wide archway to the left of the dining hall's entrance. There's a trash bin right behind me, one that's rarely used by anyone else, and if I am efficient, I can get in and out in about fifteen minutes.

Overall, I'm doing okay with my brain. Sleep is critical for someone like me, and I've become disciplined with my bedtime. There's the ten o'clock curfew after which we're not allowed to leave the dorm and a mandatory eleven o'clock lights out. When Strots finishes her homework, she usually goes up to the third floor where two of her field hockey teammates live. She stays there from ten to eleven, and as soon as I am back from my spying, I use that quiet time in our room to get settled in bed and close my eyes. Most nights, when she comes back in for lights out, I'm still awake, but I've put in my REM sleep prep time so I'm half asleep.

Today, however, in all this heat, exhaustion is something I drag behind me. I just don't have it in me to tangle with the cafeteria. I go back to Tellmer.

"No lunch for you?"

As I arrive at my dorm, Greta is coming out of it, a bounce in her step, her hair loosely knotted on top of her head, a ball of flaxen silk. Her perfume changes daily, something she accessorizes to her outfits, I assume, and today her sartorial stylings are a version of the belly shirt, short skirt, and leggings Francesca had on in geometry, only executed in bright blue and pink, no doubt to set off the tan she regularly refreshes out on the *lawn* my mother liked so much.

"You know," Greta tells me as she pauses by my side, "you're not the kind of girl who has to bother with a diet. Lucky, lucky you."

Continuing on her way, her smile, like her comment, is a casual middle finger, a screw-you that she feels the need to share but isn't inclined to put much effort into. I don't respond because my mind has gone blank and I'm therefore grateful that she seems distracted by whatever pressing matter awaits her at lunch.

In her perfumed wake, I'm even more tired.

So much for being grateful for her bullying distraction. Today, she deflates me.

On dragging feet, I go up to Strots's and my room. Given we don't have a lock, I'm instantly paranoid because Greta was here in the mostly empty dorm with access to everything I own. Gripping the knob with a sweaty palm, I open things up slowly, as if she might have jury-rigged the door with something that belongs in a Stephen King novel.

Nothing happens, and yet I remain careful as I step inside. I am also anxious for another reason. Heart in my throat, I go to my dresser. Although I don't want any of my meager belongings tampered with, there's one thing that I absolutely cannot have somebody violate. I yank open the top drawer, shove my black cotton underwear out of the way, and push my hand all the way to the back. When I feel the little cylindrical container, I shake with relief, and then I pull it out to double-check something isn't wrong with its contents.

The prescription bottle emerges from the drawer with the label facing me. I see my name, my birth date, the address of my mother's house, and the name of the drug, lithium. I see the dosage and the notation that I am to take one 300 mg tablet twice a day. Back when things were bad, I was taking pills three times a day and they were at a higher milligram count. We're on maintenance now.

Tightening a hold on the white top, I push down and turn at the same time. Inside the bottle, there are a reassuring number of the chalky white pills, perfect circles with a stamp on one side and a line on the other. I lean down and take a sniff. The chemical bouquet is faint and unpleasant, but as I've never smelled inside the bottle before, I don't know whether it's normal or not. I pour a few pills into my hand. They seem fine. In any event, I have no choice but to take them.

I look around my room. Hiding them in my top drawer seems stupid now. Everyone hides things in with their underwear, don't they? I decide to put them somewhere else. I choose the bottom left-hand side of my desk, under my extra folders and my backup notebooks. Much better. If someone comes looking for my medication, they will have to hunt and peck now, and maybe this will give me time to get back from wherever I am.

As I close the drawer on the newer, hopefully better, hiding place, I push my hair out of my face with fingers that tremble. I don't like being on lithium and I sure as hell don't like taking it here at school. I'm always afraid someone, even Strots, will burst through the door halfway through the swallow. I typically retreat into my closet and close myself in, popping the top off in the darkness and pulling them down dry, the pills getting stuck to the back of my throat so that I have to repeatedly swallow to usher them along.

Even if somebody isn't poorly opined of me, such as Strots, the news that a girl in this dorm is on a psychotropic drug is too tantalizing not to share, and share, and share.

The sound of someone talking in the hall brings my head up and I'm momentarily surprised by the fact that I've taken out the pills again and am reexamining the bottle with my door open to anyone who might pass. The lithium that helps me stay on the planet may look like aspirin, but given the orange bottle it comes in, you don't need to be a genius to know it's a substance that requires dispensing by a physician's order, and therefore treats something far, far more serious than a common cold, a common ache.

Jesus, I hope whoever was talking didn't see me.

A moment later, I hear the back door to the dorm open and close. I go over to the window and look down. Hot RA is walking to his sports car, his hair gleaming in the hot and heavy sunlight, his blue jeans once again worn and washed to the point of paling out, his shirt long-sleeved but white and diaphanous, like a veil for his torso. He looks fresh and sexy, and as my senses dance, I realize that even though he's married, I live for the moments I catch a glimpse of him.

And I ache at the thought that I am not the only one who does this. The impact of his presence is so great on me that its intensity seems to demand a special carve-out for me. I feel as though I should be the only one who is allowed to notice him. But that is not realistic, and as I consider how many others covet our residential advisor, I have a theory that part of the allure is the impossibility of it all. Nick Hollis is totally unobtainable to any of us because of his age and employment, and then there is his marriage. Plus I've heard his wife is part of a federal task force on AIDS and that she lectures around the nation to cities and hospitals. I've already decided she's a Miss America beauty queen in addition to being an intellectual giant and a resplendent humanitarian.

Even if she might get into her cups from time to time and argue with her husband over long distance.

I watch call-me-Nick unlock the driver's side door of his two-seater and insert his rangy body into the seat behind the wheel. His car is even older than my mother's, but it's no Mercury Marquis. His is some kind of vintage Porsche and it's in gleaming mint condition. It's a pale blue, with eyelike headlights offset on the flat hood, its back end curved in tight like a dog with its tail tucked under. When he starts the engine, it has a ticky, high note, and as he drives it forward with confidence—because he always parks rear fender in—I have a feeling it was probably his father's and has been passed down. From what I've overheard in the bathroom, Hot RA graduated from Yale with a master's in English, and he is only here for a year before he, and that traveling wife of his, go back to New Haven so he can get his PhD. He is going to be a professor at an Ivy League school. He is going to write important books about important books.

The fact that he is smart and wealthy as well as too beautiful to look at seems like too much good fortune for one person to possess. He reminds me of Greta.

Returning the pills to their new spot, I decide to motivate. I have some laundry that I've started down in the basement, and I should put it in the dryer before everything smells like gym clothes even though I don't take gym. I swap my geometry textbook and notebook out of my backpack, and put my French things in there. Then I one-strap the *avoirdupois* and leave.

The dorm's laundry room is in the basement, and as I descend into the lowest level of our building, I'm hit with a pervasive cool that feels good for the moment, but that will soon make me want to put a sweater on. Along with the washer and dryer facility, there's a rec room nobody uses and some storage areas that have doors that are not just deadbolted but chained with padlocks. There's also the boiler room, which wafts an auto repair shop smell of dirty oil.

As I enter the laundry, the air smells too sweet, a meadow's worth of lab-created floral scents making my eyes water because there is no ventilation. It's also toasty because somebody is using one of the six dryers. I think of that *Peanuts* comic strip: *Happiness is a warm blanket.*

Was it Schroeder who said that about his blanket? I wonder as I go over to the six washers.

There's a shelf that runs above the workhorse Maytags, and on it are various detergents, most of them liquid, all of them labeled with student names. An overflow for supplies is off to the side, the well-used,

Formica-topped table sporting a secondary fleet of bottles. There's also a vending machine that dispenses boxes of powder for twenty-five cents. The washers and dryers are free.

Naturally, there is a lucky machine for me. The one I must use is all the way down the row on the left, a random choice that is another absolute—

As I open the lid, I stop where I am, my aimless wander of thoughts ceasing in concert with my body.

A smell rises up from the belly of my machine, sharp, pungent, pool-like.

Leaning down, I pull out something, anything. What arrives at the lip of the maw is the exhausted twist of one of my long-sleeved shirts. The black of the fabric is speckled with pale brown spots and splashes, and as I flatten it out on the closed lid of the next machine in line, I do not understand what is happening. What has happened. What I am looking at.

I bring more of my clothes out, and the autopsy reveals a possible explanation. It appears that undiluted bleach was poured in after the end of the spin cycle, and the Clorox has been sitting in there long enough to stain, but not long enough to eat holes in what it came into contact with.

I look around the laundry room, as if answers will present themselves courtesy of the peanut gallery of Tides and Drefts and Persils. There are a couple of different bottles of bleach in and among the detergents and fabric softeners, and I have a passing thought that I need to check out the names on those labels. I'm utterly fatigued, however.

I assess the dryers, especially the one that is operating. Before I look away, there is a click and the carousel inside of it falls still. My heart pounds harder as I go across and pull open the door. Reaching into the hot, soft air, I pull out whatever my hand touches first. And I already know the answer. My body trembles as I turn the shirt around, and open the boat neckline to look at the fabric name tag that has been stitched into the—

Karen Bronwyn.

I don't even know her.

I look around the laundry room again as if it'll explain how the name is not Margaret Stanhope. Putting the shirt back where I took it from, I make sure the door is closed properly.

I go back to my washer. I don't move my clothes over to a dryer. I have some thought, which is expressed in the voice of my mother, that I need to rinse everything first through another wash cycle. If I put my things in the dryer with the bleach still wet on them, I'll do even more damage.

My first instinct is to ignore the advice. I want to shove everything in the clothing kiln, crank up the dial to "High Heat/Cottons," and let it all roast in a chemical bonfire.

But like I'm going to wear a towel to class?

One by one, I transfer my stained clothes out of the chosen washer into another, two units over. I can't bear to rinse them in what I thought was my anointed machine. My hands continue to shake as I gently put each shirt, and the three pairs of heavy canvas pants, and the seven underwears, and a school of black socks into their new bathing accommodation.

But maybe it wasn't Greta. Maybe this was a mistake, somebody thinking they were adding a little bleach to brighten their load in mid-cycle.

As I try on this hypothetical, every cell in me revolts at the fallacy, and I consider the practical implications to what is clearly a trend. To Greta and her backup band of suck-ups, these petty pranks are minor injuries inflicted for fun. To me, they're bombs that do structural damage, creating ragged gaps in my ability to function that I don't have the resources to patch. I can't go to the student center and blithely whisk shampoo bottles off the shelves to replace what's been washed down a bathroom sink because the bill will go to my mother and she's stretched thin. I can't go to a clothing store and buy an entire new wardrobe of long-sleeved shirts and pants for the same reason.

And I can't believe I'm stuck with no one but my unreliable self to watch over me, something that is irrespective of geographic location. Even if my mother were in the same town, that wouldn't change.

In the periphery of my vision, I note the clock on the wall, its white face and black numbers and hands proclaiming that I have twelve minutes before fourth period starts.

I want to stay to make sure no one else messes with my clothes, but I can't. We have a test in French.

Before I leave, I look at the shelf above the washers. There are three bleach bottles in the lineup on it, and all of them are nearly full. None of them have Greta's name on them. Or Francesca's or Stacia's. But when I check the trash bin, an empty Clorox container is lying on top of a bed of dryer lint bundles, cushioned and self-satisfied as a pasha. I pick it up and inspect its white body and blue product label. There is no name. I throw it out once more.

I go over to the dryers and put my hand on each of the ones that have been silent and immobile since I walked in. The one on the far end is still warm. As I open its door, the sweet-smelling, warm breath of the machine hits my face. The clothes that lie in a jumble from their tumbles are bright and sunny, tiny and pretty. I reach inside and pull out a pale orange shirt, one so small you would think it is a child's size.

The tag reads *Margaret Stanhope*.

"Bitch," I whisper.

It requires discipline on my part not to do something, anything in payback. I ultimately resist the urge. And there's no way to report this to the RAs. I'm assuming that no one saw her mess with my washer, or, if there were witnesses, they were giggling participants. And so what if my clothes were destroyed while hers were down here? That girl Karen's clothes are in a dryer as well, and the room is never locked. It could be anybody.

Even though it isn't.

As I turn to leave, I glance at my new favorite washer and pray that what comes out of it is wearable. I imagine the glee Greta will have in telling the Brunettes and the others to wait for it, wait and see what the freak is wearing now.

The idea that they consume my suffering as a snack makes me want a mother—not my actual mother, with the lit cigarette and the cheap perfume, but one of the other mothers I used to watch on the playground when I was younger. The ones who rushed over to a scraped knee, who scooped their children up and held them to a breast that was modestly covered, who rocked and cajoled and soothed. I want a gentle, Jergens-smelling hand on my cheek and in my hair. I want a soft voice telling me that it's going to be okay.

I want someone in my corner.

Anyone.

chapter
SIX

I am not going to give Greta what she wants.

It's the day after I found my laundry ruined. Wednesday. And Wednesdays we only have classes in the morning, because the afternoons are reserved for athletic games against other prep schools—or, if you're not on a varsity sport, free time. I've been to Wycliffe to eat lunch and I'm walking to the student center in the last clean, untampered-with shirt I have and a pair of pants I don't like because one leg is slightly shorter than the other. I have a five-dollar bill with me.

The oppressive weather we've been toiling under is about to break, but the heat and humidity are being stubborn about their eviction by a cold front coming down from the north. The conflict zone between the two extremes is boiling up heavy clouds that spill bowling balls of thunder out from their overstuffed duffel bags of rain. The worst of the storms are still off in the distance, but the warnings are all around, the green leaves of trees flipping to flash their silver undersides in gusty hot winds, the birds extra chatty, as if they're energized by the stir of ions in the air, a tingle on the back of my neck warning me I better be quick about what I'm doing if I don't want to get drenched.

My destination is the Petersen Auditorium, which is in the middle of campus. The building is a Victorian Gothic with a patterned red and gray slate roof, patterned gray and black stone walls, and a flourished entrance of dark gray steps and gargoyles. It's my favorite building, a marvelous Halloween-come-to-life oddball in the midst of all the prim and proper brick dorms and classrooms.

The student bookstore is in the basement. As I enter, I'm flinchy and on the lookout for pinks and pastels, for long hair and scrunchies, but there seems to be nobody inside except me and the townie clerk who couldn't care less that I've entered. She's sitting on a stool behind the counter at the cash register, leafing through one of my mother's kind of magazines. She's of college age, but she's clearly not going to a university, and she has a choppy haircut that I suspect is an attempt to elevate her otherwise cheap and uninspiring clothes. She's chewing gum and snapping it between her molars, the popping beat exactly the kind of uneven, yet repetitive, sound that goes through my body like a volt of electricity.

I have a thought that she's my mother through a time machine, twenty years erased, back at the start of things when a future that would warrant coverage in *People* was not only possible, but inevitable. My parents' whole relationship was based on her innate hunger for status elevating his garage band singing to that of a neo-Bruce-Springsteen quality. The fantasy worked for the both of them.

Unfortunately, the band stayed in the garage, and all they got as a door prize for their unrealized pipe dreams was me.

I move forward, passing through the mostly empty textbook section of the store. In the rear, I find the grocery/drugstore part, with toiletries, basic first aid medications, and rudimentary beauty products shelved next to bars of candy, bags of chips, and boxes of cereal. There's a limited choice and limited supply of what's offered, but they do a brisk business in calorie-dense, nonnutritious foods as well as no-reasonable-alternative makeup and hairstyling products.

I pause in front of the medicines because the bottles of over-the-counter pain relievers capture my attention. In the end, I keep going to my planned destination and I'm relieved I was able to move along. Aspirin and Tylenol are like sharp objects to me. They're the steak knives of pharmaceuticals, easy to get a hold of and innocuous in the hands of most.

To me, they are conduits for bad things, and I don't trust the morbid sizzle I get whenever I'm near them.

I halt at the laundry section. Sure enough, I find three one-liter bottles of Clorox, the thinner, bikini-ready versions of the big fat middle-aged bottles my mother buys for herself. I briefly revisit the idea of payback, and consider buying a bottle of retaliation brand bleach. But I know I'll never follow through on the flare of aggression, and I certainly won't ever need Clorox for my own wardrobe, even with Greta having given me a head start in the lightening department.

Disappointed by my cowardice, I search for what I came for. I'm not surprised that I'm unable to find clothing dye in what I assume is the only section in which it would be stocked.

On my way to the exit, I stop in front of the clerk to make sure I haven't missed something. It's hot outside, and I'd like to save myself the walk into town, if I can. She informs me, without looking up from an article on Ann Jillian's miracle baby, that I have to go to CVS for that kind of stuff. She doesn't acknowledge my thank-you or my departure.

Back out on the sidewalk, I frown at the sweltering temperature and think about putting off the trip. It's two miles each way and there are those storms coming. I'm running out of clean clothes, however, and I refuse to tip my hand that I discovered the damage. I start walking. For once, I will pull up my long sleeves, but not until after I step off of the Ambrose acreage.

Down at the campus's far edge, a construction project has just been started, and as I close in on the cellar hole of what will clearly be the school's biggest building, I feel a kinship with the workmen. They're all in heavy clothes just like I am, and they look hot in the sun, too.

A fancy sign mounted in front of the site surprises me.

THE STROTSBERRY ATHLETIC CENTER.

Funny, Strots has never mentioned this. And as I've had my gym requirement waived because of the lithium, I've never been close to the site.

For the first time, I wonder just exactly how much money my roommate's family has. She's so down-to-earth, but even Greta doesn't have a Stanhope Hall to brag about.

Maybe there's a level of wealth even higher up than Greta's, and doesn't that make me smile a little.

As I pass through Ambrose's gates, I shove my sleeves up and expose the scars that mark my wrists. For the longest time, they were red and angry, welts left from the lashes of my slashes and the tangle of stitches I got at the ER. They've faded a lot since then, but I know them by heart, and my obsession with how noticeable they are makes me feel like they are neon bright.

Just as I step onto the sidewalk that runs into town, one of the school's orange buses goes by. I wave as I recognize Strots in the lineup of half-cocked windows, and I see that she lifts her hand to me in response. The chanting of the girls and the sweet fumes of the diesel exhaust and the rumble of the engine all fade at the same rate as the team and their transport disappear down the road, warriors on the way to the field hockey front lines.

Fare thee well, fair Athenas, I think.

The town of Greensboro Falls isn't much more than a main street, a gas station, and a public library that's bigger than the police station that sits next to it. A ring of residential houses lollygags around the anemic suburban pimple, the tired one- and two-stories small and, in many cases, lacking garages. As I lumber by them in the blazing warmth, I reflect that my mother and I live in the same kind of place, something that's just a roof and walls to keep out the cold in the winter and the elements always.

Over my shoulder, thunder rolls through the sky. I quicken my steps and lift the hair off the sweaty nape of my neck. Even though it's cloudy, I feel as though the sun is seeking me out through the churning gray blanket that separates us. I find myself wondering whether, if I had a wardrobe similar in color to Greta's, she'd have left my washer's load alone as a chromatic courtesy. It's an inane hypothetical. Besides, bright colors make me nervous, and somehow I doubt that sartorial solidarity would have saved me.

There are two traffic lights on the main drag, one as you come into the ten-block stretch of stores and businesses, and one as you leave it. Ten blocks seems like a lot, but it's not when you consider there's no sprawl of commerce behind the storefronts, no purchasing penetration past the parking lots that skirt the back of each establishment. There are two lawyers' offices, three restaurants, a dental practice, a doctor, a movie theater with only two screens, a record store, and an H&R Block for taxes. The rest are mom-and-pop peddlers offering collections of earthy-crunchy clothes, handmade gifts, and local books, photography, and hobbyist art. There's only one national mainstay in the midst of all the town-specific, and as this CVS comes into view around the subtle curve of the street, it is a televangelist among vicars.

Inside its consumer value interior, the air smells like strawberries and wax paper, soft Muzak is piped in from somewhere, and fluorescent lights rain false sun on the thousands of products available for purchase. I wonder, if someone steals something, whether the two middle-aged, uniformed women stationed behind the mile-long candy display are rugged enough to swing their legs over their counters and chase a shoplifter down the sidewalk. Probably not. Maybe they have panic buttons to call the police, which are stationed, along with the town library, right behind the store, although it seems unlikely the cashiers have been trained for such misdemeanor emergencies. Greensboro Falls seems like the kind of town where everyone knows everybody else, and because of this, you have to be honest whether you want to be or not.

Then again, bad people travel, don't they.

The cashiers watch me as I descend on the household products aisle, and I bet they're looking to see if I am a shoplifter with my big-pocketed black pants and my lowered head. If I were to tell them the reason that I'm here, would they be more kindly disposed to my presence?

I find the shelves with laundry supplies in the back. They're by the pharmacy section, and a white-coated man looks up from behind an elevated counter. He does a double take and then resumes counting pills. Behind him, the drugs that can be given only upon doctors' orders are like soldiers ready to be called to the front lines of battles, the labels-out lineups of opaque, mostly white bottles too far away for me to read their names. This is where I will have to go for my refills, and I know he's going to look at me and not be surprised by what he must count out for me.

As I stop in front of the fabric softeners, I find the Rit brand dyes next to the bleach, and this proximity seems like a portent. The boxes are lined up like crayons, the colors cheerful and primary. There are three boxes of black available and I wonder how many I will need. I look around. There are a couple of other people strolling down the various aisles, like one with a basket full of things, another using his hands as a cart, but no one looks like a colorfast docent. I check out the pharmacist. He glances over at me as if he senses my regard—or more likely, he's waiting for me to slip something in my pocket and try to run out of the store.

After checking the price, I find that I can afford up to four boxes and be certain that I have enough left over for tax, so I clean the CVS out of its stock of three. I imagine I'll be a topic of conversation for the cashiers, probably for the pharmacist, maybe even for the manager wherever he or she is. This is a busy store, but that's a relative term in this sleepy little town, and the people who work here no doubt have plenty of time on their hands to discuss odd customers. Like a girl with black clothes buying black dye.

Just wait until I come in for my lithium.

As I turn away from the shelf, I can sense the pharmacist looking at me again, and I want to give him a little wave and tell him I'll see him soon. He and I are in a relationship.

He just doesn't know it yet.

Up at the cash registers and the candy bars, I wait in line behind a woman who is buying hairbrushes, hair spray, mascara, eyeliner, and lipstick. She's telling the clerk that she is going to her cousin's wedding.

She's frumpy and on the young side of thirty, with no wedding band. It's clear by her conversation that she's hoping to attract a specific groomsman's attention, and is placing her bets on the makeup she is purchasing and the new hairstyle she is going to try out. I feel sorry for her, and I almost wish her luck as she puts her change into her wallet, takes her white plastic bags with their red lettering, and heads off to attempt to alleviate her spinsterhood.

When the cashier's eyes settle on me, the smile she gave to the wedding guest is traded in for a professional mask of customer service. "You find what you need?"

"Yes," I say as I put the three boxes on the counter.

"You know, that's not for your hair."

So she sees my roots. Although given the amount of new growth I have, that's really not an eye test.

"Yes, I know."

When she doesn't scan the boxes, I look at the other cashier. She's staring at me, too, and I have the sense I will fare no better if I take two steps to the right and give her a try. I know what they are both thinking.

Aren't your clothes black enough, kid? Do you have to pretend you're special? God, your poor mother.

I want to ignore the thoughts going through their heads, but they're so clear to me that I can hear them in their own voices, with separate inflections and accents. And that is when a shiver of warning hits me.

What is a simple commercial transaction becomes a race against time. I take out my five-dollar bill and put it next to the boxes. This does the trick, jump-starting the process.

"You're going to use salt, right?" the cashier says as she hits keys on the register.

"What?" I mumble through the concert of voices that has started to play in my head.

"You need to add a cup of salt to the water in the washer."

This is very helpful of her and not because it has anything to do with the dyeing process. Her advice provides me with a platform on which to refocus on the task at hand.

"I didn't know that," I say.

She eyes my clothes. "Have you ever used dye before?"

"No. What do I do?"

"How much are you dyeing?"

"A big load. I have to get out bleach spots."

"Use all three then. The dye can't hurt nothing." She continues to pick up the boxes one by one and enter their price. Even though it has to be the same. "You want to prewash the clothes first. Leave 'em in wet and fill up the washer with the hottest water. Before you put the dye in with it, you need to dissolve the boxes in two cups of hot water, and do the same with a cup of salt in four cups of water—oh, and you'll want to add a teaspoon of dish soap to that. Take out the detergent dispenser tray and start the cycle. You want to pour your dye mix in where the dispenser tray goes, followed by the salt, and then rinse that with four cups of cold water. You want your cycle to last a good thirty minutes, longer if you can. Where's your ColorStay?"

"ColorStay?"

She looks at me with exasperation, as if I have forgotten how to tie my shoes at my age. "Go and get a box of ColorStay. You want to put that in with the load, too, so everything don't bleed when you wash it next."

"Okay. Thank you."

I dutifully go back and reenter the crosshairs of the pharmacist. Returning to the front, I find myself in a five-dollar predicament. But I'm still on the planet. Or at least, I think I am.

"Is it better to have more dye or the ColorStay?" I ask. "I can't afford it all."

The two cashiers lean in and whisper gravely to each other, whatever transpires between them a discussion of nuclear arms race gravity—although I don't know enough about clothing dye to tell which is the Soviet Union and which is the United States.

"Here." My cashier pulls over a clear plastic dish, like something you'd get tuna fish salad in at a deli. "Let's see what we have. You, too, Margie."

The two women count out the coppers in their *Give a Penny, Get a Penny* dishes. Then Margie chips in a quarter of her own money and my cashier, Roni, as her name tag says, does the same. I am rung up and my five-dollar bill taken, the supplemental change they provide bridging the gap between what I require and what I can afford.

I duck my head and my eyes, mumble a thank-you, and leave quickly, before they can see that I'm teary. To keep myself together, I inform my emotional side that the reason for their aid has nothing to do with me. It's not about a lower-middle-class girl who needs charity because an upper-class girl is being a bitch; it's the integrity of the dyeing process. Yes, that's why. They provided the funding because they take fabric dyeing seriously and wouldn't feel right if the project failed.

Outside, the rain has arrived, and as I step out of the cool and dry interior of the CVS, I am hit with not just raindrops, but the prevailing humidity that took me five days to get used to, and ten minutes to acclimatize out of in the store.

I turn my face to the angry sky and let the rain fall on my cheeks to camouflage my tears.

I don't have any salt and I'm out of money.

Maybe I'll just stand over the open washer and cry.

chapter
SEVEN

As thunder booms and lightning flashes, I know I must get back to campus in a hurry, but I feel very small and very weak, my Band-Aid ripped off by the begrudging kindness of strangers with name tags, my tender wound exposed. I have a thought that I need to toughen up, and the thought is spoken in my head in the voice of an older male, the one that identifies as that of my father, although I have no memory of what his voice actually sounds like.

You need to toughen up, it repeats.

I stop walking about three stores down. My feet just refuse to keep going. Standing there in the rain, I wonder how to restart my pedestrian engine and wish there were some kind of gas station for the energy I require. Unfortunately, fortitude is not something you can pump into somebody, and besides, no matter the price per gallon, I have no more money on me.

A car goes by heading out of town. A car goes by heading into town. I imagine the shop owners across the street staring out around their meager wares, pointing to the black-dressed girl who's turned into a statue.

I imagine me still here at Halloween, dogs passing by and lifting their legs to piddle on my ankles, birds sitting on my head and pooping down my back. I am here at Thanksgiving. Christmas. New Year's. Snow accumulates upon my straight and angled parts, concentrating on my shoulders where the birds perch and on the tops of my boots, over my toes. I am still here in the spring when the snow melts and the birds and the dogs come back, the former free to fly wherever they want yet subject to the cruelties of nature, the latter chained and licensed to masters who feed and care for them, lives extended through beneficent imprisonment.

As all of this rolls out not as a hypothetical, but as history about to be discovered, I am aware that my foundation is quaking again, and this scares me, especially as I feel myself step out of my body and walk forward, turning back to inspect the me statue. Especially as I picture nothing about my stance or my expression changing for decades, yet in this unaltering, altered-state reality, my hair continues to grow.

I watch as the brown roots push down the dense black ends, the length extending from my head on a fast-forward reel that has pedestrians and traffic going by at blurring speed. The ends curl up, the roots stay straight, and I see it reaching my hips, my knees, the pavement, the false black color now a minor footnote to the brown, dominant whole. I watch a municipal worker with a hose wash me down and the weight of my hair ropes with the water. I watch the water dry. The length continues to extend, even as my clothes rot off of my body, ragging away, falling free in strips like the flesh of a zombie.

My hair grows out down the sidewalk, following the gentle undulation of the storefronts. It reaches the traffic light and ignores the red signal. It grows like a tsunami, filling the valley created by the two sides of the street, and then overflowing the ten blocks of retail to submerge the tiny houses with their old cars and cheap garden gnomes. It rushes toward the border of New Hampshire. It becomes a national emergency. I must be eliminated by the government before my hair weighs so much it cracks this land mass off at the seam of the Continental Divide, this part of the country falling into the ocean and sinking down under saltwater depths—

How ironic. I'd be surrounded by the stuff and yet only need four cups.

With the snap of a rubber band, the hallucination's tensile strength fails and I reenter my body, my consciousness returning home with the sound and sensation of a door being slammed.

My head whips up to level, the muscles in my neck straining to catch the weight of my skull. I wobble in my boots and put a hand up to my head. I breathe shallowly through my open mouth, my heart playing castanets in my chest.

That is when I hear the laughter, that is when I see the bright colors and the blond hair flanked by two brunette side stones.

Up ahead of me, Greta and Francesca and Stacia have come out of a store. The music store. And by some stroke of luck, they're walking away from me and do not know I am here.

The three of them are giggling in the rain as they hold the little plastic bags that their freshly bought CDs are in over their heads, umbrellas that don't help much. As they start to run, their legs kick up the short hems of their skirts, flashing tanned thighs, and their hair, which will never, ever threaten the national security of this country, swings from side to side across their slender backs.

Their departure is perfectly timed and I thank them. Their giddy outburst brought me back to the real reality—and I have to give my madness credit. It's like a parasite that's self-aware. If I'm destroyed, the insanity will lack a host, and therefore it needs me alive and requires my rational side's help on that, at least at this point in my life.

I peel the sole of one boot free of the bolts that have kept me in place, and I studiously ignore the soft pinging sounds of screws that I know do not exist falling on the sidewalk and bouncing away. I repeat this on the other side. As I begin to move, rusty, grinding noises percolate from my joints. I am the Tin Man in *The Wizard of Oz*, needing oil after the rain froze me in position. I am the statue that should not be able to ambulate. I am . . .

Lots of things that make no sense.

And I therefore keep plenty of distance between Greta and the Brunettes and me. I am also careful that as I go along, my bag of dye and

ColorStay swings in relative silence at my side. I don't want to attract any attention, and my fear at being caught in the wake of those girls means that every sound I make is loud as a marching band.

A car passes me, hits a pothole, and throws up water that smells like motor oil, the spray speckling my left side. As I glance at what turns out to be a pale blue two-seater, I recognize the high, ticking motor, the charming color, the sloped rear end. I don't need confirmation on who's driving the vintage Porsche.

And I am somehow not surprised when it slows down three blocks ahead and beeps its horn at Greta and the Brunettes.

As the two-seater comes to a stop, Francesca and Stacia laugh and run forward, bending down and clustering around the window that is lowered. Greta is no longer laughing and she stands back, her chin lifted. I imagine Hot RA leaning across the emergency brake and the camel-colored leather seats, one tanned arm propped on top of the steering wheel, even white teeth out on display as he chides the girls for not thinking to bring umbrellas. I wonder if he is noticing their wet shirts and measuring the curves of their padded bras. I decide he is not. He's got a Miss America wife who is saving the world.

When Greta finally saunters over to the window, the Brunettes lose their excitement and their smiles collapse. Now Greta grins, but it's not a girlish expression. It's much older. It's much more knowing.

It's the kind of thing I refuse to dwell on.

The door opens from the inside.

She leaves her two best friends in the rain.

As the Porsche takes off, Greta gives the Brunettes a wave from the dry interior of the Porsche, her hand a flag of victory.

I am forced to stop walking. Even though Greta is my apex predator, Francesca and Stacia are just barely beneath her on the ascending triangle of social carnivores. I don't want their attention, either. Fortunately, I don't have to wait long. The two of them resume walking, slower now, and without the giggling or the bags on their heads. I imagine they're cursing Greta under their breath. But this is the way of things, I decide.

To retain her position, Greta must, from time to time, remind the other two that she will always be uphill of them. And jettisoning them in this storm by going off with Hot RA is a great trailhead on the way up that mountain.

I follow the Brunettes to the Ambrose gates, maintaining a four-to-five-block decontamination zone in the rain. I watch their heads turn to each other from time to time as they slash their hands angrily, their CD bags—which I am certain contain exactly what is in Greta's—jerking back and forth. I decide that this is probably the only time I will ever have anything in common with Francesca and Stacia.

I don't like Greta, either. And I'm also jealous of her.

To amuse myself, and to pass the time, I spool out fantasies of the future, and in each one, Greta is at my disposal: I'm a doctor giving her a terminal diagnosis that includes no hope whatsoever, even for clinical trials. I'm the judge whose gavel sentences her to a death penalty after she drives drunk and kills a family of four on their way home from their oldest son's high school graduation. I'm the boss who fires her from her dream job, and then the banker who forecloses on her house after she fails to make payments, and finally the mortician who does her corpse's makeup badly on purpose after she commits suicide due to her financial reversal.

I am karma. I am vengeance. I am a hundred thousand pounds of payback that lands on her head and crushes her.

For once, I am grateful that there is such a thin veil between my imagination and reality. I experience all of these vignettes as if they are actually happening, and I especially enjoy standing over Greta's cold corpse and smudging her red lipstick so that she looks like a clown who's wiped her mouth with the back of her hand, everything dragged to one side. Even though my clothes are wet and clinging to me now, I'm bummed as Tellmer Hall comes into view because I have to close the Book of Spite and return it to the library section of Never Going to Happen. These particular flights of fancy felt voluntary and highly satisfying, and I wish I could partner with my madness more often.

As I enter the dorm, I reflexively check my mailbox. There's a flyer reminding us that Mountain Day is coming soon. From what I understand, Mountain Day is a school-wide day off, called at random by the headmaster. We will know when it occurs because bells will ring first thing in the morning. Instead of attending classes, we climb a mountain, and we therefore must be ready with proper shoe wear and clothing. I'm grateful for the tips, although the idea of hiking up Pennhold Rise, whatever that is, fills me with dread. I'd prefer to stick with our regular schedule. I'm likely in the minority on this.

I'm about to follow in the damp footsteps of the Brunettes up to the second floor when I remember the instructions I was given about the dyeing process. I need salt. I look over my shoulder and see Wycliffe through the wavy glass of the phone room windows. I doubt the kitchen will give me as much as I need. I could go and steal a couple of salt shakers, but I'm not sure how to measure the required dose properly, and after the intense discussion between Roni and Margie over their dye vs. ColorStay donation decision, and the money that they gave me, I feel compelled to do things properly not just to resurrect my clothes, but to honor the two women who were so accommodating of needs I was unaware of possessing.

I look past the stairwell's banister to a closed door. As the most obvious solution presents itself, I groan, but there seems to be no other avenue. I'm too shy to approach Hot RA about anything, especially after he played chauffeur for Greta, and I have no ties to the married couple on the third floor at all. I need someone who'll be compelled into service on my behalf, and accordingly, I drag myself to Ms. Crenshaw's apartment entryway.

Knocking softly, I hope that she is not home, although this is also what I do not want.

The door opens quickly, and there is excited expectation on Ms. Crenshaw's makeup-free face, as if she's elated to finally be called upon to residentially advise.

"Sarah! How are you?"

The odor that exudes from the dark interior is musky and thick, as if she eats a lot of takeout and doesn't open her windows.

"What can I do you for?" she asks as if she hopes the vernacular will make her seem more approachable.

"May I please borrow a cup of salt?" Under the same principle, I hit back with the formal "may" instead of the casual "can" because I want there to be as much distance between us as possible.

"Of course! Come on in! Are you hungry? Thirsty?"

I step across the threshold and am overwhelmed by the amount of fabric hanging everywhere. It's on the walls, the couch, the armchair, at the windows. Everything is batiked and tie-dyed, the colors discordant, the patterns overlapping, and as if that isn't enough, Buddhist prayer flags are strung from the ceiling.

And there's weird incense burning.

"Now," she prompts. "What can I get you as a snack?"

She is standing next to the galley kitchen, her body tilted forward like she's in a stiff wind. The anticipation on her face makes me wish I'd just waited to steal some saltshakers at dinner.

"I'm okay," I say. "Thank you. Just the salt. Please."

"I have pomegranate juice."

"I'm allergic." Even though I've never had the stuff before.

"Oh, that's a shame." She turns to her countertop with a mournful expression. "It's so healthy. And I was just making some."

In the opposite direction from her den of inedibility is a set of floor-to-ceiling shelves, and I look toward them in desperation, like they're a shoal I can use to climb out of grasping waves.

Behind me, Ms. Crenshaw is opening her cupboards one after the other like she can't find that which she is certain she has. I have a thought her salt supply is hiding from her. I have no idea what she's saying, but I think it's a monologue on the role of vitamin C when it comes to boosting the immune system. I walk over to her library and look at the titles on the spines. There's a lot on meditation. Mother Nature. Animals on the verge of extinction.

"You're welcome to borrow anything you like," she announces right behind me. "Do you have an interest in meditation?"

I nearly laugh in her face. I'm interested in not hallucinating on the sidewalk. How about we start there.

"Thank you for the salt," I say, holding out my hand.

When Ms. Crenshaw's eyes drop to my soggy sleeve, I see that I haven't pulled it back into place. The scars on my wrist are very obvious, and as I yank things down, I have a thought I have just drawn a proverbial circle around them.

Ms. Crenshaw clutches the baggie of white stuff to her chest. "Sarah, I'm here for you. You know that, right."

I blink. Until now, I wasn't sure whether the RAs had been told about my "situation." But as she asks no questions, it is clear a report has been made.

"Thank you." I put my hand out again. "For the salt."

She opens her mouth like she wants desperately to jump into my madness and save me from myself. It's kind of her. But no offense, if Dr. Warten can't do it with all the pharmaceuticals and talk therapy at the mental hospital, no one who teaches geometry in a prep school is going to get far with a mind like mine.

"I'm always here for you," she says as she puts the Morton's in my palms.

As I walk out like I stole the stuff, I wave over my shoulder. I don't want to be rude, I really don't, and the fact that she probably gets a lot of hasty goodbyes makes me feel bad for her. But damn.

When I'm back up on the second floor, I take my laundry bag, which is full of bleach-stained yet clean clothes, and slip the dye, the ColorStay, and the plastic baggie of one cup of salt through the aperture created by the drawstring. After I swing the load onto my shoulder, I pick up the worn navy blue backpack that has my geometry and English homework in it. I'm bringing work with me because I anticipate I'll be down there for a while and I'm never leaving any of my washer and dryer cycles unattended again.

I struggle to get out the door with my burdens and push my damp, stringy hair out of my flushed face.

"Seems like everyone got wet today."

I look toward Greta's voice. She is sitting back on her bed, perfectly dry and happy as a clam, a closed chemistry book next to her, a notebook opened on her lap, a CD case dismantled so that she can read the album notes. She's in her silk robe, and only the corkscrew-curly wisps around her face suggest that she might have been out in the foul weather at some point. In the background, the new Guns N' Roses album, *Use Your Illusion I*, is playing, and their ilk has never come out of this Bobby Brown room before. Greta also bought *Use Your Illusion II.* It's next to her chemistry book. I didn't figure her for a Guns N' Roses fan, and I bet that Francesca and Stacia have also bought the albums. They'll all hate the music, and I'm glad the three of them wasted their money. I wonder where they got the idea to buy what they did.

As I turn away without responding to her, I picture myself as her mortician, messing up the lipstick on her gray and frozen mouth.

This makes me smile.

chapter EIGHT

The following afternoon, I'm still happily surprised the dye worked as well as it did. I am walking back to Tellmer from my last class, chemistry, and I continue to look down at my pants with satisfaction and no small amount of amazement. The bleach spots that marred the black folds are essentially gone. Yes, there are faint traces of the staining out here in the bright sunlight, but I'm very confident few will notice them.

I'm very confident that Greta will not notice.

She, of course, matters the most. And when I picture her confusion growing over the passing days as I continue to appear in all manner of freshly washed, non-bleach-speckled clothing, I chuckle to myself, and then laugh out loud.

I rarely feel this kind of accomplishment. My pride is of the weak sort, the last-ditch effort of my character to protect the fragile shell of my dignity, and in its timidity, it's always scuttling in haphazard apology for cover.

Today, however, in my resurrected clothing, I feel like I have bested Greta, and therefore I'm glowing inside. I'm radiant. I'm magnificent.

The fine day matches my mood, sure as if I control the weather with my emotions. The storms that drenched Francesca, Stacia, and me ushered out the heat and humidity, and now it is classic fall in New England, the sky a piercing blue, the sun a brilliant light bulb covered by no lampshade of clouds. With the arrival of this dry air, and the nights about to turn colder, the leaves are going to start to change fast. Soon the color show will begin, and I tell myself that this year, I will stop to enjoy the distinct seasons.

Buoyed by my current sense of accomplishment, I know that I will not miss the opportunity. In fact, I can do anything I set my mind to. My mood is an inner change of weather ushering out my dull, trudging affect. I am the brilliance that has come across this campus, across the earth itself. I am as resplendent as the sun and everyone knows this because, like the sun, I am sending out waves of energy in all directions, touching and enriching everyone's lives.

I want to feel this way forever. And ever. And ever. And I will. This is my new state of being. From now on, I will wake up every day and be in this wide open space of awesome inspiration and actualization. No more dim corridors with closed doors for me. No more grim worries about anything. No more insanity. In fact, I will stop taking the lithium for I do not need it. I am no longer crazy. I am reset to factory settings. And accordingly, I decide that these black clothes have to go. I don't want to be on the Greta side of having too much color, but enough of these dour, depressing togs. I will get a job during the month of January when we are off from school and I am back at home. I will save my money, and just before I return to Ambrose, the seat of my rebirth, I will go to the mall and I will buy blue jeans and tops in yellow and red and gold, and sweaters that have subtle patterns. I will trade my heavy black lace-up boots for more reasonable ones, ones that perhaps have a little heel on the back. I will even get my hair recolored so that it is all its natural shade of mahogany, and after that is done, perhaps I will get some strands of blond added in, just around the face.

As I picture myself in new clothes with new hair, I can feel myself sliding into place for the first time in my life, no longer half-cocked and at odd angles in the company of so many who have smooth fits around their jambs. I will be one of them. They will call me Bo, and they will sit with me at lunch, and even if I am never in Greta's group, she will be so taken by my improvement, she will not just leave me alone, she will even smile at me a little as we pass on the stairs.

When the summer comes, I will even have a proper birthday party for the first time. I will invite friends over to my mother's house and we will have a cookout. These girls and boys my own age will be everyone I meet at my paying job, not internship, at a law firm's legal library in July and August. My contemporaries will all be smart and on their way to good colleges. And I will not be embarrassed by where I live. My mother, having been inspired by my own example, will throw out her magazines and deep clean our home, no more clutter, no more frivolous purchases. She will hang new drapes and get new countertops in the kitchen before my party. She will start wearing age-appropriate clothes. She will stop smoking. She will settle down with a nice, slightly pudgy man who has a kind smile and a good heart. He will be only a year older than she is, and they will primly hold hands on the sofa and do nothing else in their bedroom.

My mother was right. Ambrose was the absolute perfect place to send me. My doubts during that first day, and in the subsequent couple of weeks, have been dashed by this uncovering of my true self, and as soon as I go home for Thanksgiving, I will make an exit interview appointment with my psychiatrist. Dr. Warten will look up in shock and awe at me as I enter his office with a confident smile on my face, a spring to my step, and nothing black on my body, not even the belt threaded through the loops on my new jeans. I will sit down across from him and place my unfinished bottle of lithium on the coffee table between us. I will tell him that I want the seventeen pills left inside of it to be given to some other patient who needs them, a donation from a previous sufferer to one who remains in the trenches. Dr. Warten will tear up at my shining example of complete recovery and my beneficence to those in need. He will take the pills and tell me that I am such an inspiration to him and so many others. I will be modest, but I will rejoice with him. I slew the beast, I conquered the enemy, and now, at the end of my book of trials, I will enjoy smooth sailing into the warmth of the setting sun for the rest of my days.

And my greatness will not stop there.

Later, after college, I will write about my hard time and my moment, *this* moment, when all became clear. I will go on talk shows like *Phil Donahue*, *Sally Jessy Raphael*, and *Jenny Jones*, and morning shows like the *Today Show* and *Good Morning America*. I will become a nationwide spokesperson, a courageous woman who breaks down prejudices and taboos to talk about mental illness. I will do speaking tours. I will advocate at the White House and in front of Congress. My entire life will be in service to others, and when I am on my deathbed, I will have nothing to apologize for, nothing to be ashamed of. I will die an old lady with a fine reputation, and my funeral will be at the National Cathedral because that is the only church big enough to handle the mourners. The anticipated weeping will require a pallet of Kleenex to be delivered prior to the service, and even still, they will run out of tissues.

It is coasting on this wave of future ensured success that I sail into the front of Tellmer Hall. Magnanimously, I hold the door open for one of Strots's teammates, who is exiting. She is Keisha. She is African American and very beautiful with her braids. She is an accomplished athlete, but I understand she's here on an academic scholarship because she is also very smart, proof that you can be both.

As she gives me a nod, I am certain that, if I followed her to whatever workout or practice she is going to, I could keep up. I wouldn't be as good as her, no, because athletics are not my strong suit. But I would not fall behind and I would not embarrass myself. Afterward, she would urge me to join the field hockey team. Strots would agree. I would demur until the rest of the team starts to chant my name, and only then, out of a feeling of obligation because I do not want to let them down or cheat them out of the benefits of my association, I would pull a singlet over my head and everyone would cheer. The singlet would bear the number two, not number one, because I don't want to be showy. I would become the heart of the team, the person who inspires all by my hard work, dedication, and calm demeanor under pressure. And when we are down by a goal with two minutes to go at the end of the state title game, I will score on a Hail Mary, and they will retire my jersey at the gym, never to be worn again.

The door closes and I turn to the mailboxes, ready to find a winning lottery ticket, a letter from my father telling me where he lives, and an invitation to meet President Bush in my slot. Mail has been delivered on time because all of that urgently needs to reach me. There are colorful flyers in all the boxes, a pretty display of pinks, oranges, whites, and yellows that is random, given that some mail we all receive, and some is specific to our particular classes, our extracurriculars, our clubs. In my cubby, I have three notices, but tragically my lottery winnings and missives from my father and President Bush have been lost somewhere in the system. They will be here soon, I am quite sure.

The top memo is in pink and has been received by everyone. It's a reminder to donate gently used clothes to the bin in the phone room so that they may be disseminated to the poor through the school's relationship with St. Francis Church in town. Upon reading it, I find myself disappointed that I cannot give away my black clothes yet, and I hope that there will be a similar drive during the second semester after the break, after I redo my wardrobe.

The second notice is white. It's a stern reminder that nothing should be flushed down the toilets in the dorm except toilet paper. All sanitary items must be disposed of in the small metal trash receptacles affixed to the insides of the stalls. The plumbers had to come again to work on the pipes and it is expensive. I promptly decide that we must convene a dorm-wide meeting about the issue. I will write up the flyers and I will work with Ms. Crenshaw, Hot RA, and the married couple up on the third floor to set the agenda and I will address the students as a peer. After the meeting, no one will flush anything but toilet paper down the pipes and we will never again need those plumbers. I will save the school so much money that I will be invited to address the Board of Trustees on cost-saving measures campus-wide and the way to get teenage girls to comply with regulations. I will be the catalyst of institutional improvement that reforms everyone from the staff to the teachers to the administrators, and when I graduate with honors two years from this spring, I will hand over the mantle of leadership to a junior I handpick as my successor. She will follow in my footsteps and be almost as good as I am.

The final memo is blue. I read it through twice. It is from Ms. Crenshaw to the members of her Geometry I class. It is dated today. It explains that due to a personal issue, tomorrow's class is canceled and the test on chapter three postponed until the Tuesday class next week.

I'm very happy with this unexpected snow day, and know that Strots will be jealous. Strots hates geometry, and based on how she struggles with her math homework, it is clear the subject is not any more favorably disposed toward her.

I turn away to the stairs, memos in hand, backpack hanging off my shoulder, smile on my face.

I stop.

I look back over my shoulder at the mailboxes. And do not move.

It is not immediately clear what's frozen me in place. I look down at the blue memo—and as I read it for the third time, that is when I see the typo. In the concluding sentence, right above Ms. Crenshaw's closing and signature, I catch the grammatical issue: "Be sure to study hard, its going to be a hard test."

Actually there are two errors. The comma should be either a semicolon or a period that splits the two halves into proper sentences. And it is "it's" as in "it is," not "its" as in the possessive form.

No, there are three errors, if you count the repetition of the word "hard."

Warning bells start to ring and I step back over to the boxes. I'm not sure what I'm looking for, but this just doesn't feel right. Ms. Crenshaw, for all her weirdness, speaks perfect English. The papers she sends home, the assignment sheets, the lists of supplies, the schedule of tests, everything is without a mistake.

But maybe this one time she was in a rush.

Francesca is in my class. I track down her box by her last name. She's emptied hers. I try to remember who else lives in my dorm. There's a

Bridget, isn't there? Yes, her room is on the first floor. But what's her last name?

I eventually find Bridget's box, but before I take out her flyers for a forensic analysis of their contents, I look around to make sure no one is in the phone room or the common area down the hall or coming out from the opposite direction. The coast is clear for this nanosecond, and I move fast before I'm caught.

Bridget, last name irrelevant, has received the donation reminder and the toilet warning, as well as a memo about soccer practice, a US Postal Service letter from what surely is her mother, and the blue flyer from Ms. Crenshaw. I put everything back but the blue flyer. Looking down at the printed words in memorandum form, I note the to and from, the date, and the subject being about the test, and I'm both instantly relieved at not being the brunt of another practical joke and simultaneously worried that my paranoia is returning.

Except then I read the verbiage. This memo says that the test, which *is* going forward tomorrow, will include an opportunity for special credit, and a problem is set out on the lower half of the sheet. Anyone who provides the correct answer will receive five bonus points.

I read Bridget's memo two more times, and then place it back in her box. There were no grammatical mistakes, and it strikes me as wholly within Ms. Crenshaw's style to actually give her students the bonus question in advance of a test. She wants us to get As. She needs us to get As. She's rigging her own system to ensure that result, or at least something close to it.

My brain processes all of this while my eyes trace across the rest of the mailboxes. I move over so that I can see the undersides of the lazy sloping notices. I find a third dorm member who's in the class. Savannah's memo matches Bridget's.

I focus on Francesca's empty box. I wonder when she got her mail. I'm willing to bet it was after lunch.

Francesca works on the student newsletter. I know this because I've seen her byline on articles about Taco Tuesday, the importance of litter pickup, and the upcoming student election. She also reported that the Board of Trustees is meeting next week to discuss tuition increases and gave ideas for entertaining our parents over Parents' Weekend. The newsletter comes out weekly, its ten or so pages stapled in the upper left-hand corner, its content more letter than news.

She's unlikely to receive a Pulitzer for her penetrating investigation into Ambrose's decision to suspend the campus-wide Sunday Ice Cream Sundae Bar indefinitely.

I've never been to the newsletter's facility. But I'm willing to bet they have reams of colored paper and serious copiers there, because all eight hundred students receive the weekly missive and white is not the only page color they use. They of course also have computers attached to printers, and cubicles in which people can concentrate on their work without interruption.

Or the eyes of others.

I turn my blue memo over. There's no label on the back where Bridget and Savannah had one.

There's a trash bin below the corkboard where tutoring notices and school club come-ons are tacked by a revolving supply of clear-headed pins. I consider going through the receptacle, imagining myself taking off its lid and dumping out its collection of crumpled colored paper, fermenting apple cores, and empty soda cans. Compulsive as I am, I nearly get on with the impulse, but someone yanking open the dorm's door snaps me out of that plan.

I hurry off for the stairs and decide Francesca wouldn't be so obvious as to rip up my real memo and toss it so close to ground zero.

As I ascend, my ebullience has disappeared as if it never existed. Now my boots weigh a thousand pounds apiece, and my black clothes are the only thing I feel like wearing. Gone are the winged fantasies of my future as a fit-in as opposed to my present lot as an outcast, the lies conceived by my hyperactive brain blown out of my air space, nothing but tufts of feathers floating down, a bird caught in mid-flight by a high-bore shotgun's blast, not just dead but vaporized.

As I contemplate my return to my dreadful normal, I have a hazy conception that the trippy, buzzy thoughts that spun out from the center of my previously singing chest were just the same as the hallucination of my hair from yesterday. More fun, for sure, and I miss them like a loved one gone too soon. But the sad reality is that I'm no more likely to sprout infinite lengths from my follicles that sink part of the United States than I am to be cured and become a spokesperson for the mentally ill as an adult.

I'm back to being me.

The idea that Greta and her Brunettes have gotten me again kicks me in the gut. The fact that I caught their trick before it hurt me doesn't matter. That they pranked anew, and in a way I wouldn't have anticipated, is what scares me, because my penchant for paranoia does not need the confirmation that my world here at Ambrose is tenuous and easily tampered with.

As I get to the head of the stairs at the second floor, I hear music coming out of Hot RA's room. This isn't unusual. He likes rock 'n' roll, no pop for him.

Going down my hall, passing our bathroom, my heart hurts, and it gets worse as I see that Greta's door is open.

"Hi, Sally," she drawls. "How are we doing? See you got your mail."

As I duck my head and ignore her, I open my door and am tired again as I enter.

"What's wrong?" Strots asks me from her bed.

I close my roommate and me in together. "Nothing."

I go over to my own mattress, sit down, and stare at the floor, my backpack still hanging from my shoulder, the fake memo in my hand along with the real notices I received.

"Jesus Christ, Taylor, did your mother die or something?"

I look across the divide of the room. Strots isn't joking. She's putting aside her hated geometry book and sitting forward, her brows bunched up hard. The fact that she honestly seems to care makes tears threaten in my eyes and I hate it.

"Why is Greta so mean?" I say without intending to. "I don't understand. Why can't she just . . . be Greta? Isn't that enough?"

Strots curses. Then she dives under her pillow for her cigarettes and her lighter. The *shcht* as she thumbs the Bic seems very loud, and I worry that Hot RA might hear it and race down here to bust us both. But wait, he's listening to rock music, and besides, I'm really not sure he'd care. As long as Greta doesn't smell anything, we're safe.

Strots cracks the window and blows the smoke out of our room. "What'd she do to you?"

I don't mean to, I don't want to, but I find myself telling Strots about the shampoo. The laundry. I hold the memo out so she can read the lie with its—not it's—grammatical errors. I turn the blue paper around and show her the lack of a label. I review my proof for all of it, which I have to admit is rather flimsy, unless you've looked Greta in the eye as one of her enemies. When I'm finished, I collapse backward and bang my head into the wall.

I'm rubbing the sore spot as Strots ashes into the muck-filled soda bottle she's been using for the last two days. Dead soldier filters float on top of the brown fluid, casualties of a flood.

"You don't believe me," I say with defeat.

"No. I do."

This is such a relief that I blink fast. "Thank you."

"But my opinion's not gonna make a shit's worth of difference."

You are wrong about that, I think to myself. *It makes a difference to me.*

Strots taps her cigarette in the opening of the bottle. And in the silence, it occurs to me that it's no small skill ashing into the Coke's little mouth. I think of the way my mom burned her hand while gesturing wildly around Greta's parents' Mercedes.

You forget that those things are on fire.

"As for why she does it," Strots murmurs.

When my roommate doesn't continue, I prompt, "She has everything."

"That's what she wants people to think." Strots pauses again. "I've heard some things about her family."

"Like what," I push when there's another silence.

"People say behind her back they aren't worth what they used to be. Guess her dad had to declare bankruptcy a couple of years ago and sold their big house in Greenwich. I don't know any details."

"They came in a Mercedes."

"Yeah, and how old was it?"

I don't know, I think. The logo mounted on that hood like the target sight of a status rifle was enough for me. Then again, I came in a Mercury that's almost my age.

"Fucking with people's a good distraction," Strots says. "It's a power trip that equalizes her dirty little secret, and she loves the chaos she creates. The suffering. The embarrassment. She feeds off that shit, the sick cunt. Makes me glad that her father's a lousy businessman."

My roommate is the Einstein of the interpersonal, I decide.

"That's fucked up," I tack on, trying to be as tough as she is.

She points at me with her cigarette. "And don't think she's going to get caught. Even if her father doesn't have the money he used to, he's still a trustee here and on the fucking admissions committee. She's the fourth generation of her family to go here, and her uncle's still got plenty in his trust fund. The school is never going to go after a Stanhope, and anyway, her powers of persuasion should not be underestimated."

We are quiet together, and then Strots says something that gets my attention.

"You want me to take care of this for you?" she says in a low, level voice.

As my eyes whip up to hers, she isn't looking at me. She's focused on the glowing end of that cigarette.

I go back to my mortician delusion. The smudged lipstick.

The dead Greta on the slab.

I have this strange, thrilling sense that Strots is talking about something so much further than going to Hot RA with the harassment.

In case I'm wrong, I point out, "But you just said she's never going to get in trouble."

"That's with the RAs and the deans. There are ways of handling things privately."

"Like you talking to her?"

One of Strots's shoulders shrugs. "Something like that."

My body goes warm and loose, as if my skin is no longer skin but bathwater over my muscles and bones, and I measure Strots's obvious physical strength. Then I picture Greta's face black and blue, swollen out of its perfection, that stick-straight nose she inherited from her father busted out of alignment.

I see blood on the back of Strots's knuckles and a flush on my roommate's cheeks, I hear heavy breathing and a pounding heart underneath her blue and gold Huskies sweatshirt.

I imagine an underdog who has no bite getting help from a German fucking shepherd.

"You would do that for me?" I ask in a rough voice.

"Yeah. I would."

"You could get in trouble."

Strots is still not looking at me, as if this conversation is all off the record provided we don't make eye contact. But the secret little smile on her face promises retribution, and this goes to my head like alcohol.

"You don't have to worry about me," my roommate says. "I'm even safer here than she is."

"The sports center," I whisper. As if it is a religious shrine.

"My father's been generous to the school," is as far as Strots is willing to go.

I struggle with my composure in this electrified moment where I feel as though we are together in a battle against injustice everywhere. Strots is my knight in shining armor, coming to protect me for no reason other than that I am being treated unfairly. She is altruism on a warhorse, thundering to the rescue of the weak and downtrodden. In her sweatshirt and with her hair pulled back, tapping that cigarette into that plastic Coke bottle, she glows with vengeance.

It feels good to have power. Even if it is only the referred kind.

"Well, let me know if you change your mind," Strots tells me as she drops her cigarette butt into the swill. "The offer stands."

As the lit end of her Marlboro hits the liquid, it sizzles like a tiny steak on a tiny grill.

"I haven't said no," I say.

"Yeah, you have. But it's cool."

My roommate truly is a genius when it comes to people, isn't she. Because she's right. As glorious as my wrath feels, it will remain only ever a potential, my roommate's offer holstered in my back pocket.

I don't have the stomach for true conflict.

Just as Strots doesn't seem bothered by it.

I look at her geometry book and clear my throat. "Do you have a test tomorrow, too?"

"We all do. We're on the same schedule for exams even if we're not in the same class."

It seems important to talk about other things, normal things, like you'd wipe down a kitchen counter after you made a sandwich and left mayonnaise smudges on the laminate.

Nice and regular. Nothing to see here.

She did not just offer to beat the shit out of the girl across the hall, and I did not just seriously consider taking her up on the kind invitation.

Strots moves the book back into her lap and pushes her hair out of her face. "I fucking hate geometry."

I try to follow her lead, but I fail and am unable to concentrate on my own test prep.

My insanity and Greta have a lot in common, I decide. Neither have I volunteered for, and both have a tendency to catch me unawares and kick me way off course.

Rubbing my eyes, I'm disappointed in my lack of courage. I am also grateful Strots has no idea where I go in my head when I get silent. Sitting across from me, she is blissfully oblivious to my struggle, in part because she's in a struggle of her own with the prospect of the test, her brows down low, her Bic pen tapping against her front teeth. She seems utterly stuck, and I envy the fact that, wherever her mind has gone, it's not to a hallucination that turns her into a statue that birds poop on.

I have the strangest suspicion she's stood over Greta Stanhope's dead body in her mind a couple of times.

"Would you like help?" I say, nodding at her textbook. "I'm really good at math."

chapter NINE

It's six a.m. The church bells are ringing. It's finally Mountain Day.

I open my eyes and try to remember what day it is. Tuesday.

It's the week following the geometry test, which I did not miss and which Strots got a B on. She's particularly satisfied with her result. I'm particularly worried about all the internal mail I receive, the good news being that there have only been generic notices in my box since last Thursday.

My roommate and I have not discussed Greta again. But when I see the girl either in the dorm or out on campus, I think of what Strots told me. I look past the expensive wardrobe and the gold bracelets, the vacation plans I overheard down by the river, the rule-the-world attitude. I wonder if Greta's hiding the kind of fear about being judged that I wear closer to the surface . . . if all her gloss isn't like my black clothes and my dyed hair, a suit of deflection.

Maybe I'm a target because I represent everything she hates about herself. Maybe she feels like an outlier because ultimately she can't keep up financially with the girls she dominates socially, and I am the living, breathing symbol of an outcast.

Maybe she's still pissed at what I interrupted that night, shortly after we all moved into Tellmer.

Ultimately, her motivations matter less than her actions. And that is why I remain on full alert.

Sitting up, I look out the windows. It's light already and very clear. Another perfect fall day. I really wish I could spend it in classrooms, and as the prospect of huffing and puffing awaits me, I don't want to climb anything, even out of bed.

"Why can't they start this shit at nine," Strots mutters. "But noooo, we gotta get the kids up at the crack of ass."

Strots shoves her bare feet into her black shower shoes and scuffs out of the room, towel looped over her shoulder. As she leaves, I eye her legs with envy. They are heavily muscled, extending out from beneath her loose boxer shorts like pistons.

She is going to have no trouble climbing anything. Even Everest.

I really should have tried to get myself out of this elevation-oriented activity. At Ambrose, we're required to take one physical education class a semester, but I got that waived because of the lithium and the way exertion affects my sodium levels and thus the drug's intensity.

It's too late now. I am going to go climb a mountain.

I change quickly before Strots is back from her shower, and I leave ahead of her so she won't have to deal with the awkwardness of walking out of our room with me. Whenever this happens, we invariably go down the stairs side by side, and make our way together to Wycliffe for food or to whatever classroom building we're bound for. But it's out of obligation on her part, and I know that her teammates would rather I get out of the way.

Besides, lately, Keisha from the third floor has been Strots's strolling companion. Strots and she are spending more and more time together, one waiting for the other at the base of the stairs by the mailboxes for meals and classes. I wonder whether this is prearranged or a habit they both fell into. Probably the latter. Strots doesn't waste a lot of time dissecting things.

I feel cut out, but it's not like Strots was walking with me much anyway. No, it is the closeness that has developed between the two as teammates that I envy, when all I will ever have with Strots is physical proximity determined by a dorm room lottery system.

As I wander alone to the dining hall, I entertain a fantasy that Greta and the Brunettes will think of some cute, girlish way of avoiding the Dickensian death march that the rest of us must face. As thin as they are, they don't seem hardy enough for mountain climbing, and given that Greta's father has been on campus for meetings with the other trustees these past few days, I tell myself that she'll appeal to him, and he'll get her excused.

If she can, I'll bet she gets Francesca and Stacia out of it, too. Rain desertions in blue Porsches aside, Greta will want her friends to stay behind as well. They'll paint their toenails in her room and listen to Guns N' Roses while the rest of us strap on crampons, kernmantle ropes, and collections of carabiners. While they lounge around, we will risk our lives over ice floes and great vertical wedges of granite, harnessed to the rock, relying on only our wits and our equipment to prevent us from plunging to our deaths. After nightfall, we'll return to Tellmer Hall dehydrated, bruised, and broken of spirit, our best efforts dashed in the face of the earth's gorgeous but cruel wiles. The three of them will not be here when we come back. They'll be in Greta's father's buttercup yellow Mercedes with the matching hubcaps, driving off to have dinner at the headmaster's house.

I know the certainty of all this as if it is an article written in Francesca's newsletter.

In Wycliffe, I eat alone at my table by the exit and the little-used trash bin. I'm not certain how long I'll have to go before I can pee, so I'm careful not to take in too much liquid. Except then I worry about dehydration. And sodium levels. And insanity.

I envy the other girls who are just bitched they're out of bed so early.

We convene at seven o'clock in front of Tellmer Hall and the Wycliffe girls join us. Hot RA is standing in front of the loose groups of students. He's addressing us, he's smiling, he's charming and handsome, his hair wet from his shower, his shoulders broad under a turquoise sweatshirt with a map of Nantucket on it. The other RAs are behind him, and Ms. Crenshaw is among them. The husband and wife who are in charge of the third floor look like brother and sister with their same blond coloring, and I recognize some of Wycliffe's RAs from campus. One of them is my French teacher, Mlle. Liebert.

We are directed to four orange school buses that are parked on the main lane of the campus. As we funnel onto them, I see Greta and the Brunettes and am surprised my fantasy about her father didn't come to fruition. She doesn't look happy and I make sure that I am not on the bus she chooses.

As we motor off in one-by-one formation, the lolling suspension of our vehicle makes me regret that I ate anything, but fortunately, in this part of New England, it doesn't take long to find a mountain. Which is how every dorm gets its own hill.

Just before I embarrass myself by throwing up, we make a wide turn into a packed dirt parking lot, and then comes the disembarking. Even though I'm right by the door, there's no chance for me to get a head start on the exodus. Others are already out of their seats before the paddle and hiss of the Jake Brakes, and I let them go ahead of me, content even in all my nausea to not get trampled by the herd.

I wonder why they're rushing. The mountain isn't going anywhere, anytime soon.

"Well, are you gonna get off?"

I snap to attention. My bus driver has turned in her seat, her thick arm draped on the back of her driving throne. She's neither annoyed nor solicitous. She's factual. She just wants to know if I'm gonna get off her bus.

I look out through the half windows. So many girls. And there, in the sunshine that is dappled as it flows through the finally changing leaves, are Greta and Francesca and Stacia.

I want to be honest with my bus driver and tell her that the last thing I want to gonna get off is her bus.

Instead, I nod and rise to my feet. As I go down the three steps and put my sneakers on the dirt, I wish I were sitting on my bed in a perfectly quiet dorm, reading something for pleasure. Like Nietzsche.

A clapping sound draws my attention and everybody else's.

"Okay, folks, who's ready to climb!"

It's Hot RA. He's pumped up for what's ahead, and his vigor once again draws the girls around him, steel shavings to a magnet. As he delivers another speech, which is a repeat of our pre-bus talking-to, I stare at him through the heads and shoulders in front of me. I'm not surprised that the gleaming sunlight coalesces around him.

When he's done with his reminders—stay on the trail, lunch after the climb, ask if you need help—he puts his sunglasses on. They are aviators like Tom Cruise wears in *Top Gun*, and the black lenses with the little gold rims and earpieces fit Hot RA's square-jawed face like his bone structure was the one they used to create the design. In this regard, the Ray-Bans are like his vintage Porsche, a nationally available item that his attractiveness makes personal to him and him alone.

He leads the pack. Two hundred girls and ten other residential advisors follow. Strots is out in front with Keisha and the field hockey team. Greta and Francesca and Stacia are in the middle, releasing a concentration of sweetly scented molecules in their wake, a Glade PlugIn with many tanned legs. I am at the back—and so is Ms. Crenshaw, but she and the married couple from Tellmer's third floor are in a clutch of conversation. I am relieved. If I had to walk with her, it would make the ascent twice as long.

It's cool under the canopy of deciduous trees, and as I trudge the well-packed dirt of the trail, I'm thankful for that. While we go along and all the others chat, I pass the time looking at the leaves and measuring the color change. It's a good distraction, my brain consuming the information my eyes provide, noting all the tiny tint variations of red and yellow that start at the tips and invade inward to drain the green.

As we approach the top, the fluffy trees fade away and are replaced by evergreens, and the climb is not as bad as I anticipated. This is what is going through my mind as I make a final turn in the ever-narrowing trail and am rewarded for my two and a half hours of effort with a keyhole view of the valley below. This tease of the horizon expands to the infinite as I finally emerge onto the flat, bald head of the mountain. Given that I am a last-place straggler, there is a crowd when I reach the trail's end, but there is plenty of space. I choose a spot off on the left, and as I stand with the wind in my hair, my hands on my hips, and my eyes trained on the graceful undulations of the peaks and valley before us, I realize that I have chosen the same place as my table in Wycliffe's lunch hall.

Voices carry and the topics of talk are varied, although almost none of them concern the magnificent sight available for us to purchase with our gazes. I am content to stand away from them all, and I am affected by the view in a way I could not have foreseen. Having faced repeatedly, and against my will, the vast landscape of what my mind insists on conjuring, I'm oddly reassured at a yawning vista that is physical. Undeniable. Experienced by others, even if they ignore it for the most part.

Hot RA is now calling for our attention. He's standing by an observation tower. He's telling us that there are drinks here, by his feet, and that we will begin our descent in five minutes. As I'm thirsty, I work my way around the periphery, the lichen-covered rocks I traverse gray and dry, and strangely slippery even though moisture is nowhere. As the wind whips my hair around and my cheeks burn from the cool air, I can't imagine what it's like up here in the winter.

I'm grateful there's only one Mountain Day a year and the next one isn't scheduled for February.

I wait in line at the three Igloo coolers by the observation tower. When it's my turn, I plunge my hand into melted ice and come up with a bottle of water. I am quick to sidestep for the person behind me, and I retreat to the exact same place I was standing before. The twist top makes a crackle as I free it from its rim, and then I am drinking, my hot and dry throat like the roots of the twiglike plants that struggle to grow up here, catching and holding the cool and the wet. My stomach is a basin at my body's room temperature, and as I guzzle, a ball of refrigeration coalesces there. I stop myself at the halfway mark. I don't want to have to pee in the woods on the descent.

Can you imagine what Greta would do with the likes of that?

The view once again commands my attention, yet I remain aware of the other girls, and soon their presence prevails over Mother Nature, my stare going to them even though I can watch their like all day, every day at school, and this mountain's offerings will only be available to me for a few minutes longer. Still, my peers are fascinating to me, alien life forms that look and sound like me, but whose inner composition is nothing like my own. Up here, in the wind and the sunshine, my contemporaries are taking group shots with cameras, cozying close and holding each other in arm links of three and four, everyone smiling at the photographer who then trades places with somebody in the lineup so they all are Kodak-accounted for. These are the pictures that will be reproduced in the yearbook and on the brochures for the school. They'll be made into posters that will hang in the Admissions Office.

"Okay, time to go!" Hot RA hollers over the gusts. "Let's do this!"

With his turquoise sweatshirt tied around his waist, he gets the descent going by standing at the trailhead and motioning for girls to drain off the summit into the mountain's pipe system of cleared pathways. The voices of my peers are loud, their energy still good because they are young, and even if they don't like climbing this mountain or going down it, it's still better than being cooped up in a classroom.

As more of them depart, the chatter dwindles. I hear the wind even more clearly now, and I am reminded that we are brief up here, and the weather, like the mountain, is permanent and unimpressed by our split-second tenure.

I take one last look at the view of the unspoiled valley. It's so beautiful, the acreage of trees nearly incalculable, the clear blue sky overhead completely incalculable. Standing alone, I am captured and held in the palms of the earth, the moment neither a curated photograph nor an imperfect, edited memory, but a pristine testament to the true power of now, of the present, of the imperial instant.

I give myself up completely to this, releasing my grasping, desperate hold on sanity for once, knowing that for this brief slice of time, I do not have to worry about traveling where I do not wish to go. I float, and yet stay where I am, because I am seamlessly connected with all that is around me, even the girls who, being so different from me, have already begun their jangling descent back to level ground, the mountaintop already forgotten.

When I turn around to go, I realize I was wrong.

I am not alone.

Off in the trees, in the shadows, two people are standing close together. A man and a woman.

Make that a man . . . and a teenage girl.

Hot RA and Greta are by themselves.

If not for her rainbow bright clothes, I wouldn't have seen them at all.

chapter TEN

My descent, unlike my trip up, is a blur. I remember nothing of the trail. My mind is consumed with what I saw. And yet what did I see? Two people standing together in and among the fluffy boughs of pine trees. That was it. They weren't kissing. They weren't touching. Maybe Greta was asking him a question about lunch, like where it was or what was being served. Maybe she had a blister. Maybe she saw Strots sneak a cigarette somewhere and was telling on my roommate.

I remind myself, quite sternly, that as prejudicial as it is for people to judge me for being unattractive, it is just as bad to assume that because Hot RA is good-looking, anytime he is alone with someone of the opposite sex, there is something sexual going on. Or anytime he happens to leave the dorm at night, at the same time a girl appears in the doorway to her room, it is something nefarious. He's a married man, for godsakes. And Greta is a child compared to him.

No matter how she fills out her clothes.

I am being too suspicious. I am looking for shadows in the darkness where there are no monsters, my brain forging chain links where there are none to be had.

I am following in the jealous footsteps of my mother, whose relationships almost always end because she thinks the man is cheating on her.

And yet as Greta gets on my bus, forcing me to choose another, I find myself checking to see if she's behaving differently. She isn't.

Hot RA and I happen to board the same bus. He is immediately swarmed with girls, the bench seats around him and across the aisle promptly three deep with nubile bodies—until he reminds them that for safety's sake, there are only two passengers allowed per row. The fact that he not only follows this rule but makes others do the same seems like a testament to his character.

His virtue matters to me, although not for a virtuous reason. I want Greta to want him and never have him.

Okay, I also might want him to find no students attractive at all, ever, because it makes my crush easier to bear.

I sit up in front again, and because no one volunteers to sit with me, I stretch out my legs across the bench seat and put my back to the window.

This is not so I can keep watching our residential advisor.

Maybe it is.

As we trundle forth to whatever destination is next, he is chatting with the girls, and I notice Francesca is right behind him. She talks over the other students. He doesn't pay her any greater attention than he does anyone else, and I become more convinced that what I saw in those woods at the top of the mountain was nothing bad, just like it was a mere coincidence that night with he and Greta appearing at the same time. After all, I do tend to see things that are not there, and not only in a hallucination kind of way. Sometimes, the connections I find among people and things have nothing going for them except the clarity with which I see the interrelationships. Which can be disorienting. There is no confusion in this case, however, and when we disembark, I tell myself to forget all about it.

Besides, I need to use the restroom, and become focused on how I can't really hold things any longer. Fortunately, we are at a county park that has a concrete kiosk of bathrooms. The line forms quickly, and when I finally get into one of the stainless steel stalls, I can smell cigarette smoke next to me. It has to be Strots, I decide, and I'm tempted to say her name. I don't. Instead, I check the dispenser to my right and am relieved to find that there is a big fat roll of toilet paper locked into the car-wheel-sized holder. There's plenty for me, and plenty to last us through the afternoon.

After I wash my hands without soap in water that's cold as a rushing stream, I use the sides of my pants to dry my palms and go out to assess the lunch situation. There are picnic tables scattered in and among a ring of trees that boundary a shorn field. Two buffets have been set up side by side, and girls are already in line, taking paper plates and piling on sandwiches, slaw, chips, and cookies like they last ate three years ago. Under an awning, backups for the food are being tended to by kitchen staff in white caps and blue and gold Ambrose uniforms.

I let the others go first, finding a trunk to lean back against. Strots and her group get their food and pick a table not far from one of the buffets, tucking into their full loads in the shade. Greta and her Brunettes exercise strict portion control and take a table in the sunlight, pushing their salad-no-dressing around, taking half bites out of sandwiches they will not finish. The RAs all sit together, and the rest of the girls pepper the other perches.

When the coast is sufficiently clear, I swoop in, take a ham sandwich and one that has turkey in it, and find an empty picnic table down at the far end. Trying to be as cool as Strots and her crew, I sit on the weathered boards of the top, not at the bench level. As I start to chew, I notice that inside the field of cut grass, there are flags set up on poles at regular intervals.

Oh, shit. Games. They're going to make us do something that involves a ball, some running, and going by the orientation of those markers, a certain amount of goaltending. This isn't good news. My legs are already tired and I hate competition, but at least it's unlikely that anyone will want me on their team. Besides, with so many of us here, there's no way that everyone will have to play. There isn't enough time, unless we go one hundred against one hundred—

Behind the buffets, over by the bathrooms, I see two girls arguing, and it takes me less than a second to recognize Greta and Francesca. The pair are leaning forward and talking fast, back and forth, back and forth. For once, it's unclear who the aggressor is. Which means Francesca's upped her game.

Trouble in paradise? I think to myself as I glance over at the table where they'd been sitting. The other girls there aren't paying any attention to them.

When I look back, the two of them are gone.

Maybe they were arguing over who will get to throw up their lunch first. As if there is ever a real debate over who's in pole position, though?

"I can't have you sitting here all alone!"

I jump and nearly drop my plate. Oh, God. It's Ms. Crenshaw.

My geometry teacher joins me on my picnic table's top with messianic glee, her savior complex triggered by my isolation. The fact that I am quite content to be on my own doesn't occur to her. I am the swimmer in the lake who drowns because the lifesaver buoy thrown at me knocks me unconscious.

It is upon this helpless note that I notice what she's taken from the buffet line. She has a disproportionate, rather disgusting, amount of coleslaw on her plate, and she dives into the huge mound of sauced-up shreds with her white plastic fork. Actually, wait. The only thing she's helped herself to is the slaw.

I hear my roommate's voice in my head. *People are weird.*

As Ms. Crenshaw carpet-bombs me with conversation, talking about the walk up the trail, the view from the top, the easy-peasy of the way down, her presence beside me, so close, so intent on communication, shines a light on the both of us, two oddballs amplifying each other's oddities, a mirror-to-mirror, *ad nauseam, ad infinitum* ping-pong of piss-poor reflections. We are a Charles Addams cartoon, except it starts ugly so there's no need for a troll to peek out halfway down the declension.

"Don't you think, Sarah? Of course you do. And that's why Mountain Day is such an important . . ."

My head spins under the gale force of her pressure of speech, and the onslaught is a reminder that while I identify as a loner, I'm not sulking at my lack of friends. I'm relieved by the solitude because I am as much as I can handle at any given time.

"—did so well on that test, Sarah. You should be a tutor for math, you really should."

Oh, she's changed subjects.

Plugging into her new line of blather, I think of Strots and how I worked with her the night before the last exam. I am not going to share with Ms. Crenshaw that I have piloted a tutoring program and it appeared to garner at least B-level success.

"Thank you," I say as I take a bite of my ham sandwich.

I have finished my turkey one, and I figure as soon as I dust the ham, I can leave under the auspices of having to get a refill of something, anything. I chew like I am in a race.

"Do you need help setting up?"

The question is such a non sequitur that I look over at her, but she's speaking to someone else. It's Hot RA. He's approaching us with a nylon net full of raw-meat-colored kickballs and what appear to be some footballs. He's ditched his Nantucket sweatshirt and I notice, not for the first time, that his Nirvana T-shirt is tight over his pecs, loose over his taut stomach.

"I can help you," Ms. Crenshaw says again.

Hot RA stops and looks over at us, although his eyes are not particularly focused. "Oh, I'm good. Thanks. Hi, Stephanie."

I twist around to see who's come up behind us. But there's no one. He thinks my name is Stephanie.

"It's a perfect day for this," Ms. Crenshaw says. "Isn't it?"

She's pushing her words, like my mother does, and her eyes are shiny as she stares at Hot RA. She's locked on at his face, but I have the feeling she's drinking in the full sight of him. *Not her, too*, I think. Then again, he does this to girls and women of any age, turning them into distracted, mooning adorers. I wonder how his wife copes. Then I think of their argument and suspect I have my answer.

"Yup." He smiles in an absent way, like he has no idea what he's replying to. "Well, if you'll excuse me, I'm just going—"

"I mean, if they had called Mountain Day last week?" Ms. Crenshaw makes a *phew* sound between her thin, un-sensuous lips. That she doesn't seem to know she has coleslaw juice on her chin makes me cringe. "What a disaster it would have been. The heat, right? Could you have *imagined*?"

Sally, have you seen this lawn, I hear in my head.

"Yup, it was a scorcher all right." Hot RA's eyes are wandering around the crowd as if he's looking for the coast guard as his boat takes on water. "So I think I'll get everybody ready for the touch football—"

"And that storm. What a storm that was. Did you remember to put the windows on your car up?"

"I did. Yup."

I can see he's annoyed at the mothering, and I want to tell Ms. Crenshaw to stop this.

She breaks out a *tsk-tsk* forefinger. "I had to remind you before."

"Yup. You did."

"Nice leather bucket seats like you have." She makes that *phew* sound again. "I mean, they have to be expensive to fix if they get waterlogged."

As if the raindrops would tear at their hides and necessitate their immediate replacement.

"Yup. Okay, time to start the game."

"I'll keep looking out for your windows."

"Yup, okay. Thanks."

Ms. Crenshaw opens her mouth to keep talking, but before I can beg her to let the poor man go, Hot RA solves the problem by turning away as if somebody, across the field, or perhaps the country, has said his name urgently.

As he walks off, Ms. Crenshaw's eyes are focused on what is below his waist on the back side, although there's no lust in her face. It's more like somebody in a museum coveting a piece of art that will never hang in their own home.

"Come on, Sarah," she says, clapping me on the knee. "Let's go play. You can be on my team and we'll do this together."

She leaves her half-eaten plate on the tabletop, all that slop fermenting in the sunshine. Eager to seize her moment, she jogs after Hot RA, ready to join him in a game I'd venture to say he'd prefer to play with anybody but her. When I don't sign on for her parade of one, she motions to me with the same hapless insistence with which she beckons me to answer her in class.

The last thing I want to do is run around after a ball, but I slink off the table and shuffle through the grass in her wake. I don't do well turning people down.

Then again, me being picked for anything happens so rarely that I am out of practice when it comes to refusing invitations.

With Hot RA involved, interest in whatever game is about to happen is strong, pulling many girls off tables and onto the field. Ms. Crenshaw inserts herself into his atmosphere as an asteroid so large it cannot be ignored by claiming the captainship of the other team, and she does this even though it is doubtful she has much experience with touch football. I can tell, as he looks over at her with exhaustion, that he wishes he'd proactively given the nod to one of the other residential advisors as his chosen opponent—like, before we even left the dorm. He's stuck now, though. And no matter the outcome of the game, this is another car-window-watch-out situation, an opening for dialogue. At least on her side.

I picture them on campus ten years from now, with Ms. Crenshaw bringing up "that Mountain Day from nineteen ninety-one." For the one hundredth time.

"Fine," he says, his smile brightening as he looks at the girls who approach. "Let's do touch football with five on each side."

"Sarah's on my team," Ms. Crenshaw announces with a smile toward me.

In her mind, she's reaching a hand across the divide of picked-last that she imagines I have always been on. She's not at all far from the truth, but I wish she'd leave me out of everything. I'm like Hot RA, manipulated and stuck.

"I'm over here."

As Greta steps free of the crowd and speaks up, I start to think of an excuse to get out of the game. With her on Hot RA's side, she's liable to come after me, tackling me into the grass, streaking my blacks now with green rather than brown—

Greta does not go to stand behind Hot RA. She comes over to me and Ms. Crenshaw. There's a confused moment of quiet in the crowd. Even Hot RA does a double take, and so does Ms. Crenshaw. The only people who don't seem shocked are the Brunettes, but then they care only about following Greta, not about any particular destination she may take them to—no, I'm wrong. Stacia is confused. Because Francesca goes and stands with Hot RA.

She doesn't look at Greta. Greta doesn't look at her. And it's then that I see both girls have scuffed knees and dirt on their shorts—and what the hell happened to Francesca's eye? Did things get physical behind the bathrooms?

The image of those two paddling their useless palms at each other is an unexpected high point of the whole day for me.

With their affiliations declared, Hot RA laughs in a relaxed way, as if everything is all right with him. "Who else wants to play?"

Stacia backs away toward the picnic table of pretties, like she doesn't want to have anything to do with the faction that's happening. Meanwhile, girls clamor to be led by Hot RA. They raise their hands and jump up and down when he's picking, sit on their proverbial palms when Ms. Crenshaw does. We end up with both teams filled, and the rest melt away to the sidelines. While the rules are being explained, I find myself searching the crowd hoping that someone will rush into the fray to insist that they be provided a spot on the field. Strots and Keisha remain on their table in the shade, and I mentally urge them to join exactly the sort of competition they so readily engage in during their practices and at their games. It's a no go. The true athletes among us are not participating with us lunch-laden amateurs.

And they are no doubt going to enjoy the show of fools.

Now we are in a huddle. Or the Ms. Crenshaw version of one, which is more like a group of strangers on public transportation, everybody trying not to catch someone else's rhinovirus. Unlike Hot RA's team, we don't link our arms around each other's shoulders. We're not chanting. We're not breaking apart with a clap of anticipatory triumph.

We are Ms. Crenshaw's team, and not even Greta's luminosity can elevate us. Apparently, being in the game is only exciting if you're on Hot RA's side of things.

"Let's just go have a really good time," Ms. Crenshaw says as she looks around at us. "That's all that matters. Just have fun, girls."

She claps, too, but not in the cool, hip way Hot RA does, palm against palm, a high five to himself. She claps in a patty-cake fashion, and Greta stares at her as if she's wondering how Ms. Crenshaw is able to put her pants on right, much less operate a motor vehicle or teach the Pythagorean theorem.

Ms. Crenshaw and Hot RA are the quarterbacks and will have to alternate possessions or whatever the hell they're called. The rest of us form lines and face off in the center of the field. Touching, no tackling, is the main rule, not that that's relevant to me because I don't intend on getting anywhere near the action. There's also some kind of system of downs, but I don't bother to track it, and there's some sort of time limit, but I don't remember what it is.

Hot RA has the ball first, so Ms. Crenshaw stands on the sidelines, and after we're all in position, he calls hike and jogs back, springing lightly on his feet, looking for a receiver. Meanwhile, girls lock against girls, and Greta is surprisingly hearty about the pushing and shoving, although she avoids Francesca or maybe it's the other way around. In contrast, I'm not enthusiastic. I don't even do my job. I let the one I was supposed to block go right by me, and as she streaks past, I watch her like a well-wisher on the dock as a boat goes off to sea, *bon voyage*, traveler.

The pass is incomplete. Play stops. We reassemble.

"Do something this time," someone snaps. "Don't just stand there."

I believe the person is addressing me, but it's not Greta, so they're easy to ignore. On the next hike or down or whatever it is, the same things happen. Hot RA gets the snap, in spite of it having a parabolic arc, and he springs backward like a gazelle, the ball cocked over his shoulder. I refuse to engage. People run by me. I let them go.

I'm hoping to be kicked out of the game. Instead, as we line up again—I'm not even sure what happened during this play—Ms. Crenshaw puts a reassuring hand on my shoulder.

"You're doing just fine."

I'm doing nothing at all, I want to say. But the woman doesn't seem to notice this. Or perhaps ascribes my failure to engage to my mental defects.

On Hot RA's third attempt to move the ball, he decides to duck his head and rush. Greta somehow reads this intention, and as he zigzags to the left, dodging girls with outstretched palms, she zeroes in on him and T-bones his body with her own. They tumble onto the grass, her short skirt flying up, their arms and legs tangling, him laughing as he loses his grip on the ball. When they roll to a stop, she is self-satisfied as she pushes herself off of him, her hands shoving against the pads of his chest, forcing him down so that he cannot get to his feet.

As Greta stands over him, she gathers her long blond hair and tosses it over her shoulder. Her scuffed kneecap is really bleeding this time, but she doesn't appear to notice.

"Well, I guess you got me," Hot RA says as he jumps up with a smile.

"Sorry. I tripped."

"On me."

"It happens."

He pulls her in for a hug in a brotherly way, shoulder-to-shoulder, not face-to-face, and he tousles her hair like she's a little kid. Greta says something that I cannot catch and they part, going back to their home teams. Everyone, including Ms. Crenshaw, is looking at them, but they pay no mind to this. Their interaction is innocent, the sort of thing that would go unnoticed if I'd been the tackler or Ms. Crenshaw the tackled. But there are implications that resonate, and I wonder if anybody else saw them up at the summit or in the middle of the night or down in town. Sidelong glances that are not as casual as they might appear arrow across the field, not only from the game's participants but from the spectators as well.

For a moment, the conclusions that I prefer to avoid stir. Except then I see how unfazed Hot RA and Greta seem. I tell myself that I am not the only one making up stories about them.

After all, beautiful people can't quarantine their attractiveness, and sometimes it does make other people sick.

The game continues and now it's our team's turn to have the ball. On our first attempt, by some inexplicable miracle, Ms. Crenshaw throws, and someone catches, and we score. This is so unexpected, we all stand around for a moment as if some referee is going to spontaneously materialize and contest the goal. When this doesn't happen—because, in fact, there is no referee—everyone except me goes into spasms of victory, the girls jumping into each other's arms. Meanwhile, Ms. Crenshaw taunts Hot RA, but Hot RA is too busy joking with Francesca, sure as if he's utterly unaware his fellow residential advisor is trying to speak with him.

The score is quickly evened, and the teams slug it out through more innings—or whatever they're called—until we are up by one goal. Touchdown. Whatever the term is. During his next possession, Hot RA tries another rush, tugging at a girl's ponytail as he slants by her, and then dodging past Greta and her outstretched hand so that she falls face first into the grass as he scores.

While his team goes ecstatic, Greta's eyes are full of cold vengeance, like he's let her down in some kind of bargain. As if he was supposed to help her tackle him for a second time. As if it was rude of him to continue to the finish line. Goalpost. Whatever.

I watch her rise up out of the meadow's sweet nap, and her anger rattles me. This is the part of her that I call forth. This is what stalks me, leaving behind the remains of my shampoo bottle, my wounded clothes in that washer, the falsified memos in my mailbox. With her mood change, this has ceased to be a game to her, and as a result, it's no longer a game to me. I am frightened by her malevolence, and I'm struck by the need to run over to Hot RA and tell him to be careful. To appease her if he is able. To redo the play and let her take him down to the ground again. He doesn't want this part of her. I know this firsthand.

Hot RA is blithely oblivious to the change he's wrought. He goes to trade places with Ms. Crenshaw on the sidelines, nodding at her as she insists on talking to him while he looks away to his players and claps his hands in encouragement. Ms. Crenshaw, eventually giving up on her attempts to open a dialogue, approaches us where we've congregated at the halfway point of the field. Her smile looks forced, and I marvel at how even grown-ups can get their feelings hurt. I believe she's finally noticed her lack of engagement with Hot RA, a door she thought had been merely shut actually locked, if not barricaded.

Ms. Crenshaw makes two attempts to score, and both go nowhere, the football bouncing out of bounds when she throws it badly. Then someone gets stung by a bee and there's a play delay. As we wait around in the sun while aid is rendered and there's talk of EpiPens and Benadryl, the day feels like August, not October. Even though I haven't been doing much, I'm panting, sweaty, and tired of the whole damn thing.

"Hey, Taylor."

I look up. Strots has come over to the edge of the field, a Coke in her hand, an amused look on her face.

"Why do you do this?" I ask between breaths so deep, it's like I'm giving myself CPR. Even though it's been a good five minutes since I actually did any running.

"Because it's fun." She puts her hand up. "Okay, fine, when we do it, it's fun. You guys are different."

"No kidding."

My roommate leans in. "Lemme give you a little tip, Taylor."

"It's too late for that."

"Don't worry about the eyes and the faces of your opponents. Focus on the body in front of you. The arms and legs will tell you where they're headed. The body never lies."

She inclines her head, like she's just given me secret insider information.

As she saunters back to her table in the shade, I hate to burst her bubble, but she's just given a fish a bicycle.

Bee sting issue resolved, we resume our lineups, a collective weariness setting in on both sides, the enthusiasm of the initial scrum of conflict long evaporated on the hot plate of our exertions. Our obligation to finish is like a bedside vigil gone bad, our sympathy for the patient now lost, impatience to have this over with so we can go about our lives all that we feel.

We slog through the motions, pathetic and slow, and Nick Hollis's team ends up making another goal. Then it's the fourth and final down of the game. When we're called into a huddle, I stand in the back of the girls on my team and only one among us is still fully engaged. Greta is in the front of the loose ring we've formed, and she's leaning forward, as if she'd like to rip the ball Ms. Crenshaw is holding out of the woman's hands and do this herself, goddamn it.

Regardless of our overall loss of morale and interest, Ms. Crenshaw gives us some instructions so we can get into overtime. I'm too busy watching the opposing team and their captain to bother listening to her. I suspect that Hot RA is also ready to end this game whether or not he wins, although I don't think the outcome ever mattered to him anyway. This was all just a way to avoid Ms. Crenshaw, one that backfired and put him exactly where he didn't want to be.

Ms. Crenshaw claps her hands in that little-girl way of hers, and the members of my team break out of the huddle, loafing into a wilted formation at the fifty-yard line. I'm getting into my space at the end when Ms. Crenshaw is suddenly right in front of me.

"Remember, just run as hard as you can," she says. "Do you hear me? No one's been guarding you, so you can get open. I'll throw to you."

My heart starts to pound. "What?"

"Come on, girls!" she calls out. "We can do this!"

"Wait—what?"

I should have paid more attention. I should have offered another idea for a play, not that my football knowledge is in any way sufficient. I should have intercepted the bee sting so that I could have taken a medical leave of yet another impending failure I was volunteered for by a grown-up.

As we set up, Greta looks down the line at me, her glare shooting across the bent backs of our teammates.

"You better fricking run," she says.

I look away in a panic. If we don't even the score and go into overtime, I'm the one she'll find responsible for the murder of her ambition in this game. If I don't do what I'm supposed to, if I don't catch the ball and haul it like I've never run before, there will be retributions, even worse than the casual, offhand pranks she's pulled so far. My throat promptly goes dry and my stomach churns on its load of ham and turkey and bread. I want to throw up, and nearly do, as a sickening flush goes through me. The sun feels a thousand times hotter on my black clothes, and I cease to be able to feel my legs, a problem as I have been commanded to be fleet of foot.

When the snap happens, all of the bodies on the field shift positions with the graceless shuffle of Claymation. Ms. Crenshaw catches the ball like she's wearing a huge set of slippery mittens, the fumbling grab nearly ending in early disaster. She looks at me, but for once says nothing, a secret kept. This is my cue to run, but I don't take it from her. I take it from Greta, who's evidently agreed this is the best strategy. Maybe this is my chance to get into her good graces. If I do score, so that she can mete out a punishment upon a married man who seems to not care she's angry at him, maybe my life will hit a flight path at Ambrose with a better cruising speed and an altitude that puts me above my current turbulence.

Calling upon my legs, I beg them to move, and shift they do, left, right, left, right. I run the way Ms. Crenshaw catches snaps, as if there are things impeding my activity, things that are weighty and take me off balance. I am a hobbling mess as I cover distance toward the red-flagged stakes at the other end of the field, but the assessment made in the huddle, that no one will see me or care about me, has proven correct. I break away as the others argue with their hands, pushing and shoving at the line.

I look over my shoulder. My hair gets in my face. My lungs burn and still I move, my sneakers trampling grass. Ms. Crenshaw is backing up, not with the bounce of Hot RA, but in the manner of my stride, nearly tripping on nothing at all. She's waiting for me to get into position, as if she can throw that far, as if I can catch anything coming at me.

This is a bad plan. This is going to result in calamity.

Ms. Crenshaw draws back and releases her throw, sending the pigskin into the air. Its path is wobbly and ugly. Her incompetence has contaminated the football through the contact of her palm, robbing it of the lilting, magical flight that Hot RA's unicorn grip brought out of its molecular makeup. Meanwhile, against all odds, I cross over into the end zone, and a saving geometric grace is served upon me, my terrible run bringing me inexplicably to the exact curving terminal of a terrible throw. All I've got to do is hold out my hands to receive the blessing.

The girls on both teams are looking at me from across the field with shock on their faces, their contorted bodies freezing in mid-scrimmage, all bad angles and off-balance stances. They cannot believe this any more than I can. On the sidelines, Hot RA's mouth is open wide, but not because he's cheering his team. He's dumbfounded. Ms. Crenshaw's mouth is also open, but she's screaming in excitement, her hands in fists up close to her chin, her body poised to jump with joy from the ground.

In the midst of this tableau depicting the win/loss tipping point between the teams, I see only Greta with true clarity. The rest are sketches; she's the full pen-and-ink drawing. She's not excited. She's not exhibiting anything even on the cusp of happiness. She's furious. I'm about to provide her with what she wants, this score to survive in a game that means nothing, and yet she's full of rage because she'd rather be the one catching the ball.

Then again, Greta would never have gotten down this far because she's not incompetent like me and would have been guarded. It's only through my lack of coordination and participation that I'm in this position, and no doubt the contradictions in all this are part of what makes her furious. Or maybe it's simpler than all that. Perhaps it's just because I am the only option to get her what she wants.

The ball is coming closer, and now that I am safely in the end zone, I turn my full body around and brace for impact. I put my hands out, cupping my palms together, my bent forearms a landing basket, my chest a brick wall. There is nothing more for me to do. The whims of fate have dictated this unlikely success, proving that, for all the possibles for which we wish that are not granted, there remain out in the ether a given number of improbables that will roost at random and without regard to our exaltations or our lamentations.

This is proof that chaos theory is a far better thing to believe in than the existence of God.

As luck would have it, Greta is in my line of sight, the flight path of the ball intersecting our stares and blocking her glare, for a moment. And while the vision of her is cut off, something rises within me, something that's been stirring beneath my fear, my worry, my cleanup of her pranks. With incalculable mental speed, I picture Greta missing the tackle that enraged her so, Hot RA skipping around her, dodging her hands and effectively landing her perfect nose in the grass. I think of her laser sight on Ms. Crenshaw in the huddle. I think of her barking at me as we lined up at center field, and then narrowing her eyes as I hobbled down here alone to get into a position to receive.

I think of her ditching her two best friends in the rain without a care.

I think of my shampoo, my clothes, and that memo.

I think of her on that mountain with Nick Hollis.

The ball smacks into my chest, the impact stinging my sternum and making a sharp noise. Distantly, I hear the cheer of my teammates, and I see them turn to each other, already celebrating, congratulating themselves for staying alive in the game. Ms. Crenshaw likewise leaps into the air as Hot RA cringes back in an exaggeration of frustration on the sidelines.

Across the field, Greta's expression does not change. And that's when I realize that if I do this for her, things'll only get worse because she'll be pissed I was the one who scored and kept us going. But if I don't even up this game for her, things'll only get worse because I'll have denied her what she demanded of me.

Succeed or fail, I cannot win.

So I don't close my hands. I don't curl my arms up to my meager chest and capture the ball. I let that which was intended by some invisible, irrational force for me and me alone to bounce free, another arc created at the transfer of energy, one that results in the football bouncing across the ground, until it comes to rest just out of bounds.

Fuck you, Greta.

There's a moment of confusion in the field. No one can understand what's happened. And then the opposing team starts jumping up and down and cheering, Hot RA running out into their midst and getting swarmed by those he chose at the beginning. Especially Francesca.

My team falls silent as their declarations of survival evaporate. They are all disappointed, but none seem surprised. Their expressions are of self-censure, as if they knew they shouldn't have trusted any job to somebody like me. These girls trudge off the field, heading for the Igloos full of iced sodas.

Greta does not leave the field. She's set her crosshairs on me, like she would blow me out of my cheap sneakers if she could.

I have no regrets. I've voluntarily placed myself in hot water, and the result of my freedom of choice improves my lot in life here at Ambrose for no other reason than it relieves the sting of randomness. Greta could have been in another dorm. I could have been born more inside the normal neural bandwidth. I could have slept through the night way back at the beginning. There could have been someone, anyone, on campus, on the planet, who she'd rather have tortured. Instead, like the ball that came to me through no skill of Ms. Crenshaw's and no finesse of my own, I'm Greta's lucky catch for the game of at least this semester, and likely the whole of my sophomore year.

But I'm choosing her ire now.

As I proceed back toward the picnic tables, no one pays any attention to me. The other girls who were uninvolved in our largely incompetent contest have transitioned quickly to other topics of discussion. Or maybe they're all studiously ignoring me, shutting me out from discourse that they neglect to recall they've not included me in thus far anyway.

There's one face that's turned to me, however, one set of eyes that meets my own.

Strots is sitting on her tabletop, her fellow athletes in a loose configuration around her, a fist not fully closed. She's looking right at me, and there's a wise light in her eye. After so many years of her being in end zones and scoring goals, she knows what I did. She knows I could easily have held on to that ball and gotten the points and kept my team alive. She knows that I made a conscious choice, that that was not a fumble.

Strots smiles at me. It's a closeted smile, a mere lift to one corner of her lips. But I catch it.

And I smile back, also in secret.

Strots gives me a nod of respect and then refocuses on Keisha, who's debating another member of the field hockey team. I continue over to the table I was at, the table on which Ms. Crenshaw's coleslaw has passed its congealed, brewing stage and is now moving on to dehydration in the sunlight.

As I resume my perch, Ms. Crenshaw does not come over to engage me and commiserate. She's received an unexpected boon. Hot RA is talking to her sincerely, his hand on her shoulder, his eyes kind as he attempts, I assume, to frame the very expected loss in a favorable light. What he fails to see, or deliberately ignores, is that his attention is the win for my geometry teacher. Her face is turned up to his with the rapture of a sunflower to the unimpeded summer sky. She's drinking in this nourishment, as for once, the object of so much of her effort—monitoring those car windows against the weather must be a lot of work—sends in her direction exactly what she's been trying to receive, a Hail Mary ball caught in the only end zone that matters to her.

I'd like something cold to drink, but Greta's by the Igloos with the cold sodas and there's a small crowd of spectators around her. From time to time, one or two of the girls glance in my direction, and then look away quickly as they see me staring. I have a feeling that Greta will not leave those coolers until it's time to get back on the bus. She knows I must be thirsty, but she also knows I won't tread into enemy territory.

But it's okay. Everything is okay. The angle of the sun has changed and my table is now in the shade, sure as if the tree beside me approves of my actions and is showing it by granting me cover. The afternoon is cool outside of the direct rays, and as my heart rate begins to return to normal, my body temperature drops.

I think back to the moment that football left my grasp and bounced onto the ground. I took something Greta wanted away from her. I thwarted her superiority. I got her back.

Even if I will pay for this, I'm quietly happy. And this version of a positive emotion is not accompanied with the clanging, hallucinatory success and mastery that I felt for those twenty-four hours after I dyed my clothes back to some semblance of wearability, the mania running amok and taking me all the way to the White House, before it was dashed just as quickly by a memo designed to mislead me.

This happiness is of a calmer nature. It's satisfaction.

And I have a feeling it's going to last for a very long time.

chapter ELEVEN

That night, I can't resist. Twenty minutes before curfew, I leave the dorm via Tellmer's front door. As I walk to the right, I hunker into my sweater and look up at the windows of the phone room. There are five girls with buff-colored receivers pressed to their ears. Two have propped a hip up on the windowsill, and the others are sitting on top of the tables that are pushed back against the walls, talking stations for the inmates. Seeing all of them sitting where they should not, their feet on chairs or wedged into the vertebrae of the radiators, makes me think about all of us out at that field on those picnic tables. I wonder whether the inability to use furniture properly is a hallmark of our generation.

There are security lights tucked into the eaves of my dorm's roofline, right above the frieze of composers, and from the fixtures flows illumination that is warm in tint but does nothing to mediate the temperature. The night is colder than I anticipated and I wish I'd brought my jacket, but one advantage to my black clothes is that I disappear into the shadows as I pare off from the walkway, my boots making no sound, as the leaves have not yet begun to fall.

I'm careful to veer far away from the parking lot, where Hot RA's Porsche is parked, along with Ms. Crenshaw's Toyota Camry and the third-floor married couple's station wagon. As I continue along, I make it seem to any casual observer as though I'm headed to Wycliffe next door. Once I am certain I've gone far enough, I double back and penetrate the brush and tree barrier, finding the dirt footpath that Greta and the Brunettes first showed me.

The path is close to the riverbed, and it must get flooded during torrential rains like the one we had the other day. This may explain why there are, from time to time, river stones embedded in the dirt, transplants from the bed that were migrated by a rushing force with sufficient power to carry them out, but not enough strength to bring them back in. The only other impediments in my way are the granddaddy trees that are spaced very far apart, their strictly enforced territories appearing to have been negotiated by virtue of the reach of their massive arms.

When I arrive at my split-trunk maple, I hide my body and lend my ear at the same time, the deciduous skyscraper accepting the lean of my weight as if I am but a newspaper section blown by the wind against its towering torso. In the icy blue moonlight, Greta, Francesca, and Stacia are where they always go, sitting on that outcropping about thirty feet in front of me. The huge stones are smooth, just like the other river rocks, but they're mesomorphs among minors, three or four enormous, mountain-worthy boulders that have inexplicably been dropped at the head of a deep and whirling pool within the river's course.

The girls are smoking, and they're tapping their ashes into the water, which, as always, makes me angry. When they're done with their cigarettes, they'll flick the filthy filters into the current as well, and I imagine if they were drinking beer, the bottles would be sunk in the pool. If they were eating chips, the bags would follow suit. So, too, would candy wrappers, sandwich sleeves, and the dead batteries of their Walkmans. They have no concept of nature, no respect for the animals and the aquatic life for whom this river is sustenance, not a moving trash can.

"—stop sulking anytime you want," Greta says. "I mean, you won. What do you have to get bitched about."

Stacia speaks up. "Everything's fine. The air's cleared. We're here together and that's all that matters."

Someone get that girl a Nobel Peace Prize, I think to myself.

"Right, Francesca?" she prompts.

Francesca shrugs and strokes her hair with her free hand. "Sure. Whatever."

In the darkness, the bruise around her eye is not very noticeable. Or maybe she's put concealer over the discoloration.

"You're such a drama queen." As Greta exhales, she lets her head fall back, the plume of smoke sent to the night sky, as if she is determined to litter up into space as well. "But I forgive you."

"Thanks."

Greta doesn't seem to notice the snarkiness. Or more likely, she doesn't care. "So let's talk about the dance," she says. "Are you asking Daniel?"

"You know I'm not." Francesca taps her cigarette like her forefinger is a hammer. "You know I can't. Mark will be there."

"It'll be fun if they see each other."

"For who."

"Me."

These are the boys they always talk about. Daniel, Mark, Todd, and Jonathon. I know all kinds of things about their other halves, except for physical descriptions, but something tells me they're the Labrador retrievers of boys, well-bred, well-mannered, and athletic. And blond.

The jury's out on whether they have webbed paws for retrieving water fowl.

"What about Todd," Stacia asks. "Is he coming?"

Greta casts her filter into the river, the stub's lit end giving off sparks until its embers are extinguished by the plunge. "I haven't asked him."

"You haven't asked him?" Francesca's head snaps around. "I thought you were going to."

"It's not an open dance. It's for St. Michael's students only."

"You were going to sneak him in."

"And now I'm not." Greta flips open the top of a differently shaped pack of cigarettes. Dunhill Reds. How fancy, and not what she usually smokes. "He's not worth the probation."

"Wow." Francesca shakes her head. "That's a change. He's really hot."

"So are a lot of people."

I close my eyes and rest my burning cheek against the maple's cool, rough bark. I'm glad they aren't talking about me, although maybe it's because Francesca benefited from my stunt—

The snap of a stick behind me brings my head around and my heart to fluttering attention. I think of every horror movie I've ever watched: Girl alone in the woods after dark, her blood splashing across a tree trunk, her body collapsing, lifeless, to the killer's feet. And here it is. A figure cut from the shadows, big and looming.

My mouth opens to scream. At least Greta and Francesca and Stacia are near—

"Shhh, it's just me." Strots's voice is dry, and soft as a breath. "Jesus Christ, paranoid much, Taylor?"

The air that I had sucked into my lungs threatens to explode in a single exhalation, but I catch it in time and ease its release so I don't make a loud noise.

"What are you doing here?" I whisper.

"I saw you leave. I decided to find out where you were going."

In the last week, Strots has been spending even less time in our room. Unless I'm tutoring her in geometry, or she's asleep, she's upstairs in Keisha's room with a couple of others who sit at her table at lunch. I miss her, even though it's not like we ever talk about anything much, and I don't blame her for bailing on me.

Strots puts a cigarette between her teeth and talks around it. "You don't seem like an eavesdropper."

As she brings up her Bic, I hiss, "You can't light that."

"Why not? We're downwind of them, and besides, what are they going to do to me. They're smoking, too. They're not going to turn me in."

As if getting caught with a cigarette is the only thing she needs to be wary of in their company. How I envy her.

I turn back to Greta and the Brunettes. It's Stacia's turn at bat. She is confessing that her boyfriend, Jonathon, hasn't called her for two nights. She further says that she went down to the pay phones in the cellar, the ones by the laundry room that you can call out on, and that she tried to reach him after dinner but was told he wasn't in his dorm. She doesn't believe the story, and Greta seems delighted by the insecurity.

"This is it?" Strots says, much closer to me now. "You stand out here in the bugs and listen to them talk about their boyfriends?"

"There aren't any bugs here."

"Only because you're buried under all that funeral draping." She slaps at something, and as I turn around to *shh* her, she rolls her eyes. "Relax. We're fine."

Strots falls silent, and so do I, as we listen to the voices that the other girls are not trying to hide even though they're smoking. Then again, the outcrop of rocks is far, far from the dorms. Well, far enough so that if one of the RAs were to look out of their window, they'd see nothing and smell nothing and hear not a syllable of the personal gossip. The same would still be true if one of the RAs were to go out to the shallow parking lot and, for example, check the windows on someone else's vintage Porsche.

And Greta doesn't have to worry about any fellow students. Everyone's too intimidated to turn her in.

For no apparent reason, I decide to tell Strots about Ms. Crenshaw and Hot RA at the game. I'm not sure why I feel compelled to share the details about her desperation and his avoidance techniques. But it's still on my mind.

"So, guess what happened between—"

I'm speaking softly as I turn my head toward her, but I don't finish my sentence. I do not make my report. Strots is staring through the V of the tree with an intense look on her face, one that has nothing to do with the conversation around the monogamistic failures of Stacia's hometown honey. Strots is staring at Greta, her athletic body perfectly still.

I've never seen my roommate like this before, but I've seen this in others. I saw it today with Ms. Crenshaw when Hot RA was talking to her after the game. I've felt a version of it myself when I crossed paths with Nick Hollis for the first time, and every time since.

"She's such an asshole," Strots says.

The words are spoken out loud, but I get the impression they are not for me to hear. They're what is in her mind. They're what has been in her mind for a while.

"I saw what you did at the game today," she says to me. "You dropped that ball on purpose."

"I did."

"Did the payback feel good?" she asks without looking at me. "After all the shit she's pulled with you?"

"Yes."

Strots laughs in a husky way. Then she glances at me. "Good for you."

Her eyes are incredibly intense, like she's somewhere deep inside of herself: Even though I'm standing in front of her, I know that she doesn't see me clearly.

Perhaps that is why she kisses me.

The last thing I expect is for her free hand to take the back of my neck and pull me into her. I'm so shocked that I don't resist as she puts her lips to mine. I can't move. I'm frozen, caught between her body and that of the tree that's been my spying refuge. Her mouth strokes against mine a couple of times, but she stops when I do not respond.

Strots jerks back. Curses under her breath. Steps away.

"Sorry," she says with a hint of bitterness. "My fault."

With that, she disappears up the path, a ghost reabsorbed into the night.

I collapse back against the tree. I am shaking.

Greta and the Brunettes leave the river before I'm able to, the girls cutting through the undergrowth and reentering the lawn somewhere downstream.

Eventually, I take the path back to Tellmer's lights. As I step out from the brush, I look up and see my room. The overhead fixture is on, but Strots isn't sitting on her bed nor does it seem like she's moving around in there. I stay for a moment where I am, watching all of the other girls in all of the other rooms.

Did Strots go back to Keisha's? I can't tell which room that would be. There are more profiles than visible faces in the windows.

I look at the Porsche and the Camry. I look at the station wagon that's owned by the married couple. But that's just to pass the time.

I'm convinced no one in any of the rooms in any of the dorms at Ambrose was kissed by their roommate tonight.

Off in the distance, an air horn sounds. It's the five-minute warning for us to be inside, on our floors, or risk probation for violating curfew. I rush in through the back door that puts me in the basement by the laundry, and I catch my breath in the scented room. When I come out, Stacia is at one of the two pay phones. She's dialing with a declarative finger, and when her call is answered, she demands to speak to Jonathon Renault. They better find him quickly if she wants to talk with him. There will be sweeps by the RAs when the next horn sounds. Or at least, Ms. Crenshaw walks around the dorm in a casual fashion. I don't know whether the duty she performs every night is to catch student violators or if she's just trolling for a Hot RA sighting.

"Well, where is he," Stacia snaps into the receiver.

She looks over her shoulder and sees me. Before she can react, I walk away in the opposite direction, as if I have somewhere to go, and I do. I climb the steps out of the basement and then continue to the main staircase, which I take to the second floor. When I get to my room, the door is shut, and for once, I knock. When there's no answer, I open things a little. The crane lamp on the edge of my desk, a holdover from the last student who slept in the bed I'm now using, is all that's on in the room now, so I know Strots has just left and turned out that overhead light.

One of Strots's bureau drawers is slightly open. It's the one she keeps her boxer shorts in. Her drawers are never left open. Clearly, she took what she needed and departed in a hurry.

I approach her bed cautiously and stand over its neat sheets and duvet, its stacked pillows. She makes the thing every morning, even though she doesn't have to.

My heart is beating fast even though I suspect she will not be back tonight. Yet, even as my instincts tell me this, my hand shakes as I reach out and lift her pillow. Her cigarettes and her lighter are gone.

She will definitely not be back tonight.

I go over and sit on my bed. I clasp my hands in my lap, as if I'm at a grown-up function, even though there are no grown-ups present and no reason I must be proper about my behavior. Our room, as I look around, seems very empty, even though the furniture count has not changed. There are still two beds, two bureaus, and two desks with two chairs. But one half of it is gone, and the hollow feeling that takes root in the center of my chest reminds me of what happens whenever I think of my father.

I wish Strots hadn't done what she did down by that tree. Not because she offended me. Not because I think less of her. Not because I'm threatened or scared by her.

I am clinically insane. Like I'm going to judge anybody for being impulsive or at loose ends?

No, I wish she hadn't because now she's gone, and gone in a way that even when she's around me again, she will still not be there. Some things that transpire between people cannot be undone, and I worry that there's no way to make what happened by the river better, no matter what is said thereafter.

And Strots was my only friend at Ambrose.

chapter TWELVE

The next morning, I awake at seven with a start, sitting up, looking over at Strots's side of the room. The bed across from mine is untouched, and the drawer where Strots keeps her boxers remains open an inch. There's no way she could have come and gone without me knowing. I slept fitfully, waiting, hoping that she might return, that we could talk it out.

I get up and go to our door. I open it a crack and look out. Girls are making pilgrimages to the bathroom, towels slung over their shoulders or dragging on the trodden carpet like the blankies of the children they were a decade ago. Strots is nowhere to be seen.

Falling in with the traffic in the hall, I enter the bathroom. Her red bucket is in her cubby, so I know she's not in one of the running showers. I use the toilet and wash my hands just to make it look like I'm here for the appropriate reasons. I'm also burning time. I want to give Strots an opportunity to come down from wherever she is so that what happened at that tree can be mutually brushed aside, as a drinking binge would be, my mouth like the open throat of a tequila bottle, never to be broached again.

As I dry my hands too thoroughly over one of the trash bins, I decide to be relieved that Strots's bucket is where it should be. I don't want her to pack up all her things and relocate off the floor, out of the dorm, even out of Ambrose itself. Somehow it'll all be my fault, and Keisha will blame me for her best friend leaving. Then I'll have two people out to get me.

I return to our room. I knock again before I enter, and there's no answer. Opening the door, I check the drawer of her bureau once more. It's in the same position. I check under her pillow. Still no cigarettes.

I pivot to her desk. What about her textbooks? What about her homework? She can't go to class in boxer shorts and a T-shirt and no bra, with nothing but shower shoes on her feet, and no work to hand in or notebooks or textbooks.

Although if anyone could get away with that, it would be Strots.

I go over and sit on my bed, tucking my legs up and linking my arms around them. My sleeping uniform consists of baggy boys' pajama bottoms and soft, well-washed, long-sleeved shirts. The idea of changing out of these comfortables and into the dark armor I wear around campus exhausts me, and as I wait for my roommate, I become utterly overwhelmed at the prospect of gathering my books and heading to class.

And forget about going to Wycliffe for food. That's like asking me to bench-press the dorm.

As I contemplate the hundreds of steps ahead of me, the weight of my backpack, the glare of the sun on my aching eyes, I feel heavy inside my skin and not from lack of sleep. My bones and my muscles throb and so does the base of my skull. It's as if I have come down with the flu in the space of a minute and a half, my immune system caught unawares, my corpuscles overrun and defeated by a microscopic invader. Except this is not really anything physical. This is an infestation of regret.

All I can think about is how I messed everything up and ruined my living situation. Last night, I should have run after Strots and told her right then and there it was okay, it was no big deal, it didn't bother me, I was only surprised. And all of this is true, not a constructed reality I discipline myself to believe in.

I am not bothered or freaked out. I have other things to worry about. Besides, I like Strots, and nothing changes that.

If only I had caught her before everything solidified overnight, I might have had a chance at undoing it all. At first she maybe wouldn't have believed me, but I could have pressed the issue, and revealed to her how cool I actually am. She could have been surprised, relieved, perhaps we would have had a short, hard hug to put it to rest, never to be thought of or worried about again. And then we could have returned to the split sugar maple, and she could have stared at Greta some more, and I could have supported my roommate in some way, and we both could have condemned all three of those litterbugs for mistreating the river with their ashes and their filters. After the girls finally left, Strots could have made a joke and we could have sauntered back here, feeling superior to those negligent pretties, Strots because she actually is, me because I'm with Strots. We could have become closer, even if Strots continued to go up to see Keisha every night after dinner, because whenever my roommate and I found ourselves together, we would have two secrets that bound us, my being pranked by Greta, and her having a crush on the girl.

Except that's not what happened.

Instead of being cool, I fumbled the ball, and this time, it was not on purpose.

I just can't get along with people my age. I can't get along with grown-ups, either, but that's not a value judgment against a person when you're fifteen. It's the relating with our peers that counts, and I fail across the board. I've always failed. I was the three-year-old in the sandbox who couldn't understand how the games were played and why. I was the six-year-old at my cousin's birthday party who no one wanted to get stuck sitting next to because of a rumor I wet my bed. I was the ten-year-old in gym class in mismatched socks and orange shorts because that was all I had to wear. And now I'm here, at fifteen, facing the prospect of being alone in this two-sided room, having driven away the most charismatic girl on campus.

In retrospect, I was stupid to think this Ambrose experience would go any other way, even if I'd been assigned to room 214.

And I will always fail. I will never have friends, and as I age, I'll just increase the breadth and scope of the categories of people with whom I cannot manage to engage. I'll be an eighty-year-old in a nursing home who no one wishes to sit next to because, even though we're all wetting our beds, my bladder's incontinence is the only one that is seen as a referendum on character.

As I contemplate my bleak, lonely future, my thoughts become tangible and they increase in weight geometrically, not just subject to gravity, but linking hands with the force that keeps all objects on the earth to pull hard, lock tighter. I gather tonnage at an incalculable rate, my thoughts leaping past the laws of physics, going quantum, absorbing dense energy that makes them infinitely solid. Unable to sustain the load, I warp in on myself, a black hole forming here on my bed, on the second floor of Tellmer Hall at the St. Ambrose School for Girls. With this change in my form, the momentum accelerates even further, and the more darkness I collect within the boundless funnel of my mind, the faster I increase the concentric circle into which all things are sucked and never released.

I consume light and matter. I consume time itself. I disappear into a cosmos of my own creation, taking everything into the void that is me.

I am so dense, so heavy, that I am the heft of the entire earth with a surface area one-tenth of the head of a pin, and the only way I can be measured and still preserve some of the structure of the universe is by pain.

Pain is what I am, no longer possessing features or form. I am the emotion that we all seek to avoid. And because this is my basis, and I'm hardwired the way I am, I feed my status like it's a boiler furnace, shoving into the burning, intolerable suffering load after load of coals in the form of thoughts: I am crazy. I am insane. There is no chance of me ever becoming better. I will never be like other people and they will always know this. I am broken, I am bad, I am worthless.

I am the reason my father left. I drove him away with my insanity.

He was a smart man, so he knew where I was going to end up well before I did, well before my mother did. He knew I was going to be an irredeemable failure on all fronts, and that I was not worth the investment of time and energy. Therefore, he got off at the next train stop, and never looked back. My mother, stuck with a malfunctioning freak for whom no one else would care, did the best she could with what little she had, and had to regress into the pretty pages of magazines to keep from losing her own mind. I am the reason all her dreams were denied. Without me, my parents would never have split up. My father's band would have succeeded and she would have gotten more beautiful with age, instead of less so. Without me, they'd be living in Bel Air, and they would have a pool, and my mother would be in *People* magazine not only because she became a successful actress, author, and daytime talk show host but because my father's band would be bigger than the Rolling Stones, the Police, and Genesis combined. He'd be touring his classics all over the world and she'd be the poor man's Joan Didion, and they'd be Linda and Paul McCartney except with more leather and a harder, edgier sound. And probably none of the vegetarianism.

My birth cheated them of all of that. I was the anchor that didn't secure them against the storm, but rather kept them too close to the rocky shore as the tide roared in and the waves got worse. I splintered and sank them.

And now I am sinking Strots. Driving her out of her room. Making her ashamed of something that is not shameful—

From somewhere within the morass, a thought occurs from a different dimension, a dimension of buoyancy rather than burden.

It's a thought I have had twice before.

It's what brings me back.

The thought, the pure, incandescent thought, returns me to the true present, to my bed, to my dorm room, to the dorm, the campus, this small Massachusetts town in the middle of the mountains. It resets everything, it returns everything, it resumes everything. And in the manner of my mis-wired brain, the thought, which unlike the others has absolutely no physical substance, which is just ether of the mind, comes with the sound of Tibetan singing bowls, a strike and then a resonance that calls me to lift my head. Or perhaps it is not an actual thought at all, it's the sound of the singing bowl itself, and my brain, which speaks the basin's melodic language, has translated the tone into a purpose that presents itself to me as a solution that is perfect.

As I look around, I am aware that the light in my room is different and I decide that it's the tail end of my hallucinatory stroll into the womb of the cosmos. Except it's not. According to my alarm clock, it's after one o'clock in the afternoon.

I have been on this bed, in this position with my knees to my chest and my arms linked around them, for six hours.

Other things have changed, besides the angle of the sun: The drawer in Strots's dresser is closed. Books that were on her desk are moved, and some are gone. She's been here. Sometime during my lock-in, she's come and gone.

The reality that she must have seen me, tucked in as if I were yet to be born, on my bed only in a physical way, which is the least significant manner of existence for any person, confirms that I must act.

Enough of all of this. This school and this roommate. My over-present mother and my absent father. My suffering that cannot be elevated no matter how much lithium I take, or group meetings I go to, or hospitals I am committed to.

Everyone will be better off without me. Except for Greta, of course, and as with my letting that football fly free of my grip, I'm emboldened by the idea of cheating her out of the pleasure she gets from hurting me.

It's what Strots said as I first arrived here.

Do not give her what she wants.

The idea of releasing people, especially my mother, from the burden of me has long been a motivator, and further, the release from my own inner pain and the terrifying trips I take inside my mind is also a blissful prospect. But what truly motivates me to stand and get dressed is the idea that I can take me away from Greta.

I can take her toy away. I can break it so badly that it doesn't work anymore and she's got to find another, more inferior thing to play with and take her petty revenge out on.

I will not give her what she wants.

Spurred on by my anger and a growing, maniacal need for retaliation, Greta becomes the sole focus of my energy, the dark thoughts that collapsed me transferring onto her, tentacles attaching and tightening. I am moving faster now, eager to mete out a punishment the likes of which that pretty girl, with her flicked cigarettes and her nasty smile and her malicious ways, is wholly unprepared for. This loser, this freak that she so disdains, is going to even the score, and ruin her in the process: I'm going to blame my death on her. I'm going to leave a note that details it all, and I'm going to make it clear that my corpse is her trophy.

She'll never recover from this. Even if it doesn't bother her, the adults in this institution won't have it. I've read enough *People* magazines to know that this kind of juicy tragedy sustains the national news feeds. Ambrose's reputation will be on the line, and there's no way this school and its long, proud legacy will go down with the ship of a one-hundred-and-ten-pound, blond-haired bully.

Even if her name happens to be Stanhope.

She'll be dealt with accordingly, and I cannot wait.

Faster and faster I move, so hungry for the end result, so impatient, that I'm unaware of putting on my clothes. I just discover, some minutes after I rise stiffly from my bed, that I'm pulling on my coat and shoving my remaining five-dollar bill into my pocket. Even as I make a brief, inconclusive assessment as to whether or not I need to pee, I remain mostly disconnected from my body. I'm no more aware of the status of my internal organs than I am of the constriction of the boots upon my feet or the weight of the clothes on my back.

All I know is my vengeance, and oh, how I am more than willing to sacrifice my pathetic life at the foot of Greta's downfall.

chapter
THIRTEEN

The next thing I know, I'm in the CVS. I remember nothing of the walk down into town because I've spent the trip lost in images of how it will all happen. The boiler room in the basement is where I'm going to do it, and I see my body being found by a workman servicing the furnace. I see him tripping over his own feet as he rears back in horror. I see him calling Hot RA down, and it's my beautiful residential advisor who kneels by my remains and picks up the handwritten note in which I state all my reasons why. Administrators are called, the big ones, who have offices on the other side of campus. The police are called, and they come with an ambulance even though it's too late. I see my note being read by the adults with badges, their brows down low, their offense over Greta's actions both personal and professional.

Greta is called to the headmaster. She arrives, confused, because news of what has happened has been strictly quarantined. She's summarily kicked out of school, and when she protests that she's a Stanhope, she's cut off with the announcement that her father has been forced to resign from the Board of Trustees as a result of her actions. While the others in my dorm gather in the common area for a special meeting, at which grief counselors are made available, she's upstairs packing her things under the furious glare of her father, who cannot fathom how he managed to bring such a horrible child into this world, his bankruptcy now not the worst thing that's ever happened to him.

In the aftermath, the girls in my dorm will sink into the role of victim/bystander and all of the adults in their lives will minister to the tender hearts affected by my tragedy; not because their elders care about me, but because they're terrified that I'll start a trend. The emotional outpouring my peers feel will be both honest and dishonest. They'll pitch forward authentically into their sadness, exploring the landscape of loss and the fragility of life on a cursory level, although it will be in inverse proportion to what they felt for me while I was walking among them. Living, I am a ghost. Dead, I will finally have substance. I will finally be accepted and I will be epic in my absence.

Greta, meanwhile, will be relegated to a life of shame in the less-than house her parents had to move into after their own downfall. She will have to go to a public school because no other preparatory institution will take her for fear of an exodus of current enrollees and a dearth of potential applicants. Colleges will not touch her, either. She will while away her mortal years in the invisible prison of the cautionary tale, no longer someone with a future, but a person irrevocably tied to a single, shattering event that occurred when she was fifteen.

As I return to the present, I find that I am standing in front of the over-the-counter analgesics, the kind of low-level pain relief medicines that you have to take some number of in order to get the result I intend. I'm unaware of whether Roni and Margie, who helped me with the dye, are behind their cash registers, and I don't sense the pharmacist anywhere in the store. Nor am I cognizant of any other shoppers. It's just me and the display of pills.

I am really planning now, getting into the nitty-gritty. After I write my note up at my desk, I'll go down to the basement and sit on the concrete floor by the boiler. I can swallow the chalky pills in two small handfuls. The bitter taste that takes root on the back of my tongue and the burning that goes down my throat will make it hard not to retch, and retching has to be avoided because it can potentially lead to vomiting, which I cannot permit. Fortunately, I remember a solution for the taste problem, a best practice. At the mental institution during my second stay, one of the girls gave me a helpful tip: Swallow the aspirin with an orange soda. Even if the taste of fake Florida doesn't appeal, she told me, it'll be enough to mask the bitterness, and make the soda cold, too, to settle your stomach as much as possible.

Oh, and above all, be certain you do it first thing in the morning, before you eat anything. Empty is best, a clean foundation on which to build your mausoleum.

It's now quarter to two in the afternoon, but fortunately, I missed breakfast by becoming a black hole and going back to the start of the universe.

I picked up some other handy information during my stays at the institution. For a girl of my weight, I should need only ten to fourteen pills to get the job done, and I used this base of knowledge two weeks after I was released the first time. Unfortunately, however succinctly something can be calculated in theory, reality tends to be more messy and unpleasant, and I failed because I vomited. This will not happen now, thanks to the Orange Crush girl and her helpful refinements.

And I really would owe her, except she killed herself six months after I met her. Not with pills, though.

My plan is set. I have my place, the boiler room. I have my timing, which is as soon as I get back to the dorm. With these two things decided, I reach forward to get a box of aspirin and am surprised to find that there's a cold Orange Crush soda already in my hand. Apparently, I was prescient enough to grab one from the cooler on the way back here to the pain reliever section.

I switch the Orange Crush to my left hand, and pick up a box of extra-strength aspirin. It's the generic brand, the kind with a label that's been designed to mimic the leading national product's. I have a thought that I am totally my mother's daughter. As she wears almost-there perfume, I will kill myself with knockoff aspirin. I check the milligram dosage and then see that there are fifty pills in the bottle inside the box. I think about the cost of the soda. I do some math. I pick up a second bottle of aspirin just in case.

The challenge is going to be keeping the pills down long enough so that the acetylsalicylic acid has time to be absorbed into my bloodstream. Even though I only need about a dozen pills, I will try to take half the bottle. This strikes me as a nice medium, providing a suitable cushion upward from what my body weight requires, without putting so many in that my stomach becomes irrepressibly irritated. As I contemplate the self-control that's going to be required not to give in to gag reflex, I try to reassure myself that anything is possible if you put your mind to it—

Without warning, a sadness creeps up on me, and like a stranger tapping me on the shoulder to ask for directions, it's the sort of thing I cannot ignore. Even as I'm so far into the approaching attempt that my salivary glands are tingling sure as if the nausea is already starting to hit, even as I contemplate with grim, excited purpose my end goal of showing Greta that her favorite hobby of fucking with people can backfire big-time, a small part of me is aware that I'm here once again. I'm on this precipice, staring down into another grave.

How am I here again? I wonder.

But that question is a stupid one to ask. I have bipolar with mania. Crashes happen. I'm crashing now.

But at least I'm finally fixing the problem so I won't ever have to worry about doing this again—and Greta is going to help me. The statistics, after all, aren't in my favor. According to an article I read after my second attempt, the suicide success rate of aspirin in adolescents is only between one and two percent, not the kind of odds you want if you're way past the cry for attention stage and on to bigger and better things. And perhaps it's because of this high failure rate that guns and suffocation are more typically used. Here at Ambrose, however, there are no guns to be had, and hanging myself isn't something I want to rope myself into. I like the idea of simply going to sleep and not waking up, although I know that I'm looking at convulsions first before the calm of stage two sets in—

I cannot believe I am here again.

I promised myself I would not, no matter how bad it got, do this to myself anymore.

This is the danger of my disease, though. For normal people, deep depression is a descent down a long, slow trail. It takes time to set in. This is not the case for me. With my disease, clinical depression is just a slip and fall away, its flimsy triggers totally disproportionate to how far and how fast I can decline. In a matter of hours—sometimes minutes, or even moments—my brain can plunge me into territory it would take others years of suffering to get to. It's the same for the mania. And both extremes, regardless of their lickety-split arrival, are things I experience as if they are the culmination of decades of emotional shift.

I am here again.

I think of my mother, though I don't want to. I think of her alone in that house we have lived in all of my conscious life. I tell myself that her magazines will keep her company, that they are her family anyway. I try to jump-start the motor of a happy future for her, my father and her resuming their relationship as if nothing has happened, the fifteen years of my existence scrubbed clean by the elbow grease of my suicide, the stain gone, the floor tiles of the rest of their days and nights as well as the grout of their attraction and feelings for each other gleaming cleanly in the bright light of promise once again. And then I try to reconnect with my image of Greta in the headmaster's office, the confusion on her face as she is told she must leave the school a blazing satisfaction as my spirit watches from one of the corners by the ceiling, a floating sentry enjoying the success of my plan.

I get nowhere with any of it. Instead, I become too acutely aware that I am holding aspirin in one hand and an Orange Crush in the other, and that I'm going to go kill myself on a dirty floor that will smell like old motor oil.

I think of the way I stood alone on the summit of the mountain as the girls funneled back onto the trail, my eyes drinking in the majesty before me, my soul joining in with everything around me, even Greta. I remember the wind on my face and the sun on my back and the cold water bottle in my hand, all of my senses receiving an unexpected gift, my mind calming, for once. I didn't expect that moment. And when I follow through with this, and I will, there will never again exist the possibility for my set of eyes, for my pair of ears, for my skin and body, to feed on the beauty around me. I will be over. I will be nothing.

After years of being at the mercy of my hallucinations, I know for a fact that there is no such thing as God, and I miss me already. Everyone and everything else will go on, but I will be gone—

A hand taps me on the shoulder. I turn sharply and look up.

It is not a metaphor this time.

The man looking down at me is the pharmacist. I recognize him from my first trip here. He has thick salt-and-pepper gray hair that is brushed back from a shiny forehead. He's wearing a white coat over a tie and button-down shirt. His lips are moving. He's speaking to me.

So much of me is tied up in my attempt that I can't decipher his words. I figure he must be warning me not to think I can get away with shoplifting. I put my hand into my pocket, take out my last five-dollar bill, and thrust the crumpled wad to him.

"What's this?" he asks as he glances at what I'm pushing on him.

It's strange to have his voice register, my hearing coming back with no warning. I open my mouth to tell him it's a five-dollar bill, the last one I have, as well as the last one I need, and isn't that a lucky coincidence. Except as I look down, I see I am not holding out something that has Abraham Lincoln's face on it. I'm offering the pharmacist a slip of paper. He takes it and reads whatever it is. Then he looks into my eyes again.

"Come with me," he says, taking the bottles of aspirin from my hand, and putting the Orange Crush down on the floor even though it's two aisles away from the cooler I got it from.

"Margie!" he calls out. "I'm taking a break for ten!"

"Yeah, okay, Phil," comes a response from the front of the store.

Phil, the pharmacist, leads me behind his counter and through a door in the wall of the elevated platform from which he dispenses pills and potions more dangerous than the aspirin I'm trying to buy. That I *will* buy. As soon as he lets me go from whatever he has in mind.

He's out of luck if he's trying to bust me. I didn't put anything in my pockets. He can pat me down. And you can't call the police and turn someone in just because you think they *might* steal something.

Phil the Pharmacist is nothing but a speed bump in my road, not a dead end in the progression to my dead end.

"Here," he says. "Let's sit down."

I look around and don't see much of the rough-walled break room area. He's brought us to a card table that has four folding chairs around it, and I take a seat because I am suddenly exhausted. He joins me and offers something forward. It's a paper towel that's folded in quarters.

When I look at him in confusion, he says, "You're crying."

I fumble to get the Bounty to my cheeks. I'm ashamed. It's one thing to melt down on the inside. Showing this kind of emotion outwardly, I'm naked in front of a stranger.

As we sit in silence, I sniffle. I don't want to look at him, but I have to check to confirm that I'm being judged.

I'm not. His eyes are kind. And sad.

So is his voice. "You go to Ambrose, don't you."

I nod. I don't answer him verbally because I'm unsure of my voice.

"I've seen you in here before."

I nod again.

"Can you tell me what's going on for you?" When I shake my head, he says softly, "What do you need all the aspirin for?"

As he poses this question, we both know exactly what they're for. He probably knows exactly why I chose the Orange Crush, too, some kind of continuing education he's forced by the state to take flagging the soda when it's purchased along with two bottles of fifty-count 325 mg pills of aspirin by fifteen-year-old girls in all-black clothes who are in tears and don't even know it.

"Were you going to fill this?" he says.

I stare at him blankly. He's holding out the piece of paper that I thought was a five-dollar bill, and when I don't respond, he turns the slip around to face me. It's my lithium prescription. The one that I've been meaning to bring down here for how long now? As my mind does a quick calendar check, I'm shocked at how many days it's been since my supply of pills ran out. How did I lose track of the time?

"Who can I call for you?" he says.

"Nobody." I clear my throat as the implications of going off my medication start to roll in, and I must reject them one by one to stay on track with my boiler room plan. I also have to get out of this conversation. "I'm okay. My roommate is on the field hockey team. She needs the aspirin. It's not for me."

The lie flows off my tongue smoothly, and I'm impressed with my destructive side's ability to cover for itself.

Across the card table, Phil the Pharmacist looks doubtful. Perhaps the lie isn't as convincing as my need for it to be tells me it is.

"Do you want me to call your doctor?" He points to the top of the prescription where the address and phone number of Dr. Warten are printed. "It's inside of business hours."

"I'm fine." Of course I am. Even if I'm still catching tears with the paper towel he gave me. "I've just had a bad day. I'm not suicidal, if that's what you're worried about. I swear to God, I'm not going to hurt myself."

It's easy to back up a lie with that kind of vow when you're an atheist, and yet throwing a little religion at the situation seems to relieve Phil. He sits back in his folding chair.

"How long have you been off your meds?" he asks.

"I don't know."

This is because, rather than counting the calendar, I'm trying to calculate what will appease him more: the idea that I've missed only a few days or that I've missed a few weeks. The former suggests I may be very mentally ill, but perhaps he'll feel as though I can quickly get back on track. The latter would mean I'm less mentally ill, but may have a harder course to return to the stasis point that allows me to be out in the world under my own auspices. I can't decide which is better, what is worse.

"You need to take these pills every day."

"I know. I won't make the mistake again."

I have no idea what I am saying. I'm just trying to agree with everything that comes out of his mouth because I'm hoping he'll take acquiescence as a sign that I'm open to his advice and will follow it. This is what adults want to hear from girls like me who are in a crisis. They want to believe that they've had a positive impact and effected a change of course away from impending disaster—and if you can't impart this illusion to them with your words, your tone, and your affect, then they'll escalate the warfare and call in for reinforcements. You've got to make sure they feel heard and give off the impression that their well-intended logic is the sort of thing that you're uniquely struck by, some combination of their syllables knocking down the barrier to your recovery. It's the way they live with themselves after a bad result, the solace they take as they go home at night to be with their spouses and children and mortgages and groceries.

At least I tried, they tell themselves.

"If you could fill my prescription now, that'd be great," I say. "I'd really appreciate it. I'll even take one of the pills right here, right now."

Phil gives my face a good, thorough examination, and I make sure that my features are arranged in a pleasant mask, as if there's nothing going on behind my eyes and between my ears that should worry him: I have no suicide plan. The Orange Crush is because I like orange soda. The aspirin really is for my roommate. And the tears are because I'm a hormonal teenager and about to get my period.

"Suicide is not the answer," he says. "It really isn't. It's a permanent solution to a temporary mood."

Bingo.

I almost smile because I've heard this preamble to a release from custody before, but I make sure I retain the receptive, open expression I'm faking. *Temporary mood, huh*, I want to say. I've had two years of hell, preceded by a decade of a lesser version of the torture, and I'm staring down a double-barreled, normal life span loaded with only more of the same. Even on the lithium, my disease is getting stronger, and if I don't put the boiler room plan into action today, it'll happen sometime in the near future.

This inevitability is typical of patients like me. What I have, I overheard Dr. Warten once say to my mother, is like childhood cancer. Sooner or later, the drugs won't work anymore, and then I'll die.

"The thing is," Phil the Pharmacist hazards, "you have to think of what you leave behind. How the people you love will feel."

Nice advice, Phil, I say to myself. *But with the way things are going right now, I don't have room in my brain to consider the ramifications of my funereal pursuits on anybody but Margaret Stanhope.*

"What will your mother feel? Your father?"

They'll be fine, Phil. They're going to get back together and move to Bel Air—hey, can I call you Phil? Is that okay? I figure, given what we're discussing, we might as well be on a first-name basis even though you're a grown-up and I'm a kid.

"How about your roommate? How will she feel?"

My roommate will be—

Abruptly, I frown. "I'm sorry, what did you say?"

I'm so busy conversing with him in my head that it's hard to hear what he's actually speaking.

"Your roommate. How will she feel?"

An icy dread comes over me, hitting my head and flowing throughout my hot, numb body. The change in temperature wakes me up, the feel of the hard chair beneath my bottom, the run-down interior of the break room, the smell of Phil's vastly diminished aftershave, all of it barging in, as if the sensations have broken through a door.

My iron-clad purpose, my clarity of mission, is shaken.

Strots. What about Strots.

I put my hand to my mouth, horrified.

I've been so focused on taking Greta's toy away that I've forgotten Strots. If I leave this store—and buy two bottles of aspirin somewhere else—and go back to my dorm, and take the pills in that boiler room, and hold them down, and am in that lucky one to two percent who get the job done, Strots will think it's her fault. She'll think her kiss was the reason. She'll blame herself for the rest of her life.

With ultra-clarity, I see my roommate's face as she pulled away when I didn't respond to her kiss. I relive the shame and blame in her eyes. Jesus. If she can't handle the repercussions of what she perceives as a relatively minor violation of personal boundaries, she'll never make it through my dead body, and nothing I can say in my suicide note will expunge her of this sense of false responsibility. What's more, she'll feel that guilt even if I'm in the open field of ninety-eight percent who can't get the job done. If I'm found unresponsive in the boiler room in a pool of my own vomit, and I'm eventually revived, waking up in a hospital bed with charcoal in my stomach and bags of saline being forced through my veins, she'll still feel responsible. With Strots's sense of honor, she'll view a failed attempt as something that's just as bad as an actual success.

For godsakes, the girl offered to beat up Greta for me. She has principles.

"So who can I call for you?" Phil says. Like he's had to repeat the words a couple of times.

I gather he's been speaking to me again and I haven't been responding, and as a result of this, what little persuasive ground I've gained on the I'm-not-crazy front has probably been lost. But that doesn't matter now. My course has changed, and it is because of something he's said, although not in the manner I'd assume he intended. This isn't a permanent alteration in my goal. Only a delay so that I can set a different foundation for my actions.

"I'm not going to kill myself," I tell him. "That is not what's going to happen."

As I stare the pharmacist right in the eye, I'm lying about absolutely nothing at all.

Well, almost nothing. I will not kill myself right *now*.

Right now, I have to talk to Strots. Immediately. I don't know how long I have before the darkness comes back for me, and I've got to find my roommate before the shifting decks of my mood tilt at the plunging angle again.

Phil nods slowly. "Okay. I believe you."

chapter

FOURTEEN

I'm racing up Main Street, heading back to campus, my refill of lithium in the pocket of my jacket, absolutely no aspirin or Orange Crush on me because Phil is not as dumb as I thought he was. I'm on Medicaid because of my mother's low income and my diagnosis, and I was able to cover the co-pay for my prescription refill with my five dollars. On my way out of the CVS, I put my forty-three cents in change on the counter in front of Margie, the cashier. She seemed surprised. It's a shame that I couldn't promise I'd be back to repay the rest of what I was given to meet the cost of the Rit dye and the ColorStay, and also that I didn't have the time to report on the success of the advice she and Roni had given me.

I have no idea how long I'll be able to keep the wolves away, and making preemptive peace with my roommate is my paramount purpose.

As words that start with the letter *p* circle my mind like a flock of birds, all flapping wings and squawks, I steam up the hill to Ambrose, chugging along in my heavy boots, making good time that nonetheless feels slow. It's two fifteen in the afternoon. I want to get my pills hidden and be in position on my bed well before Strots returns to drop her books off and have a cigarette before her home game starts. She does this because she can't smoke anywhere near the playing fields. And her cigarettes were under her pillow when I left, a first base that she will have to slide back into.

As I pass by the theater building and zero in on Tellmer, there are no students walking around. This seems right, as I feel utterly alone.

I am on the swinging pendulum between the living and the dead, and this is not an experience I believe I am sharing with many of my cohort here. It is also not hyperbole. When you begin to dance with the idea that you can take your own life, when you have tried on a number of plans for size and not talked to anyone about them, when you've actually attempted to kill yourself a couple of times, when you are mentally ill and messing around with your brain chemistry with mood stabilizers because it's the best of the bunch of weak solutions that the doctors can give you, you're very aware that what drove you to go down to CVS one hour ago is a switch that gets flipped with greater ease every time it's used. The first crank is rusty and there's some resistance; you may have to put both hands into it. But you quickly wear that off until the gear is smooth and the toggle itself entices.

That's where I am now.

The realization that I'm in a separate class of citizens makes me feel self-important. I'm a critical problem, not just an alienated girl on scholarship at a fancy prep school who wears black clothes and is growing out a drugstore dye job on her brown hair. Still, beneath that surface gleam of special status, I'm absolutely terrified.

I'm completely out of control. And in spite of this insight, I'm not sure whether I'd want to take the wheel if I could.

Arriving at Tellmer, I surmount the steps up to my dorm's front entrance, and as I wrench open the shoulder-straining weight of the door, I think about Ms. Crenshaw. Shit, I pray that she's not lying in wait for me at the base of the stairs, or in the open doorway of her apartment, or, even worse, leaning against the wall next to my room upstairs, all because of some loser simpatico that has her instinctually aware of my trip down into town.

There's no one at the bottom of the stairs, and her door is closed. I don't waste time. I don't check my mailbox. I take the staircase two steps at a time, the loose pills chattering in their hard-sided bottle in my pocket as if they're clapping for me, cheering me on. Up on the second floor, I speed down my hall. No one is around. I stop at the bathroom because I don't want to be disturbed by a call of nature once I get to my room.

I'm still drying my hands with a paper towel as I come up to my door. I knock. There's no answer. A flash of panic goes through my body as I enter and close myself in. Her bed is still made, the pillow still in place. I open her closet. Her team jackets and her jerseys and the one dress she brought with her are where they've always been. Thank God. And her bureau is still full. Lastly, I revisit her cigarettes, which are exactly where they're supposed to be.

Relieved, I fall onto my bed, letting my limbs lie where they land. I should take my jacket off, but I'm breathing hard and dizzy from not having eaten. It's also hot in our room, that boiler I intend to die next to doing its job. But so much for the maintenance man finding me; he's already turned the great beast on for the season. But at least, when I follow through with my plan, I'll be warm.

The pills. I need to put my lithium away.

Sitting up, I shed my jacket and open the bottom drawer of my desk. I put the full bottle next to the one that I emptied without being aware of it, and I'm relieved there's no crinkly little white bag to throw out. I refused one when Phil the Pharmacist handed the prescription over to me.

It's too much effort to lie back on the bed. I stay at the edge of my mattress, propping my head in my hands.

The lithium is supposed to ward off the mania, and it seems silly to take a pill now when I'm at the low ebb of mood. What exactly am I bringing myself down from? More to the point, if I'm just going to kill myself later, why do I care what my mood's trajectories are?

But some quiet, rational voice is talking to me, and it forces me to recall what Dr. Warten said about the highs and the crashes that follow. I've been overstimulated with change, with Greta, since coming to Ambrose, and my efforts to keep a semi-regular sleep schedule have clearly not provided enough support to the adjustments I've been required to make to my new environment. I see now that I've been kindling, my thoughts racing, my inner life so much more involved and involving than anything I find in outside reality.

Surrounded by fresh faces and unfamiliar territory, I've fallen back on the only friend who's never deserted or judged me. Too bad she is so destructive.

And the fact that I forgot to refill my prescription and keep to my medication schedule has allowed my madness to get a serious foothold on me.

As I reach this conclusion, it should be the end of the analysis. I should stop right here, take my medication, and call Dr. Warten, which was the plan he and I agreed to when he signed off on me attending Ambrose. My illness, however, likes to argue with facts and it's a debating expert that always wins. Even when its logic is ridiculous, the lilt of its faulty reasoning is a song I find irresistible, and I'm not even sure what it is telling me right now. I just know that resuming the medication is not a good idea. It won't really help me. It offers nothing but side effects, whereas my boiler room plan is a slam dunk, a certain score, a predictable win. Provided I do it right this time.

I stare down at the drawer I just closed. I think of the empty prescription bottle that's already in there, and recall my anxiety over its disposal. I'd decided that I was going to take it home with me out of an abundance of caution. Not during the upcoming Columbus Day weekend, though. I've already set it up with my mother that I'm staying and working in the dorm for some money. No, I'm going to wait until Thanksgiving break to throw it out, and I try to find optimism in the fact that I am contemplating anything in November, even a hypothetical. Yet the thought of home brings up the futility of my considering any sort of future. Even on the lithium, I've only made it for a year and a month without having any major suicidal thoughts.

And you'll get more of them tonight, someone in my head points out. *And tomorrow. And every day until you take care of this problem—*

My hand plows into that desk drawer and I grab the pills like they have an expiration date measured in seconds, not years. I pop the little lid, check they are the right ones—not that Phil would have made a mistake—and I take one, swallowing it dry. When it gets stuck, I go into Strots's closet and I borrow one of the bottles of Coke she keeps there. I twist off the top, suck some gulps that sound loud in the quiet room, and I'm shaking when I sit back down.

I'm not sure where the impulse to take the pill came from, but it feels like a flimsy savior compared to the glaring, blaring force of the suicidal thoughts and their rugged, persuasive logic.

I drink some more, the bottle vibrating in my grip from the tremors that rack me. The sugar perks me up and sort of clears my mind, and I grasp on to the revival of both body and consciousness, telling myself that it is my pill already going to work. This is a lie. There is nothing therapeutic going on, at least not in a medicinal sense. It'll take time to rebuild the levels of the drug in my body, to get to a saturation point where my mood is chemically altered for the better. But the placebo effect is real. I feel as though I have taken a treatment for suicide that is fast-acting and dispositive. With it in my system, I will not go into the boiler room.

Glancing around my room, I think maybe it's best that I leave St. Ambrose. For one, Strots doesn't know what town I'm from. She's never asked. I've never told. If I go back home to take care of business, she may never hear about my death. And even if she does, I'll be sure to wait long enough so that she'll ascribe the bad outcome to someone or something else's fault. For another, it will be a relief for her to not have to be the one who leaves this room. She can stay here by herself until somebody transfers in next semester or the school year comes to its natural conclusion.

Problem solved without my having to reveal anything. This is a good result for a lot of reasons. Dr. Warten says that inherent to bipolar with mania is both lack of self-awareness and impeded decision-making. He often maintains, at least to the parents of the kids he treats, that he must repeatedly convince the sick that they are, in fact, sick. I say I have too much awareness about myself. I say that in this moment, my disease is all I see, a shroud between me and everyone else, and it has been a lifetime since twenty-four hours ago, when I was down by the river watching those girls flick ashes into the current and feeling indignant at their lack of ecological awareness.

Sitting here in my dorm room, in a sunken pit of my madness, I long to get confused by the sight of our residential advisor standing with Greta in the trees. Or to become annoyed by my geometry teacher's lunch of coleslaw and only coleslaw.

But there is nothing I can do. I am where I am. At least I have a new plan, and any minute, Strots will come through that door.

Any minute—

When I hear her knock, I sit up straighter and consider hiding the bottle of Coke, but I don't think she'll mind. I hope she doesn't mind.

"Strots," I say. "I'm here."

The door opens and a dark head of luxurious hair leans in.

It's not Strots.

Hot RA's brilliant green eyes seek me out and his smile is tentative. "Hey. You got a minute to talk?"

I jump to my feet, even though he's not a sergeant, and I haven't been called to attention. "Strots isn't here."

"I'm not looking for her. I'm looking for you."

My heart speeds up, spurred on by the sugar and caffeine hitting my empty stomach. And maybe this older married man's presence.

In the back of my mind, I think, *You want to talk about good medicine?*

I am suddenly very plugged into the people around me. Person. Whatever.

"Is Strots okay?" I ask. "Has anything happened to her?"

Wouldn't it be a twist of fate if my roommate accomplished what I'd planned to do? And all because she's worried she hurt or offended me?

"This isn't about her. Come on, let's go down and talk in my apartment."

I look around my room suspiciously, as if someone might have planted contraband, like two kegs, four bottles of vodka, and some kind of illegal substance like cocaine or heroin, somewhere obvious that I missed in all my distraction.

"Am I in trouble?"

One advantage of having no friends is that I've told nobody about what anyone else is doing. Nor have I discussed the little mental joyrides I've been taking on my bipolar bicycle. But this is why I wonder what I have done wrong.

And then it clicks. "I only missed classes today because I was having stomach issues. I'm feeling better now. I should have gone to the nurse, though, shouldn't I. I'll be sure to go there now. I'll get my note or whatever I need—"

"You're not in trouble. I promise." His smile, that arrestingly beautiful smile, makes me feel like I'm sunbathing. "Come on, let's take a little walk down to my place."

Well. When he puts it like that, I feel like I've been asked on a date.

I nod and I follow him out of my door. As I close things, I glance across to Greta's room and wish she were seeing this. Although given the hot water I'm already in with her, like I need more crap for her to get pissy about?

"Great day, isn't it?" Hot RA says over his shoulder. "I like the contrast of the sun with the cool air. Do you?"

His door is open, and though he strides right in, I slow down, as if I am entering a chapel. And what do you know, all of my woes are totally sublimated as I look around his apartment. He has the same Nirvana poster I do, the one that hangs over my bed at home, the one that my mother refused to let me bring to Ambrose because it would "set the wrong tone." If only I'd known Hot RA would have it, too. There are also two of Guns N' Roses, and I think about the CDs Greta bought. In addition to his concert art, there's a slouchy sofa, a chair, a desk, and the same galley kitchen that Ms. Crenshaw has.

His windows look out over the river, just like mine do, just like Greta's do not.

All of it seems so much . . . younger . . . than his title of Married Man.

"Here, have a seat." He closes the door and points to the chair by the sofa.

Where's his wife now, I wonder. DC, I decide. Meeting with President Bush. Whose letter to me, extolling my virtues as a mental health advocate, I no longer think I will receive.

I do what Hot RA says and sit like the Queen of England, knees together, back straight, ankles crossed and tucked under me. He takes the couch and sits forward, his hands linking loosely, his elbows on his knees.

"I'm really sorry I called you Stephanie," he says. "Out at the field yesterday."

I'm so surprised by the apology, that he even remembers the exchange, that I don't know what to do with myself.

"And it's especially rude after you introduced yourself when we both couldn't sleep that night." He smiles some more. "I'm just terrible with names. I get it from my father."

Looking at his handsome face, with its tanned planes and angles, I decide that he got a lot more than just a totally forgivable slip of the memory from the man. Those green eyes . . . are like nothing I've ever seen, and they're even more attractive close-up. In fact, all of him is even more attractive close-up, something that's not always true about beautiful people. Some are like pointillism canvases, best viewed from a distance. Not him.

"It's okay, Mr. Hollis."

"Call me Nick." More with the smiling. "As I told you, that mister stuff feels weird."

"But you're married." Wait, that doesn't make any sense. "I mean—"

"I am." He lifts his hand and flashes his gold ring. "I don't think you've met Sandra yet, have you?"

I've barely met you, I want to say.

"No, I haven't." *Although I heard you arguing with her.*

And I'm on your side, I tack on to myself.

"She's an amazing woman. I love her very much."

"What does she do?" Check us out, having an adult conversation. And I ask this just to keep him talking, as I already know at least parts of her résumé. "I think she's gone a lot, isn't she?"

"She's one of the leading AIDS researchers at Yale. She does a lot of outreach with city governments, especially ones with bigger underserved populations. So it requires travel."

"Wow." Yup. Brilliant and a humanitarian. I start to surreptitiously glance around, looking for a photograph that confirms the Miss—no, Mrs.—America thing. "That's really impressive."

"She is."

When he smiles, I want to smile back, but I am afraid I have something in my teeth even though I haven't eaten today. I will also not smile because I have not brushed my teeth and I can't make an assessment of my breath after my lithium-with-Coca-Cola-chaser. Bad enough that I have roots in my hair, and desperate-girl noir clothes that are like Goth tarps on my shrinking body. Halitosis in his presence would sink me worse than my depressive episode.

Especially given the singularity of his wife.

Nick pauses. Like he's waiting for something from me. Meanwhile, I become frozen. I want to say the right thing, give him whatever he needs from me, sure as if this interaction is my one moment to be existentially judged, my single, solitary second of reckoning that will determine the course not just of the rest of this year at Ambrose, but of all the decades that follow.

If there are to be any.

"Sarah," he says, "I just want you to know that I'm here to help."

"Thank you?" I say, in the form of a question. Because I have no idea what he's getting at.

As he becomes quiet again, I decide I'm content to sit here for however long he wants. I'm in the *sanctum sanctorum* and also allowed to stare at him, and it's all so very deliciously distracting that I decide even Strots can wait.

Hell, even suicide can wait.

"So, the pharmacist down at the CVS called the school's health clinic," he says finally.

I stiffen and forget all about what he looks like and what he sounds like and what kind of posters are on his walls and what a hero he has for a wife. Now we're getting down to business, and as I curse Phil the Pharmacist for being so very much smarter than I gave him credit for, I know I am back in territory where I must consider my responses carefully.

From a clinical perspective, not an existential one.

Although with me, I suppose they are the same thing.

"I didn't steal anything." I lead with this even though I know it's a lark that will not fly. "I did not."

"That wasn't what he was worried about."

Nick is speaking softly, and I don't know whether it's because he doesn't want to spook me like I'm a wild animal or if he knows what came through the wall that night when he was fighting with his wife.

"Sarah, I know that you have some . . . special circumstances . . . in your background."

At this, I bolt up and start pacing around his apartment, my mind running at a thousand miles an hour. I picture myself paraded in front of the entire dorm in the common room, shown off as an example of how Ambrose takes care of the less fortunate, the less sane, my secret not just laid bare but promoted officially as a virtue of the institution.

"The administration wants to be sure you're okay." Nick gets to his feet, too, and casually goes over to the door. There's a long shelf directly to the left of it and he moves some books around on the levels, but I'm not fooled. He's going to stop me if I try to bolt. "We've called your mother and she's on her way."

"What?" I bark. "You can't do that."

Okay, that's a stupid thing to say. They can do anything they want.

"We need to make sure you're all right."

I put my hands to my head. No, no, no, this is wrong. Enough with the green eyes and the Guns N' Roses crap. "I have to go. I have to find my roommate."

"Sarah, what you were thinking about doing . . ." He clears his throat, and as he turns and looks at me, his eyes are a little scared. Like he's out of his professional depth, but really wants to help me. "That's not the answer. Trust me. It's not."

Doing the math in my head, I figure the earliest possible time the school could have called Tera Taylor, undiscovered movie star, is maybe forty-five minutes ago because that's when I left the CVS. It'll take her at least that long to get herself organized to leave the house. She'll have to change into one of her dresses and do her hair and makeup. She won't know where her keys are. She'll need to put gas in her Mercury Marquis because she drives around our little town on fumes. I have about three hours.

If they are shipping me out of here—which is likely not the wrong idea for my welfare—I need to get to Strots before she goes to the game, and I have about ten minutes, maybe fifteen.

"Can I go back to my room now?" I say.

"I just . . ." As Mr. Hollis—Nick—struggles for words, it's clear that whatever training he received prior to becoming a residential advisor is wholly insufficient to handle the problem I represent. "It was just a game. It doesn't matter who won or lost. No one blames you, okay? You did the best you could, and you almost caught the ball."

I blink, his words making no sense at all. And then the syllables process. He thinks it's about the loss yesterday? He and the administration think I'm killing myself over yesterday's touch football game?

I want to laugh, and I very nearly open my mouth to set the record straight, to tell him that I meant to drop that ball, and given Greta's expression as she lost, I'm quite satisfied with my choices. Hell, maybe the confession will get me off the hot seat. Except, no. I'm still stuck with the fact that Phil the Pharmacist was a rocket scientist who saw behind my okey-dokey façade and called the Ambrose equivalent of the cops on me. No matter what I say about that game, I was still caught trying to buy too many aspirin. I was still crying as I stood in front of the display. And I did present Phil with a valid prescription for a highly powerful mood stabilizer, one that they only put children on if they really, really have to, one that you have to take every day for it to work properly.

I am still insane.

Then it dawns on me. If I don't accept the football-game-loss-as-trigger conclusion the grown-ups have come up with, I'll have to explain the truth, and I will not betray Strots like that. Besides, none of this is about the fact that she kissed me. It's the bad way I handled the moment and the trickle-down implications of my utter failure as a human being.

There's a soft knock and my eyes shoot in its direction, focusing over Hot RA's—Nick's—shoulder. How did my mother get here so fast? Have I lost track of time again?

As Nick cracks the door, my eyes go to the analog clock on his stove, the one that is in the center of the dials that work the four coiled elements, like a pendant above the ornate collar of a blouse. No, I have not lost track of time. This cannot be my mother, so maybe it's something worse. Perhaps it's some white coats from a local psychiatric hospital about which I'm unaware, the orderlies coming to put me in a straitjacket and carry my trussed body out of Tellmer like a side of beef.

Except then I smell sweet perfume. Nick's beauty queen, brilliant wife arriving early for the weekend? No, she would just come in.

He talks quietly, and then closes the door. Turning back to me, he leans against what he shut. "Sorry about that."

There's great pity on his face as he stares at me, and it's sincere and unpatronizing. He does feel sorry for me, and not in the sense that I'm an irredeemable social misfit. He feels sorry for me because he's peeked under my outer layers to the stinking mess beneath, and he wouldn't wish what he's discovered on his worst enemy.

The idea that someone, anyone, knows my secret here at Ambrose, and has not shunned me, takes the air out of all my plans, both of the Strots variety and the boiler room kind. I cannot say I am relieved. But I'm grateful.

"You won't tell anyone, will you," I say in a wobbly voice.

Nick shakes his head. "No one."

As he makes this vow, I wonder if he knows that it's Greta specifically I'm worried about. But it doesn't matter. I believe him.

A wave of dizziness comes over me, and it's so pronounced that I must grab on to something, anything, or I'm going to do a pratfall on his coffee table.

Nick lunges forward with the grace of an athlete and captures my body in strong arms. As he pulls me against him, I feel his muscles. I smell his clean soap. His clothes brush against my bare midriff as my shirt is wrenched up.

"It's just the lithium," I mumble as he guides me over to the sofa. "I took my pill twenty minutes ago."

This is not magical thinking around the placebo effect. I'm very familiar with this specific kind of light-headedness, the vertigo coming on strong because I haven't eaten in a while, the lithium's been out of my system, and my emotions are playing with my blood pressure to begin with.

As he lays me out on his couch, I give myself up to the cushions and cannot look at him because this is too intimate for me to bear without blushing. Instead, I stare at his ceiling. There are beams that intersect the expanse, and they're painted white to blend in. Every once in a while, there's a hook screwed into them as if one of the RAs who lived here had a thing for hanging baskets of flowers or ivy. Except that can't be right. The meat-locker-worthy seimicircles seem too hearty for that kind of job, and my mind toys with hypotheticals, a lackadaisical cat with a largely uninteresting toy.

Meanwhile, Nick is leaning over me like he wishes he had a medical background, like he isn't sure what to do at all, and I'm surprised by the show of incompetence. He's so attractive that I have ascribed to him broadly applicable superhero powers that he evidently doesn't have. Then again, he's just an English teacher at a prep school. Maybe if he already had his PhD, things would be easier for him in this situation.

Or perhaps he would handle this better if I were Virginia Woolf.

I grab his arm. "Promise me, before my mother or a hospital takes me away, promise me I will get to talk to Strots alone. Promise me."

There's a pause. Then Nick nods once. "You have my word. But you need to stay with me right now."

Like I have a choice, I want to say as I close my eyes.

It seems odd to be in the position so many girls would envy, all Victorian-vapor'd on Hot RA's couch, him crouched beside me on tenterhooks.

In a cruel twist of irony, my illness's severity and implications deprive me of enjoying this fantasy made manifest. Then again, if I were fully present, I would likely implode.

Boiler room, indeed.

chapter FIFTEEN

Tera Taylor, undiscovered movie star, arrives just as everyone my age is leaving to go next door to have dinner at Wycliffe. She's shown into Nick's residential advisor apartment by an administrator I do not recognize, and I'm surprised by her lack of flourish and dramatic fanfare. The role of Fantastically Worried Mother has apparently been turned down even though it would arguably have played to her femme fatale strengths and also provided her with a conquest platform, given that both Nick and the administrator are men well over the age of consent in the Commonwealth of Massachusetts.

Except then I remember her coming to the hospital after my second suicide attempt. She was curiously calm then, too.

She hasn't dressed for attention, either. She is not in some figure-hugging wraparound, her cleavage not on display, her still shapely legs not set off by a flouncing hem, but rather one that is straight as a ruler and well below her knees. She hasn't dressed at all, actually. She's in her lunch lady school uniform, with its bright blue-and-white-checked gingham underlay and its white, Mother Goose apron. She hasn't even removed her little plastic name tag that is pinned to her modest lapel, the one that reads *Ms. Taylor*. Her hairnet is off, however.

And that's when I realize she was not home when she got the call. She was at work. How could I have forgotten? She didn't lose her keys in the midst of her magazine collection or stop to do her hair or change into a dress. She came directly to me, her daughter, who's in trouble once again—and not the kind of trouble that's easily dealt with, like skipping class or refusing to turn in assignments or smoking in her dorm room. I bring the kind of trouble that halts the workday and makes you drive over the speed limit to your kid, heart in your throat.

I feel awful about everything.

"Hi, Mom," I say as I sit forward on Nick's couch.

"Hi," she says without moving from the doorway. She's too busy looking me over, no doubt searching for outward signs of catastrophe like bandaged wrists. Ligature marks. IV bags.

In the tense silence that follows—which I feel like lasts for days—I think of the importance I put upon relieving Strots of any misplaced sense of responsibility for my death. I think of the focus the goal gave me, the purpose that was strong enough to pave over the best-laid plans of a bipolar patient out alone in a big, bad world full of aspirin. Unfortunately, the Strots sidetrack, as dispositive as it was, is only short-term, and in the same vein, my mother's normal way of operating—the dress, the cigarettes, the flirtation—has merely been temporarily wiped clean by yet another crisis of mine. As long as the outcome is good, she'll return to her usual ways.

And as long as I'm not put on a psychiatric hold, so will I—and there are an infinite number of bottles of Bayer available for purchase and a boiler room in the basement of this dorm that's going nowhere fast.

Assuming she doesn't take me home right now.

I remember what Phil the Pharmacist said to me about how I must think about those I leave behind, and I am suddenly protective of all my mother's affects and affectations that annoy me so much. I have a sense, with a sudden, shocking clarity, that if I take my own life, I will rob her of them. She will not recover to the odd place of functioning she has now. She'll be ruined.

I know this to be true as I look into her eyes. She is terrified. And she, like Strots, will blame herself if I do anything rash and irreversible. It was her choice to send me here, her engineered result, and the fact that she has had to race out of the Lincoln Elementary School's cafeteria, risking her job and no doubt her life, as she drove to get here, makes me feel ashamed. As Greta torments me, I torment my mother, although clearly there are limits to that comparison. Greta enjoys her outcomes. I am submerged and drowning in mine, all of which are involuntary.

My eyes tear up as Nick turns off the television that he and I have been watching to pass the time, and he and the administrator duck out of the apartment.

"Sarah," my mother says, like she was waiting for them to go.

She never calls me Sarah.

She rushes over, dropping her handbag on the floor like she doesn't care what's in it or where it lands. At the couch, she drops her body beside mine in the same dismissive manner. She takes my hand and pulls it to her chest. As my sleeve rises up toward my elbow, I tug it back into place so that my scars at my wrist do not show. She doesn't need a reminder of the times we have been here before. Neither do I.

"Are you okay?" she says with urgency.

Three words. Like *I love you*.

I want to tell her the truth. I want to tell her that I don't think I'm handling this Ambrose thing too well. I want to tell her about Greta and the Brunettes, and Strots, who I'm now worried about as my mother worries about me. The problem with honesty that goes that deep, however, is that just as Phil the Pharmacist can call in reinforcements—and did—I cannot control the fallout of any such core-level revelations. I cannot trust my mother to stay in this connected, concerned space. I cannot make her see these events as I do, as things that are passing through my life, and my life alone. As much as my choices affect her, they aren't emergencies to be solved by her and her army of adults. They aren't blizzards that bring snow requiring her removal. They aren't windstorms that knock down trees that she must chainsaw through to clear roads. They aren't floods she must remediate from basements and low-lying areas.

They are my weather-related disasters, not hers, and I want to control how they are dealt with. Even though I am not handling any of this well. Even though I tried to buy the aspirin and the Orange Crush. Even though I am only a child still.

I close my eyes. Put like that, I should tell her everything. As unpleasant, invasive, and commandeering as adult solutions have proven to be, at least none of what the older generation has done to me involved my dying on the floor of the boiler room down in the Tellmer dorm's basement.

"Do you want to come home?"

I'm so surprised she asks this that I turn my face to her. "What?"

"Do you want to just pack up your things and come home?"

I think of our house full of magazines. And of her exciting new boyfriend she told me about when we spoke on our regularly scheduled call this past Sunday. I imagine her smoking inside with the windows all closed up because the weather is turning cold and we have to save money by conserving heat. I hear her voice, calling out to me through the little rooms, pushing words about some article covering the love life of Kevin Costner. I picture whatever middle-aged man with an alcoholic's florid complexion and blooming nose tissue that she's pulled out of the plenty-of-fish sea sitting on the sofa, smoking with her in his undershirt.

I would rather roll my dice with Greta.

As I tell her no, I do not want to leave, a prevailing sense of helplessness comes over me. I do not want to be here, no. But there's no home I want to be at, either. And no matter the school I attend or the bully in my class, I will still have my head attached at the top of my spine. I will still take my illness with me wherever I go. There's no relocation that can solve what is wrong with me.

Other than that of the grave variety.

"Do you want to talk to Dr. Warten?"

"No," I tell her. "And you really didn't have to come."

She drops my hand and sits back a little. I can't tell what she is thinking, but I'm not surprised by what she does. She reaches for her purse, catching one of its straps and dragging it across the floor not because it weighs much, but because I suspect she feels the same kind of helplessness I do and impotence does tire a person right out. That she lights a cigarette in this apartment that isn't her own will likely be forgiven considering the circumstances of her daughter, but I wonder if it would have occurred to her for even a second to ask permission. I wonder if Nick will resent the smoke. I wonder all kinds of things that are hardly relevant to my situation because I am overwhelmed by the issues at hand.

Still, no is the only answer I will give her right now. No, I don't want to go home. No, I don't want to go to a hospital. No, I don't want to leave this dorm.

"I don't know what to do with you," she says on an exhale of smoke.

The secondhand intrusion of what she expels from her lungs makes my eyes water and my nose itch. I sneeze and sit up higher, no longer slouching.

"You don't have to do anything with me." I shake my head, as if that will dismiss everything: Phil the Pharmacist's phone call to the school clinic, the nurse's call here to the dorm and elsewhere on campus, the administrator's call to my mother at work. "This is all a lot of nonsense."

I try to sound adult. I try to sound secure. I create a repeating ticker tape of thoughts in my head that I am adult, I am secure, I know me better than everyone else. I tell myself to fucking concentrate on these statements and make them real, goddamn it. Otherwise, I'm going to lose my shot at talking with Strots as well as my exit stage left in the basement, which remains my ultimate goal.

"I'm taking my medicine." I shrug. "I'm going to class. I'm happy here."

I have not been taking my medicine, I missed class this morning because I fell into the Big Bang while sitting on my bed, I am unhappy here.

"You are?" she asks, covering all three lies at once.

"I am."

She lets herself fall back so she is nearly lying down on Nick's sofa. As she smokes and stares at me, I know she is reviewing old tapes in her head, the home movies not pleasant in the slightest. I regret this. I wish she had more of what she had no doubt hoped and dreamed for out of a daughter. Instead, she got me.

"Sarah," she says softly, "you're so much more than that shitty little town we live in."

My mother does not swear. Ever. It's the cheapest and easiest way for her to deny how cheap and easy she can sometimes be. And just as shocking, she's used my given name twice now.

She exhales smoke from her un-lipsticked lips. "I know you got angry at me for sending that essay I found in your room to the admissions committee here. I get it. And I'll tell you I'm honestly sorry for the invasion into your privacy. But I won't apologize for the opportunity it got you. This place. These people . . ." She looks around and then sits forward again so she can pick up a book that's lying on Nick's coffee table. Turning the spine toward herself, she frowns. "*An Artist of the Floating World*. Ka-kazuo Ishi . . . who is this author? What's it about?"

"Ishiguro," I say. "And it's an examination of postwar Japan and intergenerational conflict."

"And how do you know all this?"

"I read it."

"See?" she says as she tosses the book back on the table, the bang it lands with like the period at the end of her statement of proof. "You belong around people like this. You belong around books like that. Your mind is something else, Sarah."

This is a conclusion I have heard before, usually from teachers, and always spoken in the same awe-tinged tone, as if I've done something remarkable to earn the IQ I happen to have been born with. As if that IQ in some way makes up for all problems that come along with the intelligence. Not for the first time, I want to tell someone who's passing that pablum off on me that I would trade those high numbers for normal functioning ones in a heartbeat if I had the choice.

"And you even know what the book is about." She exhales up to the ceiling this time. "Not just the plot, but what it *means*."

I have to give her credit. There's no undercurrent of envy or jealousy. I suspect this is because, given that she birthed me, she has a claim to fame on my brain: Even though I didn't get this intelligence from her, I wouldn't be here without her.

Or maybe that's an unkind conclusion. She doesn't look grasping in any way right now. She just looks exhausted. Confused, exhausted . . . and scared.

"It's about an unreliable narrator," I say as a way to apologize for thoughts she's unaware I'm having. "And how an artist translates his life and actions into a present where he has culpability, but no accountability."

"Huh?"

I nod to the coffee table. "The book."

"Is it any good?"

"Some people consider it one of the great novels, so yes, it is."

"See. I told you."

My mother is seemingly unaware of possible parallels, and I'm not surprised when she doesn't ask anything further about the novel. Though she will explore all manner of details concerning Hollywood's elite and their revolving bedroom doors, she is uninterested in any literature whatsoever. This pick-and-choose is a little incongruous, given her upwardly mobile aspirations. You'd figure she'd prefer the binding of a hardcover over the flimsy staples down the center crease of an *Us Weekly* magazine, but this is a reminder to me that people are incongruous. None of us are all one thing or another, and sometimes our incompatibilities are at fundamental levels.

Except for Greta, of course. She seems very solid on what she is.

My mother looks around for an ashtray, as if everyone smokes so there must be one here. When she doesn't find what she seeks, at least she doesn't ash on Ishiguro's masterpiece. She gets up and goes over to the sink in the galley kitchen, leaning her hip on the counter and tapping her cigarette into the drain.

"You're better than I am," she says in a small voice. "I wish I were like you, but I'm not and I never will be. What I can do, however, is get you where you need to be, where the education is, where the opportunities are. And that is here."

I blink. There has never been any hint of her thinking like this, and I am not referencing the education part.

"I'm not better than you," I tell her. Because I know what she just said is true, and she has suddenly become incredibly vulnerable to me. I will never abuse an underbelly. Not when it comes to my mother, not when it comes to anybody. I'm vulnerable all the time, everywhere, because of the way my brain malfunctions. I'm too familiar with how an exposed weakness gets kicked.

"We both know that's a lie," she says.

She takes another drag and taps her long forefinger on the dwindling length of the cigarette. As she stares into the drain, I wonder if she is looking down it and seeing her youth and ambitions, her fantasies about who and what my father was, her excitement and her optimism, all of it long since masticated by time. She looks old, standing beneath the harsh lighting of a ceiling fixture that has no shade. She looks like a failure.

"I'm going to be okay," I say forcefully. "I really am."

As I stare across Nick and Sandra's apartment at her, I become very certain that if anything happens to me, Tera Taylor's brilliant, broken daughter, there will be no more annual subscriptions to any number of magazines that will distract her, and her never-ending supply of below-average boyfriends will do no better a job than they do now of giving her steady purpose.

If I commit suicide, I'll also be committing murder.

Tera Taylor will be dead, too.

My mother shakes her head. "You have to understand . . . that I believed it happened because of the town we're in."

"I'm sorry, what?" I say.

She shrugs and continues to focus into the sink, into the drain. When she runs some water, I imagine her salt-and-pepper gray ashes melting down and disappearing.

She clears her throat. "I thought that you were driven . . . you know . . ."

"Crazy," I provide. "You can say the word."

"I don't like to. It gives everything too much power. You're not crazy, you're just different."

Okay, now I know where I get some of my magical thinking from.

"When you had to go away . . ."

"To the mental institution," I supply.

"It was a clinic."

"For people who are crazy."

"Stop it," she snaps as she looks over at me. "You don't have to be so damned blunt."

A broken bone is a broken bone, I want to say. Calling it an "ouchie" doesn't change the necessity of a cast—or what happens if you can't put one on the injury.

"When you went away," she repeats firmly, "I thought there was a chance that you needed so much more than you were getting and that that was what drove you to . . ." She puts her lit stub under the faucet's water, dousing the glow. "I thought you did what you did because you couldn't stand the monotony. The lack of opportunity. The lack of challenge and engagement."

No, I think to myself with a chilling realization. *That is everything* you *feel about where we live.*

That is everything that has ever made you consider the idea of killing yourself.

And you have, Mom, haven't you.

I don't say any of this out loud. I am rattled to my core that my mother might have visited the same desperate, desolate places I have, where pain is the only thing you know and you can see no way of getting free from it. My mother is supposed to be superficial. She's supposed to float above the depths of life, riding on a raft made out of issues of the *National Enquirer*. She's supposed to make snap, two-dimensional judgments about people and places and things, and smoke too much, and flirt too much, and walk a path that has absolutely nothing to do with my trail of spectacular suffering.

"A town like ours can kill someone's whole life." She crosses her arms and turns to me, a forty-year-old woman in a lunch lady outfit with two hundred dollars in the bank, a ten-year-old car, and a new boyfriend she'll probably be supporting in another week and a half when he moves into our little house. "It can just eat you alive, and I can't let that happen to you. You've got so many things going for you, and my job is to get you a toehold to something better. You're nationwide smart, Sarah, not small-town bright. There are so many places you can go, so many things you can learn, because you're *that* special."

All I can do is stare up at her. I can't remember her ever saying anything close to this.

And I'm so struck by her sincerity that I'm compelled to leave the couch and go to her, my body moving on its own with no explicit commands.

As I put my arms around her, she's shocked, and I realize that I never hug her, at least not voluntarily. Any physical contact between us is her touching me and my bearing it because I must.

"It's going to be okay," I say as I hold on tight. "I promise."

I speak the words strongly because I suddenly need them to be true. Both for her sake, and for mine. The pendulum has swung back to my wanting to still be on the planet, the to'ing and fro'ing part and parcel of my disease.

"Please," my mother says in a voice that wavers, "don't make me regret this Ambrose thing, I will never forgive myself." She pulls away and grips my upper arms. "And you have to know, if you want to come home, you can. As much as I want you to have all of this, I'd rather you be alive. Anything else is so terrifying to me, I can't think about it. If things are getting . . . out of control . . . you have to let me know. This is a lot to handle, for anyone, but especially someone like you. Being away from home, being in a different environment, you have to remember what Dr. Warten said. If you have any hallucinations, if you struggle to stay connected to the people and things around you, if you're having suicidal thoughts or ones that spin out of control, we need to bring you back home. That was our agreement, remember?"

As her eyes implore me, she reveals, yet again, her powerlessness. As she lists all of the symptoms I've been having, I have my own powerlessness revealed to me.

I feel as fragile and ancient and worn out as she appears, and with this communion, a ghostly umbilical cord links us together, replacing in a metaphysical way the one that is long gone in fact.

I've been so busy judging her that I've missed the opportunity to know my mother. I've been so busy being crazy and getting taken care of by her that I've failed to recognize she requires tending to as well. I've been so focused on our differences that I've been blind to the fact that we are both broken in our own ways and that we need each other.

As these things are revealed to me, I recognize that of the many cogent and piercing insights I've had with regard to all manner of people up until this moment, these are the first truly adult thoughts I've ever had.

"Okay, Mom," I say. "I promise to let you know if I need to come home."

As I make the vow, I mean it, and not because I'm trying to snow her like I did Phil the Pharmacist. I feel like I owe her the integrity because she's just shown me some of her own—and she must sense my resolve, as her relief is so great it changes the air temperature around us, taking the bonfire of emotion that roared and reducing its heat to a simmer of ennui.

Or so I guess. I don't really know. Even though I'm on the front lines of this invisible, potentially catastrophic battle, I'm not the best person to judge the situation.

But I have reset things. And life will go on for a little longer. At least . . . I hope it does, I think to myself, when my mother and I step out of Nick's apartment shortly thereafter. As the administrator takes her aside, I am left standing next to my RA.

He's smiling at me, as if he believes that he might, possibly, in some small way, have improved my situation. The fact that this matters to him at all makes me smile shyly back to him.

Except then I remember.

"Oh, God, she smoked," I say softly. "I'm so sorry, my mom smoked in your apartment. She does that when she's nervous or upset."

And when she's happy. Sad. Bored. Tired. Anxious. But I suggest to him a specific linkage with this difficulty I'm in, in the hopes that it will predispose him to forgiveness.

"It doesn't bother me in the slightest. Sandra smokes sometimes."

How does that work, with her being into public health, I wonder. But I don't bring that up.

"I wish I had you as my English teacher," I blurt out.

I'm horrified that I've spoken the admission aloud because I'm worried that my mouth won't stop there and the next thing I know I'll be talking about his Ray-Bans and the size of his shoulders and how much I like his hair.

"Me, too," he says. "But we can talk books on our own."

"We can?"

"Sure. I'd love to. We'll start our own private book club."

As I begin to glow like a night-light, I wonder how I could ever have thought of killing myself. If I had bought those aspirin and that Orange Crush, and taken them down to the boiler room? I would have missed this chance to talk books with my new friend Nick.

All things considered, Phil the Pharmacist should have played this card above all others, and as I consider the pure radiance running through my veins, I take note, in the back of my mind, that this wild elation spinning through my chest, just after I was prepared to kill myself, is as close to a diagnostic criterion as having the word "bipolar" stamped over my eyebrows when I came out of the birth canal.

To distract myself, both from this confirmation of my condition that I didn't need, and from an asinine urge to giggle, I take note of the girls coming up the stairs. Going down the stairs.

Their curious stares are a grim re-grounding, and I can't decide whether there's been an uptick in traffic or not, whether my dorm mates are making excuses to go check their mailboxes so they can spy on me and my mother and Hot RA and the administrator or if they are, in fact, simply going about their business.

My mother and the administrator come back over. Both are looking calm in the manner of adults when a crisis involving a child under their care has been resolved. A plan of action, which I am required to agree to, is spelled out—I will take a call from Dr. Warten tomorrow morning in Nick's apartment for privacy, I will check in at the clinic tomorrow afternoon for blood tests to monitor my sodium levels, I will talk to Nick if I have any problems with anything.

After all that, my mother suggests the two of us go into town and have dinner, and I readily agree, not because I am hungry, but because I find myself wanting to spend some time with her. I'm interested in exploring this new, unanticipated territory that has opened up between us. I also don't trust my mood in the slightest.

At the restaurant she chooses and parks behind, we sit in a booth and eat Italian food that has been prepared with such haste and lack of skill that it has almost no flavor. My mother promptly falls back into her normal ways, updating me about people neither of us know, people who lead glamorous lives, people who are in those magazines. The difference now is that I forgive her for the banal conversation. I listen and I nod, and I'm content to let her go on without any judgment whatsoever.

You're more likely to forgive people if you respect them, and you tend to respect people because you've seen their strength revealed in a moment of struggle. After the self-sacrifice I have witnessed from her, there's a new, more solid platform for our relationship on my side.

Whether I make it through the rest of my sophomore year here or not, this will be one good thing that comes out of Ambrose.

When she takes me back to the dorm, pulling around to where Nick's blue Porsche is parked on its lonesome, my mother turns to me and brushes my hair back.

"I wish you would just let that black color grow out," she says.

"Maybe I will."

"Listen, I'm not sure I can come up for Parents' Weekend. I don't think I can get the time off from my cleaning job."

"It's okay."

"Are you still going to stay here over Columbus Day weekend?"

"I could use the money."

"So I guess I won't see you until Thanksgiving."

Unspoken in this pronouncement is her hope that she won't have cause to see me. That I won't crack and call her and ask to come home. Also unspoken is the fact that she will come and pick me and my stuff up anytime, without questions or censure, no matter what her job says or what she's told people in our small town about where her talented daughter is going to school.

"I love you," I say.

Her eyes flare, like they did when I hugged her. And then they get teary. As she pulls me across the seat against her, I find that I like the smell of her Primo. What I didn't like was that I assumed she was wearing it to show off and pretend like she was someone else. Now I recognize that it's all she can afford, the closest she can ever get to Beverly Hills, and that she has no choice but to accept this vast distance between where she is and where she wishes she were. I find grace in her resignation. I trust it, too, far more than superficial posturing.

I get out of the car and shut my door. She backs in and out a couple of times to turn around in the tight space. As she takes one more lingering look at me from her window, I am reminded of the way she stared up at me as she departed the day she dropped me off.

Even if I have a breakdown and have to pull out of Ambrose, I'm left with the very clear impression this school has been good for us.

And I know, without a doubt, that I will never, ever refer to her in my mind or anywhere else as Tera Taylor, undiscovered movie star.

"Bye, Mom," I say.

"Bye, Sarah."

And just like that, she is gone.

chapter
SIXTEEN

For all my time at Ambrose, I've never been up to the third floor of Tellmer. I hear the girls moving around above my room occasionally, but it's rare, so either they are very quiet, which is unlikely, or the dorm was built very well seventy-five years ago, something that's quite likely given the standards here. As I mount the apex series of landings, I feel like a trespasser, especially as I emerge in front of the residential advisors' door. Fortunately, they don't have a check-in roster or something you've got to put ID into to walk down the hall. On the contrary, the RAs up here have accessorized the entryway to their suite with a welcome mat and a seasonal wreath in autumnal golds and red. This strikes me as something married people do. They tend to have the stability and dual incomes to support things like mats and wreaths, plus they live in homes no matter if they are in an apartment or a house because they're a family.

Nick and Sandra are too cool for that, though. They're intellectuals busy analyzing great literature and saving the world. I want to be like them.

Which is probably my mom's point.

I glance left and right. I have no idea what room I'm looking for so I'm forced to wait for someone to stroll by—which turns out to be a girl on her way to take a shower, given the towel on her shoulder and her flip-flops. I know I've seen her on campus and in dorm meetings, but I don't know her name. I'm certain she feels the same about me.

"Do you know where Keisha's room is?" I ask as she gives me the once-over.

"Down there. Three seventeen."

"Thank you."

I proceed in the direction she came from, and I can feel her staring at my back. I want to tell her if she thinks only my clothes are out of whack, she's got no clue about the real weirdness, given the way I have spent my morning and afternoon.

As I go along, I am nervous, my palms sweaty. I'm heading for a bad number, according to my OCD, and I have no idea whether Strots is in there. It's just before seven p.m., so she's usually back in the dorm after dinner, having a cigarette before she starts her homework. In the beginning of the semester, she performed this ritual in our room. Lately, she's transitioned up here. Now, because of what happened last night, I gather she will move heaven and earth to avoid our room for any reason whatsoever.

317.

I stand in front of Strots's best friend's door. As I rap with my knuckles, my suicidal depression knocks on my consciousness, a squatter who's been evicted but believes it can wheedle its way back in with protestations of homelessness and perhaps the promise to do light housework.

Keisha opens the door. Her face is set and her eyes angry, and she blocks the entry with her strong, athletic body.

Before I can ask about Strots, and before Keisha can tell me to get the hell off the third floor, my roommate says from inside, "It's all right, let her in."

Strots's voice is tired, and as her teammate steps aside, I'm unsure exactly how much has been shared between the two. Did Strots tell her what happened by the river? Or is Keisha just guessing something bad went down by the contours under the blanket of Strots's change of affect, change of location, change of pattern?

Strots is sitting on a bed, underneath a black-and-white poster of Muhammad Ali in the ring, the great boxer standing over his opponent, the other man sprawled at his feet, knocked out cold. My roommate's—former roommate's?—hair is wet, and she's wearing an Ambrose field hockey sweatshirt and sweat pants. She will not meet my eyes. She's flicking the strike wheel on her red Bic lighter, and my instinct is to tell her not to waste the flint. Except Strots doesn't have to worry about money like I do, and besides, it's her lighter. She can do what she wants with it.

Keisha shuts the door and leans back against it, crossing her arms. But I can't do this in front of her. I just can't. The girl's well known to Strots, but she's a stranger to me—and besides, I feel like she wants to throw me out the window for doing something to her best friend.

Even though it was the other way around. Or started that way.

"Can we go talk downstairs?" I ask.

Keisha shakes her head, but Strots puts her hand up. "No, it's okay. Yeah. Let's get this over with—"

"You went to Mr. Hollis," Keisha says. "You went to the fucking RA—"

"It's fine, K," Strots cuts in. "Let me deal with this."

I start shaking my head. "No, I didn't go to Mr. Hollis—"

"Shut the fuck up—"

"Okay, okay." Strots talks over Keisha. "I'll handle this."

Strots shifts off the bed, and even though this is dire stuff, she takes the time to smooth the blanket and arrange the pillow properly.

I look at Keisha and figure the gossip tree has reported all that was witnessed by the stairwell on the floor below. "I didn't talk to Mr. Hollis or the administration about Strots. That wasn't what was happening."

"Really." Keisha stares me down. "What were you doing in that apartment all afternoon, watching TV?"

I debate telling her the truth. The weight of everything I'm keeping to myself is enormous and it would be a relief to get it off my chest. But I can't go that far, not when I don't know how much Keisha's been told about the kiss. Besides, if all I say is that I was on the path to the boiler room with enough aspirin to overdose ten of me, Strots won't have any context for such a revelation and will figure it was her down by the river that did it. Unlike the administrators, she knows I meant to drop that football.

"I had to wait for my mother to come," I say.

"Is she taking you home?" Keisha demands. Like unless that's the outcome, she isn't interested in any reports from me.

Strots puts her hand on the other girl's shoulder, and Keisha curses before falling silent. "I'll be back, K."

"Lemme know if you need me."

"Yeah. I will."

Strots leads the way back to the second floor. I am behind her and I have flashbacks of kids going to detention, not that that was something I ever did. I was always too busy trying to keep my head in line to have the time or inclination to break school rules. But I've seen plenty of others take this walk of shame.

As Strots and I enter our room, I note that Greta's door is open and I'm betting she's watching. I don't look, however. I don't need the image of her face as I go into this.

I close our door. Strots goes over to her bed, sits down, and takes her cigarettes out of the center pocket of her sweatshirt. She cracks the window and lights up.

When she doesn't say anything, my mouth goes utterly dry. But I know she's not manipulating me or playing a game. Strots isn't like that. She's a decent person. Moreover, she has no time for that kind of bullshit.

"I . . ." *If I kill myself, it's not because you kissed me*, I want to say. "I mean, I just . . ."

I wish she would take control of this conversation. Provide me with a framework to speak what I need to. Lead the way as she usually does not only with me, but everyone she comes into contact with.

Instead, she takes a deep breath, her lungs deflating on a long sigh, and I have a thought that I'm well familiar with what she's feeling.

She's here, once again. Wherever "here" is for her. I recognize the status, although not her particular location.

As I try out and discard strings of words, I think about the composers on the dorm's frieze. I feel for their struggles to set music to the page as none of my chords fit, but my roommate and I can't sit here forever, silent on a precipice neither of us wants to jump off of.

Before I know what I'm doing, I go over to my desk. I open the drawer on the bottom left. Then I walk across to Strots.

I hold out my prescription bottle of pills. As I realize what I'm doing, my overriding instinct is to yank back and slap my own hand for its independent thinking.

She looks up. "What's this?"

When I shake the pills, because I don't trust my voice and I need them to speak for me, she takes the orange bottle and reads the label.

"Lithium?" she says. "I don't get it."

"Do you know what it's used for?" I hear myself say. Which is stupid. "Do you know what it treats?"

As she shakes her head, I pull up both of my long sleeves and present my wrists with their lines of scars. Her eyes widen and then she looks up at my face, her stare moving around my features as if we're being introduced for the first time.

When I go to take the pills back, her hand releases them freely. My heart is pounding as I return them to their hidey-hole in my desk, and after they're safe, I sit down in my chair. I'm horrified about doing this, but I'm compelled to speak for reasons I cannot fathom.

Or maybe the reasons are so simple, I miss them in my quest for complication.

Strots may not like me after this. She may want to switch roommates. She may never speak to me again. But she will not betray me. She will not use this against me. And she will never tell anyone.

And those convictions as to her character are the only reason I can go on.

"I need you to know," I say clearly and calmly, "that it's not about you. No matter what happens, none of it's your fault and you bear no responsibility. And it's got nothing to do with what happened down by the river last night."

Strots takes a draw on her cigarette, and as she exhales, the guarded look on her face dissipates along with the smoke. "What exactly are you talking about?"

I can't bring myself to say all of it. But I try to say enough.

"It doesn't matter that you kissed me." I shrug. "I know it wasn't me you were kissing. I was just surprised and I didn't know what to do. But I'm not upset, I'm not freaked out, and I didn't say anything about it to Mr. Hollis."

I keep the call-me-Nick part to myself, protecting the space he and I shared this afternoon.

"The last thing I ever want to do," I say, "is have anyone know the truth about me. I want to keep it quiet. I have to keep it quiet. People already think I'm a freak. If they find out I'm crazy? It's all over for me."

I have to shift my eyes to the floor as I consider the ramifications of Greta finding this out.

"I don't know if I can make it at this school." I shake my head. "It's hard for me. But I want to try."

I realize this is the first time I have an opinion about my time at Ambrose, and I surprise myself. I do want to stay, although not because I have friends. Not because I enjoy myself. Certainly not because I think I can win against the self-destructive side of me. I want to stay because my mother may be right. The part of my brain that functions well may need this, and I will do anything to encourage the non-insane pathways under my skull. Provided I can keep things level.

"Wait, so you're . . ."

"Bipolar. The lithium keeps me . . . normal. Well, normal-ish."

At least in theory. At least if I take it.

"I'm not dangerous to anyone," I rush to add. "Definitely not to you."

Although this is another stupid thing to say. Strong as she is, Strots can snap me like a twig if she wants to.

"So why did your mother come today?" Strots asks.

"She was worried about me."

"I saw you sitting on the bed. Earlier." She bends down and takes her soda bottle ashtray out from under the mattress. "I thought you didn't want to talk to me. I thought you didn't want to see me."

The pain in Strots's face is something she hides by making a production out of uncapping the Coke, ashing into it, and taking another drag.

I am shocked that she cares one way or the other.

"It wasn't that at all." I shake my head even though she's looking at what her hands are doing. "I'm sometimes not here. I sometimes go away."

She looks up. "And that's part of the . . ."

As she motions in the air next to her head, I nod. "Yeah. It is. It's what the lithium helps with."

"You tried to kill yourself?" she says as she nods at my wrists.

I resist the urge to pull my sleeves back down. But why bother? The cat is out of the bag. Or its scratches, at any rate. "Yes. Twice."

Her eyes flare. "Twice?"

"I've been institutionalized a couple of times."

"Jesus Christ." She taps her ash into the narrow mouth of the bottle. "That's fucking awful."

As she stares across the divide between our two sides of the room, she's calm and interested, but not rattled. She is also sorry. She is very, very sorry.

I feel the tension leave my body. I have done the right thing.

"I don't want to freak you out by all this." I shake my head again. "It's just I don't know how things will go for me, and that's true wherever I am. It's important to me that you know it's not about you. It's not about anybody. It's not even about me. I'm sick where it doesn't show on the outside, and the illness I have isn't curable, only treatable. And sometimes treatment doesn't work. And sometimes things happen."

She frowns at the end of her cigarette. "I'm sorry I did that. Down at the river."

"It's okay. I was just surprised, honest."

"I thought that maybe you'd told them." There is no reason for her to define "them." "And you know, if it gets out, I'm out. No matter who my family is. People don't want gays here. Hell, it's even in the bylaws or whatever the fuck they're called. Christian values, you know."

"But they'll keep the Gretas around. That's stupid."

She laughs without smiling. "That's the world. And goddamn, my father would be *pissed*."

"So you told Keisha what happened?"

"Not about the, you know, by the river. I just said you'd found out what I am. That I'm gay."

"You can tell her about me. If you want." I pull my sleeves down over my scars. "I really don't want her to beat me up."

"She won't." Strots looks over at me. "And I trust her with everything."

"If my illness gets out?" I shake my head once again. "I won't survive."

The two of us stare at each other. And then she nods.

"Don't worry. You're safe."

The words are spoken directly and she's looking me right in the eye. In response, I rub my face to cover my emotions. She's going to protect me, and not just by staying silent.

She is truly my friend.

Strots refocuses on the bottle in my hand. Funny, I wasn't aware of taking it back out. When did that happen? I return it to where it belongs a second time, and as I close the drawer, I am wondering how to wrap this up—

"Greta was my roommate last year," Strots says softly.

My head whips up to level. "Really?"

Strots nods. "We lived together on the first floor."

"I didn't know that."

It's always interesting for me to watch someone else recede into their own mind, a view from the outside of myself when I disappear. And as I witness her go deep into her own memories, I'm glad that Strots does not travel to the places I go, the fantasies, the distortions, the worlds away. She's merely in her own past, remembering events from the previous year.

I think back to her staring through the V in that tree last night, her eyes on Greta, the yearning on my roommate's face not subtle in the slightest.

"You fell in love with her, didn't you."

Strots shrugs and looks down at her cigarette. "It is what it is."

"Did she know?"

"Yeah." The laugh is bitter. "She knew."

"Did anything happen between you guys?" We're getting way personal now, but I jumped into that pool first, and though Strots is not required to join me, I feel comfortable enough in calling out to her from my submersion. "I won't tell anybody."

She swishes her Coke ashtray around, the butts that float on the flat dark soda like dead bodies in a pond.

"Yeah," she says in a small voice. "Things . . . did happen between us."

A broken heart changes the appearance of a person's face, altering their features: Strots's chin disappears and her eyes get sucked back into her skull and that healthy athletic complexion is replaced by skin the color of stationery.

"Here's the thing," she says as she drops what's left of her cigarette into the soda bottle's graveyard. "Like I told you, Greta uses people for a power trip. She gets off on the games. I thought I was the exception, but it turned out I was just the rule."

"You thought she was in love with you?"

"Yup. 'Cuz that's how she acted when we were alone." Strots shakes her head. "The things she said . . . the things she did to me when we—"

When Strots stops short, it's like she's pulling the curtains closed on a window, no more landscape for me to see—or for her to, either. Abruptly, her eyes lose the faraway cast, returning to their laser-sharp normal.

"We kept it wicked quiet, of course," she says. "And besides, who'd have believed it? She's like the poster child for a quarterback's girlfriend."

I think of our school handbook. Strots is right about the Christian thing. It's in the part that covers student conduct and core values. I remember reading the relevant passage and not thinking it applied to me one way or another. I'm not having sex with anybody. Probably ever.

But under the rules, you can get kicked out for being gay.

I should have thought the rule was wrong before. Funny, how knowing someone changes how seriously you take things. Fairness is not just relative, it's relational.

"She can't mess with you," I say. "She'd have to turn herself in for the conduct violation."

"Exactly. And it's fine. It's good. It's fine." Strots lights another cigarette. "At the end of last year, we went our separate ways. She got back with her boyfriend, who she never stopped dating anyway. I went home. I try not to show anything around her. I don't want her to know she broke me and I'm still broken."

At that moment, I know I hate Margaret Stanhope more than anyone I've ever met. I also get a feel for why Strots was willing to "handle" things for me. Two birds with one stone, and I don't blame her.

Strots exhales a plume of smoke out the window. Then she points at me with her cigarette. "It's just what I told you back in the beginning. Don't give her what she wants. I'm not going to let her see the lesbian crumble—and that was the whole point of last year for her. I just didn't know it until it was too late. I didn't know until her fucking boyfriend came to pick her up." Strots shakes her head slowly. "I'll never forget it. We had a room that faced out the front. I still remember watching her from the window as she ran across the lawn and jumped into his . . . you know, his arms, or whatever. He was older. Eighteen. Going to college. Had his own car. It was a Range Rover. His parents gave it to him, I'm guessing. He was hot. Really good-looking."

"Oh, Strots," I say.

"You know what the kicker was?" She looks to our door like it's open and she can see across the hall to Greta sitting on her bed. "And it's a good one, a real twist the knife, break the hilt off kind of thing."

When Strots doesn't go on, I say, "She brought him in and introduced you, didn't she."

There's a pause. "Yeah, she did. It was allowed because, you know, everyone was there with their families packing up and leaving. She walked right into our room with him, her arm around his waist, her face glowing as she stared up at her Superman. 'This is my roommate.' Jesus Christ, I wanted to hurl. I hadn't had the courage to ask her what was going to happen with us over the summer, but in my mind, I was going to go visit her in Greenwich. Stay at her house as a friend. Float under the radar." Strots curses. "And you know, my family's got a place or two. She would have really liked my grandmother's in Newport. But seeing me during the break had never been her plan. None of what I thought we had was real. All along, what she'd been after was that moment right there, when she brought her boyfriend into the place that was ours. It was all to set me up."

Strots rubs her thumb over her eyebrow. "As I shook her boyfriend's hand? I saw the satisfaction in her eyes, and I realized, it had all been engineered for that instant. Everything we had said to each other, everything we had . . . done . . . was so she could feed off of my shock, off of all that pain and shame I had to try to hide. It was a long game, played by a master. I almost respected her for it, if I hadn't been so busy feeling like shit."

"She's evil," I whisper. "She is really evil—"

"What did I expect, though, you know?" Strots looks down as she talks over me. "I mean, really, where did I think it was headed? The whole time, we kept apart outside of our room because we had to. Because it was safest that way and it was easy. She had those two suck-asses of hers, and I got my sports. With the code of conduct, it felt like a smart move to stay under wraps, but again, that was only on my side. For her? She was living her real life with those girls, that boyfriend, the perfume and the short skirt shit. I was the lie. So what did I honestly think was going to happen?"

"You can't blame yourself."

"I absolutely can. She might be a bitch, but I let her in, knowing what she was. A girl like her? You can see her coming a mile ahead."

We both fall silent. I don't know where Strots is in her mind, exactly, but for me, I'm envisioning another round of scenarios where Greta gets her comeuppance. She is married, but her husband is cheating on her. She is rich, but someone is stealing her fortune from her. She is pretty and gets caught in a house fire. Snippets of these hypotheticals flip-card through my mind, animated sequences that move in blocks.

"I won't tell anyone," Strots says. "About your shit."

I refocus on my roommate. She's staring at the drawer of my desk.

"I won't tell anyone about yours," I say back.

Strots nods. "Good. And Keisha doesn't know about Greta, by the way."

I think of how protective Keisha is of my roommate, and enjoy a momentary image of the girl picking Greta up and throwing her through that third-story window. Or a second-story one.

Any window is good, actually.

"Someday, Greta'll get hers," Strots says. "I have to believe this, or God doesn't exist."

I nod, even though I disagree with my roommate's if-this-then-that: If somebody as evil as Greta gets what's coming to her, then the corollaries must be true as well. All her victims must deserve what they get, and how is that right? And likewise, all innocent people must have good things come to them—and how do you square that with the fact that I was born the way I am? I'm not bad. I don't enjoy the suffering of others, as Greta does. And yet I'm stuck with my messed-up mind. Meanwhile, that girl across the hall is fucking with people's lives, and she has a suntan and backup singers.

Still, it would be nice to think Greta will get her reckoning, if only because it gives Strots and me something else in common.

When my roommate smiles at me, I smile back.

That's when I realize that we're a kind of kin now.

Which is so much deeper than friends.

chapter
SEVENTEEN

It's Saturday night. I'm in the old gymnasium at the Fall Fling, a school dance for which we get gym credit if we attend. Given that I have been excused from the year's physical education requirement, I'm not sure why I'm here.

No, that's not true.

My internal life has quieted, thanks to me being back on the lithium, and because cognition is like nature and abhors a vacuum, I find myself more outwardly directed and curious about my peers—and also more lonely at the prospect of everyone on campus being at a party without me. I don't really enjoy my oddball version of extroversion as I don't like the feelings of sadness and sense of separation that come with it. But it's better than boiler rooms, I suppose.

I am standing off to the side, leaning against a concrete wall that's been painted so many times, it's as smooth as icing on a carrot cake. The lights are dim and music is playing and the bleachers that funnel down to the honey-colored playing floor are largely empty. Girls from Ambrose are dancing with each other as blue-blazered boys who have been imported from St. Michael's Prep stand in tight groups of shifting eyes. From what I understand from Strots, dances like this happen two times per year, fall and spring.

As Marky Mark and the Funky Bunch are piped in from overhead, I look at the strict separation of the sexes and decide that all these "Good Vibrations" are a waste of a bassline if the desired result is any kind of commingling. But maybe as the night progresses things will change, although no doubt the administration is hoping they stay like this. Separate is better, even if you're heterosexual.

The DJ who's in charge of the music is stationed behind a folding table in the opposite corner from me, and he alternates between CDs that go in and out of a player, and vinyl records that go round and round on a turntable. He's a robot, unaffected by the beat, although I don't think it's because he's being professional. He appears to be bored out of his mind as he keeps the succession of tracks going, queueing up pop music for rich kids. There's no Nirvana. No Guns N' Roses. It's Color Me Badd, Vanilla Ice, Madonna, C+C Music Factory, Mariah Carey. Every song is something that you've heard on the radio in the last twelve months, although evidently not on the stations the DJ likes to tune to.

There's no theme to this dance. No streamers. No banners. No one being crowned, no court of scepter-holding princesses accepting the steady arms of their princes and forming a promenade of teenage beauty. For this, I am grateful. Although I'm even less integrated into this happening than the landlocked groups of boys and girls, I'd feel totally alien if there were formal dresses and a stage and some kind of value judgment being applied to the pretty girls, another standard I will fail to meet.

As I observe the two separate camps, I note the behavior of both and find the posturing a colossal waste of energy. The girls, as they dance in front of the boys, seem wholly disdainful of the very thing they appear to be trying to get the attention of. Moving their bodies in time to the music, they wear haughty expressions, turning down offers they are not being presented with. The boys, on the other hand, in their clutches of lanky frames, act as though they are completely unaware that there's anything going on outside of the conversations they're having with each other and the push-and-shoves they become entangled in from time to time. And yet the girls keep dancing and the boys keep sneaking glances.

I wonder where the night will end for them. Still apart? Or locked in desperate, fleeting grabs under the bleachers where the chaperones won't see them? I know where my night will end, and it is not going to be anywhere near a warm body other than my own. As this prescient knowledge sinks in, I find myself worrying about my lack of response to Strots's impromptu kiss. I felt nothing. No spark. No interest. Considering it was my first kiss, I become concerned that I will never respond to anybody, male or female.

As this prospect fills me with I'm-a-freak dread, I remind myself I should be encouraged by my introspection. It's normal to wonder and worry about your sexuality when you are fifteen. I was told this in sex ed class last year. Plus anything that isn't me going back to the beginning of the universe or growing hair that takes over a small Massachusetts town or being inside a coffin at a Kleenex-deficient funeral at the National Cathedral in Washington, DC, should be rejoiced.

The lithium is definitely working.

I try to locate Greta in the crowd. It's difficult to isolate her among all the other blondes, and I wonder to what extent the admissions committee favors those with Anglo-Saxon coloring. Judging by this crowd before me? I would say that that particular gene pool and look are nearly a requirement. No doubt my mother failed to disclose what I do to my brown hair or I would never have gotten one foot through the door. Even with the perfect SAT score I got on that test I took last year just to see if I could beat it.

Oh, there she is. Greta's with her two best friends, and I'm initially surprised she's not dancing. But then I see why she isn't on the floor. There are boys with her. Three very tall, very handsome ones. The conversation in the group appears to be flowing easily, as if they all know each other well, and I remember what Greta said about not importing Todd to this event. I thought she wasn't bringing him here because he wasn't worth the probation? But maybe these are other boys, boys who she knows from somewhere else like an exclusive camp, a ski resort in

Colorado, or summer houses in Maine or upstate New York . . . places that it may be harder for her to get to as often as her family did before the bankruptcy.

I wonder if she feels lesser than the rest of them, having to hitch rides to destinations she used to be able to arrive at on her own. And they must all know about the financial reversal. How can they not? The rich and powerful community can't be any different from the small town I grew up in, where everyone knows everybody's business.

And yet, if she does feel inferior, she isn't showing it. Greta is smiling. She's petting her own hair, as if trying to subdue the strands that are not, in fact, out of order in any way. And then she touches the forearm of one of the boys, the tallest one. Other boys come over and kibitz on the periphery, probably because she is so beautiful, definitely because the ice has been broken. The purpose of the dance is finally being served.

As my eyes track her movements, I picture her running out of our dorm and throwing herself into the arms of her hometown honey. I see Strots standing in the center of their room, staring out through the windows, breaking on the inside as spring sunlight falls like a blessing on the golden couple out on the lawn.

I cannot fathom that kind of cruelty.

Something hot curls deep inside of me.

I can't see Greta without thinking of Strots's suffering, and whereas before, I was unable to muster anything more than self-pity in my role as that pretty girl's target, such passive endurance goes right out the fucking window when it comes to my roommate. I feel rage.

I feel hatred.

And I feel like protecting Strots, in the visceral way she offered to protect me—

"Hey, Sarah, not going to get your groove on?"

I jump in surprise. And then try to pretend I didn't. "Oh, hi, Nick. How are you?"

I'm grateful that the lights are dim because I don't want him to see that I'm flushing. Part of the reason I am is that I'm happy to see him, but I'm also ashamed by my uncharitable thoughts about Greta, regardless of what she's done. I'm fairly sure Nick Hollis hasn't hated anything or anybody. Things go easily for people like him, and it takes strife and hardship to breed what I'm feeling toward my tormentor.

"I'm good." He smiles. "So you don't feel like dancing?"

"No. Are you going to?" What am I saying?

"I'm just here doing my job as a chaperone." Nick leans in. "Also, I can't dance."

I am shocked, in the manner I would be if he told me he was missing a kidney. "I'm sure that's not true."

"It is. I got my two left feet from my dad as well."

He and I stand together and watch the dance, and I try not to notice the subtle scent of his aftershave. He's wearing a pale blue button-down with the sleeves rolled up, and the shirt is tucked into slacks the color of Cream of Wheat. He looks sophisticated and polished, his hair pushed off his high forehead, his strong forearms out on display.

As I consider the drift of my previous thoughts, I return to what happened between Strots and me down by the river, except I now edit in Nick Hollis kissing me—purely as a hypothetical construct to test my libido. I am instantly on fire, and I nearly swoon, so overcome with a full-body response that I wonder if I'm not coming down with food poisoning. And when the rush of blood pressure and heart rate stabilizes some, I decide that, if a man like Nick Hollis were to do what Strots did to me—or, conversely, if I ever, in some parallel universe of my mind's creation, did what Strots did to him—I am totally convinced that lack of sexual response on my part would not be a problem.

It's unclear whether this is good or bad news.

"So, what do you think of *American Psycho*?" he asks me.

I glance over at him and try to form a cogent thought. "It's raw. Savage. I love it."

Nick throws his head back and laughs. "Me, too."

"I'm almost done."

Our private reading club is the high point of my days now. The book I borrowed, and the prospect of taking more out of his lending library, light me up inside in a way that's even better than when I'd catch glimpses of him before. And it's the same when I get to go to his apartment to have my now three-times-per-week check-ins with Dr. Warten. It's reliable contact that's deep and meaningful for me.

"I'll bring it back to you when I'm finished," I tack on.

"Take your time. I'm into *The Kitchen God's Wife*. During this year off from studying, I'm going to read as much contemporary fiction as I can before I sink back into the old stuff."

Nick's demeanor is so easy, so comfortable, that I wonder how I ever assumed he was standoffish. If anything . . . he seems lonely.

He must miss Sandra.

"Are you going to teach English at the college level when you're finished with your doctorate?" I ask, feeling like he and I are at a cocktail party while the rest of my peers and these imported boys are playing with finger paints.

"I don't know. The old man's footing the bill for my PhD, so I'm not in a hurry. Of course, all he cares about is that I finish what I start, so I will need to get through my dissertation." Nick's face grows remote, but then he snaps out of it. "Afterward, I can always go to New York and work in publishing if I decide I don't want to read student papers for a living."

"Wow. New York City."

He glances over and smiles that smile of his before returning to his perusal of the dance. "Just because it's big, doesn't mean it's a big deal."

"How can you say that? New York is so full of . . . everything."

"When were you there last?"

"I haven't ever been. Only read about it and seen it on TV and in the movies."

Nick nods as his roaming eyes settle on something and stay there.

"You shouldn't believe all the hype," he murmurs. "It's only shiny from far away, like so many other things."

Overhead, the song gets slow. "Rush, Rush." Paula Abdul. As lyrics about summer breezes and kisses that put souls at ease wash through the gym, wash through me, I stare at Nick while he stares at the dance. The dichotomy of our diversions should be a reminder of reality to my heart. But when has the distance between what I see in my mind and what really exists ever changed anything for my brain?

How I envy his wife.

"Well, I'm going to go for a wander." He puts his hand on my shoulder. Like a residential advisor. Like a friend. "I'll see you later."

"Thank you," I say. "Sorry, I mean, see you later. Too."

As he walks away, I picture myself returning at the end of next summer as a junior, with him no longer in Tellmer on the second floor, but at Yale with his old books and his PhD track and his beautiful, traveling wife. His looming, inevitable absence dims my future. I've enjoyed reading his book in my bed at night, knowing that my hands are where his have been on the hardcover, my eyes on words he has read. What Bret Easton Ellis conceived of is so much less important than the identity of the book's owner, although as I put the novel under my pillow and close my eyes, I'm uneasy that its title is also a descriptor for me. I wonder if that's why I chose it out of all of Nick's collection after I finished my first phone call with Dr. Warten.

I'm willing to guess that my next book will be Amy Tan's newest release, the novel he's reading now. I like the idea that I'm following in his footsteps in some small way. Greta can have all the rides back to campus in his car that she wants. I'd rather ambulate myself up that hill from town a thousand times if it means I can hold Nick Hollis's books in my hands.

It's strange the connections that emotions create out of thin air.

It's also isolating to be the only one who sees them, and I think of Ms. Crenshaw.

As the dance continues, I note a change in the gym. It's as if Greta paved the way for the others. Integrated groups are now forming everywhere, the girls' expressions not so haughty, the boys' eyes more direct.

There's less dancing, too, as if the former were working off their anxiety that way, and there's more strolling, as if the latter are becoming less frozen from fear.

Prospects do not improve for Nick, however.

He's now standing next to Ms. Crenshaw in front of the bleachers, and it's a repeat of the Mountain Day picnic scenario, just with a bigger crowd, a music track, and a teenage dating movie unfolding around them. I can imagine the conversation, and I'm willing to bet it started with another entrée about car windows and weather. With the winter coming, she'll have a problem. It'll be cold enough so that he'll want to conserve interior warmth when he drives. What will she monitor so that she has something to discuss with him, some new kind of update she's got to share? She'll need something more current than that touch football game I lost for Greta. Maybe this dance?

As Ms. Crenshaw chatters at him, Nick's focus is on the crowd again and his hands are in his pockets. He is jazz music, I decide, cool and smooth and sexual. Ms. Crenshaw is the theme to a sitcom with a laugh track, choppy and desperate and falsely cheerful. I don't understand why she keeps throwing herself at his wall of polite disinterest, and then I recall his book in my hands and my eyes tracing those words that I cannot say I'd otherwise choose to read. I realize now that I didn't pick the Ellis book, he picked it for me in a roundabout way. I was leaving his apartment after speaking with Dr. Warten, and I trolled Nick's shelves because I wanted an excuse to stay a little longer. He pointed out to me what he'd been reading in the last six months, indicating various spines with his long, lovely forefinger. He stopped at the Ellis book. He said it had come out in March and he'd devoured it even though he'd had schoolwork to do for his master's program. I was motivated by his enthusiasm, by the look in his eye as he took it out of the lineup and fanned its pages. I wanted to feel like that when I read it so I could feel him inside of me. So I could have a part of him even if he was unaware of the piece that was borrowed.

Nick's books are my car windows.

But at least I am not going to be cut off as the temperature drops.

I'm no longer looking at the girls and boys melding around the dance floor, groups now splintering up into pairs that move together to the music. I'm staring at Nick and Ms. Crenshaw. I want to tell her to stop, just like I did on that picnic table. But then I want to borrow another book from him, and another, and another, carving out a special space that is unique to him and me in comparison to all the other girls. In this pathetic folly, I completely understand where Ms. Crenshaw is coming from, and I'm sad for the both of us. We're window-shopping with no cash in our pockets, no hope of even trying on that which is so far outside of our price range.

When Nick takes his leave of Ms. Crenshaw, his departure reminds me of someone peeling a name tag off a lapel. There's great resistance, and what comes off is thrown away and forgotten.

I, too, am nearing my limits with the dance, both in terms of invested time and sensory overload. I have learned the hard way that there's only so much loud music I can take, only so many flashes on a movie screen or strong smells in a kitchen before my brain begins to think independently. I'm surprised I made it this long. I think I was waiting to see Nick and talk to him. Now that I have done both, my reason for being here has been served.

"Hi."

When the greeting is spoken to my left, I pay no attention. It is then repeated: "Hi."

I look over. There's a boy standing next to me. He's tall and he's wearing the navy blue blazer with the St. Michael's crest on the breast pocket. He's paired this with a white shirt—they're evidently allowed to choose between white and pale blue—and khaki pants that have been pressed. His tie is a black/blue with interceding, angled white stripes that sport a repeat of that crest. His shoes are polished loafers and there's a pop of red color from his socks. I focus on his clothes because I don't want to look at his face.

"Yes?" I say. If he asks me to move, I'll tell him I'm leaving anyway, although I can't imagine what personal space I'm infringing on in this far-off corner.

"I'm Reynolds." He puts out his hand and smiles. "What's your name?"

I glance around the dance. Some version of this introductory interaction was what spread throughout the crowd about twenty minutes ago, the boys going up to the girls and sticking out their hands, growing some forced confidence because they realize they're running out of time if they're going to kiss someone tonight.

Reynolds is late to this stage of things. But being out of better options is not why he approaches me.

Through the crowd, I see Greta standing with her back to me in a new co-ed group of which she is, naturally, the leader. But the Brunettes are staring over in my direction, and their faces are rapt with banked delight. They're watching me, watching the boy.

He drops his hand. "So, what grade are you in?"

I look at him properly. He is very handsome, with sun streaks in his hair that probably came from sailboat excursions off of Cape Cod. His eyes are blue as a summer sky and his cheeks are bright and marked with the occasional mole.

"I'm a sophomore." He pauses. "At St. Michael's?"

My eyes narrow as I think of Strots. As I think of myself. "Tell Greta to fuck off. Does she think I haven't seen *Carrie*?"

I walk out of the dance, leaving him, and so much more, behind.

chapter
EIGHTEEN

It's Saturday of Columbus Day weekend, late in the afternoon. I'm in my dorm room alone and it's eerily quiet. I'm one of the minority of students who are in Tellmer over the three-day break, most of the girls having been picked up to go home or to head off on a last-gasp vacation at a summer country house somewhere. Strots took Keisha away with her, and I gather they were bound for Newport, Rhode Island.

Before Strots left, she told me that they've decided to, as Strots put it, "You know, be together."

So this is a romantic weekend, not just one for friends, and I'm glad because then I don't feel left behind by my roommate. I decide that Strots telling me about Greta freed her heart for K. I don't know whether this is true, but it makes me feel helpful. They're going to stay at Strots's grandmother's house. Given that she thought Greta would be impressed with the place, I'm guessing it's big as a football field and has more columns than the White House. Strots said that she only likes going there in the off-season. In season, evidently, there are too many parties.

Wow, is all I can think.

And there's been another reminder of my roommate's wealth, in addition to the ever-gestating gymnasium going up at the edge of campus: A long black limo has been spotted at the construction site and around the administration buildings. I've overheard it belongs to Strots's father. She hasn't mentioned anything about it, and she also hasn't talked about seeing her dad. But how could she not, if he's here at the school? Fathers and daughters . . . see each other, right?

As if I would know.

What I am certain of is that just as I have kept Strots's secret, she has kept mine. I can tell she's honored our pledge to each other because none of the other girls in the dorm, even Keisha, are treating me any differently—which is not to say they're welcoming me into their cliques, but they haven't shunned me like I'm a ticking time bomb about to go certifiable.

I'm well familiar with the look people give me when they know my truth. I was the recipient of plenty of those wide eyes and hissed whispers in my old school after my breakdowns. In my small town, Tera Taylor's daughter going nuts was big news. That was why I ended up writing the essay my mom submitted to Ambrose's admissions committee. "How I Spent My Summer" by Sarah M. Taylor. I'd gotten tired of the speculation, and decided to set the record straight with brutal honesty, even though I never had any intention of anybody actually reading it.

And then my mom found the thing. After which, Ambrose.

Returning to the present, I look down to my lap. As I sit on my bed, leaning back against the bare wall behind me, I have another book of Nick's in my hands. It is *The Plains of Passage* by Jean M. Auel. It's part of a series and a novel that, I gather, has sold very well. I'm interested in, but not gripped by, the content and prose, and I find myself curious as to why Nick has read the novel and is keeping it. It's kind of pedestrian, for entertainment rather than depth, and there are other books on his shelves that go to this populist vein. What's more, and this surprises me, he's written notes in the margins, keeping track of the plot, which strikes me as wholly unnecessary. But maybe he's practicing his skills as an editor, honing things so that his fallback to being an English professor is strong.

Although if you're in your early twenties and your father is still paying your school bills, how much of a fallback do you need?

The idea Nick could be anything less than the intellectual titan I've made him out to be fills me with a strange dread. Because he *is* wonderful and he *is* smart, and I can make these declarations because I now feel as though I know the man. In the last couple of weeks, I've been going in and out of his apartment regularly, and he visits me as well, like stopping by to share the *New York Times* best-seller list with me this past Sunday afternoon, and on Wednesday coming to see what I thought about Auel's work so far.

Courtesy of our relationship—friendship, I mean—I've totally restructured my college trajectory. Previously drawn to math and science, I now pay extra attention in my English classes, and I've decided I'm now going to be a literature major for undergrad, go on to Yale to get my master's, and then finish up inside those ivy walls with my doctorate.

After which, I will end up teaching wherever he does.

Oh, and I'm not like Ms. Crenshaw, on a solo mission monitoring the windows in his pale blue Porsche. These works of fiction that Nick and I discuss and dissect are a two-way street. We both talk. We both ask questions. We both listen to each other's opinions and care about what they are. And people are noticing. The girls in Tellmer were confused at first, shooting curious looks in my direction as I knocked with growing confidence on his door, and then, when he began to seek me out, jealousy entered their eyes. Misfits are not supposed to ascend. They're supposed to stay put underfoot, to be trod upon at leisure. But my peers' issues with me are not my problem, nor do I give it much thought. I'm only interested in developing my relation—my friendship with Nick.

In truth, I sense that he's lonely with his wife being gone so much, and I also feel that he's lost in this sea of teenage girls who find him attractive and dote on him. On his side, he treats them all like little sisters, bundles of charming energy he must safeguard, and now that I know him so much better, I am certain that whatever anything with Greta looked like, nothing untoward was going on. In all our interactions, never, not once, has he ever done or suggested anything inappropriate, and I get the solid sense that it's not about who I am. It's about who he is. It's such a relief not to worry that he's capable of things that are wrong.

But he's definitely starved for real conversation, and, his collection of popular works aside, he does have good insights. He really does. And he honestly cares about what I have to say. My ability to recall passages word for word, to synthesize plot into theme, to defend my perspectives, seems to captivate him. I feel sometimes that he's testing me, although not to trip me up. He wants to feel out where my intellectual end points are, and the more he's unable to find them, the more fascinating I become to him.

That this spectacular man, who is worshipped by so many, chooses to seek me out sustains me to such a degree that my madness has gone blissfully quiet, cowed by my focus on him. The retreat of my disease in deference to Nick Hollis is the very best gift that my brain has ever given me, and it suggests my mother's purpose in sending me here to Ambrose is being well served. This connection, these conversations, would never have happened in my small town.

And he's had another magical effect. Greta has been leaving me alone. In fact, I haven't really seen her much around the dorm or elsewhere. All of her tormenting, along with my fantasies of being her undertaker, feels like the distant past.

I did not give her what she wanted so she moved on.

Or maybe Nick Hollis is a talisman that has recalibrated my whole life.

The church bells start to ring six o'clock, and I close his book.

I am tired. I spent the day on my hands and knees, washing all the woodwork on the first floor with hot water and Murphy Oil Soap. I'll do the same tomorrow down my hall and should finish upstairs by noon on Monday. I'm earning five dollars an hour and cannot guess whether this is charity in the guise of a job or if any of the elbow grease is in fact necessary to the functioning of the dorm or the school. Whatever the case, I'm grateful for the money I'm earning. It'll cover the co-pays on my prescription, something that's necessary as I'm taking my lithium scrupulously as directed.

As I watch my pill supply dwindle in its little orange bottle, I find myself looking forward to my next interaction with Phil the Pharmacist. I'm doing so much better. I can't fathom a return to the depths that took me to his CVS, to the boiler room plan, to my almost-grave. It's like with Greta's aggression. All of my angst and my disease seem like a dreamscape I've woken up out of. History has certainly proven that this current mental stability should not be trusted, and yet that's a hard truism to remember now that my daily routine is so . . . well, normal.

On that note, I've got laundry to do.

I take Nick's book with me along with my bag of dirties, and as I approach the main staircase, I slow down just in case there's an opportunity to cross paths with him. In my mind, I see him opening his door right as I come up to his apartment. He smiles and says that he was coming to look for me anyway. He's cooked too much spaghetti for himself, as his wife was supposed to be back but has been delayed by bad weather in Minnesota. He'd like to know if I can join him? I say yes, of course, even though I already ate my brown-box dinner at Wycliffe an hour ago, a fact I do not share with him because this is a realistic fantasy, not a hallucination, and I would lie like that in real life just to spend time with him. I tell him I've got to start my laundry downstairs first, and he tells me he will get my place setting ready. When I come back, his door is open, and there's a lit candle on his little table. We talk until three in the morning about books, and before I go back to my room, there is a meaningful pause as our eyes meet in the doorway at my departure.

In that moment, he communicates wordlessly that he wants to kiss me. In that moment, I communicate wordlessly that I want him to kiss me. We stand there like a pair of Victorians, kept apart by student/teacher propriety, his wedding ring, and the distance of our ages. Even though grown-up lust simmers below our surface, we respect the boundaries that we must not, and will not, cross, because we are two righteous, principled people who would never violate such strictures.

And the recognition of this shared and indelible self-control is part of our attraction.

This vital exchange, as powerful as it is silent, alters everything and nothing at all. As fall turns to winter, and winter warms to spring, we continue our connection on an intellectual plane. When he goes off to Yale for that PhD, he writes to me. I write back to him. Our ties deepen as I enter college. Finally, I'm of age, and he and Sandra split up because she's never around. Nick's and my relationship is consummated in a blaze of passion. We marry the June after I graduate as an English major from Yale. We live a life full of books and learning, our conversations what we nurture, no noisy children interrupting the literature that brought us together and sustains us still. He dies first. It's quick. He barely manages to tell me he loves me one last time before his heart stops. I linger for exactly three more years, limping along, half of me gone, and yet I must step into his shoes to usher the last class of freshmen he taught through their senior thesis. Upon their graduation, my job done, I graduate to the other side, where I meet him again in the company of angels in heaven—

Wait, am I actually getting religious here?

That man truly has transformed me.

Back in the real reality, I stare at Nick's closed door for a little longer, to see if he comes out, to see if we can jump-start my spaghetti fantasy into action. When nothing happens and I hear no sounds inside his apartment, I'm crushed, sure as if we had a date and he stood me up.

I force myself to descend the stairs—because how embarrassing would it be to get caught standing on his doorstep with my sack of dirty clothes hours from now?

Down on the basement level, I walk past the boiler room and proceed to the laundry. I flip the switch with my elbow as I enter, and I'm surprised that one of the washers is on a spin cycle. It's the third one from the left, the one I've been using ever since the bleach tragedy. I'm forced to take the machine all the way on the right, as I don't want to be too close to anybody, and I'll never use that other one on the far end ever again.

I portion out the contents of my laundry bag, and as I fill the machine with a single serving of my dark load, I recognize, not for the first time, the ease that comes with having an all-black wardrobe. No reason to worry about color leaching.

Provided no one gets creative with the Clorox.

As I go over to the vending dispenser and purchase a small box of Tide, regular scent, I think of Greta and feel bad for whatever target she's moved on to. But I have to acknowledge my relief. I was unaware of how much I tracked her every movement, in the dorm, in the cafeteria, around campus. Paranoia, however, has a half-life. When it isn't validated, eventually its potency decreases.

I train the machine's knobs on normal wash cold, cold rinse, and single spin, and then I go over and sit on one of the metal folding chairs at the table that holds the overflow of detergents and fabric softeners. It's not lost on me that, despite Greta forgetting about me, I remain unable to leave my clothes down here unattended. But the protective impulse is easy to give in to, and I was just reading alone upstairs, anyway.

I reopen Nick's book on my lap. I'm loath to put it on the table for fear of damaging the spine or staining the cover with some sweet-scented liquid detergent I'm unaware was spilled. Even with all his notes in the margins, he's still managed not to crack the spine. I see this as a sign of his sensitive nature and his respect for the things he pays for. It's a nice change from the girls here for whom everything is disposable.

I'm reading, and enjoying the pleasant waft of Tide rising from my machine, when someone enters the room.

"Oh, my God, we're doing the same thing tonight."

I look up in surprise and fumble to keep the book in my lap. Nick's smiling and his hair is damp from a shower. He's wearing those slouchy, faded jeans that ride low on his hips along with an Ambrose sweatshirt that sits on his strong shoulders like they're a display form.

"We are," I say in a coquettish voice. Or at least my version of one, which is probably not all that coquettish. "Party animals."

"It's true."

He checks his machine, the one that's running. The one that I've been regularly using. It's like he knew my Maytag habits and wanted our clothes to be in the same washer. I am suffused with happiness.

Nick, on the other hand, seems frustrated, although in a good-natured way. "I was hoping this load would be done by now."

"Going somewhere?" I ask casually. I make sure to duck my eyes back to his book so that I appear only moderately interested. In reality, I'm waiting for his response like it's the result of a pathology report.

I remind myself it's inappropriate to be jealous of the woman he walked down the aisle with.

"My father's passing through town."

I look back up. "Your father?"

As a tight expression crosses Nick's face, he links his arms over his chest and tilts a hip against our machine. While he seems to be composing a careful reply, a rush of thoughts goes through my head. I wonder whether his load is a light or dark one. I wonder if he uses scented or unscented detergent. I wonder if his boxers are in there. Whether he wears boxers. What he has underneath those jeans right now.

That last one floods my face with heat and I cover it up by pretending to sneeze.

"God bless you," he says as I fake-itch my perfectly content nose. "And, ah, yes, my father's driving through and we're meeting for dinner."

"Are you going to Luigi's?"

As if that hole-in-the-wall where my mother and I ate is a three-star Michelin restaurant, and because I've gotten the jump on him, I can thus recommend the reheated chicken Parmesan over the microwaved spaghetti Bolognese.

"That's the one. You've been there?"

"My mother and I have." I don't mention it was after she came on the emergency basis, and I hope that he assigns her and my patronage of the establishment to sometime around the first day of school.

"It's a terrible dive, isn't it," he says with a laugh. "We just don't have anywhere to eat out here in the sticks."

"Horrible."

I mimic his tone of benign exasperation, as if I, like him, have a palate well familiar with the likes of first-rate sushi, imported caviar, and French dishes prepared by Le Cordon Bleu chefs. But it's okay. Soon we will be back in the cosmopolitan environment our tongues prefer.

"It's nice that your father's come to see you."

"He loves Sandra. And the feeling is mutual. She's very excited."

"She's going out with you, too?"

"She's in for the weekend, yup." He nods to my lap. "Are you liking Auel any better?"

I am instantly nauseous as I revise his shower scene to include a woman with a brilliant mind and long dark hair and a smoking habit that's a necessary flaw. Because without that personal failing, she'd be too divine to exist outside the pages of the Bible.

"It's . . ." I flounder, and hope that he ascribes the awkward silence to a gathering of my thoughts about the book. As opposed to a grappling with his sex life with his wife and the tension with his father. "I think the author has a great knowledge of the prehistoric period and likes to share what she's researched with her readers."

"You find the information parts tedious, too, then?" he asks with a smile.

"I think they're heavy-handed, yes. But the plot does move along."

"Not into any new territory." Oh, how I love to hear him dismiss that which I find dismissible. "It's just interesting to deconstruct things that work in the market, you know."

I find myself narrowing my eyes on him, and I partly close the book, saving my place with my forefinger. I tap on the author's name on the cover.

"You want to write one of these, don't you," I say to him. "You're reading these commercial books and analyzing the plots not to become an editor, but to become a writer. And you're starting with this kind of fiction because you think it's easier to break into."

His face flushes, and I feel Einstein brilliant for having guessed an inner truth of his—plus the fact that I've seen behind his proverbial curtain wipes away all the wife stuff. I am special once again. I am on his radar once again. Even though Sandra is in town and the pair of them probably just had sex in his shower, I have secret knowledge of his inner workings. His thoughts and fears. His goals. His motivation.

"That sounds like I'm selling out, doesn't it," he hedges.

And his conflict.

"I don't think so." Short of him becoming an axe murderer, I'd support any career choice of his. "Not if you believe in what you write."

"I've taken a stab at a couple of stories, actually. Much to my father's disapproval, none of them are the great American novel. For him, it's Scribner's or it doesn't count. Going on to get my PhD is a negotiated way of not disappointing him again."

I suddenly want to read what Nick's put to the page with an unholy desperation. "I'm sure your books are very good."

"They're not. But I feel like they might be good enough for commercial stuff. I'm not going to live off my father forever. I'm not a child."

Now his voice becomes bitter, and I welcome the show of honest emotion.

"You can do it. I believe in you."

"You're sweet, Sarah." Nick checks his watch, which is gold and has an alligator band that is brown. The fact that he can wear something that expensive with a sweatshirt makes me feel like he is a down-to-earth man of character. "Crap. I've got to go get into a suit."

"I'll put your things in the dryer if you like? I'm just going to be waiting down here while my stuff gets done."

"You'd do that? Oh, my God, that would be great. I use unscented detergent, and if the clothes sit wet, they start to smell pretty quick. Just regular heat, please."

"Absolutely. I'll take care of everything for you."

He takes a moment to stare at me. Then, tilting his head to the side, as if he's seeing a new angle to my face and he likes it, he says, "You're the best, Sarah."

My entire body blooms from the compliment. And even though he leaves, his presence stays behind with me in the sweetly scented laundry room.

I look to the detergent dispenser. I am never using something with a fragrance again.

I get so distracted playing and replaying each syllable and every glance of the interaction that before I know it, his washing machine ceases its spin with a click and a deceleration of its drum. While my load churns on, I place his book carefully aside and rise to my feet, wiping my hands on my pants to make sure they are clean.

As I pop the lid to our machine, I glance around. There isn't a plastic basket of his that I can see and using my bag feels too intimate, like I'm stroking the back of his neck. I decide I'll makeshift one of his T-shirts as a net to carry his clothes across to the dryers.

Before I reach in to touch the things he wears on his body, I take a deep breath and have an uncharitable moment of feeling so much more superior to Ms. Crenshaw. Nick would never allow her to do this. No way.

For one, he'd never hear the end of it.

Bending over, I extend my hand into our Maytag and I pull out the first piece I come in contact with. It's the Nirvana T-shirt he wore the first day we all arrived. As I spread the wet bundle out on the closed lid of the machine to the right, I allow my hand the scandalous pleasure of skating lightly over the damp fibers, the lettering, the image. The fact that I know where he saw the concert and under what circumstances—during one of our chats, he told me he went with his college roommate—gives me another secret thrill. I have personal knowledge of him. I've pierced his privacy boundary, and not as a trespasser, but an invited guest.

Pulling out another piece of his clothing, I blush. Boxers. In a dark color. I don't inspect these, as that would be indiscreet. I'm quick to grab something else, teasing it free of the wet twist formed by the spin cycle. Jeans. Like the ones he's going to change out of so he can wear a suit for his tyrant of a father who fails to recognize his genius.

As I transfer the Levi's over to the pile I am making—and note how much I'm titillated by the incredibly sexy denim that has clad his long, strong legs—something slips free from the back pocket of the jeans and falls to the floor.

I immediately turn to pick it up. But I freeze.

At first, I cannot understand what I am looking at.

In contrast to the dark clothes, whatever was in that pocket is pink. And it's silky. And it's—

A pair of panties.

I take a sharp step back, like the delicate, feminine flush of lingerie is a hissing snake.

My heart pounds. I breathe in and out. I feel my head swim as if I'm a girlfriend, betrayed.

But then I remember . . . he has a wife. These are Sandra's.

I need to calm the hell down. Even as irrational pain lances through the center of my chest, I know that this bucket of cold, foul-smelling reality getting dumped on my stupid fifteen-year-old girl's head is a good thing. My fantasies have created a double life that is curated for a fulfillment that can never, ever translate.

Nick Hollis is not my boyfriend. He is a married man who is my residential advisor. Instead of feeling two-timed, I need to do what I agreed to do for him and put his clothes in a dryer. And then when my load is finished, I need to leave his where it is, even if his things get the equivalent of a permanent press's worth of wrinkles from cooling in a jumble inside the machine.

He's done nothing wrong, and this is none of my business, and I'm way over the line with my feelings.

This rational pep talk lasts about ninety seconds. Almost immediately, I am reassuring myself that he and I still have our special wavelength in spite of his wife. I am still important to him. I am still more significant in his life than all the other girls in the dorm who look at him all the time.

I begin to feel a little better, but I decide to stop being so nosy with his clothes. I reach into the machine, grab an armful, and walk across to the dryers. I do this two more times, and make sure I don't look at anything. Then I peel the concert shirt off of the machine and toss Nirvana and his boxers across the space, almost making it.

After which, I'm stuck with the jeans that I've left draped on the lip of his washer. And the panties.

I can't leave them on the floor.

Why didn't I come down here with that French homework? I would have had a pen.

Taking a deep breath, I bend at the waist and, holding my hand out to the very farthest reaches of my arm, I angle my body back as if I am trying to protect my internal organs from a chain saw. My forefinger and thumb are likewise fully extended and tense, tweezers that only happen to have blood circulation and feeling. Or at least the circulation. I cannot feel a thing anywhere on my body—

My hand goes limp and I feel the world spin like I am on a rinse cycle.

The panties have fallen in a random orientation of pink folds created by a handshake between gravity and dumb luck: The back of the waistband just happens to be facing up at me, and there's a name tag that has been sewn into it, no doubt by a maid's needle and thread.

Stanhope.

These are Greta's.

chapter NINETEEN

It's Monday afternoon now. I've finished washing down the third floor, and I'm checking in with the married couple up there, standing on their welcome mat and asking them if there's anything else I can do. They're the ones who've been coordinating my work, and who will be issuing me a check that I can cash at the student center with my school ID. I'm hoping they tell me I should go wash down the entirety of Wycliffe.

I'm denied that distraction. I'm told I have done a great job. I'm issued an order payable in my name for ninety dollars. I take my check and turn to the main stairs. I dread using them. I don't want to be on my floor, or even in my room.

I decide to head down the hallway instead of descending the center staircase.

As I pass by Keisha's room, number 317, I hope that she and Strots are having the best weekend away ever. I hope they ate good food, and learned new things about each other, and planned a future that spans decades. I want them to have a perfect destiny. I want them to be the lovers embracing in the sun on the front lawn of this dorm in the springtime, even though the school will never let them.

I think of that dance in the gym, and how neither of them went. There's no place for them here on campus and that's unfair.

At the end of the hall, there's a fire door with a red glowing EXIT sign above it, and I push through so that I can begin the change in altitude. I pass my own floor's fire door, and when I get to the first level, I shove its reinforced steel panel open.

As I scoot out the front of the dorm, I feel pursued even though there's no one behind me, and I'm tense as I hook up with the concrete path that I take at night, the one that brings me around our phone room's windows and then skirts the back of Wycliffe to lead me toward the river. Before I veer off from the sidewalk, I look around to make sure I'm not being seen, but this is stupid. Even if all the RAs in both dorms were pressed up against their windows, spying on me like I'm a criminal as I step off onto the mowed grass and head for the slim cutout in the trees, what can they do to me? There aren't any *No Trespassing* signs posted by the river, and it's nowhere near close to curfew.

But everything's changed. Even as the buildings stay in their same alignment on campus, and the trees remain plugged into their same root systems, and the sky is blue and the grass is green, there's a dirty cast to it all, grime in the corners and in between the floorboards of the whole world.

I'm not wiping everything down anymore, trying to clean what's right in front of me.

After I duck through the break in the foliage, I stop as soon as I am hidden. It's much colder in here, and I note the change in temperature, as well as the intrusion of the earthy smells that congregate in this place where nature is not clipped and pruned. Looking around, my tension does not leave me. There is no relief to be found in the burbling of the brook or the embrace of the autumnal leaves.

I go down to the bifurcated tree where Strots kissed me, where I used to hide and listen to Greta talk to her friends night after night. Through the V in the trunk, I stare at the rocks that the girls sit and smoke on. I find myself resenting every single filter Greta flicked into the rushing water, and revisit my familiar outrage that she cares nothing about where what she throws out will end up.

So careless. Just a user who doesn't give a shit about the messes she creates for other people.

Nick Hollis should be very, very careful.

I step out from behind the tree. Walking forward to the congregation of boulders, my heart pounds. I feel as if I have gone across a hostile country's borders without a passport. As if Greta owns these rocks.

I stand on them. I look at the weathered stone beneath my boots. I try to see in the veins of the mineral deposits the answers to the questions that have kept me up for the last two nights.

Why does she have to ruin everything? This first line of inquiry has driven the most highway miles, even though it cuts out half of the participants in question. It is just easier to focus on Greta. The nuances beyond that take me into a swamp that I would rather not trudge through.

Not that there are many nuances when an underaged student's panties are found in the back pocket of her residential advisor's well-washed jeans.

I sit down in exactly the place Greta always parks it. I look up to the sky. The sunlight splicing through the canopy of changing leaves dances upon my face and my shoulders and reminds me of Mountain Day. I am taken back to when we disembarked from the orange buses and stood on the packed dirt of the parking area, listening to Hot RA lay out the rules for the ascent a second time. I remember noting the way the morning sun, razor bright and laser precise, fell upon him, turning him and his Ray-Bans into a religious painting come to life, God blessing the beautiful, youthful man in his role as protector of us.

I want to go back to that moment in time. I want to return exactly there, to that point in the procession of events, when things, in spite of Greta's tormenting, were so very much easier than they have become.

Over the past two nights, I have worked so hard to sculpt an innocent explanation for it all, slapping together hypotheticals in an attempt to construct a three-dimensional representation of a reality I can live with—and once again, I answer the siren call of that myth-building. Maybe her panties were somehow left inside the washing machine, and just happened to commingle with his clothing. Yeah, but then how did they end up inside a pocket? How could that happen? Okay, fine. Maybe she dropped them on the stairs while taking a load down to the laundry and he picked them up as a Good Samaritan. And because he couldn't very well walk around with a student's pink silk underwear in his hand, he stuffed them into his pocket with the intention of giving them back to her—

Bullshit.

And the idea that Greta seduced an innocent married man, plying him with wiles so beguiling that in spite of all his principles, he couldn't help but give in to them?

That's also fucking bullshit.

After forty-eight hours of dissatisfying dissection, I'm beginning to get angry with Hot RA's role in all this. Something as fundamental as a residential advisor not sleeping with a minor under his supervision is like gravity, a law of physics that everyone understands because its purpose and properties are vital to the way the world works.

And just in case there was any gray area as to where that line is for Ambrose, I checked our student handbook. Section IV, paragraph 13 spells out the no, not ever, not in any fashion, at all when it comes to adults fraternizing with students.

So I'm left with the conclusion that Nick Hollis did a very, very bad thing, one that cannot be excused by whatever invitation, however intentional and manipulative in nature, Greta presented to him. He did something utterly against the rules, something that, again, can never be explained away by how hot and sexy Greta can be, or what her desires might have been, or how lonely he was with his wife away.

Oh, and screw the handbook. In the eyes of the law, no matter how many times Greta may have begged him for it, he committed statutory rape. While he was married. And to hell with how often Sandra is on the road, saving the world while she gives herself lung cancer.

The facets of this reality the three of us are in—and yes, I'm now stuck with the pair of them because of those panties—are ugly, and they make a hypocrite out of me. Wasn't there a sexual component to my own fantasies? A physical connection I dreamed of, I relished, even though he is an adult, I'm a minor, and he's married?

The difference is that my transgressions with him were in theory, Greta's in fact.

I think back to that day in the rain, her ditching the Brunettes to hop into the Porsche with him. Had it started back then? And what about on Mountain Day, when the pair of them were up on the summit in the trees? And then when Greta defiantly chose Crenshaw's team and got pissed when Nick outplayed her?

And what about her and Francesca arguing. Maybe the other girl found out.

No, I know when it started. I just hate to contaminate a moment I had with him . . . with everything that is Greta.

But if I'm really being honest, I think things started back on the third night I was in the dorm, when I woke up without a reason and went to the bathroom and heard my residential advisor arguing with his wife on the phone.

After which I emerged to find my residential advisor leaving his quarters with his car keys in his hand.

I recall his eyes bouncing around, focusing on the hall behind me. I had ascribed the distraction to him battling his emotions after a rough call with Sandra, but no, that hadn't been it. Greta had come out of her room at the prescribed time and he hadn't been sure how to handle it.

With the clarity of a memory revisited in another light, I see Greta fully dressed in her doorway, clear as if she were standing before me.

And then there had been that curling iron left on in the bathroom.

It had been planned. The two of them had arranged to meet up and go for a drive in the moonlight—but his wife had called unexpectedly, and then I had been another monkey wrench in the works with my appearance in the hallway. He'd had to leave by himself because they both knew I was awake and my room faced the parking lot. It was too much risk, and they'd had no means by which to make an on-the-fly adjustment to their meetup.

So, yes, I believe they started things almost immediately. Maybe not with the actual sex. Maybe that had taken time to enter the picture. But the tracks had been laid for that horizontal destination right from the beginning.

As I ponder how any married man could think of this dorm as a dating pool, the dance in the gymnasium comes back to me. I remember Nick searching the crowd as we were talking, and his eyes seeming to focus on something specific. Had it been Greta? Had that comment about New York not being as good as it seemed been about the girl?

My head's ability to extrapolate endlessly is well suited to precisely this kind of persistent recasting of recollection. I've been looking under every single rock to probe the truth, and the result is the mental equivalent of finding pink panties all over my dorm, my hall, my classrooms, my meals, and my interactions with people. It's exactly the kind of egg hunt I do not need to go on.

I wish I had someone to talk to about this. I wish there was somewhere to go. But as I sit on Greta's rock and hate her to my core, I'm unwilling to end Nick Hollis's marriage and his entire professional life on the basis of a pair of underwear in his laundry, no matter what their presence in that pocket so strongly suggests.

And I'm crushed as I reaffirm my conclusion that I will not act upon my constructive knowledge of the affair. Crushed and saddened.

After battling with my hallucinations for so many years, you'd think I'd be used to reality shifting and changing in front of my very eyes, yet I find that all my training in this regard helps me not one iota: My residential advisor is not who I thought he was, and there's no going back from this realization. No changing it, either.

And I miss the fantasies I had of him sure as if I've broken up with a real person.

With a nasty edge, I find myself hoping that in this go-around of

Greta's game, she'll lose and lose hard. I can't imagine Nick Hollis leaving his wife for a student. But maybe Greta's just trying to pull another Strots, this time with higher stakes. Not a lesbian, but a married man.

He needs to be really, really careful.

I sit for a while longer on the rocks. Then I get to my feet and wander back in the direction of the dorms. As I emerge from the river path, I look to the parking lot behind Tellmer. The pale blue Porsche is gone, and I wonder how he can be around his wife. How he can put on a suit and go out to dinner with her and his father and pretend that he doesn't know a damn thing about the pink panties of a fifteen-year-old.

I go around to the front of the dorm, because Ms. Crenshaw's car is also missing, and I don't want to get trapped by an ill-timed confluence of our schedules.

Girls are beginning to arrive back after the long weekend, cars pulling up on the lane out front, students disembarking with their travel bags, parents taking a stretch before hitting the road once again.

I'm looking forward to seeing Strots, although I will not be talking about anything related to the color pink or intimate apparel of any variety. Although my roommate has kept the secret of my illness very well in hand, I cannot tell her about what I found down in the laundry and what I know about Greta and our residential advisor.

It's not to protect the guilty, although that's the end result, and I hate that I'm complicit in their whatever-it-is. I just don't want to let anybody in on the secret world I created in my head between me and Nick Hollis, and I know I can't tell the story without that coming out. It was all so truly pathetic on my end, and I should be relieved that my crush is over, even though the mourning hurts.

Ascending Tellmer's center staircase, because I know the coast is clear, I go to my room. *The Plains of Passage* by Jean M. Auel has been on the floor under my bed since Saturday night.

Taking it out, I remove the plain index card I was using as a bookmark from its pages. I'm three-quarters of the way through the story, but I'm not going to finish it. Not now. Not ten years from now. Not ever.

With sorrow, I leaf back through what I have read and feel as though I'm looking at photographs of a couple that has since split up, the romance, once so promising, now over as if it had never been.

I return the book to its owner by leaving it propped up against the Tellmer second-floor residential advisor's door.

I don't leave a note because I don't want any contact between us ever again, but there's a pattern to be broken. When he comes to me to ask what I thought of the book, and he will, how am I going to look him in the face and pretend all is well, I'm just busy with schoolwork?

I better figure that the hell out.

chapter
TWENTY

It's the following afternoon, the Tuesday after Columbus Day weekend. It's three thirty, and I'm walking back to the dorm from chemistry lab alone because I helped my teacher clean up after class was dismissed. Overhead, the sky is gray, November briefly stepping in and relieving October's sunshine and blue skies for a shift, the cold wind brooming the first of the fallen leaves across the lawn, across the concrete path at my feet, across my boots.

Everyone came back after the mini break, and by this, I mean Greta, of course. The entire dorm could have forgotten the directions to Ambrose or been expelled for whatever reason, and as long as she returned, it would feel like a crowd was once again under Tellmer's great slate roof. And she was very chatty last night. I gathered from the volume that permeated my closed door that she was holding court right in the hallway itself, sitting against the wall directly outside her room, girls circled round her, a campfire's worth of captive audience that provided her with a laugh track and theme music to the tune of adulation.

She seemed excited, happy, pleased with where she'd gone and what she'd done. It was the kind of thing that I otherwise would have taken no particular note of, but that I reconsidered in light of what I know. I decided she was chatting it up next to her room so that her voice and the details of her break traveled down to Nick's apartment, a songbird chirping to its mate.

There wasn't one mention of Todd, the hometown honey, something that, given the cruelty of her nature, struck me as an underutilized opportunity to stir up some jealousy on Nick's part. But what do I know.

As I close in on my dorm, I reexamine the timeline I've been constructing with all the fastidiousness of a model-ship-maker working on 1:50 scale. I've decided that after their affair all started that moonlit night, it intensified with the ride home in the rain, that sliver of privacy in the Porsche opening the door to their physical expression. And then in spite of the trials of Mountain Day, including whatever happened with Francesca and then that touch football play, things must have continued apace. The underwear must have changed hands relatively recently, however. Given the risks of exposure, it's hard to believe he was just walking around with them in his pocket for a month. I decide Greta gave them to him right before the three-day break, as a reminder of what he's missing while she is gone and his wife is home.

Or . . . perhaps were they removed from her teenage body by his passionate hands and retained as a keepsake by him for when she was away for those seventy-two hours? Or was it a case of them having only a brief moment during which they could entwine in the basest of ways, and he forgot to give them back? Does she even know they're missing, then?

And what if his wife had found them?

Jesus Christ. He was lucky it was me.

You're the best, Sarah, I hear in my head.

"Fuck you, Nick," I say under my breath.

Lost in my lingerie reverie, I barely notice all the girls standing around Tellmer's entrance. They're dispersed in random groupings on the stone steps and they're reading the newsletter that would have been put in all our boxes around two p.m. Some of them have book bags at their feet, some have one-strapped loads hanging off a shoulder, all of them are raptly absorbed to such a degree that I wonder what story has broken in the *Ambrose Weekly*.

One by one, the girls glance up at me. One by one, they do a double take and stare, halting in the course of their reading.

I glance down at myself, wondering if I've inadvertently lost my pants and not noticed.

No, I'm fully clothed and nothing is out of place.

As I look back up, I see in the central bank of windows on the second-floor landing a figure in white. No, there are three figures. And the trio are staring down at me, ghostly specters that cause me to lose my stride for a brief beat.

Are they real? I wonder. I've been taking my lithium.

Chilled, I refocus on the entrance of the dorm. The congregated girls on the steps are still looking at me, but this changes as my eyes return to them. They fold up the newsletter and scatter in every direction, leaves carried away by a gust of wind.

At the door, I grip the brass pull where the hands of all the girls do, the section on the graceful curve rubbed to a high shine. Putting my shoulder into the draw, I open the way in and stop between the jambs, a photograph framed.

There are girls around the mailboxes, at the base of the stairs, in the phone room. And they're all reading the newsletter, heads of mostly blond hair tilted downward, the top page pulled back, other pages pulled back, one page left, depending on how far they've gotten, how long they've been reading. These girls do not look up as I enter, so engrossed are they.

After everything that's been crowding my mind since Saturday night, I'm eager for a distraction that's verified and shared by other people. And as I'm incapable of instigating mass hallucinations, and the students around me are real, whatever they're captivated by is safe for me to get pulled into.

As I step up to my mailbox, eyes begin to rise around me and there's a collective shuffling of pages of which I am only dimly aware. Reaching out my hand, I take the stapled sheaf of papers out of my designated slot, and expect to see the familiar masthead of—

It's not the newsletter.

At first, I do not know what it is. I'm confused. My name is at the top: Sarah M. Taylor.

There's a title above my name, and I read it only once. By the second word, I know what this is, although my confusion is not cleared up.

What is "How I Spent My Summer" by Sarah M. Taylor doing in my mailbox?

I look back at the lineup of boxes, and it's then that the horror begins to manifest in my gut. Two-thirds, perhaps three-quarters, of the cubes are emptied, and my brain connects what's in my hand with what everyone in the dorm seems to be reading so intently.

I snatch another set of the pages from a random box. "How I Spent My Summer" by Sarah M. Taylor. And another. "How I Spent My Summer" by Sarah M. Taylor.

They're all reading about me. They've all received in their mailboxes the essay I wrote just over a year ago, the essay that detailed my two suicide attempts, my stays in the mental hospital, my psychiatrist, my drugs, the orderlies—God, the orderlies, who I devoted an entire page and a half to.

My first inclination is to vomit, and I lurch toward the trash bin to do that. But then someone comes in through the dorm door and I realize there's no time to waste. Frantically, I begin to pull the remaining copies from the boxes that have yet to be emptied. I must save what's left of my privacy, rescue it, shade it, from the blinding heat and light of all the eyes that are upon me. My shaking hands do not work right, however, and copies of the essay fall to the floor like snow, covering my boots. And still I try to clean out, take back, safeguard—

Somebody captures my arms.

It's Strots.

She's just come in. She's the one who came in.

She is speaking to me, but I cannot hear her. I cannot hear even my pounding heart or my wheezing breath, and then I cannot see my roommate, either. Tears have formed and are falling down my face. The fact that I do not know how the essay was found is secondary to my terror that it has been, and now my secret is exposed in the worst way, not just as words whispered into a cupped ear, but with a bullhorn of my own creation: These girls, none of whom care about me, none of whom like me, have all my facts, my details, my entire timeline.

Strots's attention is suddenly diverted to something over my shoulder, and even through the chaos inside of me, the change in her expression registers.

In slow motion, I turn and look to the staircase.

Greta is coming down the steps, the Brunettes behind her. The three are dressed in all white, from their shirts to their kicky skirts. White. Like the orderlies I wrote about. Just like the orderlies who tortured me when I was at my sickest. Who wore all white.

Of course it was her. Who else could have done this?

Sealing the deal that she's the perpetrator are the affects of the two behind her. Though Greta is smiling widely, the two Brunettes are not. Francesca and Stacia have lowered their heads, and they have wrapped their arms around their middles. They're clearly uncomfortable with this. They don't feel this is right and know it's gone too far. But as usual, they're swept up in the plan, and see no way around their participation in it. They're as ashamed as I am, just for a totally different reason.

Greta steps off the staircase and puts a hand on her hip. She looks directly at me. "Anything wrong? You look like you're hallucinating or something."

I can't reply. I have no power, no voice, no recourse. She's won, not by a margin but by an atomic bomb's ring of devastation. And she knows this. Her eyes are lit up with victory, and her smile is so real that she's radiantly beautiful. This is the predator with a full belly. This is the competitor who's got all the trophies. This is the self-satisfaction that comes with the mastery of hurdles and the attainment of a goal.

As I remain silent, Greta shrugs. "Well, let me know if I can help with anything. We're just off to play a little tennis—"

I'm not exactly sure what happens next.

One moment, I am breaking down . . . the next, there's a flash in front of me, and it moves so fast that my addled brain can't identify it. And then my view of Greta is blocked by something—no, by someone. Immediately after that, Greta is no longer standing triumphantly before me, at the base of the stairs. She's being thrown into the wall.

Gasps from the other girls. People jumping back. Greta's blond hair flowing up and out as she is banged into the wall a second time. And the attack doesn't stop there.

It's as she's propelled through the open doorway of the phone room that I realize Strots has her hands around Greta's throat and, with her much more powerful body, is pushing the girl, shoving her, taking her down. They land on the hard floor, the rug between the tables offering no cushioning at all. Strots is on top, straddling Greta, dominating her. Greta's legs are extending out from under her crouched attacker, kicking, splaying, losing a white sneaker.

I have a thought that I need to stop this. I stumble into the phone room, but I can't go any farther. Strots is pounding the back of Greta's head into the carpet with a look of cold intensity. And Greta is clawing at Strots's locked hold on her throat as her skull is nailed to the floor over and over again.

My roommate is going to kill the girl.

Greta's luscious mouth is wide open, gaping, gasping for air that cannot get down into her lungs. Her eyes are peeled even wider, the whites showing around the blue in a full circle. Her spun-gold hair is tangling in a blur. And that sound, that hollow, horrible sound of a head impacting solid wood, is the loudest thing in the universe.

"Stop," I whisper, too scared to yell. "Please . . . stop—"

I am shoved out of the way, my body ricocheting off to the side and banging into a table, hitting it so hard that I dislodge one of the phones' receivers.

It's Keisha. She's jumped into the fray and now she's forcing her arms around Strots's rib cage, her body bulging with muscle as she hauls back, using her powerful thighs, putting all of her strength into it, her athletic build in direct battle with Strots's. As girls watch in a crowd at the archway, and I brace myself against the table I fell into, no one knows whether Keisha will drag Strots back in time.

There is an eternity before we have our answer.

With the same abruptness the attack began, its ending arrives in the blink of an eye. One moment Strots is still trying to crack the back of Greta's cranium; the next, Keisha's determination overrides Strots's urge to kill. The two of them go flying backward, the energy necessary to break the bond with Greta's cervical column so great that they pinwheel across the room and slam into the far wall.

Keisha doesn't let go. Even as she hits the hard-stop of the plaster, and a sharp sound suggests something might have been broken and not necessarily the laths, her dark forearms remain belted around Strots's torso right below the breasts, her knees extending out on either side of Strots's thighs, her legs braced so that her feet get the most traction.

Over in the middle of the room, Greta curls onto her side on the floor, her sloppy hands pawing at her neck as if she has no idea the constriction is gone. As her long, bare legs swing over the floor, I see her underwear beneath the hem of her skirt. They are pink. They are silky. They are a reminder I do not require for so many reasons.

Strots points a finger at Greta. In a booming voice, she says, "You stay away from her! You leave her the fuck alone!"

As the words register, I look over at my roommate. There are tears on her face. She's crying in fury, and I know it's from pain that only the three of us know the source of. Yet I'm very sure that she attacked only to defend me. Just as I could only really despise Greta after I knew what she had done to Strots, my roommate's the same way.

It's hatred, not unrequited love, that burns in her eyes.

"You leave her alone!" she hollers again.

Greta lifts her head from the carpet, and I'm prepared to see tears in those blue eyes. Except there are none and she doesn't appear to be afraid. She is absolutely furious in spite of the fact that she's still coughing, still gasping for air.

Even though she has to know that, if Keisha hadn't interceded, she wouldn't be alive right now.

Francesca and Stacia fight through the tightly packed bodies and run over to their friend, their despotic leader. In their white outfits, they're like nurses to a patient, but as they reach out, Greta punches their concerned hands away.

"Don't fucking *touch* me," she spits at them.

As they rear back, Greta plants her single shoed foot on the rug and stands up on her own. Her hands are trembling, but she doesn't seem to notice as she jerks her white skirt down, yanks her white shirt back into place. After this, she gathers her hair and sends it back over her shoulders with impatience. The sight of the marks on her neck makes my stomach roll anew. The brilliant red band that encircles her throat is neon against her delicate skin, and there's blood on her lower lip where she must have bitten herself with her front teeth.

But she doesn't appear to care.

She takes a step toward me. And another. And another. In the background, the receiver I knocked off when I hit the table begins to let out a *beep-beep-beep-beep* of alarm. But it's not as if we need further notice that this is an emergency, this is an awful emergency, this is a really, really terrible emergency.

I cringe back and shield my face with my arms, thinking that Greta is coming at me.

She is not coming at me.

She's going to Strots, who's still fighting to get at her, and I measure Keisha's strong arms. I pray that she can keep holding on because if my roommate gets loose, there's not going to be a second chance for a rescue. She's going to drag Margaret Stanhope across to the table I hit, and she is going to use the edge of it to snap that girl's head off at the top of her spine. After that, she's going to hang up the phone with the same steady hand she uses to make her bed every morning, that which was messy taken care of.

I can see it happening, clear as day. Yet none of the still-imminent threat seems to register on Greta. Her head must be hurting, her throat must be on fire, her lip must be throbbing, but none of that seems to matter, either.

She stops right in front of Strots, and puts her finger in my roommate's face. In a low voice, she says, "You shouldn't have done that. You should have just left it alone."

As she speaks, a single, bright red drop of blood falls from her lower lip and lands on the front of her bright white shirt.

She turns away. The crowd parts for her. Francesca and Stacia look at each other, and then run after their leader.

I look at Strots, who finally looks at me. My roommate just shakes her head once, like she doesn't want me to say anything.

With a shaking hand, I am the one who hangs up the dislodged receiver, cutting off the high-pitched, urgent beeping that fills the tense silence like a scream.

There's going to be no setting what just happened to rights.

Ever.

chapter
TWENTY-ONE

It's the next day. It's nearly twenty-four hours exactly from the moment I returned to the dorm after chemistry lab and found that my essay had been Xeroxed and put in all the mailboxes. Twenty-four hours from when I tried to take back the copies that had yet to be read, as if that would create some kind of magical reversal of it all. Twenty-four hours from when Strots nearly killed Greta in the middle of the phone room, in front of half of Tellmer.

I am alone in Strots's and my room, sitting on my bed, my back against the wall, my legs stretched out perpendicularly. I check the clock that rests on the windowsill, even though its numbers can provide no insight into the wheels that have been set in motion, no prediction as to what's going to happen next.

The truth about teenagers is that we have more privacy than the adults around us know. The vast majority of our daily and nightly interactions with our peers, and with others, are outside of the earshot and the eyesight of our elders. We're independently functioning entities under an umbrella of supervision that cannot possibly monitor every nanosecond of our lives, and this zone of secrecy tends to be protected by everyone in our age group. Tattletales, whether they sit at the cool table or are losers like me, are ostracized fast, and the adage about loose lips and ships is never more true than when you are fifteen.

All of that being as it is, there are times—rarely, and usually around circumstances that are dramatic and dangerous—when the collective discretion of youth shatters and grown-up intervention is sought. It's the equivalent of an adult calling 911 after they're assaulted or their home is broken into: An event has arisen that we are not capable of dealing with on our own, and we must seek help from people who have the legal authority, and often the medical or psychological training, to render aid, guidance, and the opportunity to redress the situation.

Strots and I did not sleep last night. We just sat here in this room, on our separate beds, staring into space. The only thing she asked me was whether I needed to call my mom. I said no. The only thing I asked her was if she was all right. She said no. Other than that, we were silent, and that was because we were waiting for the consequences to come knock on our door. Until such time as they did, there was nothing to discuss.

I knew what had been done to me and by whom. She knew what she had done and to whom. It was the future that mattered to both of us, that scared both of us, and for some portion of the dark hours, I harbored a secret hope that Greta would do nothing, given her complicity in what had occurred with my essay. But I saw the fearless look in her eyes when she spoke to Strots. Clearly, she's hidden her tracks well. And the Brunettes are not going to break ranks and betray her.

Strots is in trouble.

Dawn's arrival bathed our grim vigil in golden light, and sure enough, our residential advisor came to us first thing in the morning. Although I'd been avoiding him since Saturday, I looked Nick Hollis right in the face, the imperative about what was going to happen to my roommate wiping away even my heartbreak and baseless sense of betrayal at what he'd done and to whom.

He'd been serious, and he'd shut the door. He'd stated to us in a low voice that the administration had become aware of a "goings-on"—his exact verbiage—in the phone room and that both of us were going to be expected to tell our sides of things. He then asked Strots to leave so that he could talk to me alone. I didn't want Strots to go, but I could tell she was ready to check in with Keisha anyway. After her departure, our residential advisor's mask of professional reserve melted away. As Nick's compassion came out, it offered a pool to immerse myself in, a way to be cleansed of my mourning of our non-relationship, but I resolved to stay strong. I'd been in the process of working through my grief and I wasn't interested in a regression that would require reintroduction to my disillusions. The path out of what we'd had, such as it was, was proving hard enough to tread just once.

He asked me if I wanted to see my mother. I said no, as I had to Strots. He asked me if I wanted to take the day off from classes. I said no. He asked if I'd like to speak to Dr. Warten. I said no.

I knew I was being a pain in the ass. But I didn't want to give anything to him, and that meant that any idea posited by him, even if it was in my best interests, was going to be shot down. His final offering was presented as an alternative to the rest: He wanted to know if I wanted to come hang out in his suite and watch TV or read.

The offer took me back to Saturday night, and I had a brief diversion into the land of wishing my lack of clean shirts had not required a trip down to the laundry so I could find someone else's panties in his jeans.

"I need to go to class."

Our residential advisor nodded. Then he asked, "Are you going to be okay?"

I'd be much more okay if you weren't sleeping with Margaret Stanhope, I'd thought as I forced my shoulders into a shrug.

"They already think I'm weird," I said. "Now they have a concrete reason why. It really makes no difference to me."

This was a bald-faced lie. It makes all the difference in the world to me.

But at least there's a corollary to this catastrophe that is a help. Nick Hollis will not wonder why my affect has changed around him. He will attribute the shift in my patterns to this crisis, and I am tired enough, and overwhelmed enough, to use anything as a shield.

"You're so strong," he said to me. "And I'm always here if you need me."

At this point, I'd wanted to ask how his wife was. Traveling again? Or asking questions about—what was her name again?

Mollyjansen. Like it's one word.

After he'd closed the door, I spent some time staring out the window. I realized then, and continue to realize now, that I'd have asked for his help with this back before Saturday night. I would have used him as a resource to deal with the fallout of my essay being distributed so widely without my permission or foreknowledge, something that, considering my mother's illicit use of it to get me into Ambrose, seems to be the damn thing's destiny.

So I went to my classes and could not concentrate. I took notes I had no idea I'd written. I answered questions I was not aware of being called on to address. I paid particular attention, while coming and going from my dorm, and during my classes and at lunch, to how many girls looked at me and then pretended not to have done so.

And now, I'm here. Waiting. I have no idea whether Strots made it to class, and I worry that she's being held for moral deviancy in a barred cell down at the police station. As the seat of law in Greensboro is located next to the library, behind the CVS, I'm of half a mind to walk into town and see if Margie and Roni can help with her bail. But I worry that I'll miss my roommate arriving back here.

Meanwhile, I have seen and heard nothing of Greta. Her door was closed when I left, and closed when I dropped off my backpack before lunch. It was still closed when I returned here about twenty minutes ago. Has she gone off campus? Is she in the infirmary? Did she die because of some rare complication as a result of having almost been strangled while the back of her head was banged into the floor ten times?

I think of my mortician fantasy. I think of Strots's offer to hurt her. I am glad no one from administration can read minds.

I did catch sight of Francesca and Stacia at one point in the day. They were at lunch, leaning in toward the center of their pretty girls' round table, talking in an intense fashion to the others who were dressed in the colors of sorbet and paying rapt attention to a critical update.

I'm certain Greta has gone to the administration and reported the attack. And she's done this despite the fact that she got those essays into the mailboxes, and without regard to her history of pranking me. For anyone else, I'd say it's a bold move to play victim in a situation in which you've worn the mantle of a charging bull, but Greta strikes me as the kind who can manufacture tears when the need arises. Besides, as it relates to me, her hands have always been clean, no traces of what she's done left behind, her supposed guilt resting only on inferences and conjecture on my part, accurate though I am convinced my conclusions are.

For example, when it comes to the essay? I have no idea how she got ahold of my involuntary manifesto, but as with the geometry memo, I suspect Francesca of being in on the photocopying because of the *Ambrose Weekly* connection and also because of the ashamed look on her face as she came down those stairs in Greta's wake, dressed in white like the orderlies I hated so much.

Will Francesca crack under questioning? I wonder. Will she break ranks and be truthful about her best friend? Surely, she'll be asked for some sort of testimony—

The door opens and I jerk up. It's Strots.

"Oh, thank God," I say as she closes us in and drops her book bag at her feet. "What happened? Are you okay?"

Strots leans back against the panels and crosses her arms over her chest. She becomes utterly still, as if she's not even breathing, and I know from the look on her face that she's not actually in the room with me. The static mask of her features bears only a passing relationship to my roommate's normal countenance, everything three-dimensional becoming two because of her critical distraction. She's somewhere else.

She is scaring me.

As my fear hits properly, she shakes herself and her eyes come to meet mine. There is no light in her stare. It's as if she's died.

"You just need to be honest with them," she says in a hollow voice.

"What?" I try to swallow, but my throat is too tight. "And who is them?"

"I don't want you to lie for me."

"Who did you talk to?"

"The dean of students."

"Of course I'll be honest. I'll tell them Greta somehow found my essay and she gave it to Francesca and told her to copy it. Then they put it in the mailboxes when everyone was in class—oh, and Stacia has to be in on it, too. Maybe she was lookout when they—"

"It's too late for that." Strots rubs her eyes, but not because she's crying. "None of that matters."

I recoil. "Of course it does."

When she says nothing, I shuffle off the bed and go over to her. "We can't let her get away with this. She's taken too much from both of us. Now's our chance."

My roommate still doesn't respond, and I begin to get energized in a way I have not been. Maybe ever. "We just need to tell the administration what happened—"

"It's not going to go down like that."

"Yes, it is. It has to. I'm smart. I'll find a way to prove to them it was her. I'll make this right!"

"I gotta go talk to Keisha," Strots murmurs. "I just . . . I gotta go talk to her. They're coming for you, by the way. Right now."

"Strots, I'm going to tell the truth. About everything Greta's done to me. All of it. Then they'll understand why you did what you did."

"Do you really think it's that simple or that that's an excuse they're going to buy?"

"Greta's won too many times," I say. "She can't get away with this."

Strots stares into my face. "None of it is your fault. Just remember that. I don't want you to blame yourself and do something stupid, okay?"

"It's not either of our faults, Strots. All of it's on Greta, and it's time people know what kind of person she is."

Strots reaches out and puts a hand on my shoulder. "Promise. After the dust settles, promise me you won't do something stupid."

My body goes still. As we stare into each other's eyes, I find myself thinking of all the times I've lied to protect my internal reality, attempting, and often succeeding, to derail my mother, my doctor, the nurses, from what's really going on inside my head. Phil the Pharmacist. Our residential advisor. The divide between adult and teenager has always made the falsifying easier, a fact that I was unaware of until right this moment.

Meeting Strots's steady regard, I find myself wavering away from the kind of smooth lie I've used on my elders. I've never before had a peer confront me like this, as someone my age who cares deeply for me and worries about my future. Strots really is my first true friend. And for this reason, the consequences, if I can't make this vow and stick to it, seem very real, more real than even the ruination I'd bring to my own mother. After all, we as children aren't responsible for the well-being of adults—the system is set up to be the other way around. Friends are not the same as the adults we love, however. I know I cannot let Strots down.

"I promise," I say.

Strots nods, gives my shoulder a squeeze, and then leaves.

After her departure, I stay where I stood in front of her. A toilet flushes on the other side of our wall. I hear distant voices.

Down below in the parking area, someone pulls in—no, they're pulling out, their engine sounds fading rather than being cut off sharply.

I look around our room. Then I go over to Strots's bed. I lift her pillow. Her cigarettes and lighter are right where she keeps them. I have a thought that I should run after her and bring them to her. If there's ever a situation that calls for nicotine, it's now, and besides, I want to do something, anything, to ease the burden she's under.

She says this is not my fault, but I'm very confident that if she hadn't been paired randomly with me as her roommate, she wouldn't be in this mess.

Ultimately, I decide to leave her pack of Marlboros and her red Bic where they are for fear of interrupting a private moment between her and Keisha upstairs. As I feel like a sitting duck doing nothing while I wait for whatever administrator is coming for me, I open our door and lean out into the hall. I frown. Greta's door is open, and I see her moving around in her room. She's talking to someone, her back toward me, her blond hair swinging loose at waist level, the ends curling up in a pretty fashion. She's wearing her pink silk robe. When she laughs to whomever she is speaking with, my blood goes cold, and I close Strots's and my door quickly.

My heart speeds up and my mouth goes dry.

My brain, which is both my best and my worst asset, does a lightning-fast calculation of the entire situation. There are many ways this can go, and none of them are good news for Strots.

There's a knock on the door. I brace myself and reopen things. There is a man I do not recognize standing out in the hall, and he looks annoyed.

"Sarah?" he says to me. "Sarah Taylor?"

As if this is the front door of my house and he has a delivery for me. Or, given the suit he's wearing and his pinched, unkind face, an official summons of some sort.

"Yes," I reply.

"I'm Mr. Anthony Pasture, the dean of students. I need you to come talk to me down at my office. Now."

Over his left shoulder, I see Greta. She's twisted around and is staring at both me and the administrator. Her lip is swollen and the red marks around her neck are transitioning to a purply rose. The injuries are not what I focus on. It's the look in her eyes.

She's got the same one she had as she came down to the bottom of the stairs and smiled at me yesterday afternoon.

She's triumphant.

And once again, I want to vomit.

"I just need to change," I blurt out. "Can I have a minute?"

"I'll be waiting for you."

This is spoken in a dire tone, as a warning in case I decide to try to leap out my second-story window and run. I briefly entertain the idea that there's a gun somewhere under his suit, one that he'll point at me and pull the trigger of, perhaps even if I do not try to escape his authority. I don't believe he'll be the one who tracks me as a fugitive, however. In spite of his official capacity, one that would, I imagine, include some kind of training with regard to students with mental and emotional challenges, he seems not to want to be anywhere near me, as if I'm diseased in a communicable fashion.

After I close my door, I look around frantically as I gather my thoughts, as I try to orient myself . . . as I attempt to give me a pep talk along the lines of yes, I can tell my story without breaking down to a man who already seems not just unprepared to hear anything from me, but unwilling to get in an enclosed space with me.

And that is when I realize he is blaming me for something. Not for being mentally ill and writing about it, no. Not that. It's something else.

Oh, God. Where has Greta gone with this?

I focus on the closed door and see her triumphant face through the panels. And suddenly I know what she's done.

With the same clarity and confidence I've had about the pranks the girl has pulled on me, I know exactly what she's told the dean of students. It explains the way he looked at me. As if I'm contaminated.

A split second later, I follow an impulse that's born of my brain's superior ability to connect dots that, in some cases, has taken me into madness and ruin, but, in this instance, allows me to forge a path forward. Literally.

I run over to Strots's pillow, take her cigarettes and her lighter, and transfer them to the top drawer of my desk.

Then I smooth the clothes that I did not change, put on my jacket, and emerge from my room, secure in the knowledge that the disapproving man in the suit, who is indeed waiting for me outside in the hall, will not be able to tell that the components of my black outfit have not been altered.

"Let's go," I tell him. "I'm ready to talk."

chapter
TWENTY-TWO

Mr. Pasture's office is in the administrative building down on the very edge of campus. It's the only modern construction inside the iron gates of Ambrose—other than the Strotsberrys' nascent sports complex—and the two-story structure appears to have been punished for the temerity of having been born in the seventies by its banishment to the fringes. With brick walls and thin, metal-trimmed windows, it's stylistically unoriginal and unremarkable, even as it hearkens back to a specific era in American architecture.

The steps are concrete and take us beneath an overhang to a set of glass doors onto which the crest of Ambrose has been etched. Inside, I recognize the flooring immediately. It's the pressed commercial-grade ceramic tiles that I trod over at my schools at home, flecks of various beige extraction forced to marry for life in squares that are cemented into place.

"I'm down this hall."

These are the first words he's said to me since we left my room, and his air of disapproval, which seemed to intensify during our promenade, is so pronounced, I wonder if he hates his job in addition to me.

I follow him past fake-wood doors that have black-and-white nameplates on them with titles like *Comptroller*, *Faculty Liaison*, and *Associate Dean of Students*.

So there's an understudy of him? I think. *Bet that's fun.*

Mr. Pasture's office is at the end of the corridor, just as he's promised, and its glass entrance is embellished by the Ambrose flag on one side and the American flag on the other. Both standards are hanging off poles set into heavy bases, and they are so large and grandly out of proportion, they make me think of ball gowns. Inside, there's a little waiting area with a lot of dark blue carpet and walls hung with pictures of students in matching frames. His secretary is behind her desk, typing something. When the phone rings, she answers it in a dead voice.

"Mr. Pasture's office, dean of students."

Twisting her chair toward her orderly blotter, she moves a pad closer, wedges the receiver between her shoulder and her ear, and makes *mm-hmm* sounds as she writes. I'm not sure of her age. She could be forty, she could be sixty. Maybe she's twenty and the heavy atmosphere here has depressed her to such a degree that she's lost her will to live.

"In here," Mr. Pasture informs me.

He opens a fake-wood door with a flourish, as if he's revealing something he regards with great pride and expects others to as well. It is a corner office, it's true, but the windows are small and offer a lackluster view through the campus fencing of the sporadic traffic into Greensboro Falls's meager town center. But perhaps he's showing off all his framed degrees. There are a lot of diplomas hanging on the fake-wood-paneled walls. Or maybe it's the objects on his desk that he's preening over?

He has many pictures in fancy frames facing out into the room, and they all feature him with people I recognize from television news broadcasts.

Where are the ones of his family, I wonder. Then again, they must be in frames he faces toward himself while he sits behind the desk—oh, wait. There are none of those.

Mr. Pasture closes the door behind me and I look to a sitting cluster of a couch and flanking chairs, its coffee table bearing copies of a tome on Ambrose's history, its area rug like a plate serving up the balanced meal of the furniture arrangement.

But he doesn't want us over there. He goes around behind his desk, and indicates the chair opposite him, as if I need the direction to quell any confusion about where I must be. As I take the seat he directs me into, we're separated by all of his photographs, as well as a telephone, a lamp, a coffee mug on a coaster, and a stack of reports in folders. He couldn't be behind a better firewall if he'd built one of cinder blocks.

He does not even spare me a professional smile. "So I understand yesterday there was some unpleasantness in Tellmer Hall."

Directly behind him, hanging on the wall, is an antique oil painting of a man draped in red robing, with a shepherd's crook in one hand and a Bible in the other. His vestments and bishop's hat are marked with symbols of the cross, and in the background, there are Gothic arches that recede in perspective as well as a beehive that suggests his cathedral needs an exterminator. I don't need to read the little plate on the ornate frame to know it is St. Ambrose, the man whose life-example of Christian leadership is the basis of the school.

As I regard the somber portrait that sits at Mr. Pasture's back as both a guardian and a warning not to violate tradition, that's when it hits me. This man intends on becoming the next headmaster. He cannot wait to give the reins of this also-ran position to his associate dean, and leave this crappy building and second-tier job, and install himself in the headmaster's house, which is a grand white wedding cake of a mansion with its own garden, cooking staff, and office facilities. This venerable and somber painting and these photographs that face outward and the diplomas with the school names of august places of highest learning are not for the students, but for the parents of the students as well as the staff he oversees.

I'll bet he takes his buddies in the gold-leafed frame with him.

Looking away from the piercing eyes of the saint, I clear my throat. "A copy of an essay I wrote was—"

"That is not relevant to why we are here."

I'm taken aback by his starchy comment. "But it is. That's the reason why Strots—Ellen, I mean—"

"I am uninterested in the particulars of what was put into those mailboxes. What matters is the fact that one of *my* students was physically attacked in her very own dorm."

Something about his tone as he emphasizes the "my" before "student," coupled with all those pictures of himself with important people, makes me wonder whether he'd have such a personal stake in this matter if Greta were not the daughter of a trustee of the school, Mr. Stanhope's bankruptcy aside. And this dean is wrong about what matters. My essay, served up as it was with malicious intent to everyone in my dorm, is a boxing match of over five thousand double-spaced, twelve-point Times New Roman body blows, against which I had, and have, no defenses to offer.

"Provocation is very much the issue," I say. "Strots had a reason for what she did. She was protecting me."

"There is no excuse at the St. Ambrose School for Girls for settling any disagreement with bodily harm." His brows go down. "And let us talk about Ellen Strotsberry. It has come to my attention that there have been difficulties with her during the previous year. I gather that the student affected did not feel comfortable coming forward about them until the attack yesterday, at which point she believed that she could no longer handle matters privately. Given the deviant nature of the complaint's details, I do not blame her."

Damn you, Greta, I think to myself.

And I hate that I was right.

"I have no idea what you're talking about," I say.

"If you lie, it will not reflect favorably upon your record here at Ambrose."

"I don't even know what you're asking me."

He steeples his hands, and his distaste of me is simmering below the surface of his brisk, professional demeanor. I take both the revulsion and his composure as signs that I'm a perfunctory visit for him. He's already made his mind up about everything.

"I understand that the door to your room is closed a lot," he says.

"Excuse me?"

"This is unusual in the dorms, is it not."

Maybe for "his" students it is. "There's no rule against privacy. And it's not always—"

"Why exactly do you and your roommate feel the need to have your door shut all the time."

This is not a question. So I answer the statement with an inquiry just to keep the conversation balanced. "What are you suggesting, exactly?"

"Are you and your roommate behaving inappropriately behind that closed door?"

"Are we having sex, you mean?"

I take a mean-spirited thrill at how his eyes dart away and an ugly flush colors his face. It feels good to make him uncomfortable.

"Have you read the student handbook?" he says as his stare returns to mine.

"Yes, I have." I decide to stop playing games. "And no. We are not having sex. The door is closed for another reason."

"And why is that?"

"What is Strots being accused of exactly?"

"Why is your door closed, if there is nothing inappropriate happening."

"Tell me what Strots is being accused of."

We both lose our questioning inflections and turn to declarations because we have exited rhetorical territory as well as any semblance of polite behavior. We are arguing, and I have a thought I need to keep this hard-line going. I have to be strong, for Strots.

Mr. Pasture sits back in his padded leather chair. "Do you want to stay here at Ambrose?"

"Yes." The definitiveness of my answer surprises me. "I do."

I cannot imagine going to school anywhere else at this point, even with Greta and everything she has done. Even with Nick Hollis. Even without—no, I will not think like that. My roommate cannot be expelled.

"If you want to stay, then tell me why your door is closed."

"I smoke. It's closed because I smoke."

Mr. Pasture smiles a little, and almost, but not completely, manages to keep his nastiness out of it. "You realize that is a violation of school rules."

"Yes, and for a first offense, I am to be put on probation. You can't expel me. It's in the handbook."

"If you smoke frequently, it is not a first offense."

"Then I'm only admitting to doing it once, and by all means, try to prove it's a habit. I've never been caught."

The dean of students studies me for a long moment, and I sense a shift of position in him, but it's not one that will help me. "Has Ellen Strotsberry ever made any advances toward you?"

I purposely recoil. "Absolutely not. She's not gay. Are you serious?"

His eyes narrow. "Yes, I am very serious."

"Well, I've never seen anything to suggest that, and she certainly hasn't done anything inappropriate toward me. Now, come on, what's she really being accused of? Because you aren't asking me anything about what happened yesterday in the phone room."

Mr. Pasture continues to stare at me for a while. Then his disdainful demeanor eases, as if he has come to the conclusion that not only am I not attractive enough for even a lesbian to bother with, I have no such immoral tendencies myself. This makes me wonder what he would think of the impure fantasies I had about my residential advisor. Then again, no doubt they are preferable, on the sliding scale of wickedness, because at least they are not against God's word.

I consider making a revelation about the marriage vows that have been broken at his school of lofty Christian standards. But my roommate's sexual orientation is at the base of all of this, and going into the Greta and Nick affair would be a distraction I'd have trouble backing up with solid evidence. I must present my case solely as it relates to me, and do it quickly, as I sense that, now that I'm not an avenue to further condemn my roommate's behavior, he is going to kick me out of his office pretty quickly.

"Greta Stanhope has been bullying me since I arrived here on campus."

Mr. Pasture frowns and leans forward in his chair, as if I've addressed him in a foreign language and he is trying to place my nouns and verbs somewhere in the context of the Latin tradition.

"It started with my shampoo," I hurry on. "She emptied it out and put water in the container. Then she poured bleach into the washing machine my clothes were in. She put a falsified memo about a geometry test in my mailbox, and she tried to get a student from St. Michael's to ask me to dance at the Fall Fling to embarrass me. She's been coming after me this whole semester, and yesterday was the final straw. She got ahold of my essay, the one that was used to get me in here, and she had someone make copies of it. She filled the dorm's mailboxes, all of them. Everyone read—" As the horror of that moment comes back, my voice wavers, but I force myself to go on. "Everyone read it. Everyone knows that I have bipolar—I mean, that I am bipolar."

I could have done without the hiccup at the end. Otherwise, it's a pretty good speech, considering how scared I am. How lonely. How sad. This man, this officious, disapproving man, managed to beat down even Strots, so it's no surprise I'm losing my momentum. But I have to go on.

"I told Strots about what Greta has been doing to me a while ago. I told her everything. She knows what Greta is like, and she—"

Mr. Pasture holds up his hand. "I'm going to stop you right there."

"But it's the truth—"

"Is it?"

"Yes! I'm telling you, you're blaming the wrong person for what happened in the phone room! You're totally wrong. Greta deserved what she got and—"

"May I remind you for a second time that here at St. Ambrose, we do not promote physical violence as a method of conflict resolution," he says in a bored tone. "And as for your accusations, Miss Taylor, they are quite serious. Where's your proof?"

"I know what happened when I squeezed my shampoo bottle. I know what was done to my clothes—"

"What shampoo bottle? Which clothes?"

"I can show you the spots." I stand up and pull my black shirt out between the halves of my jacket, pointing to the bleached areas that I'd had to dye black. "See? They're right here."

I lean over his desk, pushing at some of the frames, holding the shirt forward, knowing it is the vital clue that will save Strots, that will take down our tormentor.

Mr. Pasture glances down. "I see nothing."

I jab my forefinger at the subtle variations in the color. "It's right here."

"That does not look like a bleach spot to me. And sit down. Now."

My legs go weak and I fall into the chair. Dropping my eyes to the front of my shirt, I see what he does. Or rather, everything that he does not. The variation in the black is so minor that it could be explained away by wear and tear or manufacturer's error.

I never in a million years thought my solution to the problem Greta created, the one that she intended to throw me off my wardrobe stride, would prove to be too successful.

"I am not unaware of your . . . difficulties." Mr. Pasture's voice shifts away from disapproval to a chilly kind of dispassionate compassion, as one might feel for a squirrel that has ended up under the tires of one's Mercedes. "I realize that you have struggles other students do not."

I look back up at him. "That has nothing to do with what Greta has—"

"Doesn't it?" He puts his hand on the stack of folders. "You're subject to hallucinations. It is in your medical release."

I shake my head. "No. I know what happened to me. I know what Greta did to me, to my things."

"Do you? Are you sure? Or is this all in your mind."

"I'm not making anything up," I breathe.

For a moment, I'm stripped naked again, just as I was when I entered my dorm and realized what those girls were reading. I am beyond disarmed. I am dismantled, in pieces here on the far side of Mr. Pasture's pictures and position of authority. I am a glass shattered and falling onto his carpet.

Because . . .

The truth is, I am only ninety-nine percent sure about the series of events that have occurred since my first day here, since the moment Greta stuck her hand out to me by our parents' cars, when my mother declared she and I would be best friends and I knew that that was never going to happen. I am merely ninety-nine percent sure of what was in that shampoo bottle, of how my clothes were ruined, of what I read in that geometry memo, of the motivations of that boy from St. Michael's.

I'm even using the fact that I am currently in this office, speaking to the dean of students about an attack that was witnessed by easily twenty other girls, as a way of grounding myself in what I think happened yesterday.

Assuming I am actually sitting here. Assuming that this is reality.

With a shaking hand, I reach out and touch the front of his desk. It seems solid. It really does.

"Miss Taylor," the dean says in a gentler voice. "If you're not hallucinating, then the only other explanation is that you're fabricating things to try to save your roommate. Why else have you not told anyone? Why have you not gone to your floor's residential advisor and made a report of the incidences?"

Because he's fucking the girl who's doing it all to me, Mr. Pasture.

The bald truth rides up my throat, but it stays in my mouth. If I can't be completely sure about the torment, I can't trust the pink panties. And in this minefield of allegations of misconduct, tossing Nick Hollis's reputation into the mix is something I can't do given my mind's ability to conjure events out of thin air. It's just not fair to him, in the event my mind made it all up.

I raise my eyes. The dean's change of affect is pronounced and totally devastating to me. He is no longer hostile because he's no longer dealing with a student who is being deliberately oppositional. He has softened because he is dealing with a disabled person, someone from whom it would be cruel to expect normal functioning.

Of all the things my illness can take from me, I never expected it would be my credibility.

And certainly not when such a thing matters most.

chapter
TWENTY-THREE

I return to Tellmer by myself and have no memory of the trip back. The fact that I am suddenly at the door to Strots's and my room supports the dean of students' position that the reliability of my testimony is suspect. Opening the way in, I find my roommate dismantling her bed. She's lifted the mattress up off its seat of springs.

She looks over at me. "Have you seen my cigarettes?"

That this is the first thing she asks does not offend me. Nothing has changed in her situation as a result of my going off with Mr. Pasture, and I'll bet she didn't have any hope in that regard as I was leaving.

"Sorry. I took them."

As her face registers surprise, I close the door and go over to retrieve the Marlboros and their matching red Bic lighter from my desk.

"I didn't smoke any," I say as I hand her things back to her. "I moved them to prove I was smoking."

The statements, taken at face value, make no sense, but neither of us is in a rush to sort it all out. I sit on my bed. She sits on hers and cracks the window.

"You want to be a smoker now?" she says in a conversational tone, as if we're waiting in a doctor's office or perhaps at a beauty parlor, as if she doesn't care about the answer particularly, but feels the need to make neighborly talk.

"I figured out what Greta was going to tell them, how she was going to spin everything. I figured they would ask about the closed door, so I wanted to have an excuse. I told them I was smoking and that's why it was closed. Not because we were . . . doing anything."

I'm as defeated as she, but for a different reason. In her case, the truth has been used against her. In my case, the truth does not exist.

She looks up from the lit end of her cigarette. The smile that touches her face is sunlight breaking through dark clouds, a welcome slice of golden warmth that does not last.

"You did that?" she says.

"I wanted to help. Any way I could." I shrug. "But it didn't matter. They don't believe me—not about Greta's pranks or anything else."

Strots exhales toward the window. "They want to kick me out."

I close my eyes. I am going to cry. "Greta deserved what she got in the phone room."

"Not because of that."

I glance over. "Because Greta told them you hit on her last year?"

"She said I forced myself on her. They called it sexual assault."

This freezes me, even as I tell myself I should not be surprised. But I just assumed Greta would play the made-a-pass card, although why should I have underestimated her. Of course, she would take it further.

"That's a lie," I say.

I have seen the heartbreak in Strots's eyes. I can guess the illusion of mutual love Greta engineered, and having to use her own body to do the job would be totally irrelevant to her.

"I thought we were in a relationship," Strots says as she bends down and untwists the cap of her soda ashtray. "She saw things very differently, at least according to what she told them."

"Oh, God . . . Strots."

"The charge against me—how did they put it? 'Conduct unbecoming an Ambrose girl.' I believe that's the gay part, but it covers the sexual assault, too." She laughs in a hard rush. "Get this, though—Greta is refusing to press charges."

"She better not. She'd have to lie to the police."

"She says she's too traumatized, and the school wants to cover it up anyway. Oh, and the physical attack downstairs? They didn't even bring it up. Then again, they have more than enough against me already. Jesus Christ, to think that I nearly killed her and that's no big deal compared to this school's Christian values being offended. Unbelievable."

"When are you leaving?"

Strots laughs again without smiling. "Well, see, that's the thing. My father being who he is, and that sports center only half finished? They're 'meeting' with him."

"Who is?"

"The headmaster. I don't know what's going to happen. They want me gone, but they like that new weight room and gymnasium and the endowment. They're going to try to negotiate to keep the project going."

"So maybe you'll get to stay," I say hopefully.

"Doubt it. My father is *pissed* at me. If the administration doesn't kick me out, he'll probably pull me himself."

As she taps her ashes into the Coke's narrow neck, I cannot fathom that we will not sit like this ever again. I begin to tear up.

"I tried," I say as I look down at my shirt, at the black expanse that has been so completely and competently dyed. "I really did. Maybe if I hadn't bought the ColorStay . . ."

"What?"

"I doesn't matter." I shake my head, and correct myself. "*It*. It doesn't matter."

"You're right about that." Strots stares out the window, one arm tucked around her middle, the other up on the vertical so that her hand with the cigarette is right by her tanned face. "I really hate her. I really fucking hate Greta Stanhope."

Strots drops her butt into the bottle and exhales in exhaustion as she looks around. Then she gets up, goes to her closet, and pulls out the camping backpack and the duffel she walked in with that first day.

As she tosses them on her bed, I say, "Why are you packing? You don't know you have to go."

My tone is pleading. I feel like a small child, staring up into the face of an adult who has the power to ruin my life.

"Might as well be ready. And I can't sit still."

I take care of the stationary side of things while Strots makes an efficient decampment from her bureau, her desk, and her bed. Even as I keep out of her way, I'm participating in the preparation for her departure: I'm the one doing the crying. Tears are rolling off my face and landing on the dyed shirt that did us in.

I'm crying for Strots. For Keisha. For me.

It's all so wrong. However, I think that Strots wants to leave. Not because she doesn't like me or love Keisha, but because she's done with everything here. I can't blame her.

When my roommate has finished with her packing, she puts her load by the door. "Listen, I have a favor to ask."

I sniffle and drag my palms down my eyes and my face. "Anything."

She points to a plate and a chef's knife that she took out from under her bed and left on the corner of her desk. "Can you return those to Wycliffe tomorrow? I feel bad throwing 'em out. I shouldn't have taken them in the first place."

"Yes, of course."

"Thanks." She looks at the ceiling. "Anyway, I'm going upstairs."

As her voice gets rough, more tears fall from my eyes and I wipe my face again, this time on the rough sleeve of the jacket I've forgotten to take off.

"What do I do if someone comes for you?" I ask.

I'm thinking of her father. In my mind, Mr. Strotsberry looks like Ronald Reagan but has a temper like Hulk Hogan, and whether I am right or wrong about either, I do not want to have to see him or talk to him.

"You better bring me back down here," she says. "My father doesn't know about Keisha."

In this, I know she's talking about the relationship, not the friendship.

"Okay."

She nods and leaves, shutting the door quietly. I panic that we haven't said goodbye properly, but her stuff is here. She'll be back for her things. I'll have my chance, I tell myself.

Then again, knowing my roommate—my ex-roommate—her request to take the plate and knife back and my agreement to do so is going to be the extent of our parting, the mission assigned and accepted, a substitute for the tight, disconsolate embrace I have in mind.

In Strots's absence, I look at the now-barren side of the room. The end of the year seems decades away, and I have no idea how I'm going to do this alone. We've known each other only six weeks, but in so many ways, she's been my partner in a wilderness we've had to protect ourselves against. Now I am without any backup whatsoever.

The prospect of going solo fills me with a cold dread that is not relieved as I consider what my mother said. Yes, I can always go home—but if I leave like this, Greta has beaten me. I'll be giving her the trophy in her game against me, my capitulating exit something she can inscribe with her name. As I consider my choices, Strots's initial advice remains as excellent as ever.

I must not give Greta what she wants, and from now on, I'm denying her the prize of me not just for myself, but for Strots—

Through the window Strots opened, I hear a car pulling into the parking area. I lean over the corner of my desk and look down. It is long and black, a limousine, and a driver is getting out from behind the wheel. He's wearing a uniform, like something out of a *Dynasty* episode. I have a thought that my mother would love this sight. Like the *lawn*, it's everything she admires about Ambrose.

My heart pounds so hard I cough.

The driver doesn't make it down to the rear door in time. Then again, the limo's flank seems of football-field length. From the back, a man dressed in a dark blue pinstriped suit emerges. He is facing away from me, toward the wild foliage and the river. He is tall and his hair is the same color as Strots's.

There's a shout from above my window. The man turns and looks up. His face has all the same angles that Strots's does, her features passed through a transforming filter of masculinity and middle age. And he is nothing like Hulk Hogan in his obvious anger. He is ice cold, not red hot.

He nods curtly and points at the ground in front of him.

A minute later, Strots emerges down in the parking area. The driver gets back behind the wheel and closes his door. I do a quick check of the faculty cars. They're in their proper places, Nick Hollis's, the married couple from the third floor's, and Ms. Crenshaw's. I pray that no one has to go out for a gallon of milk right now. My roommate looks humiliated, and I don't want anyone to get close enough to hear whatever words are exchanged. The visual is more than enough for all the eyes that are no doubt staring out of the rear of our dorm.

Mr. Strotsberry does most of the talking and Strots, for all of her athletic strength, seems to get smaller, even as she remains the same height and weight. I want to go down and demand that her father hear me out. I want to tell him his daughter is my only friend, my one champion, a source of kindness in a place that so often feels hostile. If she gets kicked out, the wrong side wins.

But I cannot move. I witness the whole thing, a bird's-eye view of an argument that is almost exclusively one-sided. When it's done, Strots turns away and disappears into the dorm. I expect the limo to wait for her to bring down her things. It doesn't. Immediately after her father reenters its dark confines, the black Lincoln oils away, making wide, ocean-liner turns that nearly score the front grille of Nick Hollis's Porsche and the back corner of Ms. Crenshaw's beater.

Strots comes into our room moments later. Her eyes are red-rimmed and her cheeks are pale. "Well, there we are."

The door is still open behind her, and as she avoids my eyes, I know she doesn't want to get emotional and she needs the threat of her vulnerability showing to others to help strengthen her self-control.

"Why is he leaving?" I ask. "Is he making you take the bus home?"

Or perhaps forcing her to walk back to Boston?

Strots stands over her packed duffel as if she doesn't know what to do with it. As if she's never seen one before. "I'm staying."

"Wait—what! You are?" I jump up at the same time my voice soars into a lilt. "They're letting you stay?"

"My father told them that if they expel me on hearsay, he's pulling everything. The sports center, the endowment, the scholarships. At the end of the day, it's her word against mine. Personally, I think it's a cost/benefit thing. There's not as much money on the Stanhope side of things, not anymore."

I clasp my hands in front of my chest, like I'm in prayer. "But what about the phone room?"

"I'm on probation for that. The shit Greta pulled with your essay made it easier for them."

Apparently, Mr. Pasture was wrong. There is a justification for violence at St. Ambrose, and it's money.

As Strots falls silent, I expect more of a happy reaction. I expect any reaction at all. She just stares at her packed clothes.

"What's wrong?" I ask.

"It's hard to let someone down just by being alive." Strots shakes her head. "Especially when it's your father."

I think about how many times I've made my mother come to a psychiatric hospital—once even in the back of an ambulance. I am unsurprised at her father's prejudice, but also very, very sorry.

However, because my survival is at stake, I feel the need to pin down what affects me the most. "You're staying in school, though."

"He doesn't want me back home, so . . . yeah. I am."

As the words drift, a familiar scent of perfume wafts into the room. We both turn our heads to the open door. Out in the hall, Greta emerges from her frilly lair, fresh as a daisy, her hair curled at the ends, her Calvin Klein outfit worthy of an ad on a billboard in Times Square.

When she sees us, she focuses only on Strots. Then she looks at the duffel with satisfaction. "That's a little much just for an away game, isn't it."

Strots only stares at her.

I walk over and stand between my roommate and Greta. "It didn't work. She's not leaving."

I want to spray-paint the words on the wall above the bitch's bed so that the neon drips onto her monogrammed fucking duvet cover and ruins it.

"Well, then, we're not done," she says softly. "Are we."

There is a long pause and I search Greta's face for any kind of hint about how she'll escalate things. She is like a marble statue, however, nothing but a faithful representation of her features. I tell myself she must be seething inside.

I look back at Strots. She is also still, so still, in the manner of an animal. But not because she's scared. Her stare is locked on the other girl like the sight of a gun.

I have a thought that Greta should watch what she says. And maybe where she goes after this. What is a game to her . . . does not look like hopscotch to my roommate.

Strots takes the cigarettes I was prepared to pose with to protect her, and as she crosses over and steps out of our room, she says something to me, but I don't hear it.

Greta smiles as my roommate goes by her. "Going upstairs to see your girlfriend? Say hi to Keisha for me."

Strots is already out of the scope of our doorway so I can't catch her reaction. But Greta's feigned look of innocence, as if she's responding to a glare, makes me furious. I'm also worried about who might have overheard her.

Before I know what I'm doing, I am standing in front of the girl as my roommate walks off. "What is wrong with you."

Those beautiful blue eyes shift over to me. And then she laughs. "This. Coming from somebody who's certifiably insane? Hey, do they give you a little certificate when they tell you you're nuts? Is that how the term got started—"

"Why do you have to do this to people?" Tears make my vision wavy. "Why do you have to be so cruel? Is it because your father spent all your inheritance?"

Her hitch of breath suggests that the cheap shot hit deep. "You don't know anything about me."

I think of the night I interrupted her and Nick. "Yes, I do."

As her eyes narrow, she manages to look downright ugly, and I wonder whether she, too, is back at the nocturnal interruption that seemed to start it all between us.

"Like what," she demands.

For a moment, I almost say it. But then I shy away. "You're fucking mean."

I just can't do it when it comes to our RA. I don't trust him. I don't trust her. Unfortunately, I don't trust myself.

"I'm not mean," she says. "I just like playing with dominoes. The cascade is so much fun to watch."

As she turns away, I put force in my voice. "Leave Strots alone."

"Or what."

"I'm going to hurt you."

Greta stares over her shoulder. "Sorry, reject. Dominoes can't fight falling. But go on and try. Let's see what happens with that."

I really want to reveal what I know about her and our residential advisor. But suddenly, my mind breaks free of the commonly experienced environment and takes me on a trip to an alternate version of our hallway, one where blood flows, red as the ruby studs in Greta's earlobes, glossy and thick as maple syrup. As the girl takes her leave of me, the scent of copper floods my nose, replacing her flowery perfume, and I look down to find the carpet soaked with plasma. My sneakers *schmuck-schmuck-schmuck* through it as I turn and go back into my room.

I slam my door so hard, I make myself jump.

As I look around, I see walls running with blood. There is so much of it, there are pools forming on the floor, licking up the feet of our bed frames, swamping Strots's still-packed luggage, seeping into our closets.

I feel the cloying squeeze around my ankles as the levels rise. I slosh over to my mattress, searching for higher ground. I open my window, so that it will run out and not drown me, a river's worth of Greta's blood flowing freely down the back of Tellmer, landing on the cars, making its way to the low point of the streambed in a tsunami that knocks over trees and consumes the straggly brush.

My last cogent thought is that I'll bet Ms. Crenshaw never thought she'd have to roll up Nick Hollis's windows against the likes of this.

chapter
TWENTY-FOUR

When I finally return to my body and my version of normal awareness, I am sitting on my bed and it is dark out. In the glow from the security lights, I can tell that the walls of my room are once again white, the floor is dry, and my roommate's packed things are not sponges to be wrung out for the benefit of the Red Cross. I lift my hands. There is no blood on them. I inspect my sneakers. They are free of the kinds of stains you have to call the police about. Likewise, my pant legs are clean.

As I go to close my window, I nonetheless have to double-check the parking area. Thanks to the outdoor illumination, I can see the faculty cars. The back lawn. The trees and the ground cover that obscure the river's edge. Everything looks right.

I am so relieved that I begin to shake. I am also disoriented and weak, as if the hallucination required calories even though my physical body didn't go anywhere.

I look at the time on my alarm clock. Dinnertime is almost over. I have been gone for nearly two hours. In an effort to ground myself, I force my brain to enter into an elaborate assessment of the pluses and minuses of a trip over to Wycliffe for food. This is not because I'm hungry, but because I'm scared of where my mind has taken me this time.

I am afraid of the violence.

Suicide is one thing. Murder, another.

I go back to inspecting my hands and wonder, as if they belong to someone else, exactly what they're capable of. I consider using them to unpack Strots's duffel and backpack for her, but the butler-ing seems intrusive, even though it would provide me with proof that I have control over where I place my palms and what I grip with my fingers.

I picture Greta standing in the open doorway of her room, all gift-wrapped in her superiority and her *Seventeen* magazine clothes. I have spent little time thinking about her motivations, her origins, her own perspective on her behavior, particularly as it all relates to me. When you are in wartime, you do not pause to dissect whether the bullets coming at you have been shot out of something made by Smith & Wesson or Remington. And in fact, the question I posed to her was not actually an inquiry into her backstory. By asking her why she behaves as she does, I was begging her to stop in a pathetic rhetorical.

I think of my meeting with Mr. Pasture, and the self-doubt that kept my mouth shut.

I consider Nick Hollis that first night, fighting with his wife over the phone.

I remember the unshed tears in my roommate's eyes as she talked about the girl who didn't just break her heart, but shoved a lit stick of TNT into her chest cavity.

Finally, I hear Greta's voice in my head: *Well, then, we're not done. Are we.*

My eyes go to the bank of windows. I note the thin, single-sheet panes of glass. The fragile old crosshairs made of wood and putty. The drop down to the hard, cold asphalt of the parking area. To reaffirm the height at which I am above the ground, I lean forward to look over the lip of the sash and then I create an *in vivo* physics problem to solve. If I had enough of a running start, I believe I could land on Nick Hollis's Porsche.

The idea that my body's last earthly mission would be to smash the sports car's hood and blow out all its safety glass has electric appeal.

The impulse stays in the holster, however.

Because for once, I want to hurt someone other than myself.

When I finally stand up, it's not to go eat at Wycliffe. I walk to my closet, crossing the ghostly chessboard pattern of the windowpanes on the floor, and I am ultimately not surprised at my destination. I suppose it's kind of inevitable.

There is only one thing that I can do in this situation, one piece of leverage I have against Greta. But it is a warhead that will be sure to cause considerable collateral damage—and, going with that unoriginal metaphor, it has a somewhat unreliable guidance system.

Once I let it loose, I will not be able to control the aftermath.

But I cannot let this stand. I cannot sit on the sidelines and watch Margaret Stanhope further escalate things with my roommate.

As my closet door opens before me, I am called by a higher purpose. Onto my knees I drop, landing on my backup pair of black boots, which I push out of the way even though the hardwood is just as uncomfortable. Breaking into a nervous sweat, I pat my palms along the dusty floor until I reach my ugly suitcases. I shove them off to the side.

For a moment my heart stops because I don't see anything there—

Wedged into the dark corner . . . is something small and silky and soft.

And pink.

Exhaling in a rush, I wad Greta's panties tightly in my palm and I am dizzy with relief as I extract myself and stand back up.

I stay where I am, panting and shaky, until I hear a voice right outside my door that recedes down the hall. This refocuses me. Shoving the underwear into the pocket of the jacket I haven't taken off since I went on the promenade to Mr. Pasture's office, I stumble out of my room. It is then that the limits to my planning become apparent.

I only have relative evidence and I'm not sure how to fix that. The panties don't prove anything, really. Their context was the thing, not their existence.

And I still have my credibility problem with the administration.

In the hall, I head for the main stairs because I am distracted and it is a habit, but I stop as I come up to the steps. Down below, I hear many voices, and the volume of them is doubling and redoubling.

I forgot. There's a mandatory dorm meeting now. To discuss community expectations and standards for behavior.

I look over my shoulder to Nick Hollis's door and think of that portrait of St. Ambrose. Not fucking the students is part of those community rules, but somehow, I doubt that is going to come up.

Moving quicker now, I head for the far end of the hallway, to the stairs that will take me all the way down to the basement. I'm not clear what I'm doing, and this adds to my sense of urgency because action *must* be taken. Wrongs must be righted, yet I am an unreliable and feeble white knight. The dean of students isn't going to suddenly believe me, even if I drop this wisp of Victoria's Secret with the Stanhope name tag into the field of framed photographs on his neat desk.

The next thing I'm aware of is that I'm in the basement, and when I open the dorm's back door, the cold slaps at me. The shallow parking lot has two cars in it now: the couple from the third floor's station wagon and Nick Hollis's Porsche. I stare at the vehicles as if they might take me somewhere helpful. Which is ridiculous. You can't drive to veracity, even if "city" is part of the word.

Something hits the bridge of my nose and I look up. Rain.

Overhead, I hear the dimmed cacophony of the dorm meeting, the chatter of the girls as they assemble echoing throughout the parlor's vast open space. I imagine Nick will bring everyone to order when it is time, and I picture Greta staring at him through a logjam of heads and shoulders. Does she think about screwing him in those moments?

I step farther out onto the lawn, crossing my arms over my jacket to keep warm, the rain collecting in my hair at the crown of my head. There is that big, beautiful oak tree about thirty feet from the parking area, its tremendous branches unfurling into a canopy that doesn't reach the RAs' cars, a lucky thing given all the leaves that are dropping. I duck behind the trunk because I am not going to that meeting, and my eyes rise to our residential advisor's row of windows on the second floor. I see him walking around his apartment. He is putting on a baseball cap. I know the one. He told me he got it from his cousin who is a Cincinnati Reds fan.

When did his wife leave again? I wonder. *Right after that dinner with his father? Does she suspect anything?*

I think she does. I think that was what the drunken phone call was about.

I look away, as if Nick Hollis can sense what I have in my pocket, these panties he took off a fifteen-year-old while his spouse was away, these panties that are my leverage—if I only knew what to do with them. Who to tell. Who would believe me.

For some reason, I notice that Ms. Crenshaw's car is not in the third and final space, the one farthest from the door. The lights in her apartment are off as well. Given that she is never late for anything, and this is a mandatory meeting, she must be either hurrying back at a dead run or dead from having run into a telephone pole on a slick road.

It's probably not an accident. She strikes me as a too-careful driver, the kind who would create an accident while trying to avoid one. I'm ashamed of myself that I don't care whether she is dying or just late, and then I don't think about her at all. I'm too busy trying to find a way to use what I know and what I have. I knock on the doors of all kinds of hypotheticals, but each one of them is locked and none of my raps are answered—

All at once, I picture Ms. Crenshaw back on Mountain Day. I remember the look on her face as she sits on the picnic table next to me with her mound of coleslaw, forcing Nick Hollis into conversation. Even though he is married. Even though he is way out of her league. Even though he is clearly uninterested.

My eyes go to the pale blue Porsche. As usual, it's backed into the center spot, its sloping butt toward me. Ms. Crenshaw will have to put her Toyota in that farthest spot, the one that is just out of the range of the security lights that shine down from the roofline.

I look up to the second-floor RA's block of windows. They're dark now. He's left to go to the meeting.

I look at the Porsche.

And that's when my brain clicks with my location and informs me what I must do. The indecipherable line of algebra I am in, with only its solution extant up until now, suddenly reveals its values as readily apparent, the answer to the missing piece so facile and easy that I can't believe I haven't seen it the whole time.

As I move forward toward Nick Hollis's Porsche, I stick to the shadows, my black clothes disappearing me, especially as I pull the hood of my jacket up to cover my pale face. When I open his passenger side door, I duck down to stay out of the security lights, and I have to stretch my arm to put the panties on the seat.

Just before I shut things back up, I crank the window down four inches, and wipe my prints off the handle.

Like this is a murder scene.

The twist of pink silk glows like a gem on the caramel-colored leather.

Closing the car door, I back into the darkness like a ghost. Return to the tree. Hold my breath.

As the rain continues to come down, golden leaves fall through gnarled branches like One-Eyed Willy's doubloons, good fortune on the ground at my feet, everywhere.

This is the thought that is going through my mind as the glow from a pair of headlights pierces the night, the double beams crossing my dorm's rear lawn and penetrating the unruly foliage by the river—before swinging around and slashing at the tree I am hiding behind.

Ms. Crenshaw parks her car exactly where she must, in the last available space. In her inimitable way, she scrambles out from behind the wheel with all the elegance of a plumber, dragging along a pair of supermarket bags that clap her in the leg as she kicks her door shut.

She rounds the front of her car on the sidewalk in a rush, but she spares a glance at the pale blue Porsche. My heart pounds.

Do it, I will her. *DO IT. You always do—*

Ms. Crenshaw, with her two jangling bags, and her sloppy purse, and her flat, stringy, damp hair, keeps right on going.

She doesn't stop to put up the window. She's late. She's distracted. Either she hasn't seen the gap or she's decided that on a night like tonight, with everything else that's going on, she doesn't care about protecting Nick Hollis's vintage leather bucket seats.

Or perhaps her unrequited love has finally run its course.

She goes into the dorm.

I close my eyes and sag against the tree trunk. My mood sinks abruptly, sure as if a plug has been released and all of me is funneling out the soles of my sneakers. The black despair I feel is not just about Greta and Strots and Nick Hollis. It's everything about me, from the blood flood in my dorm room to the no-win in Mr. Pasture's office.

But I can't tailspin in this familiar trap. I've left my only leverage on the passenger seat of Nick's car. If he finds the panties there, he'll get rid of them, and I'll be left with nothing.

I step out from behind my cover. As I cross over to the cars, I am—

The dorm's basement door opens wide, and it is pushed with such force that the heavy weight slaps against the brick.

I freeze right in the middle of the grass, halfway from the tree to the parking area.

Ms. Crenshaw marches through the rain, muttering curses and tossing her damp hair. Her bags are not with her and neither is her purse. She must have dropped them somewhere inside.

Her head is down and I pray it stays that way because part of me is in the light, my right leg extended into the illumination that falls on the scruffy ground cover.

She goes around the rear end of the Porsche to the passenger side. With her back to me, she yanks the door as if it's the last thing on earth she wants to do and she leans into the car to crank the handle that operates the window—

Now she is frozen, too, the pair of us unmoving in the gentle, cold rain.

She bends down even farther and then slowly straightens, a splash of pink in her hand. She is no longer frustrated. She is no longer aware of the rain.

Ms. Crenshaw turns the panties over in her hand.

And reads the name tag.

After a moment that lasts the entirety of my life span, Ms. Crenshaw turns away from the Porsche and walks back to the dorm.

Just as she disappears into the basement, there is a silencing of the voices up above in the parlor. The meeting about conduct and behavior expectations has commenced. A moment later, the lights come on in Ms. Crenshaw's first-floor apartment. I see her go into her kitchen, put her purse and the groceries on the counter, and then just stand there, staring down at something.

I imagine it's the panties.

When something drips onto my nose, I realize that I have been in the same step-forward position long enough for the rain to have saturated the hood of my jacket, and its cotton fibers have begun out of necessity to release some of their aquatic burdens.

I look back to the Porsche.

I may have put down the window a crack, but Ms. Crenshaw has left the whole door open. It strikes me that the poor car is bearing the brunt of transgressions it played little active role in, assuming Nick Hollis didn't have sex with Greta in its interior—something I'm not sure is physically possible, even though Greta is thin as a dancer and no doubt just as flexible.

Owing to her age, and all.

It is upon this analysis of collateral automotive damage that I tiptoe over to the Porsche. There isn't time to mop up the water in the seat, which is, I see now, very accurately termed a "bucket." I also don't have a towel on me, and besides, it would be best that I'm not seen anywhere near the car.

Pulling my sleeve over my hand, I shut the door.

Oh, Greta, I think to myself as I jog off. *The dominoes have finally fought back.*

chapter TWENTY-FIVE

I can't fall asleep that night so I'm still awake when Strots finally sneaks down to our room after curfew. As she closes the door, I sit up in bed. In the dim glow from the security lights, she's a shadow that moves quietly.

"Hey," I say.

"Hey," she whispers back to me in the dark. "You didn't go to the meeting."

"No."

I was too busy planting evidence so a geometry teacher could draw lines and rays in her head and ruin the life of a future English professor. Or acclaimed novelist. Or whatever he wants to be.

Wanted, I correct in my head. And what is Sandra going to say about it all? Dear God, the man's life is over and it's my fault—

No, I remind myself, he chose the risk of exposure the moment he crossed that line. He probably just assumed that because everything has always been easy street for him, his golden-child good luck would continue no matter his actions.

And yet I still feel bad. Probably because he seemed so sincere when he was trying to help me.

"What happened?" I mumble.

"With the meeting? Nothing. Although shit got awkward when I walked in, which meant it was worth me going."

Strots changes inside her closet. She always does this, but not because she's embarrassed over her nudity. It's all about function, and since she hangs up most of her clothes on pegs in there, she can swap into her version of pj's with the alacrity of a magician's assistant between acts.

Tell her, I say to myself as I listen to the shuffle of clothes going off and on my roommate. *Tell her what you did.*

Even though I'm uneasy about what will happen to Nick Hollis, it's hard to be an anonymous hero, a Superman who works the back channels to avenge her roommate's honor and redress her own torment. Red capes fly off the shoulders of saviors for a reason and it's not to hide the light of good deeds under a bushel. Or a veil of humble secrecy.

Still, I stay silent on my side of Metropolis. Unlike Greta, I have no experience with engineering outcomes, especially not those involving underwear and Porsches and math teachers. Abruptly, I think of Ms. Crenshaw's overearnest, flurried nature, and wish I had any other messenger. But I had to work with what I had.

"G'night, Taylor."

I glance across the black and gray landscape of our room. In her bed, Strots is facing away from me, the curves of her shoulder and hip draped in bedding that's not monogrammed. I think about the other girls here, of their clothes and their jewelry, their purses and perfumes. And yet Strots's family is the one building the new sports center.

"Are you in love with Keisha?" I ask.

The instant the words leave my mouth, I want to snatch them back.

"Yeah," Strots says. "And she loves me, too. Totally."

"Be careful with her."

Strots rolls over and looks at me. "What the hell are you talking about."

"Not like that." I think of Greta, standing outside her room earlier, completely unbowed. "I don't want her to have to deal with Greta like we are, is all."

There's a long silence. "If she does anything to Keisha, I'll fucking kill her."

With that, Strots turns away again, and soon thereafter she's doing that percolating thing she does when she snores. How I envy her ability to shut herself off even in the midst of the chaos we're in. On my side of the room, that is just not possible.

I am still staring at the ceiling when the dawn's early light arrives with a blush at the horizon, as if the sky is shyly delighted by the sun's advances. Lack of sleep is dangerous for me, exactly what we bipolar patients do not need, and yet there is nothing to be done about the insomnia. My mind has been kindling all night, my silence and stillness only an exterior affect. Inside my skull, my thoughts are a heavy metal concert.

When the time comes, I go through my morning motions and so does Strots. We head to Wycliffe separately for food, and when I enter the cafeteria, I receive a lot of double takes and lingering stares. For a moment, I can't figure out why. And then the essay in all those mailboxes comes back to me. The good news is that none of that really matters now. There's another shoe that could be, should be, dropping, and I spend a lot of time glancing in the direction of Greta's table. Everything looks normal over there, but it's not going to stay that way.

Nick Hollis will catch more flak, for sure. And even if Greta doesn't get kicked out, because as a minor she really can't be blamed for the indiscretions of an adult, I will guarantee he won't have anything more to do with her. He'll be too worried about his own problems, and people who slip and fall do not want to go back and revisit their banana peel.

Talk about toys being taken away, and I wonder if Francesca is going to be pleased. I know in my gut she's not going to be surprised.

In first period English class, which I am once again grateful I do not have with Nick Hollis, I stare ahead and see nothing. I write things down in my spiral notebook that could be an adequate representation of what's covered by the teacher or might be doodles. I open my mouth and answer when called upon, and have no clue whether I'm speaking in tongues or not.

In Ms. Crenshaw's geometry class, which has been mysteriously rescheduled for a day early, I actually pay attention. Not to the material. To her. Does she have bags from lack of sleep under her eyes? Yes. Do her hands shake when she takes chalk to the board? Hard to tell, but I think so. Is her voice low-level anxious? I guess.

Except this was all true before last night in the rain, her wound-up agitation an *en tremblant* halo around her.

And there's an ironic twist to everything. She and I are truly on the same team now, really working together, just as she's always wanted—except she doesn't have any clue about the relay race we're in or that I've handed her the baton. Making things worse, I can't watch her going around the track, can't measure her stride or her stamina.

For that matter, I don't even know if we agree on the finish line.

What if her crush on Nick Hollis makes her determined to protect the man? She's already been taking care of his bucket seats this whole semester, without any encouragement from him. Quite the opposite. Maybe she confronted him and demanded a movie night in return for her silence?

I have to hope jealousy will cut that cord quickly.

At the end of the day, I take a walk around campus instead of heading back to my room. In doing so, I hope to give things a further chance to play out, as if my absence in the dorm is required for the situation to fulminate properly. The idea of passing another night in strained ceiling contemplation is torture in the hypothetical. If this insomnia actually transpires? I don't know how to get through another block of those creeping hours.

My roam takes me by the maturing superstructure of the Strotsberry Athletic Center. In spite of the late hour, there are workers crawling like ants around the site, welding, hammering, using heavy equipment. There is a long black limousine parked parallel to the construction zone, and it has to be Strots's father, still on campus after he strong-armed the administration into keeping his daughter in school. As I keep going, I find myself glad that the rich are treated differently than anybody else. Courtesy of this double standard, I'm getting to keep my roommate, and my desperation not to be without Strots makes me embrace the favoritism that inures to my benefit. To hers.

No wonder the people in my mother's magazines look so happy and self-satisfied. There is no uneven terrain for them, no matter their footwear.

As I arrive back at Tellmer, I'm not sure what to expect, and a strange, riding paranoia makes me rush up the stairs. It's hard to see how my own little game of dominoes might backfire on me and my roommate, but it could happen. Greta is far better at this kind of scheming than I. Much more practice, for one thing, and then there's the fact that the load she carries is far lighter, since she's jettisoned the weight of a conscience long ago.

Reaching the second-floor landing, I get an inkling something has changed. Nick Hollis's door is open. This is not unusual. There is, however, a pair of suitcases off to the side, like soldiers standing at attention in the presence of an officer.

Oh, shit. They've fired Nick and his wife is leaving him. I stumble and have to catch myself on the balustrade—

"Are you okay?"

A woman rushes out of the apartment as I trip, her arms stretched forward, her face concerned. She's tall and slender, with luxurious brown hair, and she smells of faded perfume and faint cigarette smoke. In her professional suit jacket and skirt, she is beautiful in the manner of a news anchor, all even, symmetrical features and innate elegance.

"Mrs. Hollis?" I say.

She smiles, revealing perfectly straight white teeth. "Call me Sandy. You must be Sarah."

Struck by how at ease she is, I look at the suitcases. Maybe she's just coming home, not leaving? So she doesn't know. Or maybe nothing's been done?

The information vacuum makes my head spin in dangerous ways. "How do you know me?"

"Nick's told me a lot about your book discussions, and happened to mention your favorite color is black. I figured it had to be you."

"Oh." Every time I blink, I see my sleeve-covered hand wiping my prints off the window crank of this woman's husband's Porsche's door.

"—surprised him by getting home early," she's saying with another open and honest smile. "It's so good to be here. I feel like I've been on the road all semester long, but I know you've been taking good care of Nick. God, you've done me a favor with talking about all his books with him. Fiction is not my thing."

I nod. I say something. I'm not sure what.

"Anyway," she says with a brisk cheerfulness, "now that my MacArthur Foundation grant has been discharged, I get to be home while I seek another round of funding. I don't know if Nick told you what I do, but I focus on municipal programming and outreach to support HIV-positive—" She waves her hand to stop herself, and I see that she wears the same kind of simple gold band that her husband does, only smaller. "None of that matters. I want you to come have dinner with us. I'm a terrible cook, but I am determined to learn more now that I have a little time off. What do you say?"

I look into her eyes. They are hazel, that catchall term for irises that are too brown to be green and too blue to be brown, and they have flecks in them that make me think of the pepper I sprinkle on my French fries.

"He told you about me, didn't he," I hear myself say to her.

Sandra Hollis's—*Sandy's*—face remains calm and composed, like a social worker who's been trained to stay calm and composed, no matter what's revealed to them. It makes me wonder what would happen if I told her about Greta's underwear. Would the expression change then?

"He said you're super smart, and that you should definitely be an English major in college. He told me that he's going to stay in touch with you after we leave at the end of this school year and give you a leg up at Yale in three years, if you want."

She's lying. Maybe not about the college admissions stuff, but certainly by omission about knowing the truth of my illness. She's too smooth, too prepared with her words.

Abruptly, she tilts her head. "Are you okay?"

As I just stare at her, she glances over her shoulder into the apartment. "Nick? Can you come out here—"

I am so sorry, I think to myself.

"About what?" she asks.

When she poses the question, I realize I've spoken out loud. I also realize how high I have raised the stakes in this game I am trying to play with Greta.

"I have to go," I say just as Nick steps into the open doorway.

He's wearing a deep red cashmere sweater, at least I think it has to be cashmere given how fine the knit is. And he's smiling as he drops a casual arm around his wife. She looks at him, her mouth moving as she brings him up to speed, and when she nestles her body into his, I doubt she's even aware of how comfortable she is with him. How loose. How unwound. The way she is with her husband is honest intimacy, and I'm the only one among the three of us who suspects it's not going to last much longer.

I look down at his jeans, and try to guess whether they're the ones I took out of the washer, the ones that Greta's panties were in. They seem similar. Don't all jeans look the same, though?

"God, Sarah, I feel like I haven't seen you in forever." Nick smiles. "And you've got to come to dinner—"

"I have to go study," I mumble.

"We'll make a date," he says as I trip over my feet again and take off.

I barely make it to the bathroom in time. Punching through the door, I go to the row of toilets, burst into a stall, and crash down onto my knees. I don't even bother to put the seat up as I retch. Nothing comes out, though, so I retch again. And again—

"Are you okay?"

When I hear the voice from up above, I have a thought that God is a female and She's checking in on me, and I promptly decide I must apologize for doubting Her existence all these years.

I lift my sweaty, flushed face out of the bowl.

Francesca is standing in the open doorway of the stall. She's put her hair up in a scrunchie and she has her toothbrush and toothpaste in her hand—and that's when I realize that she's been doing successfully what I just failed to execute: You can always tell when the pretty girls purge after they eat because they have to get their long, beautiful hair out of the way. It's the only time those locks are not down around their narrow shoulders.

"Well?" she prompts.

Even though she's inquiring about my welfare, it's not exactly with charity. From her superior, far more comely elevation, she's regarding me like a stray dog in the street that she may or may not have to call animal control about. Given her pursed lips, it's clear that she'd really rather write me off and keep going. She's not like Greta, though. If she leaves the stray with a broken leg in the middle of the road, it will bother her later. It will not sit right.

Just like putting my essay in all those mailboxes and showing up in tennis whites ultimately affected her.

"When Greta punched you in the eye on Mountain Day," I hear myself say, "was it because you knew what she was doing with Nick Hollis?"

The color drains out of the girl's face, transforming her subtle makeup job into Bozo the Clown's version of Maybelline.

"What are you talking about," she whispers.

I don't even try to get up off the bathroom floor. My legs won't handle my weight for so many reasons, and besides, I've been beneath her and her kind since the day I drove onto campus in a ten-year-old Mercury. Going eye to eye isn't going to change anything.

"It's not right," I say. "The whole thing. He's fucking married."

There are moments when the rigid hierarchy of teenage social status melts away, and this is one of them. The significance of what I've broached is so great that it sandblasts our distinctions of pretty girl and insane outcast away. We are merely human. And we are both appalled.

"How did you find out?" she says softly.

"It doesn't matter."

Francesca looks around the empty bathroom. I look at her. I realize that she, like Stacia, has been a blur to me, the unfocused background behind the object my camera's lens has been so sharply focused on. Her face is not as pretty as I've always thought it was, her nose a little too long in her lean face, her profile therefore birdlike as her chin is no match for its projection. I'm guessing she will fix this imbalance before she goes to college, and likely, too, the size of her breasts. Her skin is perfect, however, so smooth and unblemished that it is alabaster with a blood source. And of course, courtesy of her after-dinner toilet stall habits, no one can fault her body fat percentage.

Assuming a vertical yardstick is the standard you're applying to her figure.

"I caught them back in early September," she says in a hushed rush, like she's been holding on to the secret for a while. "I was in the newsletter offices alone way late."

Copying my essay? I wonder. No, given the timing, that was closer to the fake geometry memo. But I am no longer angry about the pranks or violations of my privacy. At least, I'm not angry with her.

"His office is on the same floor as the newsroom," she says. "It's way down at the end of the hall. I was leaving and they walked out of his door together. His hair was a mess. So was hers. He was tucking his shirt back into his pants." Francesca shakes her head. "Like I don't know what they were doing in there? Come on."

"They didn't see you?"

"No. They were too busy flirting with each other. And then on Mountain Day, she was being way obvious. Talking to him. Touching his arm or his shoulder. When we got to the park, I told her she better chill if she didn't want the whole school to—" There's the bang of a door out in the hallway and her head whips around. But she doesn't stop. She talks faster, like we might be running out of time. "I said she was making a fool out of herself and she needed to quit it. She went outer limits on me."

"But you kept on being friends with her."

Francesca's eyes come back to me. "What am I supposed to do? Sit at a table alone?" She looks down quickly. "No offense."

"None taken."

"So how do you know?"

"I found her panties in his laundry. It's a long story, but there's no doubt whose jeans pocket they were in."

Francesca's eyes bug out. "When was this?"

"Over Columbus Day weekend."

"Are you going to go to the administration?"

In this, I can be absolutely truthful. "No. They wouldn't believe me anyway."

"Yeah, totally." She doesn't bother to apologize for that gibe, but again, I am not offended. "Someone needs to tell on them. And it's not because I want him or something. It's just wrong. We're children, for godsakes. And he's *married*."

I nod, even though I'm not exactly sure I believe her. Given how she was looking at Nick Hollis on that bus? I think boundaries could have been crossed with her, too, if he were so inclined. Something tells me Greta's the only one he's been with here at Ambrose, though—not because he has any particular virtue, but because she wouldn't stand for any competition.

Except then there was that name I overheard him say on the phone when he was fighting with his wife.

The idea that there is a predator in our midst curdles my stomach.

"His wife is through with the traveling," I say. "I just talked to her. It sounds like she's going to be around more. She told me her grant is over. Or whatever."

Francesca stares off to the side. And then a hard smile hits her face. "This is going to be fun to watch." She glances back down to me. "Are you sick? Because you should really use the Lysol if you are."

As she points to the white and yellow aerosol can on the back of the toilet, I shake my head. "No, I'm not coming down with something."

"Oh." Her brows lift in curiosity. And then she shrugs. "If you're just starting out, you need to bring your toothbrush with you. Turn it around and put the handle deep into the back of your throat. Fingers don't always go far enough, and besides, it's gross to have your hand in your mouth."

As she mimics the motion in front of her open lips with her Oral-B, I think of stewardesses on planes showing people how to use a seat belt and where the exits are. Then she nods, like she's done what she can with the stray dog, and walks off.

I sag against the toilet seat.

A split second later, she leans back into the stall. "Have you told anybody?"

"No." I am relieved this is not a lie. "She already hates me. I don't want any more trouble."

Francesca seems disappointed by my lack of follow-through. In a low voice, she says, "Someone needs to take down that bitch."

"I thought she's your best friend."

"I found out at the Fall Fling that she fucked Mark on the Fourth of July. Just to prove she could."

Funny, how she assumes I know who Mark is. But because I used to eavesdrop on the three of them down at the river, I do.

"And it's not the first time she's stabbed me in the back." Francesca crosses her arms over her chest and narrows her eyes. "Everyone I'm with, she tries to fuck."

"Why are you friends with her?"

"Sometimes I could kill her, I really could," the girl mutters absently, as if she hasn't heard me.

For a moment, Francesca's eyes go opaque with a rage that shocks me. In spite of the plaid skirt and the navy blue thigh highs, the quilted ballet slippers with the double-Cs and the cute top . . . she suddenly looks like a boxer.

Who's wearing brass knuckles under her gloves.

As the silence stretches out, I'm willing to bet she's seeing blood in whatever fantasy she's playing in her head, and when she turns to leave, I'm not surprised she doesn't say anything else to me. She seems unaware I'm in her presence, and not just because I'm a social pariah.

Alone again, I drag myself off the tile using the toilet seat. Then I spray Lysol on a just-because, and go over to the sinks to wash my hands.

Looking at my reflection in the mirror, I see nothing of my face or hair. I am thinking about the black hatred in Francesca's eyes.

Greta has more enemies than I would have guessed. And some of them are right in her back pocket.

chapter
TWENTY-SIX

"You are *not* going to believe this shit."

Strots throws open our door in the middle of this sentence, and as I crank around in my desk chair, my lungs contract like a fist. It is the next afternoon, just before sunset. I know this because every minute of the previous twenty-four hours has been like a cut in my skin, the lashes all over my body, stinging and itching. I have tracked the passage of time in my every cell.

My roommate is careful to shut things up before she speaks, and yet she still comes over close and drops her voice. "Nick Hollis is getting fired."

I put my eyebrows up and try to look surprised. Which is not hard. *Holy shit*, I think to myself. *It worked?*

"He is?"

"He was fucking a student."

I shake my head as if I'm struggling to hear her right. "Are you serious?"

I feel weird that I've talked about this with Francesca and not with my only friend at St. Ambrose. But I've been worried that if Strots knows what I've engineered, even more bad things will come her way if it blows up.

Strots goes over to her bed, leans to the side, and in a burst of movement, throws her window open almost all the way. As she lights her cigarette, she exhales out into the middle of the room, too animated to do proper air quality control.

"Keisha's work job is in the headmaster's house, right? So she saw Hollis go into the big office there along with the dean of students after class today. Hollis came out an hour later and was all upset."

"How do you know what he was upset about?"

Strots slashes her cigarette through the air like she's frustrated with stupid questions. "After he left, Keisha overheard the dean of students and the headmaster talking. They hadn't closed the door all the way. Hollis has been fucking a student and he's out for fraternization."

"Who's the student?"

"They didn't use a name. Keisha said they referred to her as 'the minor in question.'"

"Wow." I look down at my hands, which I'm twisting in my lap. "His wife just got home, too."

As I picture Sandy trying to keep me from falling at the stairs, I feel really, really bad.

"I wonder who the hell it is." Strots points her smoldering cigarette at me. "Trust me, the name'll come out. These things never stay completely quiet."

"What's his wife going to do?"

"Divorce his ass, I'll bet." Strots laughs a little as she reaches for her Coke ashtray. "Who'd have thought the shit with me would get put on the back burner so fast. Gay doesn't look so bad when it's compared to statutory rape, right? Anyway, I thought you'd like to know the gossip."

"Thanks."

There's a hiss as she drops her half-smoked butt into the plastic bottle, and then my roommate leaves quickly and without saying goodbye. My feelings aren't hurt. She just proved she was taking me into account by reporting the news with timely gusto.

At that moment, I hear voices down below in the parking area. I rise half out of my chair and look over the edge of the big window. Nick

Hollis and his wife are arguing with each other. Her car, a Honda hatchback, is parked off to the side on the grass because there's no official spot for it, and I feel as though her presence in the world of Ambrose seems paralleled by the out-of-kilter way her Civic is jammed where it's not readily accommodated.

Her suitcase, which she's putting in the trunk, is a clear commentary that regardless of her travel schedule being over, she's hitting the road again.

She's collateral damage, I think to myself. Although she is not wounded. She is infuriated.

Still, the pair of them are pretty restrained in their discord, no doubt because they're aware they're liable to be watched. Both of their faces are bright red, however, and their eyes glow, hers with anger, his with brokenhearted pleading. I have a thought that this is not the beginning of this particular fight, but rather the culmination of something that has been going on for a bit, probably since he returned from the headmaster's office. I'm willing to bet when things were confined to their apartment, there was more volume, and maybe some shoving. I'm extrapolating this from how they tilt in toward each other, how rageful Sandy's expression is, how she gets even more flushed as the hushed volley speeds up.

I want to stick my head out my window and tell them to do this elsewhere to protect their privacy. As soon as the word gets out widely that Nick Hollis has been fired for sleeping with a student, this public display of marital conflict will become part of the story, and though none of their words carry, at least not up to my window, dialogue will be dubbed in by novice screenplay writers with soap opera tendencies.

And then something carries through Strots's open window that hits me in the gut.

Nick raises his voice sharply to talk over his wife. "My father is getting me a goddamn lawyer. I'm *not* leaving this campus and I'm going to fight this all the way. It's defamation—"

"Not if they look into Molly Jansen." Sandy's voice gets reedy. "How are we here again, Nick? Only one year later. With another fifteen-year-old."

Abruptly, they fall silent, and as the woman stares at her husband, I consider bolting back to the bathroom and kneeling in front of another toilet. No toothbrush required, Francesca.

Another fifteen-year-old?

His wife is the one who ends the argument. She backs off with a dismissive gesture, as if she's washing her hands of the whole thing. Slamming shut her rear compartment, she gets behind the wheel of her cockeyed Civic and reverses out in a herky-jerky fashion, as if her anger is being channeled through her foot into the accelerator and the brake. When she can finally tear off, there is only an anemic squeak of tires, the low horsepower of the engine failing to meet what is no doubt a stomping call to action. If she'd been in the Porsche, I bet she would have made a lot of noise and burned a lot of rubber in her wake.

Left by himself, Nick Hollis turns his back on the dorm, and he stands there staring at the brambles and the river for a very long time. Every once in a while, he pulls his hand through his thick, silken hair. I have a thought that he must be getting cold in only that red cashmere sweater, but as the sun begins to set, he doesn't seem to notice the drop in temperature.

I wonder if he is aware of anything at all—

There is a bang behind me, sharp and insistent, like a gunshot.

I spin so fast that I knock my chair over.

Greta is standing in the open doorway to my room, and for once, she is undone. Her eye makeup is smudged and her face is blotchy.

My one and only thought is that Francesca sold me out to protect herself with this girl who is not really her friend.

"Where is that fucking bitch," Greta says.

"Strots?"

"Where the *fuck* is she."

"I-I don't know. Why?"

Greta jabs a finger at me. "She's gone way too far this time. *Way* too fucking far."

My heart pounds. "What are you talking about?"

"You tell her I'm going to settle this. She takes from me, I take from her."

The door slams shut, and I hear Greta take off. For someone who weighs less than I do, her footfalls are those of a fully grown man, and her fury frightens me.

I lunge for the door, thinking I'll tell her the truth, that it was me who ratted on her and Nick. I did it, not Strots. I found what I found and I made it all happen. And then when she doesn't believe me, because no one ever does, I'll race ahead and warn my roommate, who has to be upstairs with Keisha . . .

As my hand makes contact with the cool brass doorknob, an elemental change overtakes me. I am no longer capable of moving. Confused, I look down at myself.

I expect to find a conversion occurring, my feet now stone and bolted to the floorboards, a tide of concrete-ion once again running up my ankles, over my knees, and throughout my torso, as I become a statue just as I was in front of the CVS.

I have a thought that at least here in my room in Tellmer, I will be protected from both the elements and bird poop.

Except that is not what is happening.

I lift one of my feet. Then the other. I take my hand off the knob and retract out of my forward lean.

I am not a statue of myself, and yet I cannot leave my room. I am frozen, but not inanimate.

When the explanation for my immobility arrives, I am so ashamed that a swirling self-hatred plays the role of my hair from the hallucination I had downtown. Fibers of enmity pour out of my head and coil around my body, encasing me in a mummy wrap of darkness before they go on to swamp my room.

I cannot leave because I'm too weak to stand up to Greta.

For all my background maneuvering, my pink-panty conniving, I am a coward. When it truly counts, as in right now, I cannot stand up and admit to my enemy what I have done and face her wrath. No, I must draft behind my stronger, more robust roommate, setting Strots up for a fall when she has already been falsely accused.

Greta won't believe her when she tells the girl it wasn't her. I've just taken their conflict and doused it with lighter fluid.

And Keisha is going to be the next person sucked into this.

Yet even though I know this, and even though I want to protect Strots, I can't move, and I hate myself for everything. For my illness, for my weakness, for my pussying out, once again, when it matters.

I am useless. I am weak. I am useless. I am weakIamuselessIam-weakweakweak—

From out of its period of hibernation, my illness saddles up the steed of my recriminations, the spurs of its boots digging into the flanks of my self-flagellation. In a surge of power and grace, it carries me into the abyss once again, the sparking strikes of the iron shoes on those clamoring hooves the only light in the darkness of my version of reality.

Except there is a difference this time.

From out of the conviction that I am an insane coward, something different emerges and then explodes into a blaze of heat. It is an anger that I have never felt before. No, that's not true. There have been brief flares of this fury over the course of the semester, and like kindling under dry wood, they have finally caught hold, although not just to logs stacked primly in a hearth, but to my entire house.

Fuck Greta Stanhope.

From out of this spinning referendum on my character, I become wrath. I become vengeance. I am torched to the point of a crematorium's worth of rage. Is it because of what the situation with Greta has shown me about myself? Or is it because I am done going quietly into the bad night of my madness?

Like so much of what has happened at Ambrose, the origins do not matter.

What happens next is what counts.

As I leave my room, I do not bother to have an opinion about where I go. Why should I? I am not in control as I proceed down to the basement and exit out the back door.

The last thought that I am conscious of is the dim notation that Nick Hollis is no longer standing in the parking area.

The last thing I am aware of seeing is the tightly sealed windows on both sides of his car.

The last sound I hear is the final step my right boot takes before I leave the asphalt and walk off onto the damp, cold grass.

And then I have no memory of anything.

chapter
TWENTY-SEVEN

Someone is shouting.

I open my eyes. I am groggy and disoriented, and I cannot ascertain what I am looking at as I am confronted by an expanse of white. Did I pass out and end up at an emergency room? Did I get taken to a mental hospital in Boston? Did I die and this is—

It is the ceiling. Over my bed in my dorm room.

Light is streaming through the bank of windows, creating shadows in the folds of the blankets that cover me. Morning? It must be.

As I sit up slowly, I put my hand to my face. My temples are pounding and my head feels as though it weighs as much as my entire body. Moving with care, because I worry that my skull is in danger of rolling off my shoulders and getting lost under my mattress, I look to Strots's bed, expecting her to be asleep.

She is not. Her side of the room is empty.

And who is shouting? What time is it—

Something lands in my lap, damp and heavy, and I squeak. It is the towel that evidently had been wrapped around my hair, which is also damp and heavy. I must have taken a shower before putting myself to bed. I do not remember doing either . . . the soaping and rinsing or the stretching out and resting.

Who is yelling? The words are muted, distilled through some kind of distance. At first I think they are coming from outside in the hall, maybe down by the staircase. But no. Their origin is below me.

I stand up and lean into the window. Down in the parking lot, a dark-haired man in a groundskeeper uniform the color of an ivy bed is motioning toward the river with his sweat-wrinkled cap. He is speaking to a policeman who is dressed in a blue uniform and is sporting a badge, a gun, and cuffs, all of which are holstered.

The cop is nodding and making calm-down motions with his palms, like he is patting the asphalt they are both standing on. The three cars owned by our RAs are where they always are. No other people are around.

No, that is a lie.

Two men emerge from the trees by the river, and as they walk up to the cop and the groundskeeper, their heads are lowered. One has his hands linked behind himself, at the small of his back. The other is fiddling with a notebook. They're in schlubby sports coats rather than uniforms, but the way the cop turns the handling of the groundskeeper over to them, it's clear they're in charge.

They take turns speaking to the man of the flapping cap, the groundskeeper's hands shaking as he grips and re-grips his topper, twisting the brim like it's taffy.

I look to the brambles and wonder what they have found out there.

Unable to watch for a moment longer, I leave my room, and find that Greta's door is open. Her bed is made and there are a couple of outfits, colorful as rainbows, laid out as if she's having a hard time deciding what, among all her options, she will put on for the day. Her roommate does not seem to be in there.

No doubt Greta is in the bathroom and I head there with heavy feet that become ever more weighty as I worry about my roommate.

Inside, the air is especially thick with steam and shampoo scents from the rounds of morning showers. There are two girls at the sinks, curved over the basins as they brush their teeth. Someone is still in the process of showering, the rainfall landing in a tinny rush on the drain.

I use the toilet and go to wash my hands. As I dry them off, I glance over my shoulder. At the bank of cubbies, Greta's bucket is missing, so she must be the one under the spray. Strots's is in its space, so she must be upstairs with Keisha.

The night's repose has steeled me. Once Greta returns to her room, I'm going to tell her my truth so she can be mad at the right person. And then I need to go up and confess my sin of silence to my roommate. In front of her girlfriend, too, so that my accountability is magnified. It may be too late; Greta may be gunning for Keisha already. But my conscience needs a shower of its own.

When I get back to my room, the order of my To-Do list is inverted. Strots has returned already. She's sitting on her bed, smoking, dressed in her sleeping rig of T-shirt and boxer shorts, her shower shoes on her bare feet. Her hair is wet and slicked back from a combing.

She doesn't notice me.

"Strots?" I say as I quickly shut our door to make sure no one sees her with her Marlboro. "You okay?"

Maybe she's deliberately giving me the cold shoulder? But I never told her about the panties, so how would she know that I—

Her head jerks as her eyes shift to me. "Oh, hey."

There's no anger in her expression. There's no . . . anything, really. She's like a billboard of herself, painted by an amateur.

"Sorry," I say. "I didn't mean to startle you."

I approach her cautiously. In case she wants to yell at me. When she just goes back to smoking, I'm disarmed by her detachment.

"Are you all right?" I ask.

"Oh, yeah." She taps her cigarette on her Coke bottle's opening and misses, ash spilling down onto her bare leg. "Just great. And you?"

As now really doesn't seem like the right moment for my confession, I should go on about my business and intercept Greta as she comes back from her shower. But I feel compelled to stay with my roommate.

"Um, did you see the cops out there?" I say, unsure how to break the silence.

"Out where?" she says on an exhale.

"In the parking lot."

"No." Strots taps her ash and makes the Coke goal this time. "Was there one?"

"Three, I think." I go over and tilt into the window. "They're gone now."

"Weird." Strots rubs her face with her free hand. "So Keisha broke up with me last night."

"What?" I fall into my desk chair. "Why?"

"It's just too much, you know. The whole thing about Greta and me from last year."

"But it's resolved. I mean, your father took care of everything."

"Keisha's on an academic scholarship. If it gets yanked? She can't afford to be here anymore." Strots shrugs. "Even though I didn't get expelled, I'm on probation and I'm contaminated in the eyes of the administration, so it's too dangerous for her to hang out with me. Christian values and all, you know? And the school can't sacrifice me, but she'd be out in the blink of an eye. She's right."

A chill goes through me. "Did Greta find you last night?" I ask with dread.

"Huh?"

"I think, ah, I think she was looking for you."

Strots has a faraway cast to her eyes as she glances over at me, and I imagine all kinds of thoughts fighting for airtime in her head. The same thing is happening on my side of the room.

I clear my throat. "So, um, I have to tell you something—"

"You know, I think I will leave."

"What?" My breath clogs in my throat. "What do you mean, leave. As in this dorm—or as in school?"

"St. Ambrose. Yeah. I'm just not interested in being here anymore."

"But you can't—I mean . . ." It's beyond selfish to think of my own interests, but that is instantly where I end up. "Where will you go? Back home?"

"Nah. There's a bus service down in town. I have some money. Cash, I mean. Enough to last me a month on the road."

"No." I shake my head, though she isn't looking at me. "You're not leaving. You're just not."

Strots laughs in a short huff. "So you can see into the future, huh. You know everything I'm going to do."

"I know you don't quit. And if you leave, you're quitting."

Strots stares at the end of her cigarette and the subdued nature of her face, her body, her affect, is just all wrong. This is not my roommate sitting before me.

"Things have a way of changing a person," she says remotely.

"Not you."

She smokes for a minute in silence. "Why the hell do you think so highly of me, Taylor."

"Because you're my friend and friends believe the best in each other." I lean so far forward in my chair, I'm in danger of slipping off the seat; I am begging her with everything I have, all the way down to my posture. "And that's how I know you're not going to go."

"I wouldn't put so much faith into me if I were you. You're bound to be let down."

I glance through the open door of her closet. She never did unpack her stuff from when her father came and negotiated a way for her to stay. With the exception of remaking her bed so she had somewhere to sleep, she left the rest of her clothes and things in the backpack and the duffel, using them as a bureau.

"Do you need help unpacking your stuff?" I ask as I eye the loose mess of half-folded sweatshirts and pants and shirts.

"Nope, I'm going," she says listlessly.

"No, you're not. Let's get you unpacked."

Except, typical me, I'm too timid to start without an okay from her. So we both stay where we are as she smokes the white part of her cigarette down to the orange quick of the filter.

"You're not leaving," I tell her again. Like my opinion matters. Like I can affect anything—

Now, wait a minute, I remind myself. I did manage to get a teacher fired. That counts. Of course, I've also ruined Strots's life, it feels like. And if I'd been assigned to another dorm, or even another floor in Tellmer, none of this would be happening at all.

"Don't make a permanent decision based on a temporary emotion," I tell her. Which I realize is a *bon mot* from Phil the Pharmacist. "At least give it a little time. Think things over."

"A day," she finally says. "I'll give it a day."

This is as much progress as I'm going to make on the subject, but I tell myself that my roommate will rally. That's who she is. And I'm not bringing up the Greta stuff. Not right now. I'm not going to give her another reason to go Greyhound on me.

I get up and dress inside my closet, just as she always does, although unlike her, I am embarrassed about how my body looks. Pulling on my black clothes, I note that my thoughts are consumed with both Strots's breakup and Greta's lies about the year before, and though I am sad for my roommate and worried about my having to track down our common foe, there is a measure of relief at the subject matter of my focus.

I'm plugged into a commonly agreed-upon version of reality.

It's better to be connected with the planet, even if everything feels seesaw shifty and very raw. At least we're all in this together, and by "all," I mean Strots and me.

I tell myself she's going to come to her senses. She just has to.

chapter TWENTY-EIGHT

There is yet another mandatory dorm meeting that night. The announcement for it is in my mailbox when I get back from lunch, the single sheet of paper lolling lonely in the slot with my name on it. I am not at all interested in attending if it's going to be another seminar on how to behave. After my roommate has now lost her girlfriend thanks to St. Ambrose's sanctimonious bullshit, I've had more than enough of the handbook's conduct expectations.

But what I am curious about is why there are four cop cars parked in front of my dorm. They've been there since I went to breakfast.

As a rippling anxiety turns my body into a tuning fork for all the worry in the universe, the idea of going upstairs to do some homework seems like a life sentence in solitary confinement. It's one o'clock on Saturday. Strots, I imagine, is getting ready to play a field hockey game, and I wonder how that's going to work with Keisha. Mr. Strotsberry's negotiations included keeping his daughter on the varsity team and Keisha is the captain.

It's going to be so tough on both of them. Yet it's impossible to fault Keisha for protecting her scholarship, and I hope the distancing is not too late. Greta wasn't at lunch just now and I'm terrified about what that absence means. I picture her in Mr. Pasture's office, sitting under the protection of the handbook and that oil painting, condemning a girl to an expulsion that is grossly unfair just to fuck with my roommate.

Measuring the stairs to the second floor, I know I need to go up there and wait for Greta's return so I can cop to my actions, but I'm suddenly having trouble breathing in the foyer. I wheel around and charge back out of the heavy door. The change in air temperature helps, and I start walking, resolving to clear my head a little before I face Greta.

To avoid the girls who are returning to the dorm in a steady stream, I go around to the rear, and as I arrive at the parking lot, I check the cars, as if their number and alignment means anything. All of them are where they were this morning. Receiving no clues, I continue onto the grass, and I look at the tree I hid behind that night—ground zero for everything that has now happened.

I think of Ms. Crenshaw in the rain. Those panties. The open door she left behind as she went back inside.

I keep going, down to the river's scratchy woolen scarf of brambles. Breaking through the tangle, I find that the burble over the bed of stones is still quite vigorous, even though it hasn't rained in a couple of days. Breathing in, I smell fresh dirt and know that the earthy scent is soon going to be something I will miss until spring arrives.

I wonder where all the police are. Four cop cars in front of the dorm mean there have to be at least a quartet of them somewhere. Maybe they're inside talking to people? Maybe the administration is bringing criminal charges against Nick Hollis for the Greta thing? I suppose there are two ways the school can deal with a crisis like this. Either they cram it under the rug, which was what I assumed the administration would do, or they hit it head-on, which would include prosecuting the teacher involved.

I start to walk along the river, picking my way carefully along the worn path, stepping my boots toe to heel and palming off branches so that I am soundless. I'm not sure why I feel the need to disguise my presence. Perhaps it's because everything else is so quiet around me, the current of the stream the only chatter within earshot.

This doesn't last.

I'm almost at the bifurcated tree and the huge smooth rock where Greta and the Brunettes like to meet when I hear the voices. Male ones. The policemen?

I stop, and try to hear what they're talking about. When I can't follow the words, I sneak over to the big split trunk and hide in my usual spot. Over on Greta's stone throne, there is a knot of some six or seven men standing shoulder to shoulder with their backs to me. Most are uniformed, but I recognize the two who are not by the sports coats. They're the ones who took over with the groundskeeper this morning. Some of the men are smoking. One has a pipe.

Something is on the rocks at their feet, breaking up the dull gray expanse of the stone.

As I shift my weight and try to look between the loose fabric of their slacks—

Is that a bare foot?

Through the forest of the officers' pant legs, I recognize a single bare foot that is white and immobile. It is tilted out to the side, and from my angle, I can see that the toenails are painted bright pink, and it is a manicured pink, not something sloppy and done by hand in a dorm room. There is a single gold ring on the third toe—

I step back sharply and my boot snaps a stick.

The clutch of men pivot toward the sound I've made. That is when I see whose foot it is.

Margaret Stanhope is lying on the boulder faceup, her bright clothes disjointed and stained with blotches of red, her blond hair tangled, her eyes open and staring at the sky in the midst of her colorless face. There is a man on his knees next to her and he's in the process of laying out a black bag that has a zipper that runs the length of the heavy, tarp-like plastic.

One of the policemen leaps toward me. "Hey! You're not supposed to be back here—Jesus Christ, Bob, you were supposed to make sure none of them came down here!"

I take off at a panicked run on the path, sure as if Greta's killer is on my heels, as opposed to the police. I run in terror, every pounding stride sending the image of that foot through my brain again and again, the toe, the toenail polish, the toe ring. The dead white skin. The flecks of dirt on the ankle.

Bushes slap at my face. I slip on some mud and recover my balance as if I am an athlete, instead of a mentally ill shut-in. Something slaps my back repeatedly between my shoulder blades, and I am convinced they're trying to lasso me like an errant steer. Without any plan other than evading capture, I cross the river, hopping a pattern over the rocks that are big enough to be out of the water. I fly down the other bank. When the smacking on my spine continues, I realize it is just my jacket.

All the while, the policemen following me are shouting, those fifty-year-old, paunch-bellied cops keeping up with my breakneck pace for a time, until I wear them out and their voices grow dimmer. This is going to be the first, and maybe only, race I ever win, and I am grateful that, however out of shape I am, older age is no match for youth.

I press on, heading for the outermost barrier of campus, for the chain-link fence that will become, when it is in view of the lawn and the buildings, the elegant wrought-iron production that unites in an arch over the entry into Ambrose. That expensive upgrade is not wasted on the invisible scruff I find myself in now. When I come up to the links, out of breath and in the weeds, the boundary here where no one sees it is downright ugly.

I collapse against the flexible flank and become aware of an approaching train. No, it is not a train. It is the sawing sounds of the suck and push of my lungs. My legs, weakened by the demands of my escape, give out on me. I slide down the fence until the heels of my boots catch my weight and my knees protest at the compression of my lower limbs.

I put out a hand into ground cover to keep myself from falling over. Mud oozes through my fingers. I do not care.

Every time I blink, I see Greta's face. Unblinking, unmoving. Never to blink or move again.

Pranks, I think with despair. They were only pranks. It was just water in a shampoo bottle. Bleach on clothes. A falsified memo. A setup at a dance.

An essay copied and shared among school chums.

When the harrassment had been happening, it had seemed earth-shattering. But not compared to a body bag. Not compared to all the blood on those bright clothes. Not compared to a death stare focused on the brilliant blue sky of what may well be the last warm, sunny day of the year.

"Oh, God, please don't be dead, Greta."

For so many reasons, this is the very last thing I'd ever think would come out of my mouth. And of course she's dead. The girl's makeup and hair were a fucking mess. If she were alive, she would never have let herself be seen like that.

Besides, what the hell do I think the body bag is for? If there was even a chance of life, they would have brought a stretcher and medics.

I wrap my arms around myself and moan.

And this is when it dawns on me that things are so much worse. Not only is she dead . . . clearly, she was murdered.

Fuck.

chapter TWENTY-NINE

The cops are waiting for me when I finally return to my dorm and go to my room. As I come up from the basement and emerge at the far end of my hall, I see one of the sport-coated ones standing in my doorway. I don't think of running again. I'm out of energy, and unlike Strots, who has enough cash on hand for a month on the road, I only have the money I earned wiping down woodwork over Columbus Day weekend.

And it's all in my desk.

As I walk toward the detective, he looks over at me. I expect him to rush forward and clamp cuffs on my scarred wrists like I'm a suspect. Instead, he purses his lips into a sad smile that makes me think he's trying to disarm me with sympathy.

"Sarah Taylor?" he says when I get in range.

"Yes." My voice is hoarse because of all the running I did to get away from the river. As well as all the tears I shed on the way back from that chain-link fence. "I'm Sarah."

"Detective Bruno."

First name or last name, I wonder as he puts out his palm to shake like I'm an adult or something.

"I'm sorry I ran." I put my clammy, dirty, and soft palm against his warm, clean, hard one. He's the one who shakes us, and I barely hang on for the up and down. "I didn't know what else to do."

"It's okay, sweetheart. This is your room, right?" When I nod, he says, "Come in and let's have a chat."

There's another officer inside. He's wearing a uniform and he looks me up and down like he's taking my height, weight, and fingerprints with his eyes. I feel utterly profiled.

"I have to go to a dorm meeting tonight," I tell them as I glance at the clock. "It's mandatory."

Like the police are going to give a shit about a dorm meeting?

"That's okay." Detective Bruno smiles again in that professionally compassionate way, making me wonder if he and Sandra Hollis went through the same facial training. "There's no problem with that."

"So I'm not under arrest or anything?"

"Not at all. We just want to make sure you're okay. What you saw . . . is hard enough for grown-ups to handle."

I search his face for clues as to what is really going on behind this you're-just-a-kid platitude. But he's really good at hiding tells. I can extrapolate absolutely nothing from his expression or where and how he focuses his eyes.

"Listen, can we just talk a little bit about last night?" he asks me. "About where you were and what you might remember?"

The door to my room is open and neither of them is blocking the way out. I'm glad. I may have to bolt again, even though I don't have anything to hide.

At least . . . I'm thinking I don't have anything to hide.

Instantly, I remember my visions of blood and of Greta in my morgue with her lipstick smudged.

Oh, God, I can't remember taking that shower. Or lying down to go to sleep.

But that doesn't make me a murderer. I mean, surely, I didn't . . .

In a daze, I move past them and sit on my bed. As I tuck my boots under the springs and curl my fingers into my mattress, I try to think about what I need to say. I also make sure I have a clear exit.

"I was here all night." I point to the crinkled towel on the back of my desk chair. "The only time I left my room was when I had a shower, and I fell asleep with that in my hair. I woke up at my normal time."

Detective Bruno's eyes narrow. "And what about your roommate."

"Strots?" I ask.

"Where was she?"

I glance at the other officer, the uniformed one. He's staring at the wall about two feet to the left of my head, like there's a mirror hanging there and he's checking out his own reflection.

I nod toward the other bed, and am so glad that the sheets are messy because for once, my roommate didn't tidy everything up before she left.

"Strots was here. And in the morning, too."

"You're sure about that?"

"Of course I'm sure. Where else would she be?"

Other than maybe with Keisha because they were still talking things out. Can these men arrest them for being gay? I don't think so. At least . . . I hope they can't. And I'm glad I can protect my roommate. It makes up for my earlier cowardice a little.

I resolve to keep Keisha very far out of this, to make sure these cops stay off the third floor, but I worry they can somehow see my obstruction of justice in my eyes. My heart begins to pound and I clear my throat. I try to remember what relaxed looks like on other people. *Loose shoulders*, I think. I need to loosen my shoulders.

I rotate the left one. Like it hurts. "Where else would Strots be?" I repeat.

It's at that point that I hear the crying. It's very soft. I lean forward, so far forward that I nearly fall off my bed. Across the hall, Greta's door is shut, but that's where the sound is coming from.

Her roommate, I think to myself.

As the implications of what I saw in that riverbed trickle into my consciousness, I am hit with the realization that Greta will never, ever open that door again. She will never wear her pink silk bathrobe or the Benetton clothes she laid out—or any of her underwear, no matter the color.

She will also never sleep with another married man. Or somebody Francesca is dating.

She will never again hurt anybody.

"You're absolutely sure Ellen Strotsberry was here all night," Detective Bruno prompts.

A calm comes over me, giving me the composure I was trying to fake.

"I'm a light sleeper, so yes, I'm sure. I would have heard if she left." I frown as if I am engaging in all of this for the first time. "But why are you asking about last night? Greta was alive this morning. I heard her in the shower."

"You did?"

"When I went to the bathroom first thing. Someone was in the shower and her bucket with her shampoo and stuff was gone from her cubby. It had to be her."

I state all this like it's dispositive, even though I know it's really not. Greta's bucket could just as well have been in her room for a reload of bottles or something.

As if the detective comes to a similar conclusion, he gives me a noncommittal nod. "How well do you know the deceased?"

"She lives across the hall."

"So you were friends?"

In a flash, I wish I hadn't gone to Mr. Pasture with the accusation of bullying. Maybe it gives me a motive. Then again, he didn't believe me, and as devastated as I was at the time, I am now relieved by this.

"I don't think she cared for me. I'm . . . different, you know?"

Another nod comes back at me. "It's our understanding that you and Miss Strotsberry had an altercation with Miss Stanhope in the phone room recently. Can you tell me a little bit about what happened?"

"It was no big deal." *Liar.* "Greta—Miss Stanhope—played a joke on me. That's all."

"What kind of joke was it?"

"She put an essay of mine in—well, she gave it to a couple of other people."

"We understand that your essay was shared with everyone in the dorm. And just to be clear, you believe Miss Stanhope was complicit in that dissemination?"

"Yes, it was her."

Detective Bruno's eyebrows close in on each other, two brown caterpillars facing off like they're about to wrestle over the bridge of his nose. "How can you be so sure?"

"She can be a prankster sometimes. Could be, I mean. But like I said, it was just a joke."

"Is that why you argued in the phone room? Because it was a joke?"

"We didn't argue. I didn't say anything to Greta. And what she did didn't really bother me."

"Then why did you go to Mr. Pasture, the dean, about the incident?"

I blink and try to hide the fact that I'm panicking, I'm drowning in a whirling pool of truth and lies. Except then I remember—

"I didn't go to the dean. The dean came to me."

Detective Bruno gives me a level look, like if I were his kid, he would be telling me not to be such a smartass. "When you were in Mr. Pasture's office, you asserted that Greta played a number of practical jokes on you."

"Like I said, she was a prankster."

"And you maintain you were not at all bothered by the fact that the essay you believe she put into the dorm's mailboxes contained personal and private information about your . . ."

"Insanity?" I fill in for him.

"About your mental challenges."

"It is what it is. And when I was at Mr. Pasture's office, sure, I mentioned the pranks, but he'll tell you himself, it wasn't what he brought me there for."

"Yes, it was about your roommate and Greta. Can you tell me what you know about them?"

"I wasn't here last year. I don't know anything."

"Miss Strotsberry never mentioned Miss Stanhope to you? Even in passing?"

"Do I look like someone you'd take advice from?"

As his eyes make a quick pass over me and he clears his throat, I figure I might as well use me to my own advantage.

"Miss Taylor, we've talked to a number of students about the incident in the phone room. They all say the same thing, that your roommate was trying to protect you. So I find it hard to believe you felt the pranks were no big deal."

I drift back in time, sifting through the previous few days, and then the previous two months, figuring out how to evade without lying too much. I hated Greta. I wanted to be her mortician. But that is not the banner headline you want as your newspaper is read by the cops.

I shrug in the way Francesca did with me in the toilet stall, relaxed, one shoulder only. "When it came to what Greta did to me, I guess I was just resigned. She liked to pick on people and I was her flavor of the semester. What could I do? You just have to take it and keep going." And then I tack on, "Besides, it isn't the first time I've been singled out for this kind of stuff."

"Here at Ambrose?"

"No. At my old schools."

Detective Bruno glances around the room like he's only now taking note of the arrangement of its furniture and whatever else is in it. Which is a lie. I'll bet the pair of them have been through my and Strots's things with a fine-tooth comb.

"You and your roommate are close, right?" he says.

"Not particularly." I allow honest sadness to creep into my voice. "But I wish I were more like her. Where is she?"

The detective's face shifts subtly. "Your roommate overpowered Miss Stanhope fairly easily, didn't she? In the phone room, I mean. Miss Strotsberry is an athlete. She's very strong."

"Where is Strots now?" I repeat.

"You don't have to worry about that."

"Ellen's rich, you know." I use her proper name because he doesn't deserve her intimate one. "Her father can get her a very good lawyer—which she does not need because she didn't hurt Greta down at the river."

"We're aware of Miss Strotsberry's family connections."

Given the way the uniformed cop's lips thin, I get the impression that those connections are already doing what they need to do.

"She did not kill Greta," I say. "She may have pushed her in the phone room, but she did *not* kill her."

"I never said she did, sweetheart."

"You don't have to."

The detective smiles at me, but there's a don't-get-ahead-of-yourself-kid chill in his eyes. "Miss Strotsberry did not just push Miss Stanhope. She tried to choke her."

I have a quick image of Keisha hauling Strots off our enemy. "Sometimes people snap."

"Do they? Tell me more."

"But they come to their senses. A moment of frustration doesn't lead to murder."

Now he's smiling at me in a condescending way. "So you and your roommate were here all night—"

"Greta can get pushy, too."

"What makes you say that?"

"On Mountain Day, Francesca—who's one of her best friends—and Greta were arguing. Later, Francesca had bruises on her face and her knees."

"Did you see Greta assault her?"

"They were on the fringes of the picnic. They were definitely arguing, and the next time I saw them, Francesca had a black eye. You should ask her about it."

"But you didn't witness any physical altercation between the two."

"Greta had grass stains on her skirt afterward. And a scrape on the side of her leg, too. She came back out of the tree line first."

This is a flat-out lie. I don't remember seeing either one of them emerge, but I figure the detail makes it seem like Greta's tough.

"You should talk to Francesca," I reinforce.

Sure, I'm selling the girl down the river a little. But as mad as she might have been at the park, and as much as Greta clearly pissed her off sometimes, I don't think she's capable of murder. Besides, she did copy my essay and put it in those boxes. Some payback is allowed on my side, right?

"Do you have any sense of what the two girls might have been arguing about?" Bruno asks.

I am losing threads even as I continue to weave, details slipping from my grasp. "Greta left her and Stacia in the rain once. Maybe that was it."

"Left them how?"

Now I'm stuck in what is a trivial detail, all things considered. "She got into a car and left them to walk home from town in the rain."

"When was this? And whose car was it?"

I hesitate because I'm not sure how much the school's told him. "It was earlier in the semester. Before Mountain Day. And it was our RA's car—Nick Hollis."

"He's the one who lives in the apartment just down the hall? With his wife?"

"Yes, that's right."

"And you saw Greta get into a car with him?"

I nod. "I went into town, to CVS, to buy some things. You know, just regular stuff." Not aspirin and Orange Crush, for example. And no, I'm not bringing up the bleached clothes. "It was raining when I came out of the store. Greta and Francesca and Stacia were walking together ahead of me. They'd come out of the record place. They'd bought CDs."

"And then what." When I don't immediately answer, he prompts me with, "What happened then?"

As I look down at my hands, I wonder if keeping quiet will make my diversion seem more significant.

There's a creak and I glance back up. He's closing the door. "Just for privacy. I'm not keeping you here. And whatever you're struggling with, it's best just to be honest."

I nod and look at my hands again. The right one, the one I threw out to keep myself from falling over at the fence line, is dirty. I rub it on my thigh. Not much transfers.

Detective Bruno gets down on his haunches in front of me. Both of his knees crack as he does this, and he nearly hides a wince. I decide that one or both are injured from his old high school football years.

"Tell me," he says, his eyes fixated on me.

I take a deep breath, and the image of Sandra Hollis is so vivid, it's like she's crouched in between the pair of us.

"Nick Hollis has a vintage Porsche," I say. Then I point out the window. "It's a really distinctive car. It's parked right down there. Anyway, I was behind the three girls. I saw him pull up beside them and talk to them. Greta got in with him and they drove away."

"So he gave her a ride and not the others?"

"It's a two-seater."

"And then what."

"That's it. Well, and then I saw Francesca and Greta arguing at Mountain Day."

"And that's it?"

Well, yeah. Except for pink panties. Blue Porsches. Geometry teachers. But if he knows about the phone room, surely he knows about all that.

"Yes," I say in response to his question.

The hunter light in the detective's stare dims, and he gives the floor a shove with his meaty palm as he stands up with a grimace.

"Okay. Thank you. I'll follow up on all that—"

"Greta's body is where they met every night."

"What did you say?"

I rub my eyes to try to get that image of the body out of my mind. The scrub job does nothing to help with my crystal clear memory. "The body's where Francesca and Stacia and Greta always met. On the rock at the river. They smoked there."

"How do you know this?"

"I'm new here. I had no friends at first." Still. "So I used to walk along the river at night when it was still light. I'd see them all sitting there. I never stopped to talk them because . . . well, let's face it, I'm not their kind."

In the silence that follows, I find myself mourning the sight of those three girls sitting on the big, flat boulder, smoking like they didn't have a care, their lives so bright they had to wear shades, to quote the song. And now Greta is gone.

"What was the tone of their conversations?"

I lower my eyes to Detective Bruno's shoes. Florsheim. I've seen them for sale in the mall back in my hometown. They're cheap and have plastic wedges at the heels instead of blocks of contoured wood. They have mud on them, from him chasing after me. From him trying to find clues down at the river.

"Teenage girl stuff." I rub my eyes again. "Who they were dating, what they didn't like about them, where they were going to go for breaks. You should talk to Francesca and Stacia."

"I will."

I look him in the eye. "Are you allowed to ask me all these questions? I'm a minor and I have no legal representation."

"This is just an informational interview. And we're almost done." He clears his throat again. "I understand you take medication."

"Would you like to see it?" I lean forward but can't quite reach the bottom drawer on the far side of my chair. I have to get up. "It's lithium. I take it because I'm bipolar."

When I face him again, I hold out the orange prescription bottle. He shakes his head and puts his palm up in a vertical no, like he could catch the disease if he touches the container.

"Explain to me what that means? Bipolar," he says.

"Some doctors call it manic-depressive. I have mood swings. Big ones."

"So you get sad and then happy?"

"Something like that." I almost keep the sharpness out of my tone. "I'm mostly sad, to use your word."

"Do you ever get angry?"

"Anger is about power. I have no power. Not over my illness—and not over Greta, if that's where you're going. Not over anything. I just endure. It's all I can do. She was just one more thing I had to put up with, and if you think an essay about living with my disease is a big deal, I can tell you right off that words on a page are nothing compared to the reality."

The detective stares at me. After a moment, his eyes go to the label on the little bottle, and something about the compassion that flares in his face makes me realize that he truly doesn't think I did it.

As I go to put the pills back, I start to breathe easier. It is not until this moment, when my heart rate slows and I take less-restricted breaths, that I realize I have been frightened I might have done something very, very bad.

That's why I ran away, and it wasn't from the police. They were incidental.

I was running from the terror that my mental illness might have taken the wheel not to go inward into my mind, but to travel outward, into the world. I might be powerless, nothing more than a fragile identity stuck inside the bag of skin I was born into. My disease, on the other hand? It can create a black hole out of my bed, a tidal wave from my hair, a fantasy about success just because I used some black dye.

It is so all-powerful as to be godlike.

"What are you thinking about, Sarah?" Detective Bruno asks softly.

"I didn't like Greta," I hear myself say. And then I continue, because he doesn't think I've committed murder, and I'm taking his professional opinion as fact. "I maybe even hated her, and I definitely hated what she did to me. She was like my bipolar, though. She made things harder for me, except it wasn't personal. My disease isn't personal. It's not about me, although it affects me and my life. Greta was just the same, shitting on me because I lost the residential lottery and ended up in the room across from her. But I was going to get through whatever she did to me. I was going to survive because I've already gotten through so much worse."

I think about the boiler room in the basement and am aware that that last sentence is more bravado than conviction. But I'm riding a buzzy crest of exemption, and it's making me feel optimistic.

"You've been to a place that's helped you, correct?" the detective says.

"A mental hospital, you mean." I nod. "Yes. I tried to kill myself. Twice. I was an inpatient at a facility that's an hour away from my small town."

He gets points for looking subdued, as opposed to judgmental, and I wonder, if he happens to have a son or a daughter at home, whether or not he's going to hug that kid a little tighter tonight.

"Have you ever tried to hurt someone before?" he says. But he already knows the answer.

"No. Never. You can check all my records. I have no history of violence toward anyone else."

He nods like this is new information, but I sense it's an act. He probably already has a copy of my essay. They've been here for seven or eight hours, haven't they. Talking to people, talking to administrators.

"Well, I think that's all for now. Thank you, Miss Taylor."

The other officer, the one in uniform, heads for the door like he was done with the interview about ten minutes ago. Detective Bruno talks a little bit more. I am no longer hearing him.

As he turns away, I think about Greta's domino taunt, the one she made a lifetime ago. I'm still angry at her, even though she's dead—especially as I recall her threatening to get at Keisha.

And it's easy to be courageous, given that the whole back-from-the-grave nightmare is something that only happens in George Romero flicks.

"You do know that Nick Hollis was sleeping with Miss Stanhope, right?" I say.

chapter THIRTY

The following day, everything is in chaos. Church services on campus are canceled. Grief counselors are brought in. Girls jam the phone room, crying to their parents. Several mothers and fathers even come by and remove their precious cargo from the proverbial overhead compartment. Clearly, in the minds of most of the community here, the airplane is going down in a ball of fire.

From the window of my dorm room, I am watching one such evacuation roll out. The parents are rushing around the BMW like flies on chicken salad, moving, always moving. They're inefficient as they put toiletries and a suitcase in the back seat, and then have to transfer the pink, and no doubt fragrant, load to the trunk.

Obviously, they aren't putting their darling daughter in the boot.

The girl who is getting out while she's still alive is one I recognize from my history class. She is red-eyed and puffy-faced, but her hair is curled and she's wearing a coordinating outfit of Black Watch plaid extraction.

She looks honestly scared, though. I know how she feels.

After the family unit gets into the sedan, father behind the wheel, mother on the front passenger side, progeny on the bench seat in the back, the doors of the BMW shut all at once, as if they coordinate these things as a rule. Then they do several rounds of back-and-forthing in the parking lot and take off as if there is a murderer with a raised knife about to jump on their rear bumper.

I flop back on my bed. When it comes to Greta's death, there are two camps in the dorm. Half of the girls, led by Francesca and Stacia, are the ones who once idolized Greta—and also likely resented her in private. They're vocal in their mourning and have turned Margaret Stanhope into a beacon of style and goodliness that the world has been tragically cheated of. This is a solid platform on which to shed many theatrical tears, and having watched them wrench their fistfuls of Kleenex in their hands, but dab carefully at their made-up eyes, I believe that although there is some real grief there, getting swept away in the drama is their main driver.

The rest of the dorm is quiet but respectful, falling into a line of "We didn't like her, yet we certainly didn't want her dead." The bunch of us are young, and by definition self-involved, so we're actually fairly okay now that the shock has worn off. In fact, we're doing better than the adults around us. Anybody on campus over the age of eighteen is looking like they'll never sleep again.

Come to think of it . . . there may be three groups, and it's likely that this final catchment is a subset that encompasses portions of the larger two: There probably are some people who happen to be glad she is dead. I know I'm one. I'm fairly sure Strots is, too, and of the Brunettes, at least Francesca is, not only given the skirmish at Mountain Day and the stuff about "Mark over the summer," but, more important, due to her sudden ascendance to social supremacy. Francesca has taken over the leadership of the pretty girl group, the right-hand lieutenant assuming the stars of a dearly departed general thanks to the latter's unexpected mortal wound.

"Taylor, your mom's on the phone downstairs."

I twist around from the window. Strots has come in. She's got a six-pack of Cokes, and undoubtedly some fresh packs of cigarettes in her jacket pocket.

"Okay," I say. "Thanks."

I look at my roommate and will her to meet my eyes. When she does, and seems as unflappable as usual, I take a deep breath. Forcing stare-to-stare contact with Strots is my new obsession. People who can look others right in the face have nothing to hide, and I want Strots to be hiding nothing. I need her to have no secrets about the night Greta died.

And so far, so good. To the point where I'm starting to feel like my OCD has taken over with this constant testing of a deadbolt that I know, I *know*, I locked into place.

Strots didn't kill Greta any more than I did.

As I hustle down to the main staircase, I'm ready to hear my mother's voice with a desperation that I'm unfamiliar with, but on the descent, my thoughts return to Strots. I learned late last night, during an offhand exchange with her, that she did in fact go down to the police station yesterday afternoon—which was what I was worried about when I asked the detective where she was. I asked her if she had a lawyer. She said her father was taking care of everything, but she wasn't a suspect.

And that was that. No details about what she was asked. No emotion, either, but not in a weird way. In a perfect way. My roommate is calm as a cucumber.

On my side? I'm feeling a little guilty for bringing up Nick Hollis to Detective Bruno out of vindictiveness, but of course the man already knew. And it doesn't take a genius to follow a lead like a residential advisor being fired for fraternizing right before the girl in question turns up dead down at the river: I overheard someone saying at breakfast that Nick Hollis's Porsche was parked at the police station for a couple of hours last night.

I'd like to believe it wasn't him, except then I think of the way he stood in the parking lot and stared off to the river. Was he planning it then? You'd think that he'd have enough to deal with, what with imminently losing his job and his marriage. Unless . . . well, he'd know those panties didn't just magically appear in his car, right? What if he thought Greta was trying to mess with him? After all, Sandy's grant is over, so she wouldn't be traveling for a while and her constant presence would change everything.

What if he and Greta had an argument that went too far?

As I arrive at the first floor, I am grappling with all kinds of hypotheticals and wondering how many of them I can share with my mother without making her worry. Except then I go over to the phone room and come face-to-face with an SRO situation. It's like a commuter train at rush hour, packed with bodies, and of the seven or eight phones, none of the receivers are free. Someone must have hung up on my call after Strots went to get me.

"—my best friend, Mom. I miss her so much—"

"—haven't found the murder weapon yet. But she was stabbed—"

"—want to come home now! There was a murder behind my dorm! Why won't you come and get me?"

I could enter the fray and stand in the center of the room, joining the half a dozen or so harpies ready to swoop in the second a receiver is dropped into a cradle and free to ring, but I back away. My mother will have to wait, and I'm sorry about this. I want to talk to her, even though there's nothing I can say, really. I just kind of want to hear her voice.

As I turn to ascend the stairs, someone comes at me.

"Oh, Sarah, I am *so* glad you're here." It's Ms. Crenshaw, and my thought is that she brushed her hair with a thornbush. Everything is Einstein on the top of her head. Did she just roll out of bed? At three in the afternoon? "You know you can always come see me, right? My door is always open for you."

I look around. I'm not anywhere near her door.

"Here, let's talk privately." She hooks an elbow through my own and pulls me along. "It's much easier that way."

As we do-si-do into her apartment, I see that she's propped her entryway open with a foot wedge, like she's trolling to help students, even though they really only want to talk to each other or their parents. Just my luck to get caught in her net.

"Let me get you something to drink." She points to her ugly sofa. "Sit. I'll bring you some of that pomegranate juice you liked from before."

I didn't have any then, I want to remind her. Instead, I counter with, "I have to go do my homework."

She doesn't hear me. She's already in her kitchen. Then again, I don't think she'd hear me if I were standing in front of her. She's on anxious autopilot, and I suppose, given the circumstances, I should have some compassion and understanding.

"I know it's hard on all of us, this terrible tragedy," she says. "What we need to do is pull together as a community. Help each other. Cry together."

Oh, God.

Resigned, I take a seat on her fabric-draped couch. As my body sinks into the cushion like I'm falling through the floor, I wonder if Ms. Crenshaw chose the sofa because it mirrors her own grasping desperation, the furniture equivalent to her endlessly starting conversations with people who would prefer to speak to anyone else.

"I'm just cutting up an orange for us as well," she says as she leans out from her little kitchen. "It's so full of vitamin C, you know. And the pulp is good for digestion. Fiber."

After this little infomercial, she goes back to talking about the death. She covers a lot of territory fast, and without any apparent expectation of my interjecting a response. In this, she is like a ticker tape: The police. The newspaper article in this morning's paper. The fact that it will be the lead story on the six o'clock local news tonight.

Given that the victim is a Stanhope, I think it may well make the national news, but I don't share this opinion with her. Just like I don't mention I saw the body. With her consuming oxygen as she is, I don't want to exert myself any harder than I have to for fear of passing out from hypoxia. But more than that, wandering into secrets-shared territory is going to trap me in future conversations I also won't care about.

I wonder what she would think if she knew I was the one who facilitated her finding those panties.

As Ms. Crenshaw decides that she and I need toast as well, I sit forward. Or try to. The doughy cushion I'm on has a death grip on my lower body. I glance around, looking for a rope to pull myself out—

I stop. I frown.

I become transfixed by the lowest shelf of the floor-to-ceiling bookcases.

Shoving both my palms into the couch's arm, I surgically remove myself from the sofa and double-check that Ms. Crenshaw is still working on the pomegranate juice that I lied about being allergic to, the orange I don't want, the toast I don't need. She is leaning over the toaster, as if rays from her eyes, rather than coils heated by electricity, will be what browns the no-doubt whole-wheat-whatever she put in there. And she is talking, talking, talking, her words like lemmings leaping out of her mouth.

I have to step around a magazine holder with issues of *Mother Jones* in its slats or else I will trip, fall, and end up fending her off to avoid being given CPR.

Over at the shelves, I crouch down and focus on the splash of color that caught my eye. It's a keen turquoise, an outlier in this apartment full of so many shades of browns, tans, and golds.

It looks like Nick Hollis's sweatshirt. The turquoise one with the map of Nantucket on it that he wore on Mountain Day. The one that he later complained to me was lost, back when he and I were talking about his books, and I was spinning romantic fantasies about him, and Greta was still alive.

I have to be sure.

I glance over my shoulder to the kitchen. "I'm really hungry," I say. "May I have two pieces of toast?"

"Oh, yes! You know, I made this bread myself. It's got four different kinds of hand-ground grains in it!"

Without warning, she leans around the partition.

I shove my boot out and make a show of doing up laces that were already done up. "I was just looking at your collection of magazines. And books."

She smiles and points across with the tip of a serrated knife, one that seems really big and really long for the job of slicing homemade bread.

"Did you see all my Dickens? I love Dickens."

"I was looking at them, yes." I straighten and reach for something. Anything. "But what I'm really interested in is . . . Shakespeare."

"You like the old classics."

"I do." I put the book to my heart. "They're my passion."

"Mine, too!"

She goes back to what she was doing, and I hear a sawing that suggests either she's trying to slice off a piece of the counter or that bread of hers is solid as a rock.

"You know, we should start a book club!" she says.

I wait to see if she needs more eye contact. When she just keeps talking about literature I have no interest in, I duck back down to the shelves.

There's a key by the sweatshirt. A napkin and spoon that seem like they're from the cafeteria. A glass that is empty—and given its murky contours, used yet uncleaned. A stick about six inches long. And a newspaper clipping.

With Nick Hollis's grainy picture on it.

"What are you doing?"

Ms. Crenshaw's voice is right next to me and I straighten quickly. She is standing behind me, and she has the knife in her hand. I look to the apartment's door. She's closed it.

"I was just wondering if you had any Jane Austen," I say.

I meet her dead in the eye. As if I am not lying. As if I'm not suddenly worried about making it out of here alive.

There's a pause.

"They're over on that side," she says tightly, pointing with the serrated knife.

"Thanks," I croak.

chapter THIRTY-ONE

It's the following day and classes are canceled. As it turned out, Ms. Crenshaw did let me go from her apartment, but I no longer feel safe in my dorm, and I can't decide whether that is paranoia or self-preservation. I am also aware of a simmering anxiety that seems to be expressing itself in a tic involving my left eyebrow. The thing has been going into fits all morning, like the spout cap on a boiling teakettle.

Currently, I am walking into town at a fast pace, and as I pass by the CVS, my stride gets even quicker. I don't want to go in there ever again, and my mind teases me with an unlikely scenario that its glass doors are actually a suction flow that will pull me in and never release me. All of this ugliness and deadly disruption kind of started after my first trip inside, and as much as I hated Greta, I wish none of this had ever happened to any of the parties involved.

As my brain connects dots I regret, I feel as though my role in this terrible drama is as the binder. I am the link between so many disparate people and events, and though I did not stab Greta Stanhope on the rocks down at the river, I cannot escape the sense that I am the bridge that let her killer cross onto her private island.

Feeling pursued, even though I am the one who is doing my own stalking, I cut down a shallow alley beside the pharmacy. It is clean as a city park, and I presently emerge behind the lineup of stores. The library is off to the right, forming the farthest boundary of the parking lot, and as I note its tight proximity to the police station, an irrational fear grips me. I see cuffs slapped on my scarred wrists. I see me dragged inside and put immediately into an electric chair. I picture the old-fashioned metal cap on my head, and feel the surge of volts go through me. I smell burnt hair and flesh as my fingers stick straight out of my straining hands, like spikes—

To escape my spinning mind, I'd walk even faster, but then I would be jogging. And besides, what is that saying? Everywhere I go, there I am.

I'm breathing heavily as I enter the Mercer Memorial Library's glass doors, and I pull them closed behind me, like they're a cloak of invisibility that will shield me from prosecution.

In spite of the fact that I am guilty of nothing. And Detective Bruno was the first to know this.

I need a moment before I can recalibrate and absorb my environment. When I am able to form an opinion about where I am, my first impression is that the library is over-warm, like an elementary school room where the teacher is worried her charges will come down with spontaneous pneumonia if the temperature goes below sixty-nine degrees Fahrenheit. The carpet underfoot is a speckled brown that coordinates with the seventies-era harvest gold and avocado green décor, and on this main floor, there are big windows all around, letting in gray light. The aroma is pure book, something on the nose spectrum between oatmeal and fresh paint.

The front desk is unmanned—or unwomanned, more likely—and I am glad, even though it means I'm going to have to hunt and peck for what I'm in search of. Beyond the gatekeeper station, the children's section is right up front, along with popular fiction. There's also a newspaper station, the hanging rods slung with various pulpy editions like wash that is drying in a yard. These dailies are close to what I'm looking for, but they're too recent.

After all, I already know what the current articles are saying about Greta. And yes, the murder did hit the national news. There's nothing about Nick Hollis in any of the reports yet, and I wonder how long that will last. The media are being very persistent. There are a dozen TV newscasters and reporters at the gates of Ambrose, and I don't think the school is going to be able to keep a lid on something so germane to the murder as what that man did with the student who was killed.

Especially if he becomes an official suspect. Or is it *when*? Even though I can't really imagine him killing anybody.

Which is why I'm here.

Refocusing, I find a helpful list of the library's sections and services on one of those felt signage setups with the white letters you push into soft slats. The display is mounted on the wall by the elevator, but I take the stairs down into the basement. It's a whole different world underground. The stacks here are gray metal and squeezed in tight, and the flooring is black and gray linoleum, like the gold and green up above is something that has risen to the top of a liquid suspension by virtue of its lesser, and therefore more buoyant, molecular weight.

Down here is the meat of the enterprise, home of reference volumes and the dusty, annotated scholarly stuff that I doubt gets much use. I find the microfiche stations straight ahead, and I am surprised that, again, no one is around making sure that things aren't tampered with or stolen. But maybe the library knows its clientele can handle with competence and respect whatever is under its roof.

It takes me a while to understand the cataloging of the films, but soon enough, I make some choices from the archive of the *New Haven Register*. It's a surprise that a small Massachusetts town like Greensboro stocks the paper's past issues in its library, and I feel lucky at the show of New England solidarity.

With a flutter in my chest, I sit down at the farthest of the three microfiching machines. At first, it is exhilarating to whip through the columns and pictures of previous issues. Then the whirling makes me queasy—but that could also be because I feel like I'm doing something sneaky.

The article I'm searching for is from back in early September last year, and I have a thought that I am in a needle-in-a-haystack situation. Reversing the flow, I wonder whether I'll have to consult the next reel and am frustrated that I'm going to have to wade through—

"—what Jerry said. Do you think he'd lie? And don't tell anyone this, okay."

I look up from the light box. Two women are emerging from a door marked *Staff Only*, the kitchenette behind them neat as the rest of the library. As my view of the pristine counter is closed off, I have a random thought that no one would ever reheat cod in that microwave or leave a mug in the sink.

"They got the autopsy results fast, then," the other one says.

"It's an Ambrose kid. Like they'd take their time?"

They're about the same age, fortyish, and dressed in the same version of serviceable skirt and blouse. Their hair is even similar: one's maybe a little darker, the other showing roots that need a touch-up, but both have shoulder-length blunt cuts. I think of the two cashiers at CVS. *Does the town have a rule about coordinating employees?* I wonder.

The two cluster together, heads tilted in, voices low.

"And they're going to keep this quiet, right? Ambrose will never let it out that the dead girl was pregnant—"

Both of them turn to me, startled. Clearly, I've made a sound.

I go back to the microfiche, afraid they'll kick me out for my black clothes. For my eavesdropping, even though they were in the library proper. For the fact that they've guessed I'm a bipolar Ambrose student on a mission—

Oh, God. Greta was pregnant?

I think of all the times she went into the bathroom after meals with that toothbrush in hand. Maybe she wasn't using it the way Francesca showed me.

She was *pregnant*? Did Nick Hollis know? Was that why he . . . ?

Without warning or preamble, I disassociate and float away from my own body—and in a rush of fear, I become convinced that this library trip is all an illusion in my mind. The real-reality is me back in my dorm room, sitting on my bed, my disease having created a new and different black hole for me to fall into, not a galaxy this time, but the local athenaeum.

Yes, this is all a hallucination. Mr. Pasture was right. None of this is real. Not the panties. Not the death. Not the police or Nick Hollis . . . or the two women I think I'm seeing now. After all, I am not actually in the Mercer Memorial Library, and I am not—

I snap back into focus and reach out to touch the microfiche machine. When my trembling fingers inform me that, yes, there is a three-dimensional, measurable mass in front of me, I take a deep breath and try to sort out my confusion about where I am.

In desperation, I start to move the image on the screen, and try to connect with—

And there it is. An article about a Yale University teaching assistant becoming embroiled in accusations of sexual impropriety. It's blinded of Nick's name, but I know it's him. The date is right, it notes that he's married and a master's candidate in English, and it says he comes from a prominent family. Granted, there are probably a lot of people who fit that description at the school, but there's a tell that strikes me to the core.

The girl's name isn't mentioned.

Because she's fifteen, according to the article.

Mollyjansen was fifteen. According to Sandra Hollis.

I sit back in the seat and stare at the glowing print. I wonder how their paths crossed. Was she the daughter of a professor or an administrator? No, I decide that she was a townie, someone who didn't matter, so it was easier to gloss over the whole problem, bury it in spite of this piece of nonreporting because the school worked with Nick Hollis's dad and closed the case. Was the girl's family paid off? There's no mention of charges being filed, so I'm thinking they were.

I've read enough of my mother's *People* magazine articles to know how rich people deal with things that take the shine off their reputations.

And for sure something happened with the girl. I heard an ugly truth in Sandra Hollis's voice when she brought up the whole situation in the parking area, right before she took off with her Civic and her suitcase.

But the real news flash isn't about Mollyjansen. Greta was pregnant? That certainly raises the stakes, especially as I consider payoffs to minors. Greta and the Stanhopes went bankrupt. So what if she got herself pregnant and tried to blackmail Nick Hollis? After his father had to buy silence from another girl the year before?

That might just get a guy who loves *American Psycho* to take a page out of Bret Easton Ellis's book.

"May I help you?"

I brace myself before I look up—because I'm not entirely sure what I'm going to see. The article has kind of put me back on the planet, but who the hell knows what's real.

I turn my head toward the disapproving female voice. It's not the staffer who needs to go to the hairdresser for her roots.

"I'm almost done," I say, assuming either one of us is actually here.

"Please do not try and reshelve the film," she tells me. As if she's a brain surgeon taking a scalpel out of the hands of a landscaper. "It goes in that basket."

She points to a red plastic container that belongs at a burger joint full of fries fresh from the oil vats. Sure enough, there is a wrinkled, handmade sign taped to the front of its flimsy slats: *Please Put Film Here.*

Well. What do you know. This is exactly the kind of stupid minutia the real world drowns in. Maybe this *is* happening.

"Thank you," I say. "I won't reshelve."

She nods, like we've formed a blood pact and if I violate the agreement, I'm subject to a lifetime library ban. Taking strength from the banality of our exchange, I put my head down.

And it's "do not try **to** *reshelve the film,"* I think to myself when I'm finally left alone. And the reels are in a drawer, not on a shelf.

After I make sure I've followed the rules more correctly than her grammar does, I go back up to the first floor via the stairs. The lady with the roots showing is at the front desk, but she is on the phone, taking notes on whatever conversation is occurring. I don't know where her "try and" colleague is.

I almost walk by the newspaper display, but I stop.

The local paper is the fourth in the lineup, going from left to right, behind the *New York Times*, the *Washington Post*, and *USA Today*. As I lift the rod it's bifurcated on, I wonder if I'll be allowed to "reshelve" it when I'm finished.

There's a big table with six chairs around it right next to me, clearly provided so that people can do what I do as I lay out the folio on its dowel. The front page is filled with the known details of the murder thus far, and there are plenty of photographs. The first is a shot of the river behind Tellmer, but it's a stock photo, from the Ambrose admissions pamphlet. Another image, of the school gates with all the reporters and news trucks, is a fresh one, however, and so is that of the police chief at a microphone, addressing the press at the station house next door. The last is a picture of Mr. Stanhope looking more enraged than full of grief as he walks out of the headmaster's house. This one was clearly taken with a serious telephoto lens from the iron fence, as the press is not allowed on the school's private property.

As my eyes go back and forth over the newsprint, I figure out how Greta got ahold of my essay. The reporter states that Mr. Stanhope has served on the St. Ambrose admissions committee for the last decade, and in this capacity, it is noted, he has personally reviewed the applications of every single student who has matriculated into the school.

Which means he had to have a copy of my essay somewhere. And Greta went home over Columbus Day weekend. She must have gone through his files in some kind of study or office, found it, and gotten her bright idea.

Given all the other things that have happened, the elucidation of this now very minor detail barely registers, and I suddenly remember the first time I saw the Stanhopes on move-in day. I can picture so clearly that Mercedes with its matching hubcaps, and Greta's mom with her every hair in place, and the way Mr. Stanhope looked at my mother.

And then that smile Greta gave me.

I have no sense of satisfaction that all that is ruined now. Truly. I'm not that kind of monster, to be happy a family is destroyed.

Even if that daughter of theirs is a total nightmare.

Was, I mean.

Oh, Greta, I think to myself. *What did you say to Nick Hollis about that baby you were carrying?*

chapter THIRTY-TWO

It is night now. The dorm is quieting down as everyone tries to get their homework done. I wonder if any of the other girls are having the same trouble concentrating that I am. What I'm sure of is that I'm glad there are so many people around me. That music is playing. That the walls are thin enough that I can hear the occasional volley of chatter.

I don't want to be alone. Outside the bank of windows in front of me, the darkness of eight p.m. on a mid-October evening makes me feel like total and complete isolation is only an eyeblink away.

I am obsessing over fact patterns and none of them pertain to the content of the American history book I'm supposed to be studying. I'm thinking about Mountain Day, about Francesca looking as if she had been in a fight. She hadn't been crying afterward. She had been mad. Viciously so. I think of her role in the distribution of my essay. I think of her being left in the rain when Greta got into Nick's Porsche.

What if Francesca knew about the pregnancy? What if she figured it out, based on, say, a pattern of throwing up that changed on Greta's part, vomiting that did not, as of late, have to do with an eating disorder, but with morning sickness.

Francesca strikes me as the kind of person who would notice this.

And now I think of what she said about her hometown honey, Mark, and his extracurricular activities with her supposed best friend over the summer.

"No, no," I say out loud. "That's crazy."

Maybe it's someone from outside Ambrose entirely, all these what-ifs and if-thens complete bullshit. Maybe it was a drifter and a case of wrong place/wrong time.

Or a serial killer getting started.

As my head spins and spins, I wish I had never gotten involved in any of this sleuthing stuff. It's food for the caged beast of my illness, the possibilities and permutations raw meat dangled just outside of the bars, enticing and somewhat necessary for its survival.

Just as I look back down at my textbook, Strots comes into our room. She smells like cigarettes and fresh air, which are not as mutually exclusive as one might think.

"Hey." She takes her field hockey windbreaker off and hangs it in her closet. "Man, it's getting cold out there. You hear the latest about the murder?"

Yes, in the echo chamber of my skull. All the time. "No?"

"They called Francesca down to the police station." Strots sits on her bed with a bounce. Her cheeks are flushed from the chill and she rubs her nose like it's running now that she's in the warmth of the dorm. "Someone saw her leave with the cops."

I try to seem casual. "What are they asking her about?"

Strots gives me a flat look. "Her plans for Christmas. What do you think?"

"Did they ask Stacia down, too?"

"I don't know. They probably will, though. They've got their ass in a crack until they find out who did this."

After Strots kicks off her shoes, she bends down and drags a fresh six-pack of Coke out from under her mattress. She pulls one of the plastic bottles free of the plastic loops.

"You want?" she asks me, holding it forward.

"I can't sleep as it is."

There's a hiss as Strots cracks the top of the soda. "That's not good for you, right?"

What? Oh, my bipolar.

"No, it isn't. But things have been so crazy."

"Too right." Strots settles back against the wall and looks at the ceiling as she crosses her legs at the ankles. "I just had to go out and clear my head. I couldn't stand to be in this dorm for one more goddamn second."

I have a feeling she's thinking about Keisha as she stares at the third floor.

Abruptly, she sits up properly, like she's trying to change her thought pattern by altering her posture. "They got rid of the crime scene tape, by the way. Down by the river, at the head of the trail."

She takes a sip and I think about the number of times we've done this, her having a nightly Coke and me wishing I was like her. I'm doing that again now, quietly envying her confidence in the midst of such chaotic uncertainty. Of course, we've never had murder as a topic of conversation before, not that she's doing much talking outside of her news report. She's like that, though. She doesn't deal in hypotheticals, whereas I am drowning in them. Halfway between us, on the median line of our room, is a perfectly normal person, someone who's aware of the hidden contours of situations, and willing to discuss them, but who's nonetheless able to stay focused on the concrete and the known of the given fact pattern.

"Are you afraid?" I ask softly.

"Of what."

"Getting . . . killed. Or something."

Strots recoils with a frown. "By who?"

"I don't know. Maybe we're all in danger. If somebody can kill Greta—"

"Then they killed her. It doesn't have anything to do with me. Or you. Or anybody else here. It's a one-off."

"How do you know that? What if there's a serial killer out there?"

"It was personal." Strots gives me a well-duh look. "Whoever it was stabbed her nine times. In the front of her chest and throat. The newspaper said so. The murdering wasn't the point of it. Greta was a specific target, and come on, like all of us haven't wanted to kill her at some point?"

"You shouldn't say that."

"Why? 'Cause it'll make me a suspect? Please. The police already know it wasn't me. The lawyer my father brought in from Boston already talked to them." She laughs without smiling. "Apparently, the police can't arrest somebody on suspicion of murder just because they're gay, and predictably, that was what my pops was really worried about. Not for my well-being, of course, but for his."

"I still don't think you should talk about those kinds of things."

"Fuck that." Strots takes another drink. "The facts are what they are. And if there is a murderer on the loose? I'd like to see them come after me. I'd be into the fight, for sure."

"What if someone knows, though," I choke out as my thoughts gallop ahead of my conscious control.

"Huh?" When I don't respond, Strots lowers the bottle from her mouth pre-sip. "Knows what?"

"What if the police are talking to the wrong people, and someone knows this, and—"

"I still don't get what you're talking about."

"If the murderer killed once, they could do it again. Right? To protect themselves."

There's a long silence, during which Strots stares into the open neck of her Coke bottle.

When her eyes lift to mine, they're deadly serious. "Is your brain getting into trouble? I mean . . . are you, like, spiraling?"

She motions next to her temple, her forefinger going around and around, but it's not to make fun of me. She's trying to put into movement something she is struggling to find the words for.

"I mean, I read up about the bipolar thing," she explains. "After we talked. They said it can get weird or something. Sorry if I'm not saying this right. But you just told me you're not sleeping, and I know you haven't been going to meals."

I haven't? I think to myself.

"And I guess"—my roommate clears her throat—"well, I mean, there's a lot of shit happening around here, and they say that stress can start things—what's the word? Kindling. Or something."

I look down at my history book. And realize I've been trying to work on geometry, not the Revolutionary War.

As I start to panic, I rub the end of my nose even though it's not tickling. "Can I . . ." I clear my throat, just like she did—and likely for the same reason. I don't have something caught there, I'm feeling incredibly awkward. "Can I tell you something?"

"Yeah, sure." Strots laughs a little. "And I promise to keep it to myself, but that doesn't mean much 'cuz I'm not really talking to anyone right now. Which is why I'm out walking in the dark instead of studying French."

I open my mouth . . . and it all comes out, the syllables fast like a machine gun. And the speed of my words increases as I go through Mountain Day, Nick Hollis, pink panties, Porsche, Crenshaw, sweatshirt shrine, library, pregnancy.

When I'm done, I have to recover from the exertion with a deep breath. And then I risk a glance over at Strots. I couldn't look at her while I was speaking because I was worried the you're-crazy expression on her face would keep me from revealing everything I needed to.

Except she isn't looking at me like I'm nuts.

"I'm sorry," she says slowly. Then she leans forward, as if she's not sure her ears are working properly. "*Greta* was the one fucking Nick Hollis?"

As I nod, Strots looks down at the Coke bottle like she's forgotten she had it in her hand. "Holy . . . shit."

"I didn't make any of this up." At least, I think I didn't. I'm pretty sure I didn't. "And I told the police everything about her and Nick. Well, not about my role in it all coming out. But they already knew everything that had been going on between them."

Strots just sits there with her soda, staring at the plastic bottle. I'm willing to bet the thing is like a TV screen and it's playing an after-school movie about her and Greta.

"I have a credibility problem," I say to fill the silence. "But the police have other more reliable sources. I mean, the administration investigated Nick and Greta, right? Ms. Crenshaw went to them with what she found in his car. That's why he was fired. And clearly, the school didn't—or couldn't—keep the details of it all from the cops."

Strots's eyes lift to my own. "When did Crenshaw go to the administration? After you met with the dean about the telephone room shit?"

"Yes." I can picture that open Porsche door and all the rain like the scene is right in front of me. "God, what if Ms. Crenshaw finds out I was the one who put the panties in the car and set her up—"

"Jesus Christ," Strots interrupts, "Mr. Hollis was porking Greta? Fuck. *And* he knocked her up? I'll bet he's shitting in his pants right now."

I change tracks in my mind. "His wife knows, too. I saw them arguing down in the parking lot. He must have told her who he was with, but I don't know if she's aware there was a pregnancy."

"Maybe she killed Greta."

I picture Mrs. Hollis. Sandy. "I don't think so. She looks like a mom."

A very smart, well-educated, classy, professional mom, I add to myself.

"Oh, well, then for sure she's innocent," Strots mutters. "Absolutely."

Given that cogent point, I decide not to add that the fact the woman is trying to save people from AIDS is probative of her lack of involvement as well.

"Or maybe it was Crenshaw because she's creepy obsessed and got jealous."

"What is this, Clue, girls' school edition?" Strots cocks her head to the side and affects a narrator voice. "'It was the geometry teacher with the protractor in the woods.'"

"Guess you're right," I say lamely. "I just don't understand why Nick Hollis isn't mentioned anywhere in the news."

Strots laughs out loud. "You think this school is going to volunteer to the media how an RA was fucking a minor in one of their dorms? Especially when the girl's last name is Stanhope and he's married and she turns up both pregnant and dead?"

I think of the article in the *New Haven Register*, and mention that Nick's got a history.

My roommate is poleaxed yet again, and I am so satisfied by her reaction that I have a sudden insight into why people gossip.

"You're kidding me," she says. "Fuck, this just keeps getting better."

"The pregnancy really gives Nick a motive, right?" I say this like I am Columbo and I've investigated a hundred murders. "Maybe he killed her to cover it all up."

"But he'd already been fired. What does the murder get him except prison time?"

"What if she was blackmailing him, though? And he couldn't go to his father for another payout for a girl? The Stanhopes have lost their money, and Greta never was a second-best kind of girl. Maybe she hit on him for major cash."

Strots's brows bolt up into her forehead, and it's a minute before she snaps back into focus. "Well, the Hollises have plenty of cash, for sure, and they're going to be wicked pissed at him. My grandmother knows the family from Newport, and they're part of the Old Guard, as she calls it. Those kinds of people? They're totally old-fashioned, all into propriety and shit. A son who's messing around with fifteen-year-olds? And got caught, twice? It's a goddamn stain on the name."

We both go quiet, and I'm glad my roommate has finally stepped into my realm of overthinking, not because it's a good habit that will help her in her own life, but because it's nice to not be alone.

Unsurprisingly, she snaps free of the spin fast. "None of this is our fucking problem. They're the adults. It's their job to figure it all out, not ours."

That's the thing about kids our age, I think to myself. We're all for being the big, loud noise until the repercussions get real—and then we just want to hand over situations like this to the grown-ups. It's like when we broke a toy back when we were five. Here, fix this.

Except there isn't anything that will bring Greta back. And really . . . is that so bad an outcome?

"For what it's worth," Strots says as she finishes the Coke down to the last drop, "don't worry about anybody else getting aggressive around here. I'll make sure you don't get hurt. I'm not afraid of anyone."

As a wellspring of gratitude blooms in my chest, I fidget and twitch. I don't want Strots to know just how affected I am by her heroic nature, but the truth is, I am about to fly away as a result of the lifting, soaring warmth behind my sternum.

I am never going to get used to the way Strots comes to my rescue.

Making some lame excuse about needing a shower before bed, I go over to my closet, gather my toiletries, and leave.

For the first time since the cops showed up on campus, I feel like I don't have to look over my shoulder as I walk along the hall. I am safe because Strots makes it so.

And I love her for this.

chapter
THIRTY-THREE

The following day, the local paper prints on its front page what "Jerry" had told the librarian not to speak of. I find this out at lunch as I sit alone at my table. A number of the girls have brought the *Greensboro Gazette* in with them, and they pass the first section around, table to table, everybody whispering the p-word like if they say it out loud they're going to spontaneously miss their period and start gestating.

I read the article for myself when one of them puts the headliner down to empty her tray and then gets distracted by a friend running up to her and demanding to know if she's heard the news. She becomes so busy establishing herself as a primary source that she leaves the actual news-breaking article on top of the covered bin.

I snag the soft folds. Reading quickly, I look for the name Nick Hollis and do not find it.

"Can I have that back."

The girl who forgot her copy is standing over me, utterly indignant. Like there are only a certain number of reads before the ink is consumed by our retinas and the thing is rendered blank.

"Sorry." I hand the paper back. "But you left it."

She walks off. I don't recognize her so she's probably a Wycliffe upperclassman. They all look the same to me.

I glance across the crowded cafeteria. Strots isn't around. She hasn't been sitting with Keisha, obviously, but there's a second field hockey table that has, predictably, welcomed her with open arms. She's not there now, though, and I wonder if my roommate's gone back down to the station, because she left our room early this morning without her books.

I go through the motions of my afternoon classes, distracted by the effort of trying to discipline myself against the suspect-based *Wheel of Fortune* game my brain is determined to play. According to my spinning thoughts, there are potential murderers everywhere. They are anybody who ever spoke with Greta. Took a class with her. Ate with her.

When I return to my dorm, there are police cars parked in front of Tellmer again, and I wonder who they're taking away in handcuffs.

Pulling open the front door, I hear girls on the phone in the phone room, but it's regular traffic and conversation, three of the receivers open, the girls talking about care packages and test grades with their parents. I remind myself I better call my mother back, just to reassure her I'm alive.

And then I'm at the base of the stairs.

I look down to Ms. Crenshaw's closed door, and think about her shrine. Has she dismantled it yet? It's hard to imagine those talismans mean the same thing to her now.

Hustling up the stairs, I arrive on the second floor in time to see the other plainclothes detective, the one who is not Bruno, leave Nick Hollis's apartment. Through the closing door, I catch a glimpse of our residential advisor. He's sitting on his sofa, his head in his hands. But hey, at least he's not being arrested for murder.

The detective doesn't even look at me as he brushes up against my book bag to get at the stairs. It's clear his mind is elsewhere, his middle-aged features grim.

Heading for my room, I wonder what Nick Hollis's father is saying about all this, especially given the newest, sad twist that's come out. I decide that the lawyer who was hired to fight the firing must be a good one because Nick is still on campus. This cannot last, however. St. Ambrose will really have to remove him now, and going by his obvious devastation, I don't think he'll protest the pink slip anymore.

I think of the moment I saw our residential advisor on that very first day when he'd been talking to those plumbers. Then I remember him apologizing to me for getting my name wrong. And I recall the empathy in his face when he suggested that I shouldn't feel bad for dropping the ball in the Mountain Day game.

I also think of the many times my eyes clung to him, approving of so much about how he looked and who I ascribed him to be.

It is nearly impossible to square up both his kindness and my fantasy with the situation he now finds himself in, disgraced, unemployed, and surely soon to be divorced. I think of a brand-new sedan easing off the lot at a car dealership, freshly bought and paid for, an owner's joy. But then there is the accident that crumples the front and shears off the rear, everything trashed. It's a good metaphor, although the consequences of Nick's actions are the result of choices freely made. What happened between him and Greta was wrong—and now it has become deadly and very complicated.

I go down to Strots's and my room, and am disappointed that she's not there. Then I remember the time. She has practice. She won't be back until just before dinner, and she'll be starved so she might go eat first at Wycliffe before she returns.

Though I try to focus on my geometry homework, nothing much sticks. Today in class, Ms. Crenshaw was even more scattered and wired than usual, and I found myself unable to look her in the eye. The police are going to want to talk to her, if they haven't already, and to this point, I rise out of my seat and lean over my open textbook. Peering down into the parking lot, I note that her car is gone, but the other two are there. Maybe she's at the station being interviewed right at this moment. Maybe she's relieved that she gets to talk and make sure her name is clear.

I have a sudden image of her burning that turquoise blue sweatshirt, as well as the other strange artifacts of a romance that never was. I guess there are two reasons to disappear the items, both the disillusionment and so she doesn't seem like a suspect.

As I sit back down, I knock my notebook of lined paper off my desk with my sleeve. Cursing, I bend over—

And that's when I see the dirt on the floor.

My desk and Strots's are pushed tight together under the big window, and right in between the end of hers and the start of mine . . . there is a trail of dry brown dirt particles that disappears into the shadowy seam. There aren't a lot of the specks, and they are exactly the color of the scuffed hardwood, so they're hard to see.

I look over the surface of Strots's desk. Then my own.

Nothing dirty on anything.

I look down again. In the back of my mind, I know where I've seen this type of sediment before. It's from the riverbank. I've brought it back in the treads of my boots, from when I was eavesdropping on Greta and the Brunettes. It's a pain in the ass. It's all over the bottom of my closet.

Suddenly anxious, I push my chair back, and as it squeaks, I jump at the unexpected sound. After I recover, I kneel and then get on all fours.

I can see nothing in the juncture of the desks. But again, it's dark down here.

With a shaking hand, I bring the cheap crane-neck lamp to the floor. As its blast of light penetrates the convergence, I see something between the desks.

Something dirty.

Something thin and dirty.

Something that reflects the light through some stains on its surface.

Even though I refuse to believe what I think I'm seeing, I start to make noises, soft, begging noises, even though I don't know from what source I'm searching for mercy. Maybe I am reaching out to God. I don't know.

I'm not normally strong, but a gripping terror gives me enough muscle to shove Strots's desk away.

The knife falls flat on its side.

And I recognize it.

It is the white-handled chef one that I promised Strots I would return to Wycliffe when we thought she was leaving. The one that I put, along with its plate, under the laundry bag in my closet because I wasn't sure my roommate was really going to stay and I was pulling a Crenshaw and starting a shrine to my idol.

I try to stand up, but can't make it fully to the vertical, so I slump in my chair and cover my mouth so I do not scream.

There are stains on the knife. Beneath the dirt that covers its blade and handle, there are dark red patches on the cutting surface—

Instantly, my mind reminds me of something I do not want to remember. It reminds me of the mortician fantasy I entertained, the one that had Greta's lipstick smudged. And then my awareness lickety-split shifts to the rage I felt when the girl threatened my roommate, that incandescent rage nearly uncontainable.

I did experience the very thing that I told Detective Bruno I knew nothing about. I have had moments of violence directed at others. At least in theory.

At least I think it's only been in . . . oh, God.

I remember the very last time I saw Greta alive. It was when she threw open my door and said she was going to take something away from Strots because Strots had taken something away from her.

"Oh . . . *God* . . ."

As my heart flutters in my chest, and a sickening urge to throw up churns my stomach, I try desperately to recall what happened next. I go back to that moment when Greta took off from our room. What did I do? Where did I go?

Leaving the lamp on the floor, I stumble to my closet, open it up, and yank the flimsy string to turn on the overhead light. There on the floor are the boots I wear all the time. I turn both of them over with a shaking hand. There is river mud all across the soles, the same fine silt that is between the desks wedged into the treads' pattern of valleys.

Was it just from when I saw the body and ran from the police? Or is part of it because I tracked Greta to the river and attacked her with the knife I was keeping as a tribute to my roommate—

Outside in the hall, someone shouts.

This gets my attention. Jumping up, I decide to run—but realize I have nowhere to go if I'm looking to get away from the truth.

As implications tumble down on my head like boulders from the sky, I have only one clear thought: I should have known not to put my faith in Detective Bruno's conclusion that I didn't kill Greta Stanhope. Grown-ups aren't really any smarter or more intuitive than children. They're just bigger and taller versions of us.

Now I am moving. I am yanking open the bottom drawer of my desk—

There is an Orange Crush and a bottle of aspirin right next to my lithium.

I suddenly can't breathe. Where did they come from? When did I buy them? It must have been after I went to the library. But why don't I remember?

What else don't I remember is more the question.

I hear a choked sound. It's me, but I don't bother to figure out anything anymore. I just reach down and grab the aspirin and the Orange Crush.

I don't track my trip to the basement, but this amnesia is something that has evidently been creeping up on me, the holes in my memories unnoted because I don't know what I've forgotten. I am a blind person who is unaware that their eyes don't work anymore.

Busting through the door into the boiler room, I slam myself in, barricading my own escape so that I may save the other girls in the dorm from me. I am panting now, but I am not crying. This is beyond anything associated with tears.

I don't turn the light on. There is enough illumination bleeding through the cloudy chicken-wired window of the door, the distilled glow turning everything into a potential monster. As I find a spot to hide myself, the shapes and contours of the boiler and the maintenance supplies are like things that should come at me with teeth bared—except they stay put because they know what I am just learning.

I am a murderer.

I am one of them.

chapter
THIRTY-FOUR

As I take cover behind the boiler, and the heat rolling off the great archaic hunk of metal warms my body, there is only one thing to do.

With shaking hands, I bring forward the aspirin bottle, but I can't open the child safety cap without fumbling the Orange Crush. I slide down the rough concrete wall and sit on my ass so that my lap can cradle the soda.

As I push and twist and get nowhere with the top, I probe my memory of coming back from the library in desperation, trying to recall something of purchasing that which Phil the Pharmacist doc-blocked me on earlier. But the larger question is, when exactly did my illness take the wheel without my knowledge?

Because it is in charge of all of this. It planned all of this.

I realize with a flush of dread that, in fact, it has been running the show all along.

My illness took the panties from the back of my closet and then piloted me down to the parking lot and that tree and that car before I had any conscious idea of what to do with Greta's underwear. I start to cry as I remember wondering how I'd known to go down there. At the time, it had seemed like a coincidence that had led to a logical conclusion, and I'd been grateful for the arbitrary linkage.

Now I know it wasn't any random extrapolation.

It was my illness growing and changing, maturing . . . so it could take over in a new way. I see that the panties and the Porsche were a trial run to measure how compliant I could be, one that I misinterpreted as a magical synchronicity of unconnected elements.

I bang my head back into the solid wall I am up against. I don't even feel the pain. I don't feel anything as tears roll down my face and drip onto the bottles in my hand and my lap, bottles that I do not remember buying after I murdered the girl I hated for threatening the only friend I have here at Ambrose.

The only friend I've ever had, really.

And the endgame? Well, it was all supposed to lead here, wasn't it, to this moment, in this boiler room. Because I cheated my madness out of its previous attempts to get this plan going when I decided to restart my lithium.

"Why do you want me dead?" I ask my illness. "My death kills you, too. You're so fucking stupid."

As the cap to the aspirin flies off and the bottle nearly follows, the tiny pillow of cotton wedged into the neck of the clear plastic container is all that keeps the pills in place. I try to fish the wad out, but my hands are trembling so badly, it's impossible to get a grip on the fluff. I lose patience and slap the open neck into the palm of my left hand, over and over and over again.

And then I slow down.

And stop.

An idea has formed in my mind, and the glow of its logic is so soft that at first, I cannot see much of what the cognition is. The more I focus, however, the clearer it becomes, emerging from the bog of my consciousness, coming forward to me, fully formed and somewhat beautiful.

Why do you want me dead? My death kills you, too. You're so fucking stupid.

I think I've gotten that all wrong, actually.

There have always been two sides to me. The one grounded in the common reality. The one that is not. The latter has always won when

it wants to. Even on my medication, it's never far off, only held at bay, a storm destined to break through the prevailing weather pattern and hammer at my coastal village.

I think of Greta, tormenting me. Making me miserable.

Driving me to the brink of suicide.

I look at my left hand. My skin is red from the smacking, but the cotton ball is out and there are aspirin, chalky and perfectly round, on my palm sure as if it is a plate.

I try to imagine what would have happened if Greta had survived. She would have kept coming after me, until I dropped out. Or worse.

I think of my rage at her, that unfamiliar emotion coming out of me, unleashed and thirsty for blood.

What if that anger wasn't really about Strots? What if, instead of trying to get me into trouble, my illness was determined to protect me? What if . . . it had taken the wheel and used my body as a tool for its own survival? What if it knew that sooner or later I would break under Greta's torment, and by then it would be too late. What if it knew me and my resolve better than I did.

I didn't think I could kill someone I hated. I didn't think I was physically strong enough. But what if I wasn't the one in control . . . because my illness recognized that for it to survive, Greta Stanhope had to die.

I think back to waking up that morning with the towel on my head, and I wish I had gone through my laundry bag to see where the bloody clothes I'd worn were. Except now . . . I'm thinking I wouldn't have found any. My illness would know to destroy or clean whatever I was wearing.

It is very, very smart.

And suddenly, I see how Greta was killed that night after which I woke up so confused and groggy. I know now that I took the knife that I was keeping as a shrine to Strots and followed the girl out to the river when she went to have a cigarette alone . . . because she was pregnant, and the game she had started with Nick Hollis had gotten way far away from her, and threats concerning my roommate aside, she needed to get ahold of herself and figure out what to do.

Or wait . . . no. I approached her in the hall outside the bathroom and told her we had to meet in private. I intimated that I knew about her and Nick and that she'd better be down at the river at the appointed time or I was going to tell the administration. Or her father. No—tell the press.

She'd be furious that I had something on her, but she wouldn't be scared. I'd never been a threat to her before because I'm a loser who's insane. She wouldn't be on guard at all.

When Greta arrived at the river, at the talking rock, I would step out of the shadows. She would face me and throw out an insult. About my body. My looks. My lack of prospects across all levels of the teenage experience. No one else would be down there with us because, though she isn't threatened by me, her name hasn't publicly been linked to Nick Hollis yet, and over and above that, she doesn't want the pregnancy stuff to get out. She's on a fishing expedition to learn what I know or what I think I know.

I would have the knife hidden at my thigh and I'd keep it out of sight. I would let her broaden her verbiage from an insult or two into a full-blown slam session against me, and the rant would release much of the tension she feels, given the bind she is in . . .

All around us, I hear the river gurgling softly and I smell the damp earth. I see her face in the moonlight, the tasteful makeup, the glow of her blond hair, the brightness of her red cashmere coat, one that is the same hue as the red cashmere sweater Nick Hollis has worn. I think to myself that, like the Guns N' Roses CDs, she bought this particular piece of outerwear because of him.

She's so into herself, so riding her wave of derision, that she doesn't notice me switching my grip on the knife's handle or bringing it forward. I time things perfectly, because unlike my conscious mind, my illness knows exactly what to say and when to say it:

How many times did you fuck Nick in that Porsche, anyway?

Greta stops her rant and stares at me, clearly wondering whether she's heard me right. It is in this moment of her confusion that I stab her for the first time. Right in the front of the throat.

So she can't scream.

And then I overpower her. She stumbles back off her flats—blowing out of her left shoe, which was why her foot was bare when I saw the body—and my illness uses my weight to keep her down as I mount her like I am straddling a chair. I stab her again. And again.

I smell blood and I hear a different gurgling than the river's flow over its rock bed, the sounds of death rising up through the knife wound that opened her larynx like a can of tomatoes.

I leave her a little bit alive. I sit back on her pelvis and I watch her mouth gape for air, like a guppy's. Her face is speckled with blood, and some of it is coming out of her mouth. It looks black against her pale white skin in the ambient glow of the night. The spots on her clothes are getting bigger and bigger, stains looking for more legroom.

Just before her heart stops, I take my thumb and smudge the red plasma on her lips. Like it is L'Oréal's best. Because she's worth it.

And what do you know, I really am her mortician.

Then she is dead.

I am let down at this point, especially as I wave my free hand over her open, sightless eyes.

This has been fun, I think.

And now, I have a problem.

Dismounting her, I back up to consider the scene, comparing it with things I've seen in the movies or murders that have been covered by my mom's magazines. I imagine a grainy black-and-white reproduction of what I'm looking at on the front page of the *Greensboro Gazette*. I hope they get the scoop. The killing happened in their town, after all, so if there's going to be a jump on this gruesome mess, they should have it over the national news outlets.

While I'm marshaling my plausible deniability options, I kneel down, put the knife aside on the dirt, and rinse my hands in the rushing water. I check out my black clothes and am relieved that they're not that badly marked up with blood. With any luck, I can get upstairs without running into anybody—

Shit. My face. I'll bet I have some blood on it. I got really close out of necessity, and also because I wanted to feel the pain I was inflicting. This is personal, this killing. It is about Greta.

Strots was right about that.

I fish around in the pockets of my coat and take out a washcloth that I suddenly remember putting in there. I planned this really well. I get the small square of terry cloth wet and I scrub my face and neck. Then I rinse and repeat until there is no more pink on the towel. I wring it out and I put the thing back in my pocket though it is damp.

I keep the knife. I put it in my other pocket.

It is my trophy. It is my blue ribbon prize. I've never had an earned award before so you can bet your ass I'm not leaving it out here. Besides, it has my fingerprints all over the handle.

I look a little ways upstream, to a bottleneck in the river flow that has been formed by an impaction of branches, muck, and leaves. I make my way over there and brace myself on a knobby rock above the tangle. Kicking at Mother Nature's dam, I do not care that I am splashed. Kick. Kick. *Kick—*

The tangle breaks apart and water courses through, a relative tsunami that swamps my boots.

The surge is strong enough to ride up and over the surface of the big rock Greta is lying on, the rush washing under her body. I scramble out of the way, but make sure I'm still in the river itself so my treads leave no trace. I watch over the cleansing, my hands on my hips, ready to scold the water if it doesn't work hard enough to get rid of pesky evidence like any foot- or handprints I may have left.

The stream performs its duty well. The big boulder is washed free of blood and dirt, and yet the body doesn't move. The hair does, though. It's as if Greta is standing in a breeze, her long blond locks flowing for the last time.

It is upon this image that my awareness gradually retracts from the past and grounds me in the present.

I am still in the boiler room, behind the furnace, pills in my hand, soda at the ready, tears rolling down my face.

Even if my illness was in charge, my hand gripped that knife. My arm did the stabbing. I am guilty, complicit in a way a court is going to need Dr. Warten to explain to a jury.

"I'm sorry, Greta," I choked out. "Oh, God . . . Mom, I'm sorry."

There is a temptation to fall into hysteria, but I must resist while I have autonomy. If my illness has become self-aware, the singularity has to be intercepted. Suicide has never been more of an imperative, and I curl my hand around the pills, ready to bring them to my mouth—

A vision of me appears before me.

She is sitting against the closed door in the exact same position I'm in, her legs splayed out, her torso at a right angle, her black clothes like she is wrapped in the shadows she came out of. She has no aspirin in her palm and no orange soda with her, and that is how I know she is other than me. This is not a mirror image.

This is my illness.

She meets my eyes steadily, but why wouldn't she. She is in control.

"You shouldn't have done that," I tell her. "I know why you did, but it was wrong."

She shakes her head at me.

"You know I have to end this, right." As I hold up the aspirin, I'm aware that this is a new low for me, a new high for my disease. I've never actually talked to what ails me before. "You crossed a line."

She shakes her head again. And I interpret it to mean that she's going to stop me from committing suicide.

This gives me desperate strength.

"I'll do it right now," I say. "Goddamn it, right fucking *now*."

I mean to put the whole handful of aspirin in my mouth, but I fumble with the pills, dropping most of them onto the front of my shirt. Cursing, I pour more out into my hand as the bitter taste slices into my tongue.

When I look back up, she's gone from the dim interior, and I'm suddenly terrified. Dropping the bottle, I scramble to my feet and look all around the boiler room. I can't see well enough. On shaky legs, I fumble over to where my illness was sitting and slap a hand around the wall by the door, searching for the light switch. When I find it, I turn on the ceiling fixture and rear back from the source of illumination like a vampire, shielding my eyes with the crook of my elbow.

As things adjust, I drop my arm. There's nothing in the utility space but a floor mop in a dry orange bucket, a pop-up caution flag, a stack of metal chairs, and the old boiler.

I walk around the room, aspirin dropping off my shirt and bouncing on the floor, happy little pills, skipping over the grungy concrete like it's someone's birthday party.

Boy, did they not get the memo.

I pace for a while in the small, nothing-revealed space. Then I stop in the center of it and look at the bottle of aspirin that is back where I started, lying knocked over on the floor by the soda that rolled off my lap. There are still plenty in there to do the job. But there are also the ones I've dropped, and if I'm imminently going to die, why do I care if I put dirt in my mouth?

I think of Strots and tell myself she will understand. When it all comes out, she'll get why I killed myself and be okay with it. I picture her, clear as day, saying that she isn't afraid of anyone and she'll make sure I am safe.

We did not know at the time that I am perfectly safe because I am the threat.

It's everyone else who needs to worry. My monster has found a way out of its cage, and all I have to do is think of how I stared down at Greta's body in satisfaction and how I had to keep the knife as a trophy, to know that I have to take care of this.

My illness has a new game, and it makes Greta's version of dominoes look like child's play.

I go back over to the aspirin bottle and pick it up. I find it funny that I chose the generic, not the Bayer, to save money. As if being frugal matters after you're dead?

I lick my lips and grimace at the taste that's already in my mouth. It's going to get worse. Thank God for the Orange Crush.

Tilting the aspirin bottle over my palm, I . . .

Change my mind.

"No!" I shout as I fling the stuff away.

As the CVS-branded container ricochets off the wall, pills spool out like it's the evacuation of a burning building. The bottle lands inside the mop's bucket, the hollow ringing sound almost as loud as my voice, the hole in one the kind of score I couldn't have made if I'd aimed for the thing.

I jab a finger across at the door, at where she was sitting. "I'm *not* going to fucking kill myself just to get rid of you. That's not how this ends!"

I do not want to go out a coward. I do not want the last thing I do on this earth to be dictated by my disease.

That is not going to be my final act.

I kick the plastic Orange Crush bottle like a soccer ball and the force sends it careening into the corner, after which the laws of physics take it on a tour of the boiler room, introducing it to the stack of chairs, the spindly legs of a stool, the snake of some metal pipes that run along the floor. The soda comes to rest under the boiler, like it is taking cover in case my foot gets another bright idea with its name on it.

I'm going to turn myself in to the police.

I am going upstairs to my room. I am getting the knife. I am walking down into town, to the police station, and turning myself in.

I'm going to confess and take responsibility for actions that were not my choice, but are my doing. And then I will be put away for life, after which my disease will be treated into a remission that will be permanent, because everything will be permanently managed by professionals.

I will still be alive, and I will exist to taunt my disease. Trapped behind prescription bars, my bipolar madness will be reduced to a restless tiger that paces with fanged impotence. If I have to be in a mental institution or a jail for the rest of my days to finally win? Standing up to my disease makes the sacrifice worth it.

My hand is not shaking as I open the door, and when I step out, I take a deep breath. Things shut behind me with a click, and the finality of the sound spurs me on. I am grim and focused as I march my way to the nearest set of stairs, the ones by the laundry room.

Upstairs. Get the knife. Go into town—

"Sarah?"

I ignore whoever says my name.

"Hey, Sarah, stop," the voice demands.

Now is not the time, I think as I turn around with impatience.

Keisha is leaning out of the laundry room. She looks exhausted, dark circles rimming her red, puffy eyes. She looks like she's been crying. For, like, days.

"I can't talk right now," I say. "I'm in the middle of something—"

"Wait." She comes out. She is taller than me, physically stronger, too. But she seems very fragile. "Please."

As I shake my head, I think of the way my illness just manifested itself outside of me. I don't want to hurt anybody, especially not this girl. "Keisha, I really can't be here right now—"

My roommate's ex drops her voice, even though there's no one around. Or at least no one that I'm aware of.

"I need to talk to you about Strots. And the night Greta died."

chapter
THIRTY-FIVE

As I part my lips for another I-gotta-go, something in Keisha's face makes me slowly close my bitter-tasting mouth. Her eyes are steady but scared, and her expression is like she's physically in pain even though she seems not to be injured in the flesh. More than all that, however, she is positively urgent, and I know how that desperation feels.

"Come on," she says softly. "I can't talk to anyone else. This is important."

We go into the laundry room. Her load is in the dryer, some zipper making the rounds of the tumbler, the hiss of metal on metal irregular.

Keisha's homework is spread out on the table where I did mine when I used to have to guard my black clothes against bleach. But I don't need to worry about that ever again. For a whole host of reasons.

We sit down together. I take the chair with a clean shot to the doorway because I have to go turn myself in to the police for the homicide I committed.

"I don't know where she went after she broke up with me," Keisha says.

"What?" I ask, even though I don't care and I'm not really listening. I'm just trying to figure out how to get free of this without seeming rude.

"She left my room after she broke up with me—"

I do a double take. "Wait a minute." I rub my head, which has started to ache. Good thing I took two aspirin. Or three. "You broke up with her."

Keisha frowns at me. "No, I didn't. Who told you that?"

"Strots."

"She lied." Keisha is emphatic, leaning toward me over her chemistry book. "She came up to my room and told me we had to stop seeing each other. She said she wasn't going to be responsible for getting me kicked out because of what Greta accused her of. She said . . . she loved me, but that it was over."

I recoil. "I don't understand. She told me *you* broke up with *her*."

"I didn't. Fuck, you think I don't know what it's like to be talked about? And I don't care about what Greta threatened to do. I don't care about any of these bitch asses. I'm going to be just fine, with or without Ambrose. Without Strots, though . . ." Her eyes flood with tears. "There has to be a better reason for us not to be together than this bullshit school and that whore who lives across the hall from you guys."

Lived, I correct to myself.

I lean forward, too. "What exactly did Greta say she was going to do?"

"She threatened to go to the administration about the two of us." Keisha's face hardens. "She told Strots she was going to get me kicked out because she knew that even if Strots could get around the rules, someone like me can't."

"Did Greta confront you, too?"

"No. Just Strots." Keisha shakes her head. "And right after, Strots came to my room and broke up with me. It was a fucking mess. She was crying. I was crying. I was like, why the fuck are we ending this? But she wouldn't listen to me. I begged her. I told her she didn't need to be making decisions for me. I can take care of myself. She'd made up her mind, though. And you know her. Once it's done, it's fucking done."

Keisha goes quiet for a minute and then sits back, her long-fingered hands playing with the corner of her open textbook, fanning the strict edge of the bound pages.

"When she left my room, it was, like, nine o'clock." Keisha goes back to looking at me. "About an hour later, I decided it's bullshit. So I went to your-all's place. I knocked. No one answered. I opened the door. You were asleep. She wasn't there."

"Maybe she went for a walk to clear her head and have a cigarette," I offer. "She does that sometimes."

"That's what I thought. So I came down here and went out the back door. It was too cold, though, and I needed a coat. I ran back upstairs, and by the time I came down again, someone had come in the door. There were, like, damp footprints across the parking lot and into the dorm, and then prints down the corridor to the stairs."

That was me, I think to myself.

Except . . . if Keisha said she saw me asleep, how did I get to the river, kill Greta, and go back to my room so quickly? The basement is hot and dry because of that huge boiler. Wet doesn't stay wet for long. Whoever made the prints had just entered the dorm.

"I'm sorry," I say. "When you looked in our room, I was asleep?"

"Yeah. You had a towel wrapped around your hair like you'd just taken a shower. You looked like you'd passed out before you had a chance to unwrap it."

"And after that you saw the damp footprints in the basement?"

"Yeah."

"This makes no sense," I say under my breath.

"Anyway, I followed the tracks up the side stairs. They seemed to disappear at the second floor, but I don't know if it was because the moisture had, like, worn off."

"What did you do next?"

"I checked your room again. You were still in bed, right where you'd been."

"That's impossible."

"Why?"

I wave a hand to dismiss that. "Keep going."

I hear voices now. They're muffled, like there are a couple of people on the side stairs, arguing.

Keisha glances over her shoulder and I become worried she won't keep talking. But then she faces me again. "Anyway, I found Strots in the shower. I know because I looked into your-all's bathroom and her bucket was gone from her cubby. I also recognized the smell of her shampoo in the air."

"Did you talk to her?"

"Not right away. I waited for her out in the hall." Keisha shakes her head slowly, like she's remembering something that bothered her. "She wasn't right when she came out of the bathroom."

The back door to the dorm opens and closes. I hear more voices. Then footfalls in the corridor. They don't come down toward the laundry room, though. They head to the opposite stairwell.

"What do you mean, she wasn't right?" I hear myself ask.

"She was only in a towel."

"Why's that a problem? She was just out of the shower."

"She had a pile of folded clothes in her hands." Keisha shakes her head again, like she's been over all of this a million times in her mind. "She put them behind her back. She didn't want me to see them."

"What did you say when you talked?"

"That was the thing. She wouldn't speak to me. She barely looked at me. She just walked back to your room and shut the door in my face."

"She was upset. You guys had just broken up."

Those black eyes lock on mine. "The clothes, though. They had a funny smell. They smelled like fresh mud."

I stare across the table at her, across her open chemistry book and her notebook and her two Bic pens, one blue and one red.

"She didn't kill Greta," I say.

Keisha's voice cracks: "I think she might have."

I blink and feel like I can't breathe. "You're wrong. For one thing, the timing is off." She has to be confused about those wet footprints. And what she thought she saw in my room. And also the clothes in my roommate's hands. "For another, neither you nor Strots was in a sound frame of mind that night. Everything only seems weird because you're dissecting it and looking for clues."

Keisha rubs her eyes and then drops her hands in defeat. She says something in despair that I can't quite catch.

I reach across and put my hand on her forearm. It is warm and solid underneath her Huskies sweatshirt.

"I think you're afraid that that's what happened." My tone is compassionate because I feel for her, I really do. "I think you're terrified that she did something really bad because you love her. I think your head's all fucked up and so are your emotions and all of that is a breeding ground for speculation. Trust me, I know a lot about what the mind can do of its own accord. In circumstances like this, you're liable to create connections between facts that don't actually exist."

Keisha shakes her head. "I saw what I saw."

"Your order of events and your conclusions are the issue. Not your eyes. Be logical. Do you *really* think that Strots went down to the river and murdered Greta? Like, stabbed her nine times with a knife."

I normally wouldn't have the guts to say something as confrontational as this, especially not to Keisha, who not only is a star athlete and on the honor roll, but who has absolutely no history of mental illness. But I know that the blood is on my own hands.

I give her muscular arm another squeeze and get to my feet. "Don't torture yourself with hypotheticals."

"I love her."

I don't know what to say to make the girl feel better. "She loves you, too."

I mean this, but I also know the words are not really a balm. Keisha is going to be fucked for a long time. Strots, too.

And this makes me think of my mother. Jesus, my poor mother. Sure, I'm not killing myself, but is alive and a homicide defendant really much better? How about alive and on death row? Does Massachusetts even have the death penalty? I've never had to look it up before.

This is my first, and hopefully only, murder.

As I leave the laundry room, I am a train back on track, except I go to the left, not the right, because those voices are still nattering away on the landing of the closest set of stairs and the last thing I need is to run into anybody. While I walk along, my steadfast stride shoots me past the boiler room, and I have a thought that I've left the Orange Crush and the aspirin behind.

I'm not going in there to retrieve them, that's for sure.

I take the east-side stairs up two at a time, and as I emerge onto my hall, there are more doors open than usual, more girls standing in the corridor. They're congregating in groups, three-leafed clovers occasionally interspersed with a quatrefoil clutch. They don't notice me, and that is normal. I notice them, and that is also normal.

I have a thought that this is the last normal anything for me. Yet I remain resolved.

This is my chance to be a hero, and not in the sense that I'm ridding the world, and myself, of a scourge. The court system will have to do that. Still, setting the judicial outcome into motion is a visceral victory, one that my disease, after it has taken so much from me, cannot cheat me out of.

It is upon this particular wave of surety and purpose that I surf through the door of my room to get the knife.

I jerk to a halt.

No, this is not right.

I rush over to the desks, which are, in contrast to the disorder in which I left them, back in proper position, lined up side by side. The crane lamp, which I had taken down to see into the crack, is no longer on the floor, but back arching over my textbooks. My chair is tucked into its proper spot, all neat and tidy.

My knees bang into the bare wood as I throw myself onto all fours and look at where the knife should be.

The dusting of dirt is gone.

When I push the desks back apart . . . there is nothing there. No dirty, white-handled kitchen knife with dried blood on its blade.

Like it had never existed in the first place.

"No, no, *no* . . ."

I feel reality sifting through my mind, falling like sand through the sieve of my convictions and conclusions, slipping away once again. But I know what I saw, I know what I did—

"Taylor?"

I look around behind me. Strots is standing in the open door to our room, still as a statue.

"I need your help," I say.

"About what?" She cautiously enters and closes us in. "What do you need help with?"

I flop over so I am sitting on my ass. "I killed Greta. Jesus Christ, Strots, I killed her."

My roommate's double take is not a surprise. Neither is her immediate denial of my statement, because Strots is loyal like that.

"No, you didn't," she says.

"Yes, I did. I used the knife you told me to take back to Wycliffe for you. The night she was killed, I followed her down to the river—"

"No. You didn't."

"—where I stabbed her and I left her there and—"

"You didn't kill her." Strots goes over and sits on her bed. "I don't know what your brain is telling you, but you're innocent. You didn't murder anybody."

"I put the knife here." I point to the desks that are out of joint. "I hid it—"

"No."

"—and now I have to go to the police."

"No, you don't."

"Yes, I do. I'm going to do the right thing for once—"

"So where's the knife?"

I push my hair out of my face. "What?"

"Where's the knife? If you're going to go to the police station to confess, where's the murder weapon?"

I point to the juncture between the desks. "It was right here."

"Okay. So where is it now?"

I blink. I look back and forth between my roommate and the desks. "I don't know."

"You didn't kill Greta, Taylor."

I start to mumble and shake my head. "You don't understand what I'm capable of. I've had a psychotic break, and I—"

"I killed her."

Strots is looking at me without flinching as she says the words. And then, like she knows I'm doubting what I think I heard, she repeats them.

"I killed Greta Stanhope."

There is a whooshing in my ears, the roaring sound like a tidal wave coming in, and sure enough, as it crests, I feel a battering in my body.

"No, you didn't." I am saying what she said to me, in exactly the same kind of firm voice. Except then my tone weakens. Turns pleading. "You couldn't have."

I'm thinking of Keisha now, and what she told me she saw, what her timeline was.

Strots looks down at her strong hands, splaying out the fingers. "She was going to go to the administration about me and Keisha. I couldn't let her do that. I just . . . I couldn't."

"Strots, you don't know what you're saying." My voice goes up at the end, like it's a question, because I don't want to lose my chance to be a hero, to finally do the right thing against my illness. And also because I don't want Strots to lie to protect me. And because I don't want my roommate to go to jail because then she won't live with me here anymore. "You don't know—"

"Greta was pissed off about Nick getting fired and everything. She thought I was the one who outed her even though I didn't know a goddamn thing about it. She confronted me and told me she was going to take what I loved away from me, just like I did to her. I told her to leave Keisha out of it. We got into it big-time."

"Where?"

"Outside Wycliffe. After dinner." Strots shakes her head. "It was dark. No one really saw us. I went to her room a little later. She was alone. I told her I wanted to make a deal with her, that she needed to meet me down by the river before curfew so we would have some privacy." Strots's eyes are looking toward me, but she's no longer seeing me. "I thought it through before I left the dorm. I put a hat down on my head low. I had gloves on. I had the knife in the pocket of my sweatshirt—I'd seen it on the plate under your laundry bag in your closet. I waited at the big rock for a while. I was worried she was going to blow me off. Then I was worried she wouldn't come alone, that Francesca or Stacia might be with her. But eventually she showed up by herself, and I . . ."

Strots's voice fades. When she starts talking again, she has to clear her throat. "As soon as I saw her, I chickened out. I couldn't follow through with it. Except then . . . she started talking at me, and she got into last year, all the shit she did to me. She was throwing it in my face, laughing—I just lost it."

She looks down at her hands again like she doesn't recognize them. "I didn't mean to kill her. Even after all that planning, I don't know what I was thinking. But then it happened and I just panicked. I buried the knife about fifty yards away from the big rock in a hollowed-out stump. I came back here, had a shower, and hid my clothes. The next day I took them down to the gym and washed them in the industrial machines with the towels from practice. Then when no one was looking, I threw them away in the dumpster because I knew pickup was in the morning."

Dimly, I'm aware that there are flashing lights down below in the parking area. Red and blue. The alternating colors penetrate our bank of windows and strobe the ceiling.

"But the knife . . ." I look to the space between the desks.

"I got paranoid the cops would find it out by the river. So last night I went down and got it back from the stump. I was lucky. They'd been scrambling and hadn't really searched the area properly."

I crab-walk backward across the floor, until the metal frame of my bed prevents me from going any farther. In a messy haul, I peel myself up off the pine boards and dump my body on my mattress so that I am on the same level Strots is.

"So where's the knife now?" I ask.

She narrows her eyes. "You don't know what just happened?"

"We both just confessed to murder," I mutter dryly. "I'm pretty clear on that."

"Well, see, here's the funny part," she says without smiling. "I was wondering what to do with the knife, you know, all anxious and shit. I came back right after my last class and decided I wasn't going to practice. I was going to grab my cigarettes and go down into town to look for a better place to get rid of the blade after dark. When I got to our floor, I heard this weird noise coming out of Nick Hollis's apartment. It was like a thump and then shuffling."

She doesn't go any further.

Through the open sash on her side of our window, I hear male voices. And then they cut off sharply, like the people, like the police, entered the dorm through the back door.

The hairs at the nape of my neck stand up. "What was the sound, Strots."

She rubs her face. "Anyway, I just kept on going. I went to the bathroom, you know, then came in here. You weren't back from class yet because you have chemistry lab. I got my cigs and left." Her eyes focus on the middle ground between us. "Town didn't do shit for me. When I returned, I came up the stairs again, and I couldn't get the noise out of my head. It was so . . . weird, and hell, maybe I knew what it was in the back of my mind. I knocked on Nick Hollis's door. Then I tried the knob. When I opened things . . ." Her right eye starts to twitch. "He was hanging from a belt off a hook in one of the ceiling beams. He'd knocked a chair over under his feet. I think the shuffling noise was his toes, you know . . . brushing against the side of the chair."

"Oh . . . *fuck.*" I put my hands to my face. "Oh, God, is he dead? Oh, fuck fuck fuck—"

"Yeah, he was gone by then. He wasn't moving anymore. His eyes were open . . . and he wasn't, like, twitching, or anything. No nothing." She looks down at the floor. "And that's when I realized . . ."

I blink a couple of times. "You left the knife in his apartment."

"Yeah." She takes a deep breath. "No one else was around. No one else knew what I saw. I backed out of his place, closed the door, and ran down here. When I came in, I saw the desks pushed apart and the knife lying on the floor out in the open. I kind of hoped you were the one who found it, but I prayed that you hadn't touched it. Did you? Did you touch it?"

"No," I whisper.

"Good. I got my gloves on, took the knife, and I made sure nobody was out in the hall when I went back to his apartment. I put the knife right on the kitchen counter, and then I made sure I left the door open some. I knew that sooner or later someone would look in. And that's why the police are here. Someone did. Someone called them."

I focus on the ceiling and stare at the blinking lights that flash over our heads.

"Is this real?" I ask no one in particular. "Is this actually happening?"

Strots gets up from her bed and faces the window.

When she just stands there, like a zombie, I get scared for some reason. "Strots?"

It's a long while before she answers me.

"You were right," she says in a broken voice. "There's no place for people like you and me in this world."

"What are you talking about? I never said that." Except I think she's right. I think I did. "Strots, what are you—"

"No place." She shrugs. "I don't want to do this anymore, Taylor."

"Do what?"

"I just framed an innocent man."

I get to my feet, too. Something about her is alarming me, even though I can't pinpoint exactly what it is.

"Nick wasn't innocent," I say. "He fucked a student."

"But he didn't kill anyone." She's staring out at the night, staring through the panes of glass. "He's dead, but that doesn't give me the right to ruin his life. Memory. Whatever. He didn't kill Greta."

The way she's staring at those glass panes makes me draw rays in directions that terrify me.

"Hey, Strots," I say, "how about we have a smoke, huh? I'll try a cigarette for the first time. You can show me how to do it."

I have no idea what I am saying. I'm talking fast. I am—

"I'm so done with everything, Taylor." She looks at me. And takes a step back. And another one. "I'm really sorry about this—"

"Where are you going? You need to sit down and—"

All at once, I am back at Mountain Day. I am in the too-hot sun. I am on Ms. Crenshaw's team. It is before everything got so grown-up, before people died, before any of us had any idea about how dark and dangerous things were to become.

I am panting during that time-out for the bee sting. I have my hands braced on my thighs and my torso tilted forward over the grass as I try to get more oxygen into my lungs.

Strots is standing next to me. She's leaning down and putting her face into my own. *Don't worry about the eyes and the faces of your opponents. Focus on the body in front of you. The arms and legs will tell you where they're headed. The body never lies.*

These words, dismissed at the time, become the single most important thing I have ever heard as I realize, a split second before Strots lunges, that she is going to take a running leap at the window and launch herself face-first into a free fall to the pavement below.

chapter

THIRTY-SIX

I move before my roommate does. And my body launches itself not at her, but at a point three feet in front of where she is.

As she springs forward right after I do, we become pool balls on a path of intersection—which is the only reason why I, with my lesser weight and strength, can knock her out of her trajectory. The impact is explosive and I get an elbow in the face, my jaw clamping shut so hard my molars are singing as my momentum carries both of us off our feet and onto Strots's bed.

I land on top of her, and I know I have no time. She is stunned and not fighting back, but that's going to change as soon as she realizes she's been denied her descent—and she is certainly powerful enough to throw me off of her and succeed in busting through that fragile glass and those flimsy antique struts.

"No!" I hiss as I roll her onto her back. "Not like this!"

I keep my voice down because I don't want things to carry, but as I shove my face into hers, maintaining the low volume requires self-control.

"You are *not* fucking doing that."

In response to me, her eyes get wide and her arms flop, like she cannot believe what I've done or that I'm yelling at her.

I grab the front of her sweatshirt at the neckline and yank her up.

"You're *not* doing that." I slam her head back down into the mattress. "You're *not*!"

I do it again, jerking her up, shoving her down. I start to cry, my tears falling onto her cheeks.

"You are the *best* person I've ever met—and you are not going to do that!" I'm hysterical now, and forgetting to stay quieter. "You are my only friend! Don't make me hear that sound again!"

Of a body hitting the asphalt.

Only this time, instead of it being the girl who told me about Orange Crush, it's Strots, it's the bravest, strongest girl I know, pitching herself out of our dorm room for reasons that make all the sense in the world and absolutely none whatsoever.

I try to pull it together. I stop with the pounding and I calm myself.

"I've already heard it once," I say. "I heard the sound when a girl I knew jumped off the roof of the hospital. She landed on the pavement, and I know what it sounds like. You're are *not* leaving that as my last memory of you, do you understand me? You are *not* fucking doing that to either one of us."

We're both breathing hard. And she's the next who speaks, her voice rough.

"I can't live in this world anymore, Taylor. I can't live with what I've done—"

"The hell you can't," I snap. "Nick Hollis killed Greta Stanhope because she got pregnant, and tried to blackmail him, and his life was over. He committed suicide today because he knew he wasn't going to get away with it. *And isn't that terrible.*"

When Strots just stares up at me in numb shock, I tighten my hold on the front of her sweatshirt again and grit out the words. "Isn't it fucking awful how it ended for them both, Strots. It's a real fucking tragedy. *Say it.*"

My eyes bore into hers, and in my mind, I am breaching the hardcap confines of her skull and going into her brain, rewiring things.

"That isn't what happened," Strots says weakly.

"*Reality* isn't what happens," I shoot back at her. "Reality is what our brains tell us is true. It's all just in our minds. So you are going to start telling yourself right fucking now that—"

"That's not what—"

"—*he* was a philanderer who liked young girls and was just going to keep finding them wherever he was. *She* was a bitch who played games with people and got what was coming to her. *Nick Hollis killed Greta Stanhope because she got pregnant and tried to blackmail him. Then he hanged himself in his room because he knew he was going to jail.* You are going to fucking repeat this every waking minute and through all your sleeping dreams until it is the singular truth that drowns out all others. Do you understand me? That is what you are going to tell yourself, starting right fucking now, and your mind is going to believe it because you're going to train it like a fucking dog."

"It doesn't solve anything," she says.

"Neither does you jumping out that window. You and I don't belong now, but maybe . . ." I clear my own throat. "Maybe it gets better. In the future. Maybe things change for people like you and me."

"You don't know that."

"And neither will you if you die tonight over something you didn't fucking do—"

"I did do it—"

"No, you didn't—"

"What's going on here?"

I wrench around to the door. Keisha is standing just inside our room, her eyes bugged, her arm shaking as she holds the doorknob.

"Shut that fucking door," I snap at her. *"Right now."*

She recoils. Then she steps inside and closes things up, too shocked to do anything else.

I point my finger at her like it's a gun, my voice low and threatening. "It's such a shame what happened between Nick and Greta. Can you believe he killed her. And then hanged himself this afternoon. It's really a tragedy. *Isn't it.*"

Keisha's wide eyes go to Strots. Then they return to me.

I am prepared to beat the facts into the girl if I have to. To protect my roommate, from herself, from the world, I am prepared to do whatever it takes.

Except I don't need to start throwing punches, as it turns out.

After a long moment, Keisha slowly nods. Then she crosses her arms over her chest, lifts her chin, and gives me a steady stare.

"Yeah, Nick Hollis killed Greta Stanhope and hanged himself," she says evenly. "Real fucking mess, but at least it's over now. And we don't ever have to think about it again."

I look down at Strots. "Isn't that right." When my roommate doesn't respond, I say, "Ellen, *isn't that right.*"

Strots's eyes start to water. A tear escapes out of the corner of one of them. Then she looks across our dorm room at the girl she loves.

"I'm sorry, Keisha," she says hoarsely. "I am so sorry."

chapter THIRTY-SEVEN

It's a week later before I'm able to go to Wycliffe for lunch. Over the intervening seven days, I survive on the soda, Little Debbie snack cakes, and chips that I buy every afternoon at four p.m. at the gas station down in town. I use the money I earned over Columbus Day weekend to feed myself these junk food staples. And I keep to this schedule because it's difficult to go back right after classes and settle down in my room. I need the cold air and the walk, so I buy only enough to get me through one twenty-four-hour period at a time.

But woman—or girl, as the case is—cannot live on that diet forever. For one, real food has started to call my name. For another, I feel like I'm wasting cash and I've been poor for too long to be comfortable with such extravagance.

Although I have had another windfall of money. After Nick Hollis was found in his apartment, my mom came to see me again. She was really worried about my mental health, more so than usual, that is, and it was a relief to reassure her I was honestly doing okay. That I was taking my medicine regularly and managing myself well. That, in spite of everything happening around me, I was staying level. Before she drove back home, she gave me two twenty-dollar bills. One was old and soft as a facial cloth. The other was brand spanking new, still stiff and smelling of ink.

I am going to save her money, along with, as of today, the rest of my wages. I'm determined to return home with both those mismatched twenties. Maybe I can take her out to dinner or something with them.

The nicest thing about seeing her, more than the cash or the news that she broke up with her most recent boyfriend, was that when she told me she'd see me in a month to take me home for Thanksgiving break, I found myself looking forward to the vacation. I'm going to be buoyant as I wait for her at the curb with one of my two suitcases. Probably the blue one.

Black's kind of depressing.

And you know, as I leave Palmer Hall after class and cut across the lawn, crunching through colored leaves with a clear sky overhead, I decide I'd really like a hamburger. I'm hoping they're available on the cafeteria line. If not, pizza. Or a turkey sandwich.

I glance around at the girls who are to'ing and fro'ing with me along the sidewalks. All my life, I've heard grown-ups say that youth is resilient, and I'm witnessing that firsthand. We had yet another mandatory dorm meeting the morning after Nick Hollis's body was removed from his apartment. More grief counselors came in. There was more crying in the phone room. Classes were canceled that day.

A lot of girls went home again that weekend. But they came back on Sunday.

And now, things feel pretty close to normal. My contemporaries are laughing and talking in groups around campus. Classes and tests are the same. The rhythms of the school have resumed.

It's not like nothing happened. But no one seems to be dwelling on it.

Well, not in my age group at least. The teachers and the administrators and the RAs are still stressed and strung out. You can tell because they're all exhausted and distracted at the chalkboards when they're teaching or when they're grimly striding between buildings for meetings. I'll bet parents are still freaking out. I know my mother is.

This stuff with St. Ambrose is the one story in *People* magazine that she's said she doesn't want to read. The point of voyeurism, after all, is that it doesn't happen to you. It doesn't happen to your daughter. It's not so close. She says she hasn't watched the evening news, either, and has no plans to for a while.

When she was here, she asked me if I wanted to come home.

I told her no. I wanted to stay.

She asked me if I felt safe in the dorm.

I said absolutely.

When I get to Wycliffe, I go in the front door and drop my book bag with the others in the open area. Through the arches of the cafeteria, I see girls standing in line at the buffet with their trays, and ones clustered around the milk bar, and others sitting at tables.

I venture into the cacophony, pick up a plastic tray, and get in the queue. The food is abnormally interesting to me, which is what happens when you eat the same three things over and over again for a week. I've lost some weight, and I need to get on that, but right now, I'm not inclined to push myself to do anything. I just kind of want to go along . . . and be normal. Whatever that means.

But I do snag that hamburger. And fries.

I'm on the way to my solitary table off to the left, by the trash bin, when I happen to catch a glimpse of Francesca and Stacia. They're sitting with their group of girls from our dorm, and Francesca is holding court, her hands gesticulating as she speaks to her captivated audience.

Greta's replacement has marked her territory, and successively asserted her dominion over the clique. It didn't take her long, and part of that, I suspect, is because no one else really wanted the job, considering the last head of that lofty social circle woke up dead on the big rock down by the river.

Francesca had been waiting for her chance all along, I decide as I sit at my empty table. And I wonder if she didn't attempt a coup on Mountain Day, couched in terms of threats about the relationship with Nick Hollis. Greta, unsurprisingly, defended her turf like a boxer.

But all of that competition is moot now, and at least I'm not worried about Francesca picking on me. I remember her face as she came down those stairs in tennis whites, and then when I was almost throwing up in the bathroom.

She isn't as cruel as Greta was. She's not going to give me any trouble.

The first bite of my hamburger is heaven.

I am chewing when I hear the sound of a bunch of chairs being pushed back all at once, their feet scraping and squeaking over the linoleum floor.

I don't pay the noise any attention—

When my table is suddenly surrounded, I brace myself and keep my head down. On reflex, I pick up my tray to leave, my read of Francesca clearly misinformed.

Except then I look up . . . and recognize the field hockey team's first string of players. And they all have their trays with them.

"Hey, Taylor," Strots says as she sits down next to me. "What's up."

Every one of the athletes parks it along with her, even though they have to pull up an extra chair. Keisha is on Strots's right.

"Um . . . nothing?" I say as I glance at the other girls.

They're relaxed, and they start talking about nothing in particular, picking up the strings of conversations that had been briefly interrupted by their relocation. I glance at Strots. She's making a joke with Keisha. The other girl starts to laugh, and their eyes meet for a moment. And then linger.

"Liking that hamburger?" Strots says to me when she refocuses on her own food.

"It's really good."

"I'm glad."

"Ah . . . me, too."

As the presence of these girls sinks in, I feel an unfamiliar sensation in the center of my chest, especially when the one to my left asks me about my history test, and then tells me she's impressed, but not surprised, that I was at the head of the curve on it.

"You're really smart," she announces. Like it's a fact so indisputable, it doesn't need to be spoken aloud. "Like the smartest girl in the school."

I have no idea what to reply to that.

Instead, I retreat into my own mind.

I go back to the boiler room, where I sat across from my illness and watched that version of me shake my own head. Then I think of the morning after Nick Hollis killed himself, when the truth came out in all the newspapers and on TV . . . the truth that he had been having an illicit affair with Greta Stanhope, and she'd gotten pregnant, and he'd killed her—and then, a few days later, hanged himself from guilt in his apartment.

I remember my illness shaking my head at me.

I know now that when it was doing that, it wasn't deriding me with its power. It was telling me that I got my version of events wrong. I wasn't the one who killed Greta, no matter how keenly I could envision me doing the deed.

Nick Hollis killed her.

With a white-handled knife that he'd taken out of the cafeteria.

That was found on his kitchen counter, right next to his body as it swung from the hook in the beam over the chair he'd knocked out from under himself.

And it is a tragedy.

"Isn't that right, Taylor," Strots says.

I look over at my roommate. I don't have a clue what she's spoken, but I trust her as much as she trusts me. Which is to say, completely.

"Absolutely it is," I reply as I go back to finishing my burger. "That's exactly right."

While I eat my lunch with my new group of friends, I realize what the sensation behind my sternum is. It's the banked warmth that comes with being accepted, by people who will circle around you when you need it. It's the sense of belonging you get when you know, no matter what happens, you're not alone.

This is the reality I'd have created for myself if I could have. Instead, it's unexpectedly been given to me by others. Which is a kind of magic, isn't it?

Then again, I knew Ellen Strotsberry was going to change my life from the moment she first walked through our door.

Still, in all my flushed, private happiness, I'm not ignoring the fact that very grown-up events have marked this semester—and I know that this moment of contentment, this personal Mountain Day summit of mine, will not last forever. Life is complicated by things large and small, and what has complicated the St. Ambrose campus is as big as it gets, two people dead . . . and three people knowing about a cover-up. As far as we are aware.

None of that is the kind of thing you walk away from scot-free. I've read enough books by masters to know that sins stain the soul, and what is easily swept under the rug in the first stages of "moving on" often haunts the nights of later years. But I'll take this deep breath, thank you very much.

Plus it's funny. I never expected to leave any kind of legacy behind at St. Ambrose. I never expected to even make it through my first semester. But as I glance over at my roommate sitting next to the girl she loves, I feel like I might have changed the world a little.

And I'm very satisfied with my choices.

author's note

I wasn't looking for Sarah M. Taylor when she came and found me four years ago. I have a fantastic day job penning books about vampires, and that takes up pretty much all of my time. Some stories are too compelling to ignore, however, and Sarah's was one of them.

I'm not sure what other writers do, but for me, I have pictures that play in my head, and my role is to record what I see. As long as I follow the images, and am faithful to them, the reels keep running and everybody, especially me, is happy. Sarah, and her world at St. Ambrose, was so incredibly vivid and compelling that I couldn't leave her unexpressed. From the moment I saw her and her mother in that old car going under the gates of the school—and I heard her mom talking about the *lawn*—I knew that I was in for a ride.

And then I saw what she was affected by. I was immediately aware that her bipolar disorder diagnosis and symptoms were something that had to be treated with the utmost respect. They couldn't be a plot device or depicted in a cartoonish or one-dimensional kind of way. I proceeded to extensively research the subject and speak to people who have received that diagnosis. I also made sure early on that the book was read by individuals with personal, relevant experience, to ensure that things were correct. However, I think it is very important to acknowledge that I have no direct personal experience or background with being bipolar. I really hope that the care with which I approached the mental health aspects of this book comes through. It is not my intention to hold myself out as an expert, and any mistakes are solely my own.

I want to thank an entire crew of people, starting with my editor, Hannah Braaten, who has championed this book from the start. When it comes to my vampire series, I'm pretty much a solo operator with the content part of things. With Sarah, though, I needed help and guidance to make sure the story came across properly and with the best resonance. Hannah walked me through everything, a number of times, performing a vital service with such good humor and grace. Meg Ruley, Rebecca Scherer, Liz Berry, and Jennifer Armentrout were my first readers, and they provided critical input in the early stages when things were quite rough and I needed to get my feet under me before we even showed it to Hannah. Charlotte Powell has been a sounding board and constant source of guidance in so many ways, not just with this book, but my others, and I am, as always, so thankful to her. I am also very grateful to the incredible team at Gallery Books and Simon & Schuster for their support, not just with Sarah's story, but with all my efforts that they publish so well; Jennifer Bergstrom and Jennifer Long, and everyone there, have been a total joy to work with for all these years, and I owe them so much. And thank you to Jamie Selzer, who is an incredible partner for me in production (and who puts up with my incessant, voluminous edits with fine banter and aplomb). Finally, thank you to Lisa Litwack and Chelsea McGuckin, who do all my covers and are phenomenal artists.

This book owes so much to my dearest cousin, Lucy White, who went through and vetted every single word—and offered a truly passionate defense on an issue with the CVS store! Cousin Lucy, as she is known with great affection in my family, is a titan of the written word and offered truly important edits that shaped the final version's form. She is also an incredible source of support and love to me.

As always, I want to express my gratitude to Team Waud: Nath Miller, LeElla Scott, Lucy Campbell, Jennifer Galimore, and so many more. You all know who you are.

Lastly, thank you to my family.

And the dogs, Archie, Naamah, Obie, Sherman, Bitty, Gats, Flash, and Frank.

Jessica Ward
July 2023